WEST BY NORTHWEST

BRITISH COLUMBIA SHORT STORIES

EDITED BY

DAVID STOUCK & MYLER WILKINSON

POLESTAR

BOOK PUBLISHERS

Polestar Book Publishers acknowledges the ongoing support of The Canada
Council, the British Columbia Ministry of Small Business, Tourism and Culture,
and the Department of Canadian Heritage.

Cover design by Jim Brennan
Printed and bound in Canada

The compass used on the cover, spine and interior of this book was made in
England in the early 1900s for F.W. Nolte & Co. of Victoria, B.C. It belonged to
Corporal George M. Wall of the Northwest Mounted Police, who used it for
navigating by dogsled when he established R.C.M.P. detachments in Resolute
Bay, Baffin Island and Ellesmere Island, N.W.T.
    The compass is encased in a mahogany box measuring 3.5 inches x 3.5
inches x 1.13 inches.

Canadian Cataloguing in Publication Data
        West by northwest
        ISBN 1-896095-41-0
        I. Short stories, Canadian (English) — British Columbia.* 2. Canadian
fiction (English) — British Columbia.* 3. Canadian fiction (English) — 20th
century.* I. Stouck, David, 1940- II. Wilkinson, Myler, 1953-
PS8329.5.B75W47 1998   C813'.01089711   C98-910143-6
PR9198.2.B72W47 1998

Library of Congress Card Catalog Number: 98-84379

Polestar Book Publishers
P.O. Box 5238, Station B
Victoria, British Columbia
Canada   V8R 6N4
http://mypage.direct.ca/p/polestar/

In the United States:
Polestar Book Publishers
P.O. Box 468
Custer, WA
USA   98240-0468

5 4 3 2 1

"To those roads and waters of British Columbia which we know; and to those others which we shall never see."
— Ethel Wilson
(prefatory inscription on the manuscript for *Swamp Angel)*

West by Northwest

BRITISH COLUMBIA SHORT STORIES

Preface

The idea for this story collection came to us on a summer day in 1994 when reading Vi Plotnikoff's newly published *Head Cook at Weddings and Funerals*. Set in the Kootenay Mountains of southeastern British Columbia, Plotnikoff's stories were a striking reminder that the imagination inhabits all regions of the earth. What if we looked in other areas of the province, we asked, especially so-called remote regions like the Cariboo, Peace River, or the Queen Charlotte Islands, what stories might we find? Surprisingly, on bookstore and library shelves there were no anthologies of British Columbia short fiction. There were, however, collections set in Vancouver and we have followed the path marked out by Carole Gerson who, in *Vancouver Short Stories* (1985), brought together a hundred years of story telling in the city. In our own collection we sought to bring together the many voices, aboriginal, colonial, expatriate, that have shaped the imaginative landscape of this province.

To test the range of interest in these stories and to help us make final decisions, we turned to our children, young adults themselves, for their perspectives: to Jordan and John Stouck, and Nathan Wilkinson, with questions about gender, culture and dramatic interest. We also asked Paul Comeau to assess the suitability of some of these stories for different audiences. Sandra Jung's memories of a Vancouver childhood have given us poignant insight into the need for many histories in a book of British Columbia stories. Thanks as well to Jan and Betty de Bruyn, Gordon Turner, Marianne Hodges and Pat Jacklin for their encouragement along the way. We thank our publisher, Michelle Benjamin, for giving this proposal an opportunity, and the authors (in some cases their agents and publishers) who have given us permission to reprint their work. Many fine writers, especially from Vancouver, have not been included because of our concern to represent all the different regions of the province. We hope this selection will encourage readers to go further and search out those writers.

David Stouck
Myler Wilkinson

Introduction

In "Silence and Pioneers," Emily Carr recalls her pleasure as a child in hearing the stories told by Victoria's first white settlers, not "once-upon-a-timers" but "still-fresh-yesterday" stories, about things that had happened locally, within recent memory. She was not interested, she protested, in what people told her when they came back from the Old Country, but wanted to hear about her own country. "Wild, western things excited me tremendously," she said. In like spirit we have gathered for this collection not stories of Canada, not even of the western provinces, but stories that have been told and written down about this part of the world that we know as British Columbia.

Our first concern has been to find stories from the different regions of this diverse province: stories from the sea and the islands, from the coastal cities, the mountains and valleys and northern rivers. We hold with Patrick Lane when he observes that "the land itself is the frame for ... writing," and with Ethel Wilson when she wrote that "the formidable power of geography determines the character and performance of a people," that any meeting or event partakes of place. She said of her first novel, *Hetty Dorval,* that it had "grown from the sage brush of British Columbia, from the hills and trees, from two rivers and a bridge, from a skein of honking geese," and with the stories collected here we in turn have sought to reinforce that link beween place and the imagination. Pauline Johnson's "The Sisters" and Jack Hodgins' "Earthquake" crystallize that connection as they describe transformations of the earth itself. Rebecca Raglon's "Gridlock Mechanism," set partly on Bowen Island, partly in Toronto, dramatizes the importance of place through difference. Even stories set in Vancouver depend for their drama on the details of the city landscape: English Bay, Stanley Park, the woods along the North Shore, the Lions Gate bridge.

But we have also been concerned to collect here histories of the different peoples living in this province. We open with a Haida myth, "The Raven and the First Men," as recounted by the sculptor Bill Reid, and poet Robert Bringhurst. In *Legends of Vancouver* (1910), Pauline Johnson put a colonial frame around native story telling and we have included here two of her legends, "The Sisters" and "The Lost Island," where myth yields to elegy. The colonizers and colonized people are at the centre of stories by Emily Carr and Ethel Wilson: in "Sophie," Carr dramatizes the tragic history of a native woman whose twenty-one babies have all died, while in "Down at English Bay" Wilson celebrates the life of a black man who at the turn of the century taught a generation of Vancouver's children to swim. We learn of other histories, until recently elided from our cultural consciousness: family life in Chinatown in Wayson Choy's "The Jade Peony," the dilemma of folk tradition for a Russian Doukhobor girl in Vi Plotnikoff's "Head Cook at Weddings and Funerals." And we learn about the contemporary lives of racial and sexual minorities in Shani Mootoo's "Out on Main Street" and Eden Robinson's "Queen of the North."

While the stories in this collection each reflect in some way the unique geographic and cultural conditions of British Columbia, they also embody the motives for storytelling that keep repeating themselves over time. In the Haida myth and the Johnson legends we get an epic glimpse of origins from the peoples indigenous to this place. In Christian Petersen's "Heart Red Monaco" and Robinson's "Queen of the North," youthful adventure and romance are shaped into rites of passage. The darker aspects of human behaviour are revealed satirically in Wilson's portrait of racial prejudice in "Down at English Bay" and with bleak irony in Lane's vignette of mill-town poverty; while memories from childhood are charged with pastoral nostalgia in Choy's "The Jade Peony" and Frances Duncan's "Was That Malcolm Lowry?" And there are the inventions of storytelling itself, the timeless desire to make it new, as set forth in George Bowering's "A Short Story" and Caroline Adderson's "Gold Mountain" where, as Bowering has said of Wilson, language makes brightly visible the mountains, lakes and rivers for the imagining eye. Through language and mode these stories remain fresh in the mind, urging us to look again at those roads and waters which we know, and to see for the first time those others not yet travelled.

The Raven and the First Men

BILL REID and ROBERT BRINGHURST

THE GREAT FLOOD WHICH HAD COVERED THE EARTH FOR SO LONG HAD AT last receded, and even the thin strip of sand now called Rose Spit, stretching north from Naikun village, lay dry. The Raven had flown there to gorge himself on the delicacies left by the receding water, so for once he wasn't hungry. But his other appetites — lust, curiosity and the unquenchable itch to meddle and provoke things, to play tricks on the world and its creatures — these remained unsatisfied.

He had recently stolen the light from the old man who kept it hidden in a box in his house in the middle of the darkness, and had scattered it throughout the sky. The new light spattered the night with stars and waxed and waned in the shape of the moon. And it dazzled the day with a single bright shining which lit up the long beach that curved from the split beneath the Raven's feet westward as far as Tao Hill. Pretty as it was, it looked lifeless and so to the Raven quite boring. He gave a great sigh, crossed his wings behind his back and walked along the sand, his shiny head cocked, his sharp eyes and ears alert for any unusual sight or sound. Then taking to the air, he called petulantly out to the empty sky. To his delight, he heard an answering cry — or to describe it more closely, a muffled squeak.

At first he saw nothing, but as he scanned the beach again, a white flash caught his eye, and when he landed he found at his feet, half buried in the sand, a gigantic clamshell. When he looked more closely still, he saw that the shell was full of little creatures cowering in terror of his enormous shadow.

Well here was something to break the monotony of his day. But nothing was going to happen as long as the tiny things stayed in the shell, and they certainly weren't coming out in their present terrified state. So the Raven leaned his great head close to the shell, and with the smooth trickster's tongue that had got him into and out of so many misadventures during his troubled and troublesome existence, he coaxed and cajoled and coerced the little creatures to come out and play in his wonderful, shiny new world. As you know, the Raven speaks in two voices, one harsh and strident, and the other, which he used now, a seductive bell-like croon which seems to come from the depth of the sea, or out of the cave where the winds are born. It is an irresistible sound, one of the loveliest sounds in the world. So it wasn't long before one and then another of the little shell-dwellers timidly emerged. Some of them immediately scurried back when they saw the immensity of the sea and the sky, and the over-whelming blackness of the Raven. But eventually curiosity overcame cau-tion and all of them had crept or scrambled out. Very strange creatures they were: two-legged like the Raven, but there the resemblance ended. They had no glossy feathers, no thrusting beak. Their skin was pale, and they were naked except for the long black hair on their round, flat-featured heads. Instead of strong wings, they had thin stick-like appendages that waved and fluttered constantly. They were the original Haidas, the first humans.

For a long time the Raven amused himself with his new playthings, watching them as they explored their much-expanded world. Sometimes they helped one another in their new discoveries. Just as often, they squabbled over some novelty they found on the beach. And the Raven taught them some clever tricks, at which they proved remarkably adept. But the Raven's attention span was brief, and he grew tired of his small companions. For one thing, they were all males. He had looked all up and down the beach for female creatures, hoping to make the game more interesting, but females were nowhere to be found. He was about to shove the now tired, demanding and quite annoying little creatures back into their shell and forget about them when suddenly — as happens so often with the Raven — he had an idea.

He picked up the men, and in spite of their struggles and cries of fright he put them on his broad back, where they hid themselves among his feathers. Then the Raven spread his wings and flew to North Island. The tide was low, and the rocks, as he had expected, were covered with those large but soft-lipped molluscs known as red chitons. The Raven shook himself gently, and the men slid down his back to the sand. Then he flew to the rock and with his strong beak pried a chiton from its surface.

Now, if any of you have ever examined the underside of a chiton, you may begin to understand what the Raven had in his libidinous, devious mind. He threw back his head and flung the chiton at the nearest of the men. His aim was as unerring as only a great magician's can be, and the chiton found its mark in the delicate groin of the startled, shellborn creature. There the chiton attached itself firmly. Then as sudden as spray hitting the rocks from a breaking wave, a shower of chitons broke over the wide-eyed humans, as each of the open-mouthed shellfish flew inexorably to its target.

Nothing quite like this had ever happened to the men. They had never dreamed of such a thing during their long stay in the clamshell. They were astounded, embarrassed, confused by a rush of new emotions and sensations. They shuffled and squirmed, uncertain whether it was pleasure or pain they were experiencing. They threw themselves down on the beach, where a great storm seemed to break over them, followed just as suddenly by a profound calm. One by one the chitons dropped off. The men staggered to their feet and headed slowly down the beach, followed by the raucous laughter of the Raven, echoing all the way to the great island to the north which we now call Prince of Wales.

That first troop of male humans soon disappeared behind the nearest headland, passing out of the games of the Raven and the story of humankind. Whether they found their way back to their shell or lived out their lives elsewhere, or perished in the strange environment in which they found themselves, nobody remembers, and perhaps nobody cares. They had played their roles and gone their way.

Meanwhile the chitons had made their way back to the rock, where they attached themselves as before. But they too had been changed. As high tide followed low and the great storms of winter gave way to the softer rains and warm sun of spring, the chitons grew and grew, many times larger than their kind had ever been before. Their jointed shells seemed about to fly apart from the enormous pressure within them. And one day a huge wave swept over the rock, tore them from their footholds and carried them back to the beach. As the water receded and the warm sun dried the sand, a great stirring began among the chitons. From each emerged a brown-skinned, black-haired human. This time there were both males and females among them, and the Raven could begin his greatest game — one that still goes on.

They were no timid shell-dwellers these, but children of the wild coast, born between the sea and land, challenging the strength of the stormy North Pacific and wresting from it a rich livelihood. Their descendants built on its beaches the strong, beautiful homes of the Haidas and embellished them with the powerful heraldic carvings that told of the legendary beginnings of great families, all the heroes and heroines and the gallant beasts and monsters who shaped their world and their destinies. For many generations they grew and flourished, built and created, fought and destroyed, living according to the changing seasons and the unchanging rituals of their rich and complex lives.

It's nearly over now. Most of the villages are abandoned, and those which have not entirely vanished lie in ruins. The people who remain are changed. The sea has lost much of its richness, and great areas of the land itself lie in waste. Perhaps it's time the Raven started looking for another clamshell.

The Two Sisters

PAULINE JOHNSON

YOU CAN SEE THEM AS YOU LOOK TOWARDS THE NORTH AND THE WEST, where the dream-hills swim into the sky amid their everdrifting clouds of pearl and grey. They catch the earliest hint of sunrise, they hold the last colour of sunset. Twin mountains they are, lifting their twin peaks above the fairest city in all Canada, and known throughout the British Empire as "The Lions of Vancouver."

Sometimes the smoke of forest fires blurs them until they gleam like opals in a purple atmosphere, too beautiful for words to paint. Sometimes the slanting rains festoon scarves of mist about their crests, and the peaks fade into shadowy outlines, melting, melting, forever melting into the distances. But for most days in the year the sun circles the twin glories with a sweep of gold. The moon washes them with a torrent of silver. Oftentimes, when the city is shrouded in rain, the sun yellows their snows to a deep orange; but through sun and shadow they stand immovable, smiling westward above the waters of the restless Pacific, eastward above the superb beauty of the Capilano Canyon. But the Indian tribes do not know these peaks as "The Lions." Even the chief whose feet have so recently wandered to the Happy Hunting Grounds never heard the name given them until I mentioned it to him one dreamy August day, as together we followed the trail leading to the canyon. He seemed so surprised at the name that I mentioned the reason it had been applied to them, asking him if he recalled the Landseer Lions in Trafalgar Square. Yes, he remembered those splendid sculptures, and his quick eye saw the resemblance instantly. It appeared to please him, and his fine face expressed the haunting memories of the far-away roar of Old London. But the "call of the blood" was stronger, and presently he referred to the

15

Indian legend of those peaks — a legend that I have reason to believe is absolutely unknown to thousands of Pale-faces who look upon "The Lions" daily, without the love for them that is in the Indian heart, without knowledge of the secret of "The Two Sisters." The legend was intensely fascinating as it left his lips in the quaint broken English that is never so dulcet as when it slips from an Indian tongue. His inimitable gestures, strong, graceful, comprehensive, were like a perfectly chosen frame embracing a delicate painting, and his brooding eyes were as the light in which the picture hung.

"Many thousands of years ago," he began, "there were no twin peaks like sentinels guarding the outposts of this sunset coast. They were placed there long after the first creation, when the Sagalie Tyee moulded the mountains, and patterned the mighty rivers where the salmon run, because of His love for His Indian children, and His wisdom for their necessities. In those times there were many and mighty Indian tribes along the Pacific — in the mountain ranges, at the shores and sources of the great Fraser River. Indian Law ruled the land. Indian customs prevailed. Indian beliefs were regarded. Those were the legend-making ages when great things occurred to make the traditions we repeat to our children today. Perhaps the greatest of these traditions is the story of 'The Two Sisters,' for they are known to us as 'The Chief's Daughters,' and to them we owe the Great Peace in which we live, and have lived for many countless moons.

"There is an ancient custom amongst the coast tribes that, when our daughters step from childhood into the great world of womanhood, the occasion must be made one of extreme rejoicing. The being who possesses the possibility of some day mothering a man-child, a warrior, a brave, receives much consideration in most nations; but to us, the Sunset tribes, she is honoured above all people. The parents usually give a great potlatch, and a feast that lasts many days. The entire tribe and the surrounding tribes are bidden to this festival. More than that, sometimes when a great Tyee celebrates for his daughter, the tribes from far up the coast, from the distant north, from inland, from the island, from the Cariboo country, are gathered as guests to the feast. During these days of rejoicing the girl is placed in a high seat, an exalted position, for is she not marriageable? And does not marriage mean motherhood? And does not motherhood mean a vaster nation of brave sons and of gentle daughters, who, in their turn, will give us sons and daughters of their own?

"But it was many thousands of years ago that a great Tyee had two daughters that grew to womanhood at the same springtime, when the first great run of salmon thronged the rivers, and the ollallie bushes were heavy with blossoms. These two daughters were young, lovable and oh! very beautiful. Their father, the great Tyee, prepared to make a feast such as the Coast had never seen. There were to be days and days of rejoicing, the people were to come for many leagues, were to bring gifts to the girls and to receive gifts of great value from the chief, and hospitality was to reign as long as pleasuring feet could dance, and enjoying lips could laugh, and mouths partake of the excellence of the chief's fish, game and ollallies.

"The only shadow on the joy of it all was war, for the tribe of the great Tyee was at war with the Upper Coast Indians, those who lived north, near what is named by the Pale-face as the port of Prince Rupert. Giant war-canoes slipped along the entire coast, war-parties paddled up and down, war-songs broke the silences of the nights, hatred, vengeance, strife, horror festered everywhere like sores on the surface of the earth. But the great Tyee, after warring for weeks, turned and laughed at the battled and the bloodshed, for he had been victor in every encounter, and he could well afford to leave the strife for a brief week and feast in his daughters' honour, not permit any mere enemy to come between him and the traditions of his race and household. So he turned insultingly deaf ears to their war-cries; he ignored with arrogant indifference their paddle-dips that encroached within his own coast water; and he prepared, as a great Tyee should, to royally entertain his tribesmen in honour of his daughters.

"But seven suns before the great feast, these two maidens came before him, hand clasped in hand.

"'Oh! our father,' they said, 'may we speak?'

"'Speak, my daughters, my girls with the eyes of April, the hearts of June'" (early spring and early summer would be the more accurate Indian phrasing).

"'Some day, oh! our father, we may mother a man-child, who may grow to be just such a powerful Tyee as you are, and for this honour that may some day be ours we have come to crave a favour of you — you, Oh! our father.'

"'It is your privilege at this celebration to receive any favour your hearts may wish,' he replied graciously, placing his fingers beneath their girlish chins. 'The favour is yours before you ask it, my daughters.'

"'Will you, for our sakes, invite the great northern hostile tribe — the tribe you war upon — to this, our feast?' they asked fearlessly.

"'To a peaceful feast, a feast in the honour of women?' he exclaimed incredulously.

"'So we desire it,' they answered.

"'And so shall it be,' he declared. 'I can deny you nothing this day, and some time you may bear sons to bless this peace you have asked, and to bless their mother's sire for granting it.' Then he turned to all the young men of the tribe and commanded: 'Build fires at sunset on all the coast headlands — fires of welcome. Man your canoes and face the north, greet the enemy, and tell them that I, the Tyee of the Capilanos, ask — no, command — that they join me for a great feast in honour of my two daughters.'

"And when the northern tribe got this invitation they flocked down the coast to this feast of a Great Peace. They brought their women and their children; they brought game and fish, gold and white stone beads, baskets and carven ladles, and wonderful woven blankets to lay at the feet of their now acknowledged ruler, the great Tyee. And he, in turn, gave such a potlatch that nothing but tradition can vie with it. There were long, glad days of joyousness, long, pleasurable nights of dancing and camp-fires, and vast quantities of food. The war-canoes were emptied of their deadly weapons and filled with the daily catch of salmon. The hostile war-songs ceased, and in their place was heard the soft shuffle of dancing feet, the singing voices of women, the play-games of the children of two powerful tribes which had been until now ancient enemies, for a great and lasting brotherhood was sealed between them — their war-songs were ended forever.

"Then the Sagalie Tyee smiled on His Indian children: 'I will make these young-eyed maidens immortal,' He said. In the cup of His hands He lifted the chief's two daughters and set them for ever in a high place, for they had borne two offspring — Peace and Brotherhood — each of which is now a great Tyee ruling this land.

"And on the mountain crest the chief's daughters can be seen wrapped in the suns, the snows, the stars of all seasons, for they have stood in this high place for thousands of years, and will stand for thousands of years to come, guarding the peace of the Pacific Coast and the quiet of the Capilano Canyon."

This is the Indian legend of "The Lions of Vancouver" as I had it from one who will tell me no more the traditions of his people.

The Lost Island

"Yes," said my old tillicum, "we Indians have lost many things. We have lost our lands, our forests, our game, our fish; we have lost our ancient religion, our ancient dress; some of the younger people have even lost their fathers' language and the legends and traditions of their ancestors. We cannot call those old things back to us; they will never come up again. We may travel many days up the mountain-trails, and look in the silent places for them. They are not there. We may paddle many moons on the sea, but our canoes will never enter the channel that leads to the yesterdays of the Indian people. These things are lost, just like 'The Island of the North Arm.' They may be somewhere nearby, but no one can ever find them."

"But there are many islands up the North Arm," I asserted.

"Not the island we people have sought for many tens of summers," he replied sorrowfully.

"Was it ever there?" I questioned.

"Yes, it was there," he said. "My grandsires and my great-grandsires saw it; but that was long ago. My father never saw it, though he spent many days in many years searching, always searching for it. I am an old man myself, and I have never seen it, though from my youth, I, too, have searched. Sometimes in the stillness of the nights I have paddled up in my canoe." Then, lowering his voice: "Twice I have seen its shadow: high rocky shores, reaching as high as the tree-tops on the mainland, then tall pines and firs on its summit like a king's crown. As I paddled up the Arm one summer night, long ago, the shadow of these rocks and firs fell across my canoe, across my face and across the waters beyond. I turned rapidly to look. There was no island there, nothing but a wide stretch of waters on both sides of me, and the moon almost directly overhead. Don't say it was the shore that shadowed me," he hastened, catching my thought. "The moon was above me; my canoe scarce made a shadow on the still waters. No, it was not the shore."

"Why do you search for it ?" I lamented, thinking of the old dreams in my own life whose realization I have never attained.

"There is something on that island that I want. I shall look for it until I die, for it is there," he affirmed.

There was a long silence between us after that. I had learned to love silences when with my old tillicum, for they always led to a legend. After a time he began voluntarily.

"It was more than one hundred years ago. This great city of Vancouver was but the dream of the Sagalie Tyee at that time. The dream had not yet come to the white man; only one great Indian medicine-man knew that some day a great camp for Pale-faces would lie between False Creek and the Inlet. This dream haunted him; it came to him night and day — when he was amid his people laughing and feasting, or when he was alone in the forest chanting his strange songs, beating his hollow drum, or shaking his wooden witch-rattle to gain more power to cure the sick and the dying of his tribe. For years this dream followed him. He grew to be an old, old man, yet always he could hear voices, strong and loud, as when they first spoke to him in his youth, and they would say: 'Between the two narrow strips of salt water the white men will camp, many hundreds of them, many thousands of them. The Indians will learn their ways, will live as they do, will become as they are. There will be no more great war-dances, no more fights with other powerful tribes; it will be as if the Indians had lost all bravery, all courage, all confidence.'

"He hated the voices, he hated the dream; but all his power, all his big medicine, could not drive them away. He was the strongest man on all the North Pacific Coast. He was mighty and very tall, and his muscles were as those of Leloo, the timber-wolf, when he is strongest to kill his prey. He could go for many days without food; he could fight the largest mountain-lion; he could overthrow the fiercest grizzly bear; he could paddle against the wildest winds and ride the highest waves. He could meet his enemies and kill whole tribes single-handed. His strength, his courage, his power, his bravery, were those of a giant. He knew no fear; nothing in the earth or the sky, could conquer him. He was fearless, fearless.

"Only this haunting dream of the coming white man's camp he could not drive away; it was the only thing in his life he had tried to kill and failed. It drove him from the feasting, drove him from the pleasant lodges, the fires, the dancing, the storytelling of his people in their camp by the water's edge, where the salmon thronged and the deer came down to drink of the mountainstreams. He left the Indian village, chanting his wild songs as he went. Up through the mighty forests he climbed, through the trailless deep mosses and matted vines, up to the summit of what the white men call Grouse Mountain. For many days he camped there. He ate no food, he drank no water, but sat and sang his medicine-songs through the dark hours and through the day. Before him — far beneath his feet — lay the narrow strip of land between the two salt waters.

"The Sagalie Tyee gave him the power to see far into the future. He looked across a hundred years, just as he looked across what you call the Inlet, and he saw mighty lodges built close together, hundreds and thousands of them — lodges of stone and wood, and long straight trails to divide them. He saw these trails thronging with Pale-faces; he heard the sound of the white man's paddle-dip on the waters, for it is not silent like the Indian's; he saw the white man's trading posts, saw the fishing nets, heard his speech. Then the vision faded as gradually as it came. The narrow strip of land was his own forest once more.

"'I am old,' he called, in his sorrow and his trouble for his people. 'I am old, O Sagalie Tyee! Soon I shall die and go to the Happy Hunting Grounds of my fathers. Let not my strength die with me. Keep living for all time my courage, my bravery, my fearlessness. Keep them for my people that they may be strong enough to endure the white man's rule. Keep my strength living for them; hide it so that the Pale-face may never find or see it.'

"Then he came down from the summit of Grouse Mountain. Still chanting his medicine-songs, he entered his canoe and paddled through the colours of the setting sun far up the North Arm. When night fell he came to an island with misty shores of great grey rock; on its summit tall pines and firs encircled like a king's crown. As he neared it he felt all his strength, his courage, his fearlessness leaving him; he could see these things drift from him on to the island. They were as the clouds that rest on the mountains, grey-white and half transparent. Weak as a woman, he paddled back to the Indian village; he told them to go and search for 'The Island' where they would find all his courage, his fearlessness and his strength, living, living for ever. He slept then, but — in the morning he did not awake. Since then our young men and our old have searched for 'The Island.' It is there somewhere, up some lost channel, but we cannot find it. When we do, we will get back all the courage and bravery we had before the white man came, for the great medicine-man said those things never die — they live for one's children and grandchildren."

His voice ceased. My whole heart went out to him in his longing for the lost island. I thought of all the splendid courage I knew him to possess, so made answer: "But you say that the shadow of this island has fallen upon you; is it not so, tillicum?"

"Yes," he said half mournfully. "But only the shadow."

Silence and Pioneers

EMILY CARR

THE SILENCE OF OUR WESTERN FORESTS WAS SO PROFOUND THAT OUR EARS COULD scarcely comprehend it. If you spoke your voice came back to you as your face is thrown back to you in a mirror. It seemed as if the forests were so full of silence that there was no room for sounds. The birds who lived there were birds of prey — eagles, hawks, owls. Had a song bird loosed his throat the others would have pounced. Sober-coloured, silent little birds were the first to follow settlers into the West. Gulls there had always been; they began with the sea and had always cried over it. The vast sky spaces above, hungry for noise, steadily lapped up their cries. The forest was different — she brooded over silence and secrecy.

When we were children Father and Mother occasionally drove out beyond the town to Saanich, Metchosin or the Highland District, to visit some settler or other carving a home for his family in the midst of overwhelming growth — rebellious, untutored land that challenged his every effort. The settler was raising a family who would carry on from generation to generation. As he and his wife toiled at the breaking and the clearing they thought, "We are taming this wilderness for our children. It will be easier for them than for us. They will only have to carry on."

They felled mighty trees with vigour and used blasting powder and sweat to dislodge the monster roots. The harder they worked with the land, the more they loved these rooty little brown patches among the overwhelming green. The pioneer walked round his new field, pointing with hardened, twisted fingers to this and that which he had accomplished while the woman wrestled with the inconveniences of her crude home, planning the smart, modern house her children would have by and by, but the children would never have that intense joy of creating from nothing which their parents had enjoyed; they would never understand the secret wrapped in virgin land.

Mr. Scaife, a pioneer, had digged a deep ditch round his forest field. The field was new ploughed. He showed Father with pride how few blackened stumps there were now left in the earth of it. I let go of Father's hand to gather wild flowers among the pokes of the snake fence. I fell into the deep, dry ditch. Brambles and tall grasses closed over my head, torn roots in the earthy sides of the ditch scraped me as I went down. It was the secret sort of place where snakes like to wriggle and where black hornets build their nests — nearly dark, only a little green light filtering through the brambles over my head. I screamed in terror. Willie Scaife, a farm lad, jumped into the ditch and pulled me out. He was my first hero.

The first Victorians could tell splendid stories of when Victoria was a Hudson's Bay Post, was called Fort Camosun and had a strong blockade about it with a bastion at each corner to protect the families of the Hudson's Bay men from Indians and wild beasts.

Though my parents did not come to Victoria till after the days of the Fort and I was not born for many years after that, still there were people in Victoria only middle-aged when I was little, who had lived in the old Fort and could actually tell you about it. Nothing delighted me more than to hear these "still-fresh-yesterday" stories, that were not old "once-upon-a-timers"! You could ask questions of the very story-people themselves and they did not have to crinkle their foreheads, trying to remember a long way back.

There was a childless couple with whom I was a favourite — Mrs. Lewis and her husband, the sea captain. Mrs. Lewis had been Miss Mary Langford before her marriage. Her father was Captain Langford, a naval man. I am not certain whether the Langfords ever actually lived in the Fort or not but they came to Victoria at the very beginning of its being. Captain Langford built a log farmhouse six or seven miles out from town. The district was named for him.

Sometimes when Captain Lewis was away Mrs. Lewis invited me to stay with her for company. They lived on Belville Street, on the same side of James Bay as we did, in a pretty cottage with flowers and canaries all over it. The windows overlooked the Harbour and Mrs. Lewis could watch the Captain's boat, the old paddle-wheel steamer, *Princess Louise,* go and come through the Harbour's mouth, and could wave to the Captain on his bridge. It was Captain Lewis who took me for my first trip by sea, and later, when the Railway was built to Nanaimo, for my first trip by rail. When you put your hand in his it was like being led about by a geography (he knew everywhere) and Mrs. Lewis was history. Seated at her feet before the fire among the dogs and cats, I listened open-mouthed to tales of early Fort days.

Mrs. Lewis was a good teller. She was pretty to watch. The little bunch of black curls pinned high at the back of her head bobbed as she talked and her eyes sparkled. She told how young Naval officers used to take the pretty Miss Langfords out riding. When they came to Goldstream and Millstream, which were bubbling rivers with steep banks, that crossed the Langford trails, the men would blindfold the girls' horses and lead them across the river, using as a bridge a couple of fallen logs. One night as they were hurrying along a narrow deer trail, trying to get home before dark, they saw a panther stretched out on the limb of a tree under which they must pass in single file. The bushes were too dense for them to turn aside, so each rider whipped his horse and made a dash along the trail under the panther.

Mrs. Lewis told, too, of the coming of their piano from England. It sailed all round Cape Horn and was the first piano to come into the Colony of British Columbia. It landed at Esquimalt Harbour and was carried on the backs of Indians in relays of twenty at a time through a rough bush trail from Esquimalt to Langford. The tired Indians put the piano down in a field outside the house to rest a minute. The Langford girls rushed out with the key, unlocked and played the piano out there in the field. The Indians were very much astonished. They looked up into the sky and into the woods to see where the noise came from.

The stories jumped sharply out of Mrs. Lewis's mouth, almost catching her breath as she recalled vividly the excitement which these strange happenings had brought to her and to her sister, just out from their sheltered English life.

Sometimes Mrs. Cridge, Mrs. Mouat, Doctor Helmcken, or some of Sir James Douglas' daughters, all of whom had lived in the old Fort, would start chatting about old days and then we younger people would stand open-mouthed, thinking it must have been grand to live those exciting experiences.

"It was, my dears," said Mrs. Cridge, "but remember too that there were lots of things to face, lots of things to do without, lots of hardships to go through."

I was a very small girl when the business men of Victoria chartered a steamer and, accompanied by their families, made a tour of Vancouver

Island. It took the boat, the *Princess Louise,* ten days to go all round the Island. My Father and two of my sisters went. I was thought to be too small but I was not too small to drink in every word they said when they came back.

Father was overwhelmed by the terrific density of growth on the Island. Once when they were tied up for three hours he and another man took axes and tried to see how far they could penetrate into the woods in the given time. When the ship's whistle blew they were exhausted and dripping with sweat but their attack on the dense undergrowth scarcely showed. Father told of the magnificent trees, of their closeness to each other, of the strangling undergrowth, the great silence, the quantity of bald-headed eagles. "Really bald, Father?" I asked, but he said they were a rusty black all over except for white heads which shone out against the blue sky and the dark forest. Great white owls flew silently among the trees like ghosts, and, too, they had seen bears and whales.

One of my sisters was more interested in the passengers on the boat and made a lot of new friends. The other told me about the Indian villages where the boat had touched. This was all far more interesting to me than the stories people had to tell when they came back from trips to the Old Country, bragging about the great and venerable sights of the Old Land. I did not care much about old things. These wild, western things excited me tremendously. I did not long to go over to the Old World to see history, I wanted to see *now* what was out here in our West. I was glad Father and Mother had come as far west as the West went before they stopped and settled down.

D'Sonoqua

I was sketching a remote Indian village when I first saw her. The village was one of those that the Indians use only for a few months in each year; the rest of the time it stands empty and desolate. I went there in one of its empty times, in a drizzling dusk.

When the Indian agent dumped me on the beach in front of the village, he said "There is not a soul here. I will come back for you in two days." Then he went away.

I had a small griffon dog with me, and also a little Indian girl, who, when she saw the boat go away, clung to my sleeve and wailed, "I'm 'fraid."

We went up to the old deserted Mission House. At the sound of the key in the rusty lock, rats scuttled away. The stove was broken, the wood wet. I had forgotten to bring candles. We spread our blankets on the floor, and spent a poor night. Perhaps my lack of sleep played its part in the shock that I got, when I saw her for the first time.

Water was in the air, half mist, half rain. The stinging nettles, higher than my head, left their nervy smart on my ears and forehead, as I beat my way through them, trying all the while to keep my feet on the plank walk which they hid. Big yellow slugs crawled on the walk and slimed it. My feet slipped and I shot headlong to her very base, for she had no feet. The nettles that were above my head reached only to her knee.

It was not the fall alone that jerked the "Oh's" out of me, for the great wooden image towering above me was indeed terrifying.

The nettle bed ended a few yards beyond her, and then a rocky bluff jutted out, with waves battering it below. I scrambled up and went out on the bluff, so that I could see the creature above the nettles. The forest was behind her, the sea in front.

Her head and trunk were carved out of, or rather into, the bole of a great red cedar. She seemed to be part of the tree itself, as if she had grown there at its heart, and the carver had only chipped away the outer wood so that you could see her. Her arms were spliced and socketed to the trunk, and were flung wide in a circling, compelling movement. Her breasts were two eagle-heads, fiercely carved. That much, and the column of her great neck, and her strong chin, I had seen when I slithered to the ground beneath her. Now I saw her face.

The eyes were two rounds of black, set in wider rounds of white, and placed in deep sockets under wide, black eyebrows. Their fixed stare bored into me as if the very life of the old cedar looked out, and it seemed that the voice of the tree itself might have burst from that great round cavity, with projecting lips, that was her mouth. Her ears were round, and stuck out to catch all sounds. The salt air had not dimmed the heavy red of her trunk and arms and thighs. Her hands were black, with blunt finger-tips painted a dazzling white. I stood looking at her for a long, long time.

The rain stopped, and white mist came up from the sea, gradually paling her back into the forest. It was as if she belonged there, and the mist was carrying her home. Presently the mist took the forest too, and, wrapping them both together, hid them away.

"Who is that image?" I asked the little Indian girl, when I got back to the house.

She knew which one I meant, but to gain time, she said, "What image?"

"The terrible one, out there on the bluff."

"I dunno," she lied.

I never went to that village again, but the fierce wooden image often came to me, both in my waking and in my sleeping.

Several years passed, and I was once more sketching in an Indian village. There were Indians in this village, and in a mild backward way it was "going modern." That is, the Indians had pushed the forest back a little to let the sun touch the new buildings that were replacing the old community houses. Small houses, primitive enough to a white man's thinking, pushed here and there between the old. Where some of the big community houses had been torn down, for the sake of the lumber, the great corner posts and massive roof-beams of the old structure were often left, standing naked against the sky, and the new little house was built inside, on the spot where the old one had been.

It was in one of these empty skeletons that I found her again. She had once been a supporting post for the great centre beam. Her polemate, representing the Raven, stood opposite her, but the beam that had rested on their heads was gone. The two poles faced in, and one judged the great size of the house by the distance between them. The corner posts were still in place, and the earth floor, once beaten to the hardness of rock by naked feet, was carpeted now with rich lush grass.

I knew her by the stuck-out ears, shouting mouth and deep eye-sockets. These sockets had no eyeballs, but were empty holes, filled with stare. The stare, though not so fierce as that of the former image, was more intense. The whole figure expressed power, weight, domination, rather than ferocity. Her feet were planted heavily on the head of the squatting bear, carved beneath them. A man could have sat on either huge shoulder. She was unpainted, weather-worn, sun-cracked, and the arms and hands seemed to hang loosely. The fingers were thrust into the carven mouths of two human heads, held crowns down. From behind, the sun made unfathomable shadows in eye, cheek and mouth. Horror tumbled out of them.

I saw Indian Tom on the beach, and went to him.

"Who is she?"

The Indian's eyes, coming slowly from across the sea, followed my pointing finger. Resentment showed in his face, greeny-brown and wrinkled like a baked apple — resentment that white folks should pry into matters wholly Indian.

"Who is that big carved woman?" I repeated.

"D'Sonoqua." No white tongue could have fondled the name as he did.

"Who is D'Sonoqua?"

"She is the wild woman of the woods."

"What does she do?"

"She steals children."

"To eat them?"

"No, she carries them to her caves; that," pointing to a purple scar on the mountain across the bay, "is one of her caves. When she cries 'OO-oo-oo-oeo', Indian mothers are too frightened to move. They stand like trees, and the children go with D'Sonoqua."

"Then she is bad?"

"Sometimes bad ... sometimes good," Tom replied, glancing furtively at those stuck-out ears. Then he got up and walked away.

I went back, and sitting in front of the image, gave stare for stare. But her stare so over-powered mine, that I could scarcely wrench my eyes away from the clutch of those empty sockets. The power that I felt was not in the thing itself, but in some tremendous force behind it, that the carver had believed in.

A shadow passed across her hands and their gruesome holdings. A little bird, with its beak full of nesting material, flew into the cavity of her mouth, right in the pathway of that terrible OO-oo-oo-oeo. Then my eye caught something that I had missed — a tabby cat asleep between her feet.

"Of course," I said to myself, "I do not believe in supernatural beings. Still — who understands the mysteries behind the forest? What would one do if one did meet a supernatural being?" Half of me wished that I could meet her, and half of me hoped I would not.

Chug — chug — the little boat had come into the bay to take me to another village, more lonely and deserted than this. Who knew what I should see there? But soon supernatural beings went clean out of my mind, because I was wholly absorbed in being naturally seasick — when you have been tossed and wracked and chilled any wharf looks good, even a rickety one, with its crooked legs stockinged in barnacles. Our boat nosed under its clammy darkness, and I crawled up the straight slimy ladder, wondering which was worse, natural seasickness, or supernatural "creeps." The trees crowded to the very edge of the water, and the outer ones, hanging over it, shadowed the shoreline into a velvet smudge. D'Sonoqua might walk in places like this. I sat for a long time on the damp, dusky beach, waiting for the stage. One by one dots of light popped from the scattered cabins and made the dark seem darker. Finally the stage came.

We drove through the forest over a long straight road, with black pine trees marching on both sides. When we came to the wharf the little gas mail-boat was waiting for us. Smell and blurred light oozed thickly out of the engine room, and except for one lantern on the wharf everything else was dark. Clutching my little dog, I sat on the mail sacks which had been tossed on to the deck.

The ropes were loosed, and we slid out into the oily black water. The moon that had gone with us through the forest was away now. Black pine-covered mountains jagged up on both sides of the inlet like teeth. Every gasp of the engine shook us like a great sob. There was no rail round the deck, and the edge of the boat lay level with the black slithering horror below. It was like being swallowed again and again by some terrible monster, but never going down. As we slid through the water, hour after hour, I found myself listening for the OO-oo-oo-oeo.

Midnight brought us to a knob of land, lapped by the water on three sides, with the forest threatening to gobble it up on the fourth. There was a rude landing, a rooming-house, an eating-place, and a store, all for the convenience of fishermen and loggers. I was given a room, but after I had blown out my candle, the stillness and the darkness would not let me sleep.

In the brilliant sparkle of the morning when everything that was not superlatively blue was superlatively green, I dickered with a man who was taking a party up the inlet that he should drop me off at the village I was headed for.

"But," he protested, "there is nobody there."

To myself I said, "There is D'Sonoqua."

From the shore, as we rowed to it, came a thin feminine cry — the mewing of a cat. The keel of the boat had barely grated in the pebbles, when the cat sprang aboard, passed the man shipping his oars and crouched for a spring into my lap. Leaning forward, the man seized the creature roughly, and with a cry of "Dirty Indian vermin!" flung her out into the sea.

I jumped ashore, refusing his help, and with a curt "Call for me at sundown," strode up the beach; the cat followed me.

When we had crossed the beach and come to a steep bank, the cat ran ahead. Then I saw that she was no lean, ill-favoured Indian cat, but a sleek aristocratic Persian. My snobbish little griffon dog, who usually refused to let an Indian cat come near me, surprised me by trudging beside her in comradely fashion.

The village was typical of the villages of these Indians. It had only one street, and that had only one side, because all the houses faced the beach. The two community houses were very old, dilapidated and bleached, and the handful of other shanties seemed never to have been young; they had grown so old before they were finished, that it was then not worthwhile finishing them.

Rusty padlocks carefully protected the gaping walls. There was the usual broad plank in front of the houses, the general sitting and sunning place for Indians. Little streams ran under it, and weeds poked up through every crack, half hiding the companies of tins, kettles and rags, which patiently waited for the next gale and their next move.

In front of the Chief's home was a high, carved totem pole, surmounted by a large wooden eagle. Storms had robbed him of both wings, and his head had a resentful twist, as if he blamed somebody. The heavy wooden heads of two squatting bears peered over the nettle-tops. The windows were too high for peeping in or out. "But, save D'Sonoqua, who is there to peep?" I said aloud, just to break the silence. A fierce sun burned down as if it wanted to expose every ugliness and forlornness. It drew the noxious smell out of the skunk cabbages, growing in the rich black ooze of the stream, scummed the waterbarrels with green slime and branded the desolation into my very soul.

The cat crept very close, rubbing and bumping itself and purring ecstatically; and although I had not seen them come, two more cats had joined us. When I sat down they curled into my lap, and then the strangeness of the place did not bite into me so deeply. I got up, determined to look behind the houses.

Nettles grew in the narrow spaces between the houses. I beat them down and made my way over the bruised dark-smelling mass into a space of low jungle.

Long ago the trees had been felled and left lying. Young forest had burst through the slash, making an impregnable barrier, and sealing up the secrets which lay behind it. An eagle flew out of the forest, circled the village, and flew back again.

Once again I broke silence, calling after him, "Tell D'Sonoqua — " and turning, saw her close, towering above me in the jungle.

Like the D'Sonoqua of the other villages she was carved into the bole of a red cedar tree. Sun and storm had bleached the wood, moss here and there softened the crudeness of the modelling; sincerity underlay every stroke.

She appeared to be neither wooden nor stationary, but a singing spirit, young and fresh, passing through the jungle. No violence coarsened her; no power domineered to wither her. She was graciously feminine. Across her forehead her creator had fashioned the Sistheutl, or mythical two-headed sea serpent. One of its heads fell to either shoulder, hiding the stuck-out ears, and framing her face from a central parting on her forehead which seemed to increase its womanliness.

She caught your breath, this D'Sonoqua, alive in the dead bole of the cedar. She summed up the depth and charm of the whole forest, driving away its menace.

I sat down to sketch. What was the noise of purring and rubbing going on about my feet? Cats. I rubbed my eyes to make sure I was seeing right, and counted a dozen of them. They jumped into my lap and sprang to my shoulders. They were real — and very feminine.

There we were — D'Sonoqua, the cats and I — the woman who only a few moments ago had forced herself to come behind the houses in trembling fear of the "wild woman of the woods" — wild in the sense that forest creatures are wild — shy, untouchable.

Sophie

Sophie knocked gently on my Vancouver studio door.

"Baskets. I got baskets."

They were beautiful, made by her own people, West Coast Indian baskets. She had big ones in a cloth tied at the four corners and little ones in a flour sack.

She had a baby slung on her back in a shawl, a girl child clinging to her skirts, and a heavy-faced boy plodding behind her.

"I have no money for baskets."

"Money no matter," said Sophie. "Old clo', waum skirt — good fo' basket."

I wanted the big round one. Its price was eight dollars.

"Next month I am going to Victoria. I will bring back some clothes and get your basket."

I asked her in to rest a while and gave the youngsters bread and jam. When she tied up her baskets she left the one I coveted on the floor.

"Take it away," I said. "It will be a month before I can go to Victoria. Then I will bring clothes back with me and come to get the basket."

"You keep now. Bymby pay," said Sophie.

"Where do you live?"

"North Vancouver Mission."

"What is your name?"

"Me Sophie Frank. Everybody know me."

Sophie's house was bare but clean. It had three rooms. Later, when it got cold, Sophie's Frank would cut out all the partition walls. Sophie said, "Three loom, three stobe. One loom, one stobe." The floor of the house was clean scrubbed. It was chair, table and bed for the family. There was one chair; the coal oil lamp sat on that. Sophie pushed the babies into corners, spread my old clothes on the floor to appraise them, and was satisfied. So, having tested each other's trade-straightness, we began a long, long friendship — forty years. I have seen Sophie glad, sad, sick and drunk. I have asked her why she did this or that thing — Indian ways that I did not understand — her answer was invariably, "Nice ladies always do." That was Sophie's ideal — being nice.

Every year Sophie had a new baby. Almost every year she buried one. Her little graves were dotted all over the cemetery. I never knew more than three of her twenty-one children to be alive at one time. By the time she was in her early fifties every child was dead and Sophie had cried her eyes dry. Then she took to drink.

"I got a new baby. I got a new baby."

Sophie, seated on the floor of her house, saw me coming through the open door and waved the papoose cradle. Two little girls rolled round on the floor; the new baby was near her in a basket-cradle. Sophie took off the cloth tented over the basket and exhibited the baby, a lean poor thing.

Sophie herself was small and spare. Her black hair sprang thick and strong on each side of the clean, straight parting and hung in twin braids across her shoulders. Her eyes were sad and heavy-lidded. Between prominent, rounded cheekbones her nose lay rather flat, broadening and snubby at the tip. Her wide upper lip pouted. It was sharp-edged, puckering over a row of poor teeth — the soothing pucker of lips trying to ease an aching tooth or to hush a crying child. She had a soft little body, a back straight as honesty itself, and the small hands and feet of an Indian.

Sophie's English was good enough, but when Frank, her husband, was there she became dumb as a plate.

"Why won't you talk before Frank, Sophie?"

"Frank he learn school English. Me, no. Frank laugh my English words."

When we were alone she chattered to me like a sparrow.

In May, when the village was white with cherry blossom and the blue water of Burrard Inlet crept almost to Sophie's door — just a streak of grey sand and a plank walk between — and when Vancouver city was more beautiful to look at across the water than to be in — it was then I loved to take the ferry to the North Shore and go to Sophie's.

Behind the village stood mountains topped by the grand old "Lions", twin peaks, very white and blue. The nearer mountains were every shade of young foliage, tender grey-green, getting greener and greener till, when they were close, you saw that the village grass outgreened them all. Hens strutted their broods, papooses and pups and kittens rolled everywhere — it was good indeed to spend a day on the Reserve in spring.

Sophie and I went to see her babies' graves first. Sophie took her best plaid skirt, the one that had three rows of velvet ribbon round the hem, from a nail on the wall, and bound a yellow silk handkerchief around her head. No matter what the weather, she always wore her great shawl, clamping it down with her arms, the fringe trickling over her fingers. Sophie wore her shoes when she walked with me, if she remembered.

Across the water we could see the city. The Indian Reserve was a different world — no hurry, no business.

We walked over the twisty, up-and-down road to the cemetery. Casamin, Tommy, George, Rosie, Maria, Mary, Emily, and all the rest were there under a tangle of vines. We rambled, seeking out Sophie's graves. Some had little wooden crosses, some had stones. Two babies lay outside the cemetery fence: they had not faced life long enough for baptism.

"See! Me got stone for Rosie now."

"It looks very nice. It must have cost lots of money, Sophie."

"Grave man make cheap for me. He say, 'You got lots, lots stone from me, Sophie. Maybe bymby you get some more died baby, then you want more stone. So I make cheap for you.'"

Sophie's kitchen was crammed with excited women. They had come to see Sophie's brand-new twins. Sophie was on a mattress beside the cook stove. The twin girls were in small basket papoose cradles, woven by Sophie herself. The babies were wrapped in cotton wool which made their dark little faces look darker; they were laced into their baskets and stuck up at the edge of Sophie's mattress beside the kitchen stove. Their brown, wrinkled faces were like potatoes baked in their jackets, their hands no bigger than brown spiders.

They were thrilling, those very, very tiny babies. Everybody was excited over them. I sat down on the floor close to Sophie.

"Sophie, if the baby was a girl it was to have my name. There are two babies and I have only one name. What are we going to do about it?"

"The biggest and the best is yours," said Sophie.

My Em'ly lived three months. Sophie's Maria lived three weeks. I bought Em'ly's tombstone. Sophie bought Maria's.

Sophie's "mad" rampaged inside her like a lion roaring in the breast of a dove.

"Look see," she said, holding a red and yellow handkerchief, caught together at the corners and chinking with broken glass and bits of plaster of Paris. "Bad boy bloke my grave flower! Cost five dollar one, and now boy all bloke fo' me. Bad, bad boy! You come talk me fo' p'liceman?"

At the City Hall she spread the handkerchief on the table and held half a plaster of Paris lily and a dove's tail up to the eyes of the law, while I talked.

"My mad fo' boy bloke my plitty glave flower," she said, forgetting, in her fury, to be shy of the "English words."

The big man of the law was kind. He said, "It's too bad, Sophie. What do you want me to do about it?"

"You make boy buy more this plitty kind for my glave."

"The boy has no money but I can make his old grandmother pay a little every week."

Sophie looked long at the broken pieces and shook her head.

"That ole, ole woman got no money." Sophie's anger was dying, soothed by sympathy like a child, the woman in her tender towards old Granny. "My bloke no matter for ole woman," said Sophie, gathering up the pieces. "You scold boy big, Policeman? No make glanny pay."

"I sure will, Sophie."

There was a black skirt spread over the top of the packing case in the centre of Sophie's room. On it stood the small white coffin. A lighted candle was at the head, another at the foot. The little dead girl in the coffin held a doll in her arms. It had hardly been out of them since I had taken it to her a week before. The glassy eyes of the doll stared out of the coffin, up past the closed eyelids of the child.

Though Sophie had been through this nineteen times before, the twentieth time was no easier. Her two friends, Susan and Sara, were there by the coffin, crying for her.

The outer door opened and a half dozen women came in, their shawls drawn low across their foreheads, their faces grim. They stepped over to the coffin and looked in. Then they sat around it on the floor and began to cry, first with baby whimpers, softly, then louder, louder still — with violence and strong howling: torrents of tears burst from their eyes and rolled down their cheeks. Sophie and Sara and Susan did it too. It sounded horrible, like tortured dogs.

Suddenly they stopped. Sophie went to the bucket and got water in a tin basin. She took a towel in her hand and went to each of the guests in turn holding the basin while they washed their faces and dried them on the towel. Then the women all went out except Sophie, Sara and Susan. This crying had gone on at intervals for three days — ever since the child had died. Sophie was worn out. There had been, too, all the long weeks of Rosie's tubercular dying to go through.

"Sophie, couldn't you lie down and rest?"

She shook her head. "Nobody sleep in Injun house till dead people go to cemet'ry."

The beds had all been taken away

"When is the funeral?"

"I dunno. Pliest go Vancouver. He not come two more day."

She laid her hand on the corner of the little coffin.

"See! Coffin-man think box fo' Injun baby no matter."

The seams of the cheap little coffin had burst.

As Sophie and I were coming down the village street we met an Indian woman whom I did not know. She nodded to Sophie, looked at me and half paused. Sophie's mouth was set, her bare feet pattered quickly, hurrying me past the woman.

"Go church house now?" she asked me.

The Catholic church had twin towers. Wide steps led up to the front door which was always open. Inside it was bright, in a misty way, and still except for the wind and sea echoes. The windows were gay coloured glass; when you knelt the wooden footstools and pews creaked. Hush lurked in every corner. Always a few candles burned. Everything but those flickers of flame was stone-still.

When we came out of the church we sat on the steps for a little. I said, "Who was that woman we met, Sophie?"

"Mrs. Chief Joe Capilano."

"Oh! I would like to know Mrs. Chief Joe Capilano. Why did you hurry by so quick? She wanted to stop."

"I don' want you know Mrs. Chief Joe."

"Why?"

"You fliend for me, not fliend for her."

"My heart has room for more than one friend, Sophie."

"You fliend for me, I not want Mrs. Chief Joe get you."

"You are always my first and best friend, Sophie." She hung her head, her mouth obstinate. We went to Sara's house.

Sara was Sophie's aunt, a wizened bit of a woman whose eyes, nose, mouth and wrinkles were all twisted to the perpetual expressing of pain. Once she had had a merry heart, but pain had trampled out the merriness. She lay on a bed draped with hangings of clean, white rags dangling from poles. The wall behind her bed, too, was padded heavily with newspaper to keep draughts off her "Lumatiz."

"Hello, Sara. How are you?"

"Em'ly! Sophie's Em'ly!"

The pain wrinkles scuttled off to make way for Sara's smile, but hurried back to twist for her pain.

"I dunno what for I got Lumatiz, Em'ly. I dunno. I dunno."

Everything perplexed poor Sara. Her merry heart and tortured body were always at odds. She drew a humped wrist across her nose and said, "I dunno, I dunno," after each remark.

"Goodbye, Sophie's Em'ly; come some more soon. I like that you come. I dunno why I got pain, lots pain. I dunno — I dunno."

I said to Sophie, "You see! The others know I am your big friend. They call me 'Sophie's Em'ly.'"

She was happy.

Susan lived on one side of Sophie's house and Mrs. Johnson, the Indian widow of a white man, on the other. The widow's house was beyond words clean. The cookstove was a mirror, the floor white as a sheet from scrubbing. Mrs. Johnson's hands were clever and busy. The row of hard kitchen chairs had each its own antimacassar and cushion. The crocheted bedspread and embroidered pillowslips, all the work of Mrs. Johnson's hands, were smoothed taut. Mrs. Johnson's husband had been a sea captain. She had loved him deeply and remained a widow though she had had many offers of marriage after he died. Once the Indian agent came, and said:

"Mrs. Johnson, there is a good man who has a farm and money in the bank. He is shy, so he sent me to ask if you will marry him."

"Tell that good man, 'Thank you', Mr. Agent, but tell him, too, that Mrs. Johnson only got love for her dead Johnson."

Sophie's other neighbour, Susan, produced and buried babies almost as fast as Sophie herself. The two women laughed for each other and cried for each other. With babies on their backs and baskets on their arms they crossed over on the ferry to Vancouver and sold their baskets from door to door. When they came to my studio they rested and drank tea with me. My parrot, sheep dog, the white rats and the totem pole pictures all interested them. "An' you got Injun flower, too," said Susan.

"Indian flowers?"

She pointed to ferns and wild things I had brought in from the woods.

Sophie's house was shut up. There was a chain and padlock on the gate. I went to Susan.

"Where is Sophie?"

"Sophie in sick house. Got sick eye."

I went to the hospital. The little Indian ward had four beds. I took ice cream and the nurse divided it into four portions.

A homesick little Indian girl cried in the bed in one corner, an old woman grumbled in another. In a third there was a young mother with a baby, and in the fourth bed was Sophie.

There were flowers. The room was bright. It seemed to me that the four brown faces on the four white pillows should be happier and far more comfortable here than lying on mattresses on the hard floors in the village, with all the family muddle going on about them.

"How nice it is here, Sophie."

"Not much good of hospital, Emily."

"Oh! What is the matter with it?"

"Bad bed."

"What is wrong with the beds?"

"Move, move, all time shake. 'Spose me move, bed move too."

She rolled herself to show how the springs worked. "Me ole-fashion, Em'ly. Me like kitchen floor fo' sick."

Susan and Sophie were in my kitchen, rocking their sorrows back and forth and alternately wagging their heads and giggling with shut eyes at some small joke.

"You go live Victoria now, Emily," wailed Sophie, "and we never see those babies, never!"

Neither woman had a baby on her back these days. But each had a little new grave in the cemetery. I had told them about a friend's twin babies. I went to the telephone.

"Mrs. Dingle, you said I might bring Sophie to the twins?"

"Surely, any time," came the ready reply.

"Come, Sophie and Susan, we can go and see the babies now."

The mothers of all those little cemetery mounds stood looking and looking at the thriving white babies, kicking and sprawling on their bed. The women said, "Oh my! — Oh my!" over and over.

Susan's hand crept from beneath her shawl to touch a baby's leg. Sophie's hand shot out and slapped Susan's.

The mother of the babies said, "It's all right, Susan; you may touch my baby."

Sophie's eyes burned Susan for daring to do what she so longed to do herself. She folded her hands resolutely under her shawl and whispered to me, "Nice ladies don' touch, Em'ly."

Down at English Bay

ETHEL WILSON

ONCE UPON A TIME THERE WAS A NEGRO WHO LIVED IN VANCOUVER and his name was Joe Fortes. He lived in a small house by the beach at English Bay and there is now a little bronze plaque to his honour and memory nearby, and he taught hundreds of little boys and girls how to swim. First of all he taught them for the love of it and after that he was paid a small salary by the City Council or the Parks Board, but he taught for love just the same. And so it is that now there are Judges, and Aldermen, and Cabinet Ministers, and lawyers, and doctors, and magnates, and ordinary business men, and grandmothers, and prostitutes, and burglars, and Sunday School superintendents, and drycleaners, and so on whom Joe Fortes taught to swim, and they will be the first to admit it. And Joe Fortes saved several people from drowning; some of them were worth saving and some were not worth saving in the slightest — take the man who was hanged in Kingston jail; but Joe Fortes could not be expected to know this, so he saved everyone regardless. He was greatly beloved and he was respected.

Joe Fortes was always surrounded by little boys and girls in queer bathing suits in the summertime. The little boys' bathing suits had arms and legs, not to speak of bodies and almost skirts on them; and the little girls were covered from neck to calf in blue serge or alpaca with white braid — rows of it — round the sailor collar and the full skirt, and a good pair of black wool stockings. This all helped to weigh them down when they tried to learn to swim, and to drown the little girls, in particular, when possible.

Joe had a nice round brown face and a beautiful brown body and arms and legs as he waded majestically in the waves of English Bay amongst all the little white lawyers and doctors and trained nurses and seamstresses who jumped up and down and splashed around him. "Joe," they called, and "Look at me, Joe! Is this the way?" and they splashed and swallowed and Joe supported them under their chins and by their behinds and said in his rich slow fruity voice, "Kick out, naow! Thassaway. Kick right out!" And sometimes he supported them, swimming like frogs, to the raft, and when they had clambered on to the raft they were afraid to jump off and Joe Fortes became impatient and terrible and said in a very large voice, "Jump now! I'll catch you! You jump off that raff or I'll leave you here all night!" And that was how they learned to swim.

Rose was one of the children who learned to swim with Joe Fortes, and she was one of the cowardly ones who shivered on the raft while Joe roared, "You jump off of that raff this minute, or I'll leave you there all night!" So she jumped because the prospect was so terrible and so real, and how threatening the wet sea by night, and who knows what creatures will come to this dark raft alone. So she jumped.

Aunt Rachel did not let Rose go swimming in her good blue serge bathing costume with white braid and black wool stockings unless some grownup was there. Aunts and guardians feel much more responsible for children than parents do, and so they are overanxious and they age faster. Aunt Topaz was not very much good as a guardian because she did not bathe, could not swim, was irresponsible, and usually met friends on the beach with whom she entered into conversation and then forgot about Rose.

One day, however, Rose persuaded her Aunt Rachel to let her go to the beach with Aunt Topaz who was quite ready for an outing, and in any case wanted to take her bicycle for a walk. So Rose and her Great-Aunt started off down Barclay Street in very good spirits on a sunny July afternoon. Tra-la-la, how happy they were! They talked separately and together. Aunt Topaz wheeled her bicycle, which gave her a very sporting appearance, and she wore her hat which looked like a rowboat. She carried some biscuits in the string bag which was attached to the shining handlebars of her noble English bicycle. Rose carried a huge parcel in a towel and swung it by a strap. She further complicated her walk by taking her hoop and stick. So Great-Aunt and Great-Niece proceeded down Barclay Street towards English Bay, Rose bowling her hoop whenever she felt like it.

When they arrived at English Bay Rose rushed into the bathhouse with five cents, and Aunt Topaz got into conversation with a young man called Eustace Flowerdew, with whose mother she was acquainted. Eustace Flowerdew wore a stiff straw hat attached to him somewhere by a black cord, so that if in his progress along the sands the hat should blow off, it would still remain attached to the person of Eustace. He wore pince-nez which made him look very refined. His collar was so high and stiff that it hurt him, and his tie was a chaste and severe four-in-hand. He collected tie-pins which were called stick-pins. Today he wore a stick-pin with the head of a horse.

"Oh, good afternoon, Eustace," said Aunt Topaz, "how nice you do look to be sure. How is your mother what a nice horse!"

After taking off his hat and putting it on again, Eustace hitched up each of his trouser legs and sat down beside Aunt Topaz, and looked over the top of his collar. In so doing he jiggled the bicycle which was unusually heavy and was inexpertly propped against the log on which he and Aunt Topaz were sitting. The bicycle intentionally fell on them both and knocked them down. This bicycle was very ill-tempered and ingenious, and was given to doing this kind of thing when possible on purpose. Aunt Topaz lay prone, and Eustace Flowerdew crawled out and lifted the bicycle off her and led it away to a tree where it could not touch them any more. Aunt Topaz exclaimed a great deal, got up, dusted the sand off herself, and Rose was as forgotten as though she had never existed.

"What are you doing on the beach at this time of the afternoon, Eustace?" asked Aunt Topaz.

Eustace did not want to tell Aunt Topaz the truth, which was that he hoped to meet a girl called Mary Evans in whom he had become interested, so he told her a lie.

"I have come here to forget, Miss Edgeworth," he said, looking at the ocean over his collar.

"And what do you want to forget? ... Oh, I suppose I shouldn't ask you if you want to forget it! How very interesting!"

The young man took his hat off and passed his hand over his forehead wearily. "He is good-looking, but he looks rather silly," thought Topaz.

"The fact is that I am writing a play," he said at last.

Topaz was frightfully excited. She had never before sat on a log with someone who was writing a play. Memories of Sir Henry Irving, Ellen Terry and the Lyceum Theatre in general romped through her mind and she did not know where to begin. She bubbled a little but the young man did not seem to hear. He was still looking out to sea. How beautiful it was, beyond the cries and splashings of children who crowded round Joe Fortes. There is a serenity and a symmetry about English Bay. It is framed by two harmonious landfalls. Out stretches Point Grey sloping to the southwest. Undulations of mountain, mainland and island come to a poetic termination on the northwest. Straight ahead to the westward sparkles the ocean as far as the dim white peaks of Vancouver Island. Seagulls flash and fly and cry in the wide summer air. Sitters on the beach regarded this beauty idly.

"What are you calling your play, Eustace?" asked Aunty when she had recovered.

"Break, Break, Break," said the young man. "Who is this uncommonly plain little girl standing in front of us? How very wet she is!"

"That?" said Aunt Topaz, suddenly seeing Rose. "Oh, there you are. How do you do, Rose? That is my great-niece. Yes, she is plain, isn't she? When wet. When dry she looks better, because her hair curls. Now run away and enjoy yourself and make sure you don't drown. Well, what is it?"

"May I get a biscuit?" asked Rose, who had come up full of rapture and talk now quenched.

"Yes, yes. Get a biscuit but be careful of the bicycle. It's against that tree."

Rose looked hatingly at Eustace Flowerdew and went over to the bicycle, dripping as she went. No sooner did she touch the heavy bicycle than it rushed violently away from her down the beach and hurled itself into the sand where it lay with its pedals quivering. Rose looked, but the two had not seen this. So she went and pulled up the bicycle and led it over to the tree again. She propped it up against the tree as best she could, dusted some of the sand off the biscuits, ate them grit and all, and ran off again to the heavenly waves and children surrounding Joe Fortes.

"What does your mother say about your writing a play? I should think she would feel very nervous. Are you introducing the sex element at all ... illicit love, so to speak ... or are you, if I may say so, keeping it thoroughly wholesome?" asked Topaz.

"My dear Miss Edgeworth," answered the young man pityingly, "I trust that you do not still regard Art as being in any way connected with morality!" He saw in the distance a figure that looked like Mary Evans, and his muscles were already flexing to rise. A shadow fell across Aunty and Eustace.

"Well, I do declare!" exclaimed Aunty joyously. "If this isn't Mrs. Hamilton Coffin! Mrs. Coffin, let me present to you a rising young ... " but the rising young playwright was no longer there. He was striding away down the beach.

"Do sit down, Mrs. Coffin!" said Topaz. "This is nice! How very athletic you do look!" She was filled with admiration. Mrs. Coffin was tall and the black serge bathing suit which she wore did not become her. On this fine summer day Mrs. Coffin, warmly dressed for swimming, displayed no part of her body except her face and ears and her arms as far up as her elbows. "How delightful!" exclaimed Topaz sincerely.

"I have lately, Miss Edgeworth," said Mrs. Coffin, who was a serious woman, "come under the influence of Ralston's Health Foods, and so has my husband. We are making a careful study of physical health and exercise and right thinking. We eat Ralston's Health Foods and a new food called Grape Nuts" ("'Grape Nuts!' that sounds delicious!" said Topaz) "twice a day. Already complexion is brighter, our whole mental attitude is improved, and I *may* say," she lowered her voice, "that faulty elimination is corrected."

"Faulty elimination! Well, well! Fancy that!" echoed Aunt Topaz, and wondered, "What on earth is she talking about?"

"I have also made an appointment with Mr. Fortes for a swimming lesson and I hope very soon to have mastered the art. This is my third lesson."

"Never too old to learn! Never too old to learn!" said Topaz merrily but without tact. She had no intention of taking swimming lessons herself. "I will come down to the water's edge and cheer you on." "I wonder if it's her costume or her name that makes me think of the tomb," she thought cheerfully.

Mrs. Coffin and Aunt Topaz went down to the water's edge. Joe Fortes disentangled himself from the swimming, bobbing, prancing, screaming children, and came out of the ocean to speak to Mrs. Coffin. He looked very fine, beautiful brown seal that he was, with the clear sparkling water streaming off him.

Mrs. Coffin advanced into the sea, and unhesitatingly dipped herself. "How brave! How brave! Bravo!" cried Topaz from the brink, clapping. Joe Fortes discussed the motions of swimming with Mrs. Coffin, doing *so* with his arms, and then *so* with his big legs like flexible pillars, and Mrs. Coffin took the first position. Joe Fortes respectfully supported her chin with the tips of his strong brown fingers. He dexterously and modestly raised her rear, and held it raised by a bit of bathing suit. "How politely he does it!" thought Topaz, admiring Joe Fortes and Mrs. Coffin as they proceeded up and down the ocean. When Mrs. Coffin had proceeded up and down supported and exhorted by Joe Fortes for twenty minutes or so, with Topaz addressing them from the brink, she tried swimming alone. She went under several times dragged down by her bathing suit but emerged full of hope. She dressed, and came and sat with Aunt Topaz.

"I understand, Miss Edgeworth," said Mrs. Coffin, "that you are the President of the Minerva Club!"

"I! President! Oh dear no!" said Topaz laughing merrily. "Never again will I be President of anything as long as I live! I was for a year President of our Ladies' Aid, and the worry nearly killed me! I'd as soon be hanged as be President of anything — much sooner, I assure you! No, Mrs. Coffin,

I am the Secretary of the Minerva Club — Honorary you understand — and Mrs. Aked, the President, promises that I can toss it up! toss it up! at any moment that I wish!"

Mrs. Coffin seemed to be about to say something further when a miserable-looking object appeared in front of them. It was Rose, blue and dripping.

"J-Joe F-F-Fortes s-s-says that I'm b-b-b-blue and I must g-g-go home," stuttered Rose shivering. "I d-d-d-don't want to. D-D-Do I have to?

"Oh dear me, what a sight!" said Aunt Topaz who had forgotten Rose again. "Certainly, certainly! Rush into your clothes and we'll walk home briskly and have some tea! What a delightful afternoon!"

On the way home the two pushed their impedimenta. Rose took the superfluous hoop, and Aunt Topaz wheeled her bicycle. The bicycle kicked her with its large protruding pedals as often as possible, and became entangled in her long skirt from time to time, so she often had to stop. When she was disentangled they went on. The bicycle bided its time, and then it kicked her again. Their minds were full of their own affairs, of which they talked regardless.

"A very silly young man, I'm afraid, but he may grow out of it. It is possible, however, that he has talent … "

"I swam six strokes alone. I swam six strokes alone … "

"I'm sure Mrs. Hamilton Coffin deserves a great deal of credit at her age … "

"Joe Fortes says that if I can just master the … "

"But what she meant by 'faulty elimination' I cannot imagine. It may have something to do with the Mosaic Law … "

"Joe Fortes can swim across English Bay easy-weasy. A big boy said that Joe Fortes could swim across the English Channel easy-weasy … "

"I do wish you'd stop saying 'easy-weasy' … oh … " The bicycle, behaving coarsely, swerved, turned and tried to run Aunt Topaz down.

"And Geraldine has been swimming longer than me and she can't swim as good as me … "

"As well as I. 'Grape Nuts' sound delicious! A combination of grapes and nuts no doubt … "

This kind of conversation went on all the way home, and after they reached home too, until Rose went to bed. It was plain to Rachel and her mother that Aunty and Rose had enjoyed going down to English Bay, and Rachel was greatly relieved that Rose had not been drowned.

On the next afternoon Aunt Topaz prepared to go to the meeting of the Minerva Club. She dressed very prettily, and wore a feather boa. Her success in dress was a matter of luck rather than taste, but today she looked uncommonly well. "How nice you look, Aunty!" said Rachel admiringly. Aunty was very happy. She pranced up Barclay Street, carrying her Minutes of the previous meeting — which were brief — in her hand.

There were nine ladies gathered at Mrs. Aked's house for the meeting of the Minerva Club. Tap, tap went Mrs. Aked on a little table. "We will now call the meeting to order, and our Honorary Secretary will read the Minutes of the previous meeting — Miss Edgeworth."

Everybody admired the experience and aplomb of Mrs. Aked.

Topaz arose and smiled at the ladies. Nine of them. When it came to reading aloud, even Minutes, she enjoyed herself thoroughly. But if she had to utter a single impromptu word in public, on her feet, she suffered more than tongue could tell. Therefore she was careful never to place herself in a position where she might have to make a speech. Considering that she spent her whole life in speaking, this was strange. But human beings are very strange, and there you are.

Topaz reported, smiling over her Minutes, that at the previous meeting the Minerva Club had listened to a paper on Robert Browning and that selections from that great man's less obscure poems had been read aloud. It had been decided that today's meeting should include a brief comprehensive paper on "Poets of the Elizabethan Era" by Mrs. Howard Henchcliffe who certainly had her work cut out, and that selections from the verses of Elizabethan poets would be read by Mrs. Isaacs, Mrs. Simpson, and — modestly — Miss Edgeworth. Then Aunt Topaz sat down. How she enjoyed this!

"Any business, ladies?" enquired Mrs. Aked. "Ah, yes, one vacancy in the Club. The name of Mrs. Hamilton Coffin is up for election. Any discussion before we vote Mrs. Hamilton Coffin into the Club? I think not."

But a rather pudding-faced lady raised a tentative hand. She cleared her throat. "Pardon *me*," she said. "I hope we are all friends here, and that discussion may be without prejudice?"

Mrs. Aked nodded, and the ladies murmured and rustled and adjusted their boas.

"Before voting on the name of Mrs. Hamilton Coffin," said the pudding-faced lady, "may I remind ladies present that the reputation of our members has always been beyond reproach?"

"I'm sure Mrs. Hamilton Coffin ... " began a small lady with sparkling eyes, in outraged tones. "Whatever can this be?" wondered Topaz.

The pudding-faced lady again held up her hand. "Pardon *me*," she said, "I have nothing at all to say against the personal reputation of Mrs. Hamilton Coffin. But *do* the Ladies of the Minerva Club know that Mrs. Hamilton Coffin has been seen more than once in a public place, bathing in the arms of a black man."

A rustle of indignation ran through the room, whether at the pudding-faced lady or at Mrs. Hamilton Coffin it was impossible to say.

Suddenly in that inward part of her that Topaz had not known to exist, arose a fury. She who did not know of the existence of private life because she had no private life of her own, she who feared so greatly to speak in public, she who was never roused to anger, rose to her feet, trembling and angry. She was angry for Joe Fortes; and for Mrs. Hamilton Coffin; and for herself, a spectator on that innocent blue day. She was aware of something evil and stupid in the room.

"Ladies," she said, shaking, "I shall now count ten because I think I shall then be better able to say what I want to say and because I am very frightened. Excuse me just a minute." And Topaz was silent, and they could see her counting ten. All the ladies waited; emotions were held in check. Then the plain and interesting face of Topaz lighted with its usual friendly smile.

"Ladies," she said, "I was present yesterday when that admirable woman Mrs. Hamilton Coffin had her swimming lesson from our respected fellow-citizen Joe Fortes. I know that the lady who has just spoken," and Aunty smiled winningly upon the pudding-faced lady, "will be quite properly relieved to hear that so far from swimming in the arms of Mr. Fortes, which any of us who were drowning would be grateful to do, Mrs. Hamilton Coffin was swimming in his finger-tips. I feel that we should be honoured to have as a fellow member so active, progressive and irreproachable a lady as Mrs. Hamilton Coffin. I therefore beg to propose the name of Mrs. Hamilton Coffin as the tenth member of the Minerva Club." And she sat down scarlet-cheeked, shaking violently.

"Hear-hear, hear-hear," said all the ladies — including the pudding-faced lady — with one accord and very loud, clapping. "Order, order," cried the President, enjoying herself immensely. "I hereby declare Mrs. Hamilton Coffin a member of the Minerva Club, and I instruct our Honorary Secretary to write a letter of invitation. I will now call upon Miss Topaz Edgeworth to read the introductory selection from one of the poets of the Elizabethan Era."

The ladies slipped back their boas and emitted releasing breaths of warm air (the room had become close), adjusted their positions and adopted postures suitable to those about to listen to the poets.

Aunt Topaz stood and read. This was her great day. How beautifully she read! Her chattering tones were modulated and musical. The training of the classical Mrs. Porter had made Aunty a reader in the classical style. She was correct, deliberate, flowing, unemotional, natural. She was very happy, reading aloud slowly to the Minerva Club. She read clearly —

"Even such is Time, that takes in trust
Our youth, our joys, our all we have,
And pays us but with earth and dust;
Who, in the dark and silent grave,
When we have wandered all our ways,
Shuts up the story of our days.
But from this earth, this grave, this dust,
My God shall raise me up, I trust."

Everybody clapped.

Aunty went home disturbed and happy; and that evening she told her sister and Rachel about the meeting, and her indignation rose and fell and was satisfied. She told it several times.

The Grandmother said, "I am glad you spoke as you did, my dear sister. You were right."

Rachel put down her work. She thought, "How often I am angry with Aunty! How often I scold her! She *is* aggravating, but just see this!" Rachel looked across at Aunt Topaz with eyes at once sombre and bright that were Rachel's only beauty. "Yes, Aunty," she said, "that's true. I have never heard you say an unkind thing about anyone. I have never heard you cast an aspersion on anyone. I really believe that you are one of the few people who think no evil."

Aunty *was* amazed! Rachel, who seldom praised, had praised her. She — Topaz — who was never humble and embarrassed became humble and embarrassed. What could she say. "I think," she said, "that I will go to bed. I will take the newspaper." And she stumbled upstairs in her hasty way.

Above, in her bedroom, they heard her singing in that funny little flute voice of hers.

Hurry, Hurry

WHEN THE MOUNTAINS BEYOND THE CITY ARE COVERED WITH SNOW TO THEIR BASE, the late afternoon light falling obliquely from the west upon the long slopes discloses new contours. For a few moments of time the austerity vanishes, and the mountains appear innocently folded in furry white. Their daily look has gone. For these few moments the slanting rays curiously discover each separate tree behind each separate tree in the infinite white forests. Then the light fades, and the familiar mountains resume their daily look again. The light has gone, but those who have seen it will remember.

As Miriam stood at the far point of Sea Island, with the wind blowing in from the west, she looked back towards the city. There was a high ground fog at the base of the mountains, and so the white flanks and peaks seemed to lie unsupported in the clear spring sky. They seemed to be unattached to the earth. She wished that Allan were with her to see this sight of beauty which passed even as she looked upon it. But Allan was away, and she had come for a walk upon the dyke alone with their dogs.

It was the very day in spring that the soldier blackbirds had returned from Mexico to the marshes of the delta. Just a few had come, but in the stubble fields behind the high dyke, and in the salt marshes seawards from the dyke, and on the shallow sea, and over the sea there were thousands of other birds. No people anywhere. Just birds. The salt wind blew softly from the sea, and the two terrier dogs ran this way and that, with and against the wind. A multitude of little sandpipers ran along the wet sands as if they were on wheels. They whispered and whimpered together as they ran, stabbing with their long bills into the wet sands and running on. There was a continuous small noise of birds in the air. The terriers bore down upon the little sandpipers. The terriers ran clumsily, sinking in the marshy blackish sand, encumbered as they ran, and the little sandpipers rose and flew low together to a safer sandbank. They whispered and wept together as they fled in a cloud, animated by one enfolding spirit of motion. They settled on their safe sandbank, running and jabbing the wet sand with their bills. The terriers like little earnest monsters bore down upon them again in futile chase, and again the whispering cloud of birds arose. Miriam laughed at the silly hopeful dogs.

Farther out to sea were the duck and the brant and the seagulls. These strutted on the marsh-like sands, or lay upon the shallow water or flew idly above the water. Sometimes a great solitary heron arose from nowhere and flapped across the wet shore. The melancholy heron settled itself in a motionless hump, and again took its place in obscurity among stakes and rushes.

Behind the dyke where Miriam stood looking out to sea was a steep bank sloping to a shallow salt-water ditch, and beyond that again, inland, lay the stubble fields of Sea Island, crossed by rough hedges. From the fields arose the first song of the meadow lark, just one lark, how curious after winter to hear its authentic song again. Thousands of ducks showed themselves from the stubble fields, rising and flying without haste or fear to the sea.

Miriam called to the dogs and walked on along the narrow clay path at the top of the dyke. She delighted in the birds and the breeze and the featureless ocean. The dogs raced after her.

Clumps of bare twisted bushes were scattered along the edge of the path, sometimes obscuring the curving line of the dyke ahead. In a bush a few early soldier blackbirds talked to each other. Miriam stood still to listen. "Oh-kee-*ree*," called a blackbird. "Oh-kee-*ree*," answered his mate. "Oh-kee-*ree*," he said. "Oh-kee-*ree*," she answered. Then the male bird flew. His red patches shone finely. What a strange note, thought Miriam, there's something sweet and something very ugly. The soldier blackbird's cry began on a clear flute's note and ended in piercing sweetness. The middle sound grated like a rusty lock. As she walked on between the twisted black bushes more soldier blackbirds called and flew. Oh-kee-*ree*! Oh-kee-*ree*! Sweet and very ugly.

Suddenly she saw a strange object. Below her on the left, at the edge of the salt-water ditch there was an unlikely heap of something. Miriam stopped and looked. This thing was about the size of a tremendous hunched cat, amorphous, of a rich reddish brown. It was the rich brown of a lump of rotted wood. Although it did not move, she had instant warning that this creature was alive and had some meaning for her. She called the dogs who came wagging. She leashed them, and they went forward together. The dogs tugged and tugged. Soon they too looked down the bank at the strange object. In the brown mass something now moved. Miriam saw that the brown object was a large wounded hawk. The hawk was intensely aware of the woman and the dogs. As they paused, and then as they passed along the high dyke path, the hawk's head turned slowly, very slowly, to observe them. Its body was motionless. Miriam was glad that she had leashed the dogs. In another minute they would have descended on the hawk. One brown wing lay trailed behind the big bird, but with its sharp beak and tearing claws it would have mauled the terriers, and they would have tormented it. The hawk stared brightly at her. She wished that she could save the hawk from its lingering death on the marshes, but there was nothing she could do. Motionless, save for the slowly turning head, the great bird followed them with intent gaze. Its eyes were bright with comprehension, but no fear. It was ready. The hawk made Miriam feel uneasy. She walked on faster, still keeping the dogs on the leash. She looked back. The hawk steadily watched her. She turned and walked on still faster.

One of the dogs growled and then both barked loudly. Around a thorn bush, hurrying towards her came a man. In all their walks upon the dyke before Allan went away, they had never met another human being. Miriam was startled. She was almost afraid. The strange hawk. The strange man. The man stopped. He was startled too. Then he hurried towards her. Crowded on the narrow clayey path of the dyke stood Miriam and the two dogs, uncertain. The man came close to her and stopped.

"Don't go on," he said urgently, "don't go on. It isn't safe. There's a cougar. I'm going to a farmhouse. To warn them. Perhaps I can get a gun. Turn back. And keep your dogs on the lead," he said sharply.

"Oh," said Miriam, "you must be mistaken. There's never been a cougar on these islands. No, of course I won't go on though. I'll turn back at once. But you *must* be mistaken. A dog or even a coyote, but not a cougar!"

"It *is* a cougar," said the man vehemently, "did you never hear of the cougar that swam across from the North Shore last year? Well — I can't stop to argue — there *is* a cougar, I saw it. Beside the dyke. It's driven in by hunger, starving, I expect. Well?"

He looked at her. He held her eyes with his eyes.

"Oh," said Miriam, "of course I won't go on. I should never have come! I'm so glad I met you. But it's extraordinary!" and she turned in haste.

The man paid her no further attention. He stepped down a bit from the path on to the steep grassy side of the dyke, and pushed past her and the restless dogs. He walked on very fast without another word. Miriam hurried after him along the narrow dyke path, the dogs impeding her as she hurried. This was like a bad dream. Hurry, hurry! I can't hurry.

She nearly ran along the slippery bumpy dyke path, past the brown heap of the wounded hawk whose bright eyes watched her, and past the straggly bushes where the soldier blackbirds flew from tree to tree and sang. She hurried along until she turned the curve of the dyke and saw again the mountains behind the city. The peaks now hung pink and gold in the cold spring sky. To the farthest range of the Golden Ears the sunset caught them. Miriam fled on. The leashed dogs ran too, bounding and hindering her as she ran. She crossed the little footbridge that led to the lane that led to her car.

She had lost sight of the man a long time ago. He had hurried on to give the alarm. She had seen him stumbling down the steep dyke side and splashing across the salt-water ditch to the stubble fields.

Far behind them along the dyke, the body of the young woman who had just been murdered lay humped beside the salt-water ditch.

The man who had killed her reached the cover of the hedge, out of sight of that woman with the dogs. When he reached the cover of the hedge he began to run across the tussocky field, stumbling, half blind, sobbing, crying out loud.

The Woman Who Got On at Jasper Station

HOWARD O'HAGAN

THE DAYCOACH, SMELLING OF CHEESE SANDWICHES, WAXPAPER AND OPENED POP bottles, at the noon hour was crowded with excursionists — a conducted party of young people passing westward through the Rockies — and when the conductor came by for the tickets, the woman in the sheared lamb's wool coat who, like most of those around her, had got on at Jasper Station a few miles back, asked him if there might be another seat, one which she could have to herself, "Maybe up ahead," she said, "in the next coach."

The conductor — he was "new" on the run and she had not seen him before — punched her ticket before replying. He was a stout man with a drooping brown moustache. His lower eyelids sagged, revealing their inner redness. They gave him a semblance of rage, of bafflement, and the woman regretted that she had spoken.

"Lady," he said, leaning closer to her, "there are no seats up ahead, I've just come through. And this boy" — he glanced at the sailor by the window who shared her seat — "is ready, if the time comes, to give his life for you, for all of us. You oughtn't to mind sitting beside him."

The conductor — the old fool, she thought — went his way, panting, mumbling. The woman turned quickly to the sailor. "I did not mean to be rude," she said. "I just felt it would be more comfortable — for you."

"Don't pay him attention, ma'am. He's been reading advertisements. Besides, there's lots of room." The sailor inched away from her towards the wall of the coach. The woman supposed she had sat beside him — there were two or three other seats she might have shared — because, like herself, he was separate and aloof from the prevailing hubbub of the members of the excursion, staring wide-eyed out the windows and exclaiming at the mountains.

Now, murmuring a reply to the sailor's remark, the woman wished that he had not called her "ma'am." It set a mark upon her, put her apart, stamped her age upon her brow. Her figure was firm and trim, her carriage erect, her ankles neat. It was seldom that she was taken to be more than twenty-five.

She shuffled her shoulders, settled into her seat, surrendered herself to the immobility of travel, cheeks flat and pale, framing the red wound of her mouth, lips slightly parted as if she were about to cry aloud with its hurt. She lifted her hand, smoothed the hair upcombed from the back of her neck. Her tasselled Chinese-style hat nodded with the motion of the coach, as though in assent to her journey. Other heads nodded too, bodies swayed, voices muttered, forests of spruce and fir and pine flowed smoothly by the window.

"I know ... " the sailor said.

"What's that?" The woman was startled. She had forgotten the sailor.

"I know," he said. "You're not used to riding in day coaches. I saw your suitcase when you came in. It's got labels on it. You've 'been places.'"

The woman smiled. "It's an old weekend bag," she said. She was about to add that the labels also were old. Old times, old labels — not that, these days, labels meant anything at all.

"And anyway, I've travelled in many day coaches," she continued to the sailor. "This isn't the first time. Besides ... "

The sailor interrupted. "I know. You were going to say, 'Besides, it's only a short trip I'm making.' If it were a longer trip, someone like you would have more baggage than that little bag up there in the rack above us. Of course, you may have a trunk checked up ahead ... "

"No, I haven't," the woman interjected — and suddenly wondered why she should explain herself to the man beside her. In less than an hour she would be back "home." What would the sailor think if she told him that her "home" was a three-roomed log cabin in a railroad town of three hundred by a green mountain lake? And why should she care at all what he might think? She gnawed her lip and felt a flush of blood behind her ears. The sailor, at whom for the first time she looked fully, did not smile. A young dark-haired man with pink ears — hardly more than a boy — he seemed to await her approval before he smiled. Her eyes fell away from his. She reached into her flat, black handbag for a cigarette, searching for a match. The sailor held his lighter out to her, as if so to atone for what he had said. Over the flame his blue eyes were warm, moist, fringed with long straight lashes. Something in them — friendly, beseeching, lonely? She could not be sure.

The woman and the sailor sat for minutes in silence. She noticed, close by her own, the sailor's thigh, its curve of hard muscle showing under the dark blue trouser leg. Involuntarily, she drew back. His hand rested there upon it, heavy, competent. The back of the hand was hairy. All of him, she surmised, would be furred like that — his chest, his shoulder blades, the thigh beneath its cloth. The vagrant thought sent a tremor through her body, touched her with a gentle ecstasy. She stamped out her cigarette, rose and removed her coat, folded it on the top of her weekend bag in the rack overhead. Seating herself, she smoothed her dress, observing the dimples at the base of her fingers, the tight gold band of her wedding ring. The dress was linen and of a robin's egg blue. Up its front was a line of small white buttons, joined by narrow white embroidery. She pondered again why she had worn it. Still, it was suitable for the season, a dress for early summer. Looking down at its embroidery, she felt uneasy, as if this marked the trail of a mouse which had jumped on her straight from the tin flour bin under the kitchen table, run between her breasts and over her right shoulder.

"What were you saying?" she asked the sailor suddenly.

"Me? I wasn't talking." The sailor was surprised. He smiled weakly, in indecision, in discomfiture.

"Don't you think the coach is very hot?" The woman spoke sharply, as in rebuke.

"Well ... I don't rightly know. It seems good to me. It's cold up where I've been."

"And where is that?"

"Churchill — that's on Hudson Bay."

The woman said, "Oh, up there!"

The sailor told her that he was on his way to Esquimalt on Vancouver Island "to report."

"And then?" the woman asked, and at once regretted her question.

"They don't tell us," the sailor said. "Maybe — well, anywhere. We don't really know much before we sail."

He turned to look out the window and a shadow, pooled in his lean cheek, was shed with his turning.

The woman regarded the length of the coach before her, the bobbing heads, the swarthy heads, the fair heads of the young people. No more than ten years their senior, she envied them their youth, the pageant of their youth, from which she felt herself excluded, but one of whose course she partook for the brief period of her journey. A warmth and compassion suffused her for all those within the coach and, especially, for the man beside her. His sailor's uniform, contrasting with the gay shirts, sweaters and shawls about him, was like the shroud of all his young years.

"I am sorry," she said and was embarrassed to have spoken this comment on her thoughts aloud. The woman, who was childless, guessed it was war — the constant talk of war and what war's effect would be on the sailor and upon all the young people, so secure in courage, so vulnerable in flesh — what war's effect would be upon all the earth's people.

"Sorry?" the sailor repeated the word. His voice was slow and husky and, vibrating through the seat back, caressed her spine.

"I mean … " the woman spread her hands.

The sailor did not understand. He blinked, turned away.

After a while he asked her where she was getting off. She told him it would be at the next stop. "It's a little town by a lake. It's called Lucerne."

"Like in Switzerland," the sailor said.

"The name's the same," the woman answered. "Only in Switzerland, it's a lake. Where I am, the lake's called Yellowhead."

She had not been to Switzerland. However, she had seen pictures, read accounts of its lakes, its neat villages, its eidelweiss, its cattle grazing on the alplands and of its people given to song and dance and to blowing great curved horns. Apparently in Switzerland, unlike the Canadian Rockies, there were no roundhouses belching steam and smoke, no rundown cabins and one storied frame houses with laundry strung up behind, no pool hall with lounging men outside its door, no tilted outhouses, no railroaders in oil-stained overalls, no bearded trappers down from the hills sitting jack-knifed on the rail of the station platform spewing tobacco juice. She wished that she could have said to the sailor that she was going on to Vancouver, to Seattle, to San Francisco, to some place far, far away, where there were no mountains, no railroaders, no locomotives so close that, as the engineer waited for his "orders," they seemed to be panting in her own backyard — a backyard whose only fence was the jack pine forest.

"You live there … I mean, you live there, in this Lucerne?"

The woman spread her hands. "Of course, what else? My husband is the town doctor, I left him just now in Jasper. I went with him to visit while he's on a case."

"What sort of a doctor?"

"Oh, a doctor," the woman said. "Not a specialist. A doctor for people when they are ill." She did not, at this moment, care to think of her husband, of his work, or of Lucerne. For this short hour on the train, she would partake of another life, of youth, which was slipping by her, of a promise waiting somewhere, surely, below the horizon.

She turned her eyes on the sailor, held them there. Her eyes were brown, sullen, half-lidded. She recalled in the instant what a Boer from South Africa had said to her long ago at a dinner party. It had been long ago, four years ago, in an eastern city, before she was married and came to live in a small town by the railroad tracks in the mountains. "You know," the Boer had said quietly, the tip of his tongue lightly flicking his clipped moustache, "I have been watching your eyes. They are always half-lidded, drowsy. They make one think of ... " He said no more, but hunched his heavy shoulders, pursed his lips.

Now the sailor on the train looked away, looked back at her again.

She wondered what she wanted from the sailor, this boy regarding her through a man's face. She did not know.

"It shouldn't make any difference where I get off," she said, reverting to his former question.

The sailor said, "I was only thinking ... I guess I forgot and thought maybe we might be getting off at the same place. I mean, that you might be going through to the Coast, though I knew you weren't."

Since leaving Jasper, in the valley of the Arctic-flowing Athabasca, the train had climbed the grade along the Miette river to Yellowhead Pass and the headwaters of the Fraser which emptied into the Pacific. Now on the summit of the pass, as though upthrust by the very backbone of a continent, the coach for a moment lurched over a rough piece of track. The woman was bounced on her seat and, subsiding, her knee touched the sailor's, her thigh was next to his. This time she did not draw back.

She felt his warmth against her own, sensed the hardness of his eager body and, for the first time, caught the slight, seminal smell of beer on his breath. The train rolled on, past a waterfall and by a beaver pond reflecting the chaste, white trunk of a birch tree in its placid waters. A group of section men flashed by the window, leaning on their shovels, faces upheld to the monster of speed whose roadbed they faithfully tended. Up ahead the locomotive howled, like a thing pursued. Through the trees glimmered the green surface of Yellowhead Lake.

The sailor's shoulder touched the woman's. Against her thigh he pressed more strongly. She thought she felt its pulse, the blood urgent beneath the cloth. Lulled by the train's motion, they did not speak, they did not move, involved in a slow conspiracy of flesh. Had she tried to speak, she would have lacked the words to utter. Her mouth was dry. Chills coursed her body. Her eyes misted. The coach and its people swayed as if behind a flimsy curtain and ecstasy enfolded her like a garment.

The sailor's hand touched her knee through the skirt of robin's egg blue. She started, as if awakened from sleep. "Look," he said softly, "I could get off when you do. A day or two doesn't matter to me, I've got leave coming, and there must be a hotel in this town of yours."

He was going to get off with her! Where could she take him? To the house, guarded by neighbour's windows? Should she ask him to come by later, to dinner, when her husband, returning on a later train, would be at home? One was at times expected to ask servicemen to dinner. No, the answer was not there. Of course, they could get off separately and arrange to meet, as it were, by chance. "Maybe we could go somewhere," the sailor's voice beside her insisted.

His words brought to her mind the station, now fast approaching where she would get down from the train. A red frame station with a cinder platform and beyond it, down a slope, the town. It was not so much a town as a boulder-strewn street laid out in the wilderness stretching the quarter mile from the railroad tracks to Yellowhead Lake. Along its single street were two grocery stores, a pool hall, a combined church and school. The church-school on a little rise was across the street from the cabin where she lived and where her husband had his office. The town had no hotel, though it boasted one boardinghouse for bachelor railroaders and a homeless trapper or two.

Beyond her cabin were a few more dwellings staring stolidly at one another from across the street. Past them, by the lakeshore, the descending street became a dirt road, curving westward through a stand of jack pine to the wooden bridge which spanned the narrows. Across the bridge, on the lake's north shore and under the looming Seven Sisters, was a trapper's old cabin. From it a trail led west down the lake towards its outlet into the Fraser. Along the trail, on an idle afternoon, she had occasionally strolled. One afternoon in the recent spring, she remembered, had been grey and misty with a cool east wind from up the lake. She had sat with her back against a log and watched the waves of the lake roll in. The little waves, like the sky, were grey and she listened to each one as it dissolved with a whisper into the grey sand at her feet. Above the waves, a migrating flock of small, black birds, wheeled and dipped and twittered, like a handful of music notes thrown up against the lowering sky. It was a deserted spot, less than a mile from town. Behind the log, against which she leaned, freshly-leafed willows surrounded a verdant patch of grass. The willows, shoulder-high, would enfold one, shield one, hide one — hide her and the sailor — from all but the clouds above.

The woman did not face the sailor when she said, "But my husband ... "

When she spoke, she knew that he knew that she lied. Her husband could not be home, until the earliest, on the evening train. She would get down from the train, carrying her bag, and walk alone to the cabin, nodding here and there to the townspeople she passed on the way.

The sailor said, "Oh, I thought you told me ... I mean about your husband ... " He looked away out the window to the squalid outskirts of the town — two half-dressed children playing on the steps of a tarpaper shack. A muscle quivered on his jaw.

The woman shrank back from the scene beyond the window as though the children had been her own. To the sailor, she said, "Besides, there's no hotel in the town. Only a boardinghouse — for railroaders."

In a moment, she rose, reached up for her sheared lamb's wool coat, put it on. She took down her weekend bag with its faded labels. She paused, as if about to speak again, changed her mind and walked forward down the aisle as the train came to a stop.

The Bravest Boat

MALCOLM LOWRY

IT WAS A DAY OF SPINDRIFT AND BLOWING SEA-FOAM, WITH BLACK CLOUDS presaging rain driven over the mountains from the sea by a wild March wind.

But a clean silver sea light came from along the horizon where the sky itself was like glowing silver. And far away over in America the snowy volcanic peak of Mount Hood stood on high, disembodied, cut off from earth, yet much too close, which was an even surer presage of rain, as though the mountains had advanced, or were advancing.

In the park of the seaport the giant trees swayed, and taller than any were the tragic Seven Sisters, a constellation of seven noble red cedars that had grown there for hundreds of years, but were now dying, blasted, with bare peeled tops and stricken boughs. (They were dying rather than live longer near civilization. Yet though everyone had forgotten they were called after the Pleiades and thought they were named with civic pride after the seven daughters of a butcher, who seventy years before when the growing city was named Gaspool had all danced together in a shop window, nobody had the heart to cut them down.)

The angelic wings of the seagulls circling over the tree tops shone very white against the black sky. Fresh snow from the night before lay far down the slopes of the Canadian mountains, whose freezing summits, massed peak behind spire, jaggedly traversed the country northward as far as the eye could reach. And highest of all an eagle, with the poise of a skier, shot endlessly down the world.

In the mirror, reflecting this and much besides, of an old weighing machine with the legend *Your weight and your destiny* encircling its forehead and which stood on the embankment between the streetcar terminus and a hamburger stall, in this mirror along the reedy edge of the stretch of water below known as Lost Lagoon two figures in mackintoshes were approaching, a man and a beautiful passionate-looking girl, both bare-headed, and both extremely fair, and hand-in-hand, so that you would have taken them for young lovers, but that they were alike as brother and sister, and the man, although he walked with youthful nervous speed, now seemed older than the girl.

The man, fine-looking, tall, yet thick-set, very bronzed, and on approaching still closer obviously a good deal older than the girl, and wearing one of those blue-belted trenchcoats favoured by merchant marine officers of any country, though without any corresponding cap — moreover the trenchcoat was rather too short in the sleeve so that you could see some tattooing on his wrist, as he approached nearer still it seemed to be an anchor — whereas the girl's raincoat was of some sort of entrancing forest-green corduroy — the man paused every now and then to gaze into the lovely laughing face of his girl, and once or twice they both stopped, gulping in great draughts of salty clean sea and mountain air. A child smiled at them, and they smiled back. But the child belonged elsewhere, and the couple were unaccompanied.

In the lagoon swam wild swans, and many wild ducks: mallards and buffleheads and scaups, golden eyes and cackling black coots with carved ivory bills. The little buffleheads often took flight from the water and some of them blew about like doves among the smaller trees. Under these trees lining the bank other ducks were sitting meekly on the sloping lawn, their beaks tucked into their plumage rumpled by the wind. The smaller trees were apples and hawthorns, some just opening into bloom even before they had foliage, and weeping willows, from whose branches small showers from the night's rain were scattered on the two figures as they passed.

A red-breasted merganser cruised in the lagoon, and at this swift and angry sea bird, with his proud disordered crest, the two were now gazing with a special sympathy, perhaps because he looked lonely without his mate. Ah, they were wrong. The red-breasted merganser was now joined by his wife and on a sudden duck's impulse and with immense fuss the two wild creatures flew off to settle on another part of the lagoon. And for some reason this simple fact appeared to make these two good people — for nearly all people are good who walk in parks — very happy again.

Now at a distance they saw a small boy, accompanied by his father who was kneeling on the bank, trying to sail a toy boat in the lagoon. But the blustery March wind soon slanted the tiny yacht into trouble and the father hauled it back, reaching out with his curved stick, and set it on an upright keel again for his son.

Your weight and your destiny.

Suddenly the girl's face, at close quarters in the weighing machine's mirror, seemed struggling with tears: she unbuttoned the top button of her coat to readjust her scarf, revealing, attached to a gold chain around her neck, a small gold cross. They were quite alone now, standing on top of the embankment by the machine, save for a few old men feeding the ducks below, and the father and his son with the toy yacht, all of whom had their backs turned, while an empty tram abruptly city-bound trundled around the minute terminus square; and the man, who had been trying to light his pipe, took her in his arms and tenderly kissed her, and then pressing his face against her cheek, held her a moment closely.

The couple, having gone down obliquely to the lagoon once more, had now passed the boy with his boat and his father. They were smiling again. Or as much as they could while eating hamburgers. And they were smiling still as they passed the slender reeds where a northwestern redwing was trying to pretend he had no notion of nesting, the northwestern redwing who like all birds in these parts may feel superior to man in that he is his own customs official, and can cross the wild border without let.

Along the far side of Lost Lagoon the green dragons grew thickly, their sheathed and cowled leaves giving off their peculiar animal-like odour. The two lovers were approaching the forest in which, ahead, several footpaths threaded the ancient trees. The park, seagirt, was very large, and like many parks throughout the Pacific Northwest, wisely left in places to the original wilderness. In fact, though its beauty was probably unique, it was quite like some American parks, you might have thought, save for the Union Jack that galloped evermore by a pavilion, and but for the apparition, at this moment, passing by on the carefully landscaped road slightly above, which led with its tunnels and detours to a suspension bridge, of a posse of Royal Canadian Mounted Policemen mounted royally upon the cushions of an American Chevrolet.

Nearer the forest were gardens with sheltered beds of snowdrops and here and there a few crocuses lifting their sweet chalices. The man and his girl now seemed lost in thought, breasting the buffeting wind that blew the girl's scarf out behind her like a pennant and blew the man's thick fair hair about his head.

A loudspeaker, enthroned on a wagon, barked from the city of Enochvilleport composed of dilapidated half-skyscrapers, at different levels, some with all kinds of scrap iron, even broken airplanes, on their roofs, others being moldy stock exchange buildings, new beer parlours crawling with verminous light even in mid-afternoon and resembling gigantic emerald-lit public lavatories for both sexes, masonries containing English tea shoppes where your fortune could be told by a female relative of

Maximilian of Mexico, totem pole factories, drapers' shops with the best Scotch tweed and opium dens in the basement (though no bars, as if, like some hideous old roué shuddering with every unmentionable secret vice this city without gaiety had cackled "No, I draw the line at that. What would our wee laddies come to then?"), cerise conflagrations of cinemas, modern apartment buildings, and other soulless behemoths, housing, it might be, noble invisible struggles, of literature, the drama, art or music, the student's lamp and the rejected manuscript; or indescribable poverty and degradation, between which civic attractions were squeezed occasional lovely dark ivy-clad old houses that seemed weeping, cut off from all light, on their knees, and elsewhere bankrupt hospitals, and one or two solid-stoned old banks, held up that afternoon; and among which appeared too, at infrequent intervals, beyond a melancholy never-striking black and white clock that said three, dwarfed spires belonging to frame façades with blackened rose windows, queer grimed onion-shaped domes, and even Chinese pagodas, so that first you thought you were in the Orient, then Turkey or Russia, though finally, but for the fact that some of these were churches, you would be sure you were in hell: despite that anyone who had ever really been in hell must have given Enochvilleport a nod of recognition, further affirmed by the spectacle, at first not unpicturesque, of the numerous sawmills relentlessly smoking and champing away like demons, Molochs fed by whole mountainsides of forests that never grew again, or by trees that made way for grinning regiments of villas in the background of "our expanding and fair city," mills that shook the very earth with their tumult, filling the windy air with their sound as of a wailing and gnashing of teeth: all these curious achievements of man, together creating as we say "the jewel of the Pacific," went as though down a great incline to a harbour more spectacular than Rio de Janeiro and San Francisco put together, with deep sea freighters moored at every angle for miles in the roadstead, but to whose heroic prospect nearly the only human dwellings visible on this side of the water that had any air of belonging, or in which their inhabitants could be said any longer to participate, were, paradoxically, a few lowly little self-built shacks and floathouses, that might have been driven out of the city altogether, down to the water's edge into the sea itself, where they stood on piles, like fishermen's huts (which several of them apparently were), or on rollers, some dark and tumbledown, others freshly and prettily painted, these last quite evidently built or placed with some human need for beauty in mind, even if under the permanent threat of eviction, and all standing, even the most sombre, with their fluted tin chimneys smoking here and there like toy tramp steamers, as though in defiance of the town, before eternity. In Enochvilleport itself some ghastly-coloured neon signs had long since been going through their unctuous twitchings and gesticulations that nostalgia and love transform into a poetry of longing: more happily one began to flicker: *Palomar, Louis Armstrong and His Orchestra.* A huge new grey dead hotel that at sea might be a landmark of romance, belched smoke out of its turreted haunted-looking roof, as if it had caught fire, and beyond that all the lamps were blazing within the grim courtyard of the law courts, equally at sea a trysting place of the heart, outside which one of the stone lions, having recently been blown up, was covered reverently with a white cloth, and inside which for a month a group of stainless citizens had been trying a sixteen-year-old boy for murder.

Nearer the park the apron lights appeared on a sort of pebble-dashed Y.M.C.A.-Hall-cum-variety-theatre saying *Tammuz The Master Hypnotist, Tonite 8:30,* and running past this the tramlines, down which another parkwise streetcar was approaching, could be seen extending almost to the department store in whose show window Tammuz' subject, perhaps a somnolent descendant of the seven sisters whose fame had eclipsed even that of the Pleiades, but whose announced ambition was to become a female psychiatrist, had been sleeping happily and publicly in a double bed for the last three days as an advance publicity stunt for tonight's performance.

Above Lost Lagoon on the road now mounting toward the suspension bridge in the distance much as a piece of jazz music mounts toward a break, a newsboy cried: "LASH ORDERED FOR SAINT PIERRE! SIXTEEN YEAR OLD BOY, CHILD-SLAYER, TO HANG! Read all about it!"

The weather too was forboding. Yet, seeing the wandering lovers, the other passers-by on this side of the lagoon, a wounded soldier lying on a bench smoking a cigarette, and one or two of those destitute souls, the very old who haunt parks — since, faced with a choice, the very old will sometimes prefer, rather than to keep a room and starve, at least in such a city as this, somehow to eat and live outdoors — smiled too.

For as the girl walked along beside the man with her arm through his and as they smiled together and their eyes met with love, or they paused, watching the blowing seagulls, or the ever-changing scale of the snow-freaked Canadian mountains with their fleecy indigo chasms, or to listen to the deep-tongued majesty of a merchantman's echoing roar (these things that made Enochvilleport's ferocious aldermen imagine that it was the city itself that was beautiful, and maybe they were half right), the whistle of a ferryboat as it sidled across the inlet northward, what memories might not be evoked in a poor soldier, in the breasts of the bereaved, the old, even, who knows, in the mounted policemen, not merely of young love, but of lovers, as they seemed to be, so much in love that they were afraid to lose a moment of their time together?

Yet only a guardian angel of these two would have known — and surely they must have possessed a guardian angel — the strangest of all strange things of which they were thinking, save that, since they had spoken of it so often before, and especially, when they had opportunity, on this day of the year, each knew of course that the other was thinking about it, to such an extent indeed that it was no surprise, it only resembled the beginning of a ritual when the man said, as they entered the main path of the forest, through whose branches that shielded them from the wind could be made out, from time to time, suggesting a fragment of music manuscript, a bit of the suspension bridge itself:

"It was a day just like this that I set the boat adrift. It was twenty-nine years ago in June."

"It was twenty-nine years ago in June, darling. And it was June twenty-seventh."

"It was five years before you were born, Astrid, and I was ten years old and I came down to the bay with my father."

"It was five years before I was born, you were ten years old, and you came down to the wharf with your father. Your father and grandfather had made you the boat between them and it was a fine one, ten inches long, smoothly varnished and made of wood from your model airplane box, with a new strong white sail."

"Yes, it was balsa wood from my model airplane box and my father sat beside me, telling me what to write for a note to put in it."

"Your father sat beside you, telling you what to write," Astrid laughed, "and you wrote:

'Hello.

'My name is Sigurd Storlesen. I am ten years old. Right now I am sitting on the wharf at Fearnought Bay, Clallam County, State of Washington, U.S.A., five miles south of Cape Flattery on the Pacific side, and my Dad is beside me telling me what to write. Today is June 27, 1922. My Dad is a forest warden in the Olympic National Forest but my Granddad is the lighthouse keeper at Cape Flattery. Beside me is a small shiny canoe which you now hold in your hand. It is a windy day and my Dad said to put the canoe in the water when I have put this in and glued down the lid which is a piece of balsa wood from my model airplane box.

'Well must close this note now, but first I will ask you to tell the Seattle Star that you have found it, because I am going to start reading the paper from today and looking for a piece that says, who when and where it was found.

'Thanks. Sigurd Storlesen.'"

"Yes, then my father and I put the note inside, and we glued down the lid and sealed it and put the boat on the water."

"You put the boat on the water and the tide was going out and away it went. The current caught it right off and carried it out and you watched it till it was out of sight!"

The two had now reached a clearing in the forest where a few grey squirrels were scampering about on the grass. A dark-browed Indian in a windbreaker, utterly absorbed by his friendly task, stood with a sleek black squirrel sitting on his shoulder nibbling popcorn he was giving it from a bag. This reminded them to get some peanuts to feed the bears, whose cages were over the way.

Ursus Horribilis: and now they tossed peanuts to the sad lumbering sleep-heavy creatures — though at least these two grizzlies were together, they even had a home — maybe still too sleepy to know where they were, still wrapped in a dream of their timberfalls and wild blueberries in the Cordilleras Sigurd and Astrid could see again, straight ahead of them, between the trees, beyond a bay.

But how should they stop thinking of the little boat?

Twelve years it had wandered. Through the tempests of winter, over sunny summer seas, what tide rips had caught it, what wild sea birds, shearwaters, storm petrels, jaegers, that follow the thrashing propellers, the dark albatross of these northern waters, swooped upon it, or warm currents edged it lazily toward land — and blue-water currents sailed it after the albacore, with fishing boats like white giraffes — or glacial drifts tossed it about fuming Cape Flattery itself. Perhaps it had rested, floating in a sheltered cove, where the killer whale smote, lashed, the deep clear water; the eagle and the salmon had seen it, a baby seal stared with her wondering eyes, only for the little boat to be thrown aground, catching the rainy afternoon sun, on cruel barnacled rocks by the waves, lying aground knocked from side to side in an inch of water like a live thing, or a poor old tin can, pushed, pounded ashore, and swung around, reversed again, left high and dry, and then swept another yard up the beach, or carried under a lonely salt-grey shack, to drive a seine fisherman crazy all night with its faint plaintive knocking, before it ebbed out in the dark autumn dawn, and found its way afresh, over the deep, coming through thunder, to who will ever know what fierce and desolate uninhabited shore, known only to the dread Wendigo, where not even an Indian could have found it, unfriended there, lost, until it was borne out to sea once more by the great brimming black tides of January, or the huge calm tides of the midsummer moon, to start its journey all over again —

Astrid and Sigurd came to a large enclosure, set back from a walk, with two vine-leaved maple trees (their scarlet tassels, delicate precursors of their leaves, already visible) growing through the top, a sheltered cavernous part to one side for a lair, and the whole, save for the barred front, covered with stout large-meshed wire — considered sufficient protection for one of the most Satanic beasts left living on earth.

Two animals inhabited the cage, spotted like deceitful pastel leopards, and in appearance like decorated, maniacal-looking cats: their ears were provided with huge tassels and, as if this were in savage parody of the vine-leaved maples, from the brute's chin tassels also depended. Their legs were as long as a man's arm, and their paws, clothed in grey fur out of which shot claws curved like scimitars, were as big as a man's clenched fist.

And the two beautiful demonic creatures prowled and paced endlessly, searching the base of their cage, between whose bars there was just room to slip a murderous paw — always a hop out of reach an invisible sparrow went pecking away in the dust — searching with eternal voraciousness, yet seeking in desperation also some way out, passing and repassing each other rhythmically, as though truly damned and under some compelling enchantment.

And yet as they watched the terrifying Canadian lynx, in which seemed to be embodied in animal form all the pure ferocity of nature, as they watched, crunching peanuts themselves now and passing the bag between them, before the lovers' eyes still sailed that tiny boat, battling with the seas, at the mercy of a wilder ferocity yet, all those years before Astrid was born.

Ah, its absolute loneliness amid those wastes, those wildernesses of rough rainy seas bereft even of sea birds, between contrary winds, or in the great dead windless swell that comes following a gale; and then with the wind springing up and blowing the spray across the sea like rain, like a vision of creation, blowing the lithe boat as it climbed the highland into the skies, from which sizzled cobalt lightnings, and then sank down into the abyss, but already was climbing again, while the whole sea crested with foam like lambs' wool went furling off to leeward, the whole vast moon — driven expanse like the pastures and valleys and snow-capped ranges of a Sierra Madre in delirium, in ceaseless motion, rising and hilling, and the little boat rising, and hilling into a paralyzing sea of white drifting fire and smoking spume by which it seemed overwhelmed: and all this time a sound, like a high sound of singing, yet as sustained in harmony as telegraph wires, or like the unbelievably high perpetual sound of the wind where there is nobody to listen, which perhaps does not exist, or the ghost of the wind in the rigging of ships long lost, and perhaps it was the sound of the wind in its toy rigging, as again the boat slanted onward:

but even then what further unfathomed deeps had it oversailed, until what birds of ill omen turned heavenly for it at last, what iron birds with saber wings skimming forever through the murk above the grey immeasurable swells, imparted mysteriously their own homing knowledge to it: the lonely buoyant little craft, nudging it with their beaks under golden sunsets in a blue sky, as it sailed close in to mountainous coasts of clouds with stars over them, or burning coasts at sunset once more, as it rounded not only the terrible spume-drenched rocks, like incinerators in sawmills, of Flattery, but other capes unknown, those twelve years, of giant pinnacles, images of barrenness and desolation, upon which the heart is thrown and impaled eternally! — And strangest of all how many ships themselves had threatened it, during that voyage of only some three score miles as the crow flies from its launching to its final port, looming out of the fog and passing by harmlessly all those years — those years too of the last sailing ships, rigged to the moonsail, sweeping by into their own oblivion — but ships cargoed with guns or iron for impending wars, what freighters now at the bottom of the sea he, Sigurd, had voyaged in for that matter, freighted with old marble and wine and cherries-in-brine, or whose engines even now were still somewhere murmuring: *Frère* Jacques! *Frère* Jacques!

What strange poem of God's mercy was this?

Suddenly across their vision a squirrel ran up a tree beside the cage and then, chattering shrilly, leaped from a branch and darted across the top of the wire mesh. Instantly, swift and deadly as lightning, one of the lynx sprang twenty feet into the air, hurtling straight to the top of the cage toward the squirrel, hitting the wire with a twang like a mammoth guitar, and simultaneously flashing through the wire its scimitar claws: Astrid cried out and covered her face.

But the squirrel, unhurt, untouched, was already running lightly along another branch, down to the tree, and away, while the infuriated lynx sprang straight up, sprang again, and again and again and again, as his mate crouched spitting and snarling below.

Sigurd and Astrid began to laugh. Then this seemed obscurely unfair to the lynx, now solemnly washing his mate's face. The innocent squirrel, for whom they felt such relief, might almost have been showing off, almost, unlike the oblivious sparrow, have been taunting the caged animal. The squirrel's hairbreadth escape — the thousand-to-one chance — that on second thought must take place every day, seemed meaningless. But all at once it did not seem meaningless that they had been there to see it.

"You know how I watched the paper and waited," Sigurd was saying, stopping to relight his pipe, as they walked on.

"The Seattle *Star*," Astrid said.

"The Seattle *Star* ... It was the first newspaper I ever read. Father always declared the boat had gone south — maybe to Mexico, and I seem to remember Granddad saying no, if it didn't break up on Tatoosh, the tide would take it right down Juan de Fuca Strait, maybe into Puget Sound itself. Well, I watched and waited for a long time and finally, as kids will, I stopped looking."

"And the years went on — "

"And I grew up. Granddad was dead by then. And the old man, you know about him. Well, he's dead too now. But I never forgot. Twelve years! Think of it — ! Why, it voyaged around longer than we've been married."

"And we've been married seven years."

"Seven years today — "

"It seems like a miracle!"

But their words fell like spent arrows before the target of this fact.

They were walking, as they left the forest, between two long rows of Japanese cherry trees, next month to be an airy avenue of celestial bloom. The cherry trees behind, the forest reappeared, to left and right of the wide clearing, and skirting two arms of the bay. As they approached the Pacific, down the gradual incline, on this side remote from the harbour the wind grew more boisterous: gulls, glaucous and raucous, wheeled and sailed overhead, yelling, and were suddenly far out to sea.

And it was the sea that lay before them, at the end of the slope that changed into the steep beach, the naked sea, running deeply below, without embankment or promenade, or any friendly shacks, though some prettily built homes showed to the left, with one light in a window, glowing warmly through the trees on the edge of the forest itself, as of some stalwart Columbian Adam, who had calmly stolen back with his Eve into Paradise, under the flaming sword of the civic cherubim.

The tide was low. Offshore, white horses were running around a point. The headlong onrush of the tide of beaten silver flashing over its cross-flowing underset was so fast the very surface of the sea seemed racing away.

Their path gave place to a cinder track in the familiar lee of an old frame pavilion, a deserted tea house boarded up since last summer. Dead leaves were slithering across the porch, past which on the slope to the right picnic benches, tables, a derelict swing, lay overturned, under a tempestuous grove of birches. It seemed cold, sad, inhuman there, and beyond, with the roar of that deep low tide. Yet there was that between the lovers which moved like a warmth, and might have thrown open the shutters, set the benches and tables aright, and filled the whole grove with the voices and children's laughter of summer. Astrid paused for a moment with a hand on Sigurd's arm while they were sheltered by the pavilion, and said, what she too had often said before, so that they always repeated these things almost like an incantation:

"I'll never forget it. That day when I was seven years old, coming to the park here on a picnic with my father and mother and brother. After lunch my brother and I came down to the beach to play. It was a fine summer day, and the tide was out, but there'd been this very high tide in the night, and you could see the lines of driftwood and seaweed where it had ebbed ... was playing on the beach, and I found your boat!"

"You were playing on the beach and you found my boat. And the mast was broken."

"The mast was broken and shreds of sail hung dirty and limp. But your boat was still whole and unhurt, though it was scratched and weatherbeaten and the varnish was gone. I ran to my mother, and she saw the sealing wax over the cockpit, and, darling, I found your note!"

"You found our note, my darling."

Astrid drew from her pocket a scrap of paper and holding it between them they bent over (though it was hardly legible by now and they knew it off by heart) and read:

> Hello.
> My name is Sigurd Storlesen. I am ten years old. Right now I am sitting on the wharf at Fearnought Bay, Clallam County, State of Washington, U.S.A., five miles south of Cape Flattery on the Pacific side, and my Dad is beside me telling me what to write. Today is June 27, 1922. My Dad is a forest warden in the Olympic National Forest but my Granddad is the lighthouse keeper at Cape Flattery. Beside me is a small shiny canoe which you now hold in your hand. It is a windy day and my Dad said to put the canoe in the water when I have put this in and glued down the lid which is a piece of balsa wood from my model airplane box.
> Well must close this note now, but first I will ask you to tell the Seattle Star that you have found it, because I am going to start reading the paper from today and looking for a piece that says, who when and where it was found.
> Thanks.
> Sigurd Storlesen.

They came to the desolate beach strewn with driftwood, sculptured, whorled, silvered, piled everywhere by tides so immense there was a tideline of seaweed and detritus on the grass behind them, and great logs and shingle-bolts and writhing snags, crucifixial, or frozen in a fiery rage — or better, a few bits of lumber almost ready to burn, for someone to take home, and automatically they threw them up beyond the sea's reach for some passing soul, remembering their own winters of need — and more snags there at the foot of the grove and visible high on the sea-scythed forest banks on either side, in which riven trees were growing, yearning over the shore. And everywhere they looked was wreckage, the toll of winter's wrath: wrecked hencoops, wrecked floats, the wrecked side of a fisherman's hut, its boards once hammered together, with its wrenched shiplap and extruding nails. The fury had extended even to the beach itself, formed in hummocks and waves and barriers of shingle and shells they had to climb up in places. And everywhere too was the grotesque macabre fruit of the sea, with its exhilarating iodine smell, nightmarish bulbs of kelp like antiquated motor horns, trailing brown satin streamers twenty feet long, sea wrack like demons, or the discarded casements of evil spirits that had been cleansed. Then more wreckage: boots, a clock, torn fishing nets, a demolished wheelhouse, a smashed wheel lying in the sand.

Nor was it possible to grasp for more than a moment that all this with its feeling of death and destruction and barrenness was only an appearance, that beneath the flotsam, under the very shells they crunched, within the trickling overflows of winterbournes they jumped over, down at the tide margin, existed, just as in the forest, a stirring and stretching of life, a seething of spring.

When Astrid and Sigurd were almost sheltered by an uprooted tree on one of these lower billows of beach they noticed that the clouds had lifted over the sea, though the sky was not blue but still that intense silver, so that they could see right across the Gulf and make out, or thought they could, the line of some Gulf Islands. A lone freighter with upraised derricks shipped seas on the horizon. A hint of the summit of Mount Hood remained, or it might have been clouds. They remarked too, in the southeast, on the sloping base of a hill, a triangle of storm-washed green, as if cut out of the overhanging murk there, in which were four pines, five telegraph posts and a clearing resembling a cemetery. Behind them the icy mountains of Canada hid their savage peaks and snowfalls under still more savage clouds. And they saw that the sea was grey with white-caps and currents charging offshore and spray blowing backwards from the rocks.

But when the full force of the wind caught them, looking from the shore, it was like gazing into chaos. The wind blew away their thoughts, their voices, almost their very senses, as they walked, crunching the shells, laughing and stumbling. Nor could they tell whether it was spume or rain that smote and stung their faces, whether spindrift from the sea or rain from which the sea was born, as now finally they were forced to a halt, standing there arm in arm ... And it was to this shore, through that chaos, by those currents, that their little boat with its innocent message had been brought out of the past finally to safety and a home.

But ah, the storms they had come through!

Earthquake

JACK HODGINS

DO YOU REMEMBER THE EARTHQUAKE OF '46? DO YOU REMEMBER HOW THE chimney fell through the roof of the elementary school and down through both storeys of classrooms and would have killed us all if this had not been a Sunday morning? (Would have killed Miss Gordon, too, lying out flat on her bench and fanning herself, in the midst of one of her spells.) Do you remember how the post office, which was the only brick building in the entire valley, collapsed in a heap of rubble where it had stood for twenty-three years, and how we were thrilled to think afterwards that it looked exactly as if it might have been bombed from the air? And how the bells on the little Anglican church went chiming, and the electric poles whipped back and forth like fly-fishermen's rods, and electric wires trooped low like skipping ropes and snapped tight and clearly *sang,* and how the earth came rolling up in waves and sent Cornelius Baxter's car out of control and up onto Millie Weston's porch?

Then you may also remember my uncle. Neddie Desmond? Lived just down the road a ways from us in that little farm with the buttercup-yellow house? Well my Uncle Neddie was the first one out in our part of the valley to install an electric fence. Power had come as far as Waterville just the year before and none of us had become accustomed to its magic yet, nor learned to trust it. Neddie went out that morning to pull the inaugural switch, and to prepare himself to have a good laugh at the first cow to find out what it would mean from now on to stick her nose into a field where she wasn't wanted. Well Neddie pulled his switch and immediately the air began to hum, the world began to heave and roll, the trees began to dance and flop about and try to fly. Two guernseys dropped directly to their knees and started to bawl, a third went staggering sideways down the sloping earth and slammed into the cedar-shake wall of his barn. Chickens exploded out of their pen in a flurry of squawking feathers as if the jolt of electricity had somehow jumped a connection and zapped them. Naturally he thought that he and his fence were to blame for this upheaval but he could not make it stop by turning off his switch. Poor old Neddie had never been so frightened, he started to curse and blubber, he hollered for Gracie to get out and give him a hand. Never much of a man for religion, he promised God at the top of his lungs that he would abandon his lifelong fascination with modern inventions immediately. But God took far too long to think this offer over; by the time the earth's convulsions had settled, all of his cattle had fallen and poor Ned had wrapped himself around a fence post and begun to cry.

Now the scariest thing about quakes is that they change the way a fellow looks at the world. You may also remember my other uncle. Tobias Desmond? Owned the little sawmill up at Comox Lake? Uncle Toby drove down from his mill an hour after the quake had worn itself out and told us the entire lake had emptied in front of his eyes. Truly! Right to the muddy bottom, he said — he saw drowned trees and slime. Drained entirely down a crack which had opened up in the earth, and must have gone right out to the ocean somewhere, because it came back with tangled knots of golden-brown kelp and furious crabs and bouquets of brilliant purple anemones torn off the ocean floor and flung up on to the driftwood and shoreline trees and the sorting deck of Uncle Toby's mill.

He was uneasy about going back to his sawmill after that. Though the sound of the lake emptying all at once like water down a sucking drainpipe had been horrible enough to haunt him for the next few years, it would not have the effect upon him of those remembered moments when he stood and watched the water returning to the empty lake — leaking in at first, and spreading, then racing outwards across the mud, and swelling, deepening, rising up the nearer slopes. *He* had no reason to believe it would know when to stop. By the time the first waves slapped against the pilings under his mill, he was in his truck with the motor running, yet later confessed that he knew he would not have the will to drive out of there even if that water had kept on climbing up the posts and started out over the land. He would just have to hang around to see what happened next.

Now my Uncle Toby was a truthful man. We believed him. You only had to walk along the lakeshore yourself to see things drying in the sunlight that shouldn't be there. The problem was that this incident would trouble him far too much, he couldn't stop telling people about it. And every time he told it there seemed to be something new he'd just remembered that he hadn't told before. A whole month had gone by when he turned away from the counter of the general store one afternoon, watched a car speed past outside, and turned again to Em at the till: "My God, I just remembered! Why didn't I think of this before? There were two old men in a boat — I remember seeing them just before it started — two stiff gentlemen in coolie hats out on the lake in a punt." They weren't fishing or anything, he said. Just floating, talking, way out in the middle.

When the waves started sloshing up they rocked and bobbed but didn't start rowing for shore. They started turning, slowly turning around, turning around and around this whirlpool that had opened up, this funnel that was sucking the entire body of water down a hole somewhere. They didn't stand up, they didn't holler for help, they just turned and turned and eventually slipped into the shute and corkscrewed down out of sight. "Now what do you think of that?" said Uncle Toby. "They didn't come back, they must've gone sailing out to sea." Of course no one believed this new addition to his tale. But he continued to tell his story to anyone who would listen, adding every time a few more details that would make it just a little more exciting and improbable than it had been before. He seldom went back to the mill, or sold much lumber. He spent his time on the streets of town, or in a coffee shop, talking the ear off anyone who came along. The earthquake had given him the excuse he'd been looking for to avoid what he'd always hated doing most — an honest day's work.

So you see — that's the other thing. People will use an earthquake for their own purposes. My uncle's sawmill eventually collapsed from neglect, under a heavy fall of snow, but he hardly noticed. That's the worrying part. They're telling us now that we're just about overdue for another one. For an island situated smack on the Pacific rim of fire, as they like to call it, we've sat back for far too long and smugly watched disasters strike other parts of the world. Apparently all those tremors we've wakened to in the night have not done anything but delay the inevitable; we will soon be facing the real thing all over again, with its aftermath of legend.

Myself, I was nearly eight at the time. My brother was five. My sister was less than a year, and still asleep in her crib in one corner of my parent's bedroom. My mother, who was kneading a batch of bread dough at the kitchen counter, encouraged the two of us boys to hurry and finish breakfast and get outside. It appeared to be the beginning of a warm June day. My father had gone out to milk Star, the little jersey. He'd soon begin the task of sharpening the little triangular blades of his hay mower, which would be needed within the next few weeks for the field between the house and the wooden gate. Now, he had just started back towards the house with a pail of milk in order to run it through the verandah separator, when it seemed the air had begun to hum around his ears. Something smelled, an odour of unfamiliar gas. Off across the nearer pasture the line of firs began to sway, as though from a sudden burst of wind. The hay-field swelled up and moved towards him in a series of ripples. Suddenly he felt as if he were on a rocking ship, in need of sea legs, with a whole ocean beneath him trying to upset his balance. He could not proceed. He stopped and braced his legs apart to keep from falling. The milk sloshed from side to side in the pail and slopped over the rim. Before him, our old two-storey house he was still in the process of renovating had begun to dance a jig. The chimney bent as if made of rubber bricks, then swiv-elled a half-turn and toppled. Red bricks spilled down the slope of the roof and dropped to the lean-to roof of the verandah, then spilled down that in a race to the eave where they could drop to the ground directly above the door I was throwing open at that precise moment in order to rush outside and join him. This was the end of the world he'd been warned about as a child himself; it was happening in exactly the way his own father had told him it would. In a moment a crack would open up somewhere and snake across his land to divide beneath his feet and swallow him, would swallow his house and his family and his farm and all his animals at once, but not until he'd been forced to stand helpless and unable to move on the bucking surface of earth while he watched his family bludgeoned to death by the spilling cascade of bricks.

My brother laughed, but wouldn't leave his chair at the kitchen table. The sight of a fried egg dancing on his plate was not an entertainment to walk away from. Cutlery chattered on the tablecloth. Milk tossed up bubbly sprays from his glass and splashed on his nose. His piece of toast hopped off his plate and landed in his lap. This was a matter for giggling. The world had decided to entertain him in a manner he'd always thought it capable of and this would make a difference to his life. From this day on, he would take it for granted that he might demand any sort of pleasant diversion he wished and need only wait for all laws of nature to be suspended for the purpose of giving him a laugh.

My mother screamed. Cupboard doors flew open and spewed dishes onto her counter. Drinking glasses and cups spilled onto the bread dough. Saucers crashed in the sink. Through the window she could see her hus-band swaying like a drunken man in the lane that led to the barn. When she turned — crying, "The baby!" — she saw the drying rack above the stove sway like a gentle porch swing, swishing boiled underwear and shirts back and forth over the heat. She snatched the clothing down and tossed it all in a heap on a chair. "You boys — get outside quick!" She went flying off through the french door and across the living room and into the bedroom. "I can't! I can't!" I heard her calling and ran to help. The crib had danced across the floor and was blocking the door. We pushed it open. She snatched up my sister and cried, "Grab your brother and follow." As it turned out, she was the one who would follow. The outside door of the living room was blocked by the china cabinet which had taken up the tune and gone dancing, its contents of silver and heir-loom china clanging behind the glass. The baby cried at her hip. Between us we leaned against the cabinet but it would not move. "The other door!" she cried. But we had only got out as far as the verandah, saw my father hollering something at us we couldn't hear over a clatter on the roof above us, saw him waving his arms — he might have been signalling us to hurry and join him, he might have been telling us to stay where we were — when that fall of cascading bricks came crashing down off the roof less than a running step before us. Beyond it, my father rushing towards us, fell to one knee. We looked at one another, my father and I, with that thundering fall of red clay bricks between us. He might as well have been on the opposite side of an opening chasm, he might as well have been on the shore while we were going down a drain hole, he might as well have been left behind on earth while we went sailing off into eternity. That's what he was thinking. Even trapped in a house that was shaking itself into collapse around our ears I could see what he was thinking in his eyes. What sort of a father could not put a halt to a tum-bling wall of bricks? I was thinking the same myself.

Now what does it feel like to be an eight-year-old boy on a Sunday morning in June with the world deciding to throw itself into convulsions and scare everyone half to death? Why, how had I got to such an age, I'd like to know, still believing that the earth would stay steady beneath your feet forever, fathers stay capable of heroic rescues forever, mothers stay calm in every sort of emergency forever, and houses you lived in stay solid and still and safe and true till the end of time?

Let me tell you this: When I was two my mother came up into the attic bedroom to tuck me in every night carrying a coal-oil lamp. One night when she had kissed me she turned to go down the stairs but tripped and fell, and fell down the length of the stairs to the landing. I ran to the head of the stairs and looked: there she was in a heap, surrounded by flames, with fire already starting up the trail of spilled oil towards me.

In no time at all, my father had beat those flames out with a blanket and helped my mother away. I didn't have even the time to think he might not. Let me also tell this. When I was in my first year of school my father did not come home one day from work in the logging camp at the time he was supposed to. He did not come home that night at all: He came home the next morning from the hospital with his head wrapped up in great white bandages, nothing of him showing but two eyes, two nostrils and a gaping mouth. He laughed. A falling limb had nearly taken off one ear, had opened up his nose. But he laughed. I could take him to school tomorrow for show-and-tell, he said, and tell that teacher and all those other kids I'd dug him up in the yard where he'd been buried by the Egyptians five or six thousand years before. He would lie stiff, he said, until everyone was through poking at him and smelling him and making notes for an assignment on the pleasures of archeology, and then he would let out a long groan and sit up and scare the teacher into immediate retirement. "This isn't funny," my mother said. "You might have been killed." But of course my father could laugh in the teeth of anything that would try to kill him in the world. The earth beneath our feet stayed firm.

Then this. What do you make of it? The bricks stopped falling. The house settled. Not a sound could be heard. It was as if the earth, worn out from its convulsion, had taken in a deep breath and held it, while it gathered up its strength to buck and heave some more and go into another fit. Still we didn't move — my father down on one knee with his spilled milk bucket not far away in the grass, my mother holding my crying sister in her arms, my brother no longer giggling but looking as though he just might get scared at last. We held our positions as if we waited for someone's permission to move. Something foul-smelling had been released into the air. The light was wrong. Far off, if you listened hard, a rumbling could be heard going away beyond the trees.

Inside, one final piece of china crashed to the kitchen floor. This was a signal. Now, could you heave a sigh and laugh to show that it was all right? Nobody laughed. My brother, like the baby, started to cry. My father stood up and whipped off his cap to slap the dirt from his knees. He picked up the pail, and stood looking into it. Was he wondering where the milk had gone? It was splashed out all around him and already drying on the leaves of grass and on the gravel along the lane. My mother made a tentative move down onto the top step, and staggered a little. What *was* that?" she said. "What *was* that? I thought for a moment the war might have started up again, an invasion or something."

"Quake," said my dad. He took a step towards my mother, found that he could keep his balance after all, and sort of threw himself into a lope in our direction.

"You wouldn't believe what went through my head!" my mother said. "I thought something might have happened in the barn. You and that cow — " She was almost laughing now, but almost crying as well. "Blowing yourselves to kingdom come and taking the rest of us with you!"

My father took the baby in one of his arms to hush her, and used his other arm to hold my mother against him. "You okay?" he said to me. I nodded. He didn't smile. Not yet. He would make a joke of it later but for the time being he solemnly held my gaze with his to acknowledge what we both now knew what he must have known already himself but had kept secret from me too long. What was this thing we shared? That the world could no longer be trusted to stay steady beneath our feet? Perhaps, and that a father and son in such a world must expect to view each other across a space of falling debris.

Fifteen minutes later my uncle Neddie and his housekeeper Grace were upon us in their pickup truck, to see how much damage had been done. By this time we had already heard on the battery radio that we'd been at the very centre of this quake, and that it had measured 7.3 on the Richter scale — the worst to hit the island since 1918. Grace drew fiercely on her cigarette, blew smoke down her nose, and viewed the world at a sideways glance to show she would never trust it again. She was not one to thrive on drama. Uncle Ned was white, and shaky. "My lord, I thought I'd caused it" he said. He wasn't laughing either. He looked as if he could still be convinced he'd been the one to blame.

"That sounds pretty normal," my father said. "I thought I'd caused it myself. I was just coming across from the barn and thinking how maybe we shouldn't've moved into this old house before I'd finished the renovations. Not with little kids — y'know? What a person ought to be able to do, I thought, was just pick up an old house like that and give it a shake and see what's left that's safe."

"I was making bread," my mother said. "You know how they make fun of the way I punch down the dough like I'm mad. This time I thought well *now* I've gone and done it, this dough's begun to fight back."

None of this was comfort to Uncle Ned, who was holding his hands together, then putting them into his pockets, then clenching them into fists that he pressed to his sides. "I mean I thought I'd *really* started it!" he said. "I pulled the switch on my electric fence and away she started to rip! I nearly peed my pants." So Uncle Ned told us what it was like: how he pulled the switch, and the earth heaved up, and the cows fell, and chickens exploded out of their pen, and the fence posts shook themselves free of the ground. Naturally we laughed. Naturally he had to laugh himself.

Then he said, "I guess I had to come over and find out how far my damage had spread. But that don't mean I'm gonna get up on that roof and fix your chimney!"

Apparently it was all right to laugh. No one was hurt. The house was still standing. How important grownups must think they are! It had never occurred to me to think I was at fault. "Reminds me of that time we was kids," said Uncle Ned to my father. "You remember that? You and me and Toby was sleepin' up over the garage and the Old Man he comes hollering out to wake us up? This was the time that fire got loose up behind Wolf Lake and started down across the valley towards us. The sky was red and boiling black, the whole world was lit up by its flames and you could hear them roarin' across the tops of the trees. You could hear the cattle bellowin' too, scared to death. Well you know what *he* was like, he got us up on the roof with gunny sacks slappin' at sparks that flew our way. Even when that fire'd nearly surrounded us he wouldn't let us high-tail it out of there." He was talking to my mother now. "Well it wasn't until the next day when the wind had turned it away that we found out he'd been broodin' about some little root-fire he'd started that he shouldn't have, and couldn't get it out of his head that he somehow might've sent up the spark that started that whole mountain burning — and sweeping down to give him his punishment. Hell, I bet every farmer in the valley had some reason for thinking the same! What's the matter with us that we can't believe things happen just because?"

My father looked at me for a moment before he said anything to that. "I d'know, Ned. Maybe we'd really *rather* be the cause of these things ourselves. On the other hand, maybe we're right. Who's to say it isn't a person's thoughts that do the damage?"

Uncle Ned shook his head. Of course he wasn't satisfied. He wouldn't be satisfied until he'd made some sense of this. He bent to pick up a brick from the front step, and then another, and stacked them up on the floor of the verandah. "I know this, I'll tell you for sure. I'm gonna dismantle that fence. Barbed wire is good enough for any cow, I'll just shoot the ones that don't pay attention to it. I know this too: I ain't never gonna flick a light switch on the wall of my house without flinchin' a bit while I do it. Just in case. How's a fellow s'posed to know what to trust?"

My mother took the baby back inside. The rest of us started collecting the bricks, and stacking them on the verandah, and kept on picking up bricks until my Uncle Tobias' truck came roaring in through the gate and down the driveway. We stood up to watch him approach. Uncle Toby was out of that truck before it had even come to its usual stop against the walnut tree, and was running across the yard towards us holding his baseball cap on his head with one of his hands. "You feel that?" he shouted.

"You feel that here?" I guess he was too excited to notice our stack of bricks.

"Feel what?" my father said. "What do you mean? We didn't feel anything here." He put one hand on my shoulder. "You see anything here that's *changed*?"

The Jade Peony

WAYSON CHOY

WHEN GRANDMAMA DIED AT EIGHTY-THREE OUR WHOLE HOUSEHOLD HELD ITS breath. She had promised us a sign of her leaving, final proof that her present life had ended well. My parents knew that without any clear sign our own family fortunes could be altered, threatened. My stepmother looked endlessly into the small cluttered room the ancient lady had occupied. Nothing was touched; nothing changed. My father, thinking that a sign should appear in Grandmama's garden, looked at the frost-killed shoots and cringed: *no, that could not be it.*

My two older teenage brothers and my sister, Liang, age fourteen, were embarrassed by my parents' behaviour. What would all the white people in Vancouver think of us? We were Canadians now, *Chinese-Canadians*, a hyphenated reality that my parents could never accept. So it seemed, for different reasons, we all held our breath waiting for *something.*

I was eight when she died. For days she had resisted going into the hospital ... *a cold, just a cold* ... and instead gave constant instruction to my stepmother and sister on the boiling of ginseng roots mixed with bitter extract. At night, between wracking coughs and deadly silences, Grandmama had her back and chest rubbed with heated camphor oil and sipped a bluish decoction of an herb called Peacock's Tail. When all these failed to abate her fever, she began to arrange the details of her will. This she did with my father, confessing finally: "I am too stubborn. The only cure for old age is to die."

My father wept to hear this. I stood beside her bed; she turned to me. Her round face looked darker, and the gentleness of her eyes, the thin, arching eyebrows, seemed weary. I brushed the few strands of grey, brittle hair from her face; she managed to smile at me. Being the youngest, I had spent nearly all my time with her and could not imagine that we would ever be parted. Yet when she spoke, and her voice hesitated, cracked, the sombre shadows of her room chilled me. Her wrinkled brow grew wet with fever, and her small body seemed even more diminutive.

"I — I am going to the hospital, Grandson." Her hand reached out for mine. "You know, Little Son, whatever happens I will never leave you." Her palm felt plush and warm, the slender, old fingers boney and firm, so magically strong was her grip that I could not imagine how she could ever part from me. Ever.

Her hands *were* magical. My most vivid memories are of her hands: long, elegant fingers, with impeccable nails, a skein of fine, barely-seen veins, and wrinkled skin like light pine. Those hands were quick when she taught me, at six, simple tricks of juggling, learnt when she was a village girl in Southern Canton; a troupe of actors had stayed on her father's farm. One of them, "tall and pale as the whiteness of petals," fell in love with her, promising to return. In her last years his image came back like a third being in our two lives. He had been magician, acrobat, juggler, and some of the things he taught her she had absorbed and passed on to me through her stories and games. But above all, without realizing it then, her hands conveyed to me the quality of their love.

Most marvellous for me was the quick-witted skill her hands revealed in making windchimes for our birthday: windchimes in the likeness of her lost friend's only present to her, made of bits of string and scraps, in the centre of which once hung a precious jade peony. This wondrous gift to her broke apart years ago, in China, but Grandmama kept the jade pendant in a tiny red silk envelope, and kept it always in her pocket, until her death.

These were not ordinary, carelessly made chimes, such as those you now find in our Chinatown stores, whose rattling noises drive you mad. But making her special ones caused dissension in our family, and some shame. Each one that she made was created from a treasure trove of glass fragments and castaway costume jewellery, in the same way that her first windchime had been made. The problem for the rest of the family was in the fact that Grandmama looked for these treasures wandering the back alleys of Keefer and Pender Streets, peering into our neighbours' garbage cans, chasing away hungry, nervous cats and shouting curses at them.

"All our friends are laughing at us!" Older Brother Jung said at last to my father, when Grandmama was away having tea at Mrs. Lim's.

"We are not poor," Oldest Brother Kiam declared, "yet she and Sek-Lung poke through those awful things as if — " he shoved me in frustration and I stumbled against my sister, " — they were beggars!"

"She will make Little Brother crazy!" Sister Liang said. Without warning, she punched me sharply in the back; I jumped. "You see, look how *nervous* he is!"

I lifted my foot slightly, enough to swing it back and kick Liang in the shin. She yelled and pulled back her fist to punch me again. Jung made a menacing move towards me.

"Stop this, all of you!" My father shook his head in exasperation. How could he dare tell the Grand Old One, his aging mother, that what was somehow appropriate in a poor village in China, was an abomination here. How could he prevent me, his youngest, from accompanying her? If she went walking into those alleyways alone she could well be attacked by hoodlums. "She is not a beggar looking for food. She is searching for — for … "

My stepmother attempted to speak, then fell silent. She, too, seemed perplexed and somewhat ashamed. They all loved Grandmama, but she was *inconvenient*, unsettling.

As for our neighbours, most understood Grandmama to be harmlessly crazy, others that she did indeed make lovely toys but for what purpose? *Why?* they asked, and the stories she told me, of the juggler who smiled at her, flashed in my head.

Finally, by their cutting remarks, the family did exert enough pressure so that Grandmama and I no longer openly announced our expeditions. Instead, she took me with her on "shopping trips," ostensibly for clothes or groceries, while in fact we spent most of our time exploring stranger and more distant neighbourhoods, searching for splendid junk: jangling pieces of a vase, cranberry glass fragments embossed with leaves, discarded glass beads from Woolworth necklaces … We would sneak them all home in brown rice sacks, folded into small parcels, and put them under her bed. During the day when the family was away at school or work, we brought them out and washed every item in a large black pot of boiling lye and water, dried them quickly, carefully, and returned them, sparkling, under her bed.

Our greatest excitement occurred when a fire gutted the large Chinese Presbyterian Church, three blocks from our house. Among the still smoking ruins the next day, Grandmama and I rushed precariously over the blackened beams to pick out the stained glass that glittered in the sunlight. Small figure bent over, wrapped against the autumn cold in a dark blue quilted coat, happily gathering each piece like gold, she became my spiritual playmate: "There's a good one! *There!*"

Hours later, soot-covered and smelling of smoke, we came home with a Safeway carton full of delicate fragments, still early enough to steal them all into the house and put the small box under her bed. "These are special pieces," she said, giving the box a last push, "because they come from a sacred place." She slowly got up and I saw, for the first time, her hand begin to shake. But then, in her joy, she embraced me. Both of our hearts were racing, as if we were two dreamers. I buried my face in her blue quilt, and for a moment, the whole world seemed silent.

"My juggler," she said, "he never came back to me from Honan ... perhaps the famine ... " Her voice began to quake. "But I shall have my sacred windchime ... I shall have it again."

One evening, when the family was gathered in their usual places in the parlour, Grandmama gave me her secret nod: a slight wink of her eye and a flaring of her nostrils. There was trouble in the air. Supper had gone badly, school examinations were due, father had failed to meet an editorial deadline at the *Vancouver Chinese Times*. A huge sigh came from Sister Liang.

"But it is useless this Chinese they teach you!" she lamented, turning to Stepmother for support. Silence. Liang frowned, dejected, and went back to her Chinese book, bending the covers back.

"Father," Oldest Brother Kiam began, waving his bamboo brush in the air, "you must realize that this Mandarin only confuses us. We are Cantonese speakers ... "

"And you do not complain about Latin, French or German in your English school?" Father rattled his newspaper, signal that his patience was ending.

"But, Father, those languages are *scientific*," Kiam jabbed his brush in the air. "We are now in a scientific, logical world."

Father was silent. We could all hear Grandmama's rocker.

"What about Sek-Lung?" Older Brother Jung pointed angrily at me. "He was sick last year, but this year he should have at least started Chinese school, instead of picking over garbage cans!"

"He starts next year," Father said, in a hard tone that immediately warned everyone to be silent. Liang slammed her book.

Grandmama went on rocking quietly in her chair. She complimented my mother on her knitting, made a remark about the "strong beauty" of Kiam's brushstrokes which, in spite of himself, immensely pleased him. All this babbling noise was her family torn and confused in a strange land: everything here was so very foreign and scientific.

The truth was, I was sorry not to have started school the year before. In my innocence I had imagined going to school meant certain privileges worthy of all my brothers' and sister's complaints. The fact that my lung infection in my fifth and sixth years, mistakenly diagnosed as TB, earned me some reprieve, only made me long for school the more. Each member of the family took turns on Sunday, teaching me or annoying me. But it was the countless hours I spent with Grandmama that were my real education. Tapping me on my head she would say, "Come, Sek-Lung, we have *our* work," and we would walk up the stairs to her small crowded room. There, in the midst of her antique shawls, the old ancestral calligraphy and multicoloured embroidered hangings, beneath the mysterious shelves of sweet herbs and bitter potions, we would continue doing what we had started that morning: the elaborate windchime for her death.

"I can't last forever," she declared, when she let me in on the secret of this one. "It will sing and dance and glitter," her long fingers stretched into the air, pantomiming the waving motion of her ghost chimes; "My spirit will hear its sounds and see its light and return to this house and say goodbye to you."

Deftly she reached into the Safeway carton she had placed on the chair beside me. She picked out a fish-shaped amber piece, and with a long needle-like tool and a steel ruler, she scored it. Pressing the blade of a cleaver against the line, with the fingers of her other hand, she lifted up the glass until it cleanly snapped into the exact shape she required. Her hand began to tremble, the tips of her fingers to shiver, like rippling water.

"You see that, Little One?" She held her hand up. "That is my body fighting with Death. He is in this room now."

My eyes darted in panic, but Grandmama remained calm, undisturbed, and went on with her work. Then I remembered the glue and uncorked the jar for her. Soon the graceful ritual movements of her hand returned to her, and I became lost in the magic of her task: she dabbed a cabalistic mixture of glue on one end and skillfully dropped the braided end of a silk thread into it. This part always amazed me: the braiding would slowly, *very* slowly, *unknot*, fanning out like a prized fishtail. In a few seconds the clear, homemade glue began to harden as I blew lightly over it, welding to itself each separate silk strand.

Each jam-sized pot of glue was precious; each large cork had been wrapped with a fragment of pink silk. I remember this part vividly, because each cork was treated to a special rite. First we went shopping in the best silk stores in Chinatown for the perfect square of silk she required. It had to be a deep pink, a shade of colour blushing toward red. And the tone had to match — as closely as possible — her precious jade carving, the small peony of white and light-red jade, her most lucky possession. In the centre of this semi-translucent carving, no more than an inch wide, was a pool of pink light, its veins swirling out into the petals of the flower.

"This colour is the colour of my spirit," she said, holding it up to the window so I could see the delicate pastel against the broad strokes of sunlight. She dropped her voice, and I held my breath at the wonder of the colour. "This was given to me by the young actor who taught me how to juggle. He had four of them, and each one had a centre of this rare colour, the colour of Good Fortune." The pendant seemed to pulse as she turned it: "Oh, Sek-Lung! He had white hair and white skin *to his toes! It's true*, I saw him bathing." She laughed and blushed, her eyes softened at the memory. The silk had to match the pink heart of her pendant: the colour was magical for her, to hold the unravelling strands of her memory ...

It was just six months before she died that we really began to work on her last windchime. Three thin bamboo sticks were steamed and bent into circles; thirty exact lengths of silk thread, the strongest kind, were cut and braided at both ends and glued to stained glass. Her hands worked on their own command, each hand racing with a life of its own: cutting, snapping, braiding, knotting ... Sometimes she breathed heavily and her small body, growing thinner, sagged against me. *Death*, I thought, *He is in this room*, and I would work harder alongside her. For months Grandmama and I did this every other evening, a half dozen pieces each time. The shaking in her hand grew worse, but we said nothing. Finally, after discarding hundreds, she told me she had the necessary thirty pieces. But this time, because it was a sacred chime, I would not be permitted to help her tie it up or have the joy of raising it. "Once tied," she said, holding me against my disappointment, "not even I can raise it. Not a sound must it make until I have died."

"What will happen?"

"Your father will then take the centre braided strand and raise it. He will hang it against my bedroom window so that my ghost may see it, and hear it, and return. I must say goodbye to this world properly or wander in this foreign devil's land forever."

"You can take the streetcar!" I blurted, suddenly shocked that she actually meant to leave me. I thought I could hear the clear-chromatic chimes, see the shimmering colours on the wall: I fell against her and cried, and there in my crying I knew that she would die. I can still remember the touch of her hand on my head, and the smell of her thick woolen sweater pressed against my face. "I will always be with you, Little Sek-Lung, but in a different way ... you'll see."

Months went by, and nothing happened. Then one late September evening, when I had just come home from Chinese School, Grandmama was preparing supper when she looked out our kitchen window and saw a cat — a long, lean white cat — jump into our garbage pail and knock it over. She ran out to chase it away, shouting curses at it. She did not have her thick sweater on and when she came back into the house, a chill gripped her. She leaned against the door: "That was not a cat," she said, and the odd tone of her voice caused my father to look with alarm at her. "I cannot take back my curses. It is too late." She took hold of my father's arm: "It was all white and had pink eyes like sacred fire."

My father started at this, and they both looked pale. My brothers and sister, clearing the table, froze in their gestures.

"The fog has confused you," Stepmother said. "It was just a cat."

But Grandmama shook her head, for she knew it was a sign. "I will not live forever," she said. "I am prepared."

The next morning she was confined to her bed with a severe cold. Sitting by her, playing with some of my toys, I asked her about the cat: "Why did father jump at the cat with the pink eyes? He didn't see it, you did."

"But he and your mother know what it means."

"What?"

"My friend, the juggler, the magician, was as pale as white jade, and he had pink eyes." I thought she would begin to tell me one of her stories, a tale of enchantment or of a wondrous adventure, but she only paused to swallow; her eyes glittered, lost in memory. She took my hand, gently opening and closing her fingers over it. "Sek-Lung," she sighed, "*he* has come back to me."

Then Grandmama sank back into her pillow and the embroidered flowers lifted to frame her wrinkled face. I saw her hand over my own, and my own began to tremble. I fell fitfully asleep by her side. When I woke up it was dark and her bed was empty. She had been taken to the hospital and I was not permitted to visit.

A few days after that she died of the complications of pneumonia. Immediately after her death my father came home and said nothing to us, but walked up the stairs to her room, pulled aside the drawn lace curtains of her window and lifted the windchimes to the sky.

I began to cry and quickly put my hand in my pocket for a handkerchief. Instead, caught between my fingers was the small, round firmness of the jade peony. In my mind's eye I saw Grandmama smile and heard, softly, the pink centre beat like a beautiful, cramped heart.

Was That Malcolm Lowry?

SANDY FRANCES DUNCAN

WHEN I WAS EIGHT MY FATHER DIED AND MY MOTHER BOUGHT A SHACK on the beach at Dollarton. It was green and had painted in a white horseshoe shape on the front door: DUCUMIN. The outhouse was also green and its door invited one to BIDEAWEE which, when I deciphered the curving unspaced words, delighted me with its scatological daring. It did not delight my mother however, and she threatened at least once a month for as long as we owned the shack to paint both doors, but she never did, and the shack passed out of our hands four years later still weatherbeaten green, still inviting one to DUCUMIN and BIDEAWEE.

In spite of its having a name we never called it anything but "the shack," never beach house or cottage or summer camp; my mother was a respecter of connotations and our shack would have had to be larger, neater, or more decorated to qualify for another noun. It was one of the long line of squatters' shacks stretching west from Roche Point light along Burrard Inlet and north from the light up Indian Arm to Dollarton and Cove Cliff. Ours was the third shack west of Roche Point directly across the Inlet from the railroad tracks and the oil refinery's stack of constant fire.

It was possible to drive halfway from the highway to the shack down a rutted double track so narrow the thimbleberry, salmonberry and cedar branches whipped in the open windows of our '49 Prefect and left scratches on its paint. We parked in a clearing so small that only a Prefect could turn, and then loaded our food, clothes, toys, cat, bathing suits and gumboots into a battered black baby buggy my mother had procured at a secondhand shop to solve this final transportation problem. Past my favourite climbing tree and down the trail which, in fall, the maples littered with leaves like giants' splayed footprints, winding down and down, the buggy forcing back the bushes which gained revenge on our faces, the incline gradually lessening until suddenly we stood, always newly delighted, on the narrow grassy bank between the forest and the beach.

One of the marvels of the shack was that it stood right there as well, from its back windows appearing rooted to the forest, permanent and safely anchored, yet from the front we saw nothing but water and hills across the Inlet, and the shack became a houseboat; one flip of a mooring line and it could drift forever. There was a short boardwalk from the grassy verge to the veranda and if we had arrived at highest tide when the water tried to reach the grass and missed by only inches, the boards became a gangplank and we could see crabs scuttling among the newly washed and sparkling pebbles.

I see us now on the bank, the buggy stuck on some unseen rock, my mother jiggling the handle, my holding down a struggling cat while trying to lift up the front end. The cat scratches and leaps away, the buggy bounces over the rock and onto the boards and what I remember of this, even more than how I licked the small beads of blood from the scratch, what I remember are the smells. They are still stored pure and strong in some area of my brain, recorded by an olfactory nerve not jaded with smoke and drink and aging: the tangy hot and coolness of a forest, sun on cedar, on stones, on small wild strawberries, rotting, growing earth and roots, bleeding hearts and huckleberries, all damp and acrid and warm; and then on the narrow bank exchanging this pomander of rain forest for that of the beach: shock of hotter sun on me, on pebbles, on barnacled rocks, on the sea, salt, salt, do not breathe deep at first but test with gentle whiffs, rotting crabs and fish, a dead gull perhaps, seaweed dry and peppery-crackley jilted on the beach, slimy kelp strands the tide still plays with, lush and foam collecting, wood smoke from some shack, oil and gas from a passing boat, a piece of rusted boom chain smelling like the city; then back to us, my mother's lavender, the buggy's cracked and tangy warming leather, and, if we stand here too long, the smells of cake and apples and red-running juicy beef.

Up onto the veranda then, unlock the large padlock always stiff and unyielding with its unquenchable thirst for oil; it had come with the shack and is loathe to admit us. That time for me, while my mother turns the key and pulls the lock, squeaks back the hasp, pushes hard on the moisture-swollen door, is as long and jiggly footed as Christmas Eve, but the door grudgingly opens and I dash in to check all three rooms and relief stills my impatience, allows the curled up ball of time to once again relax into the infinity of summer.

There is a special sort of mustiness in a closed-up place by the sea that is not shared by lakefront cottages nor damp cellars in the city, an acrid salty sharpness, an awareness of fecund origins and destinies perhaps. It permeates the walls and floors and furniture, pricking nostrils as the brain sorts out and rediscovers: ashes in the stove, oil cloth, linoleum, sheets and blankets, old clam and oyster shells now used for pins and paper clips, lexicon, dominoes, comic books and popsicle sticks piled on shelves, last year's shorts and bathing suits, too-small sneakers, water-whitened; odours take on shape and solidity, becoming part of a child's primeval response to a wild and changeless place.

And now quickly outside to turn the stiffened, salt-caked clasps and remove the heavy shutters so light can help explore the shack. Four windows, one in each bedroom on the side, one at the back over the dishpan sink, one at the front looking over the veranda, all with smaller panes of glass, washed inside and out and again next day salt-sprayed, so even on sunny midsummer afternoons the shack inside was cool and dark.

The main room had a large black stove which insatiably emptied the woodbox and challenged my mother to bake cakes in its unpredictable oven, counter, table and untidy shelves all covered with worn, red printed oil cloth, small pantry at the back which once the cat used for a bathroom, and everywhere unmatching chairs, wood-backed or wicker.

A double bed filled each bedroom, a foot perhaps of floor space on three sides, more bed closets than rooms, old sheets on rods for doors. My mother had one and I the other except when we had guests and then I shared her bed as I had done when my father was ill before he died. Or when we had a lot of company we children slept in blankets on the veranda, giggling, coming untucked, listening to the water lap the pebbles, to the thump and creak as the tide bunted a log into the pilings, mystified by grownups who preferred to sleep in beds.

Time at the shack stretched straight and sunny, marked by the coming and going of tides, the coming and going of friends, and each day when the water crept up the hot beach, we swam. The beach consisted of potato-sized rocks, barnacled sharp and slippery with lime-green algae. We wore old sneakers or special bathing shoes whose rubber soles whitened and cracked with the salt and the sun. Sometimes one came off in the undertow and I hobbled and paddled to shore, trying not to place my foot on barnacles or crabs or some hungry, tickley fish. Days later the tide might deposit the lost shoe, a curled-up cadaver in the line of jetsam, and I would retrieve it triumphantly, placing it to dry with others on the veranda railing.

At high tide we could swim in front of the shack, letting ourselves into the three feet of water from the railing in the space of time before the rotted screening was replaced, a biennial chore close to the ocean. We helped the screen's disintegration, poking at tender spots with surgical precision, the fine metal giving way under our fingers, not thinking we were being destructive, but rather hastening the time a hole was big enough to scramble through onto the railing. There we crouched, turned around, dangled over the edge, feet scraping the shingles, escaping from pirates, knives between our teeth, or jumping noisily from the burning warship, white-knuckled until our numb fingers slid off the railing and we splashed into the sea, that cold, clear, salt water locating scraped knees and barnacle cuts with the unerring ability of a deliberate torturer.

The beach sloped steeply so we did not have to go out very far at high tide to be up to our necks, but at low we could not go past our waists for fear of the sudden drop off into the boating channel with its undertows and whirlpools. Frequently we went around the Point to swim where the beach was pebbly as if a philanthropist had raked away the rocks. We were cautioned to stay away from the line in the water which snaked directly from the lighthouse toward Ioco — it was a rip tide.

I certainly never went near it; Rip Tide could have been some Ogopogo relative who lurked just below the surface, his thrashing tail the line in the water, waiting to eat the legs of a child who went too close. Still, I learned to swim with my eyes open underwater hoping to catch sight of Rip Tide from a distance; I never did for he was canny, slipping away when his invisibility was threatened. I did not have a face mask or snorkel; had I, I would have seen all the fearful length of him like Leviathan or Nessie, would have felt the chill thrill of terror, kicked for my very life back to the beach certain the trailing kelp's tickle was his touch — or else I would not have seen him, would have discovered Rip Tide to be only the prosaic meeting of two swirls of water, and underneath that surface turbulence only the usual and unterrifying denizens: starfish, rock cod, anemones, mussels, and the omnipresent, irritating barnacle. Had I discovered this, I might not have been considered an obedient child, trusted after one warning to stay safely east of the Point.

My mother lay on a blanket against a log protected by a large, striped canvas beach umbrella, reading Agatha Christies, Mary Roberts Rineharts or Georgette Heyers while alone, talking to the other adults when we had company. After some time she would get up and advance slowly into the water, standing with the skirt of her bathing suit floating around her, glaring at my teasing attempts to splash her, then launch herself forward into a personal combination of dog paddle and sidestroke, carefully keeping her hair out of the water. I loved it when my mother swam. I'd swim beside her with my head above the surface but I always floundered in a stroke or two; my head belonged in water as much as the rest of me. She was a good swimmer in spite of her idiosyncratic stroke, strong, steady and enduring. She'd lived in English Bay and had swum each day before school, frequently across to Kitsilano and back. "In the winter too?" I'd ask, hoping to spur on these unbelievable reminiscences, but, "the water was warmer then," was all she would say, and laugh.

I was rarely given the opportunity to see my mother as endurance swimmer for as I swam alongside, moving my legs and arms twice for each of her strokes, she'd invariably announce, "you must be freezing, your lips are turning blue," and around she would turn and head for shore, ignoring my protestations, which were false bravado, for "blue lips" was nearly as terrifying a pronouncement as Rip Tide. How long would it take the rest of me to turn blue? Would I stay blue? If lips could turn blue and Anne's hair green, what other colours might the body break out in? And how could it happen without a person knowing it? Blue lips were associated with freezing as in "freezing to death"; could I freeze to death without knowing it? I obediently trailed out of the water, but waited a few seconds to show that "blue lips" didn't bother me.

Because we were not swimming directly in front of the shack, technically we had "gone to the beach" and that entailed a picnic. I stood shivering in a towel wondering how the air had cooled so much when the sun still shone, and watched my mother put out the food. It was packed in square glass containers with carved daisies on the sides and matching lids, potato salad, devilled eggs, lettuce and tomatoes, buttered raisin bread, and I remembered a time before my father went to hospital, before he was moved into my bedroom to die, a very long time before the shack, when the three of us had gone to sandy city beaches with these same containers. I knew my father had not liked sandwiches on a picnic; it was that sort of knowledge one has always had about one's family. I assumed my mother had told me. Or maybe, now I wonder, because of the way that sort of knowledge gets confused, if it was my mother who did not like sandwiches, for although she had given away my father's suits and sword and revolver from the war, she continued to use the glass containers.

As distinctly different as the times of high and low tide were the times of having company and the times of being alone. I couldn't have said which I preferred, no more than I could place a value on the tides. Both had good aspects and bad; at low tide clams and crabs and starfish were exposed for tormenting, but high transformed the pebbles into jewels and brought the phosphorescence up the beach. What I did not like, however, was the change from one state to another, from low to high tide, from companionship to solitude. No more does my daughter now; to get ready to go out or to leave to come home provokes an irritated outburst and I still do not like the transition between holidays and routine.

Then, at the shack, the arrival of company meant my solitary activities were interrupted by noisy, excited children who claimed the forest and beach in undisciplined forays, perhaps unwittingly trampling the seedling I was nurturing into a west coast beanstalk. But a week later, the exodus of this same company left the forest echoing with boredom and loneliness, left no pirates with whom to jump into the sea, no noisy, nightly games of snap or cheat, no soldiers and so no reason to re-build the fort.

After I had grumpily waved good-bye I informed my mother so petulantly and continuously that there was nothing to do she lost patience and I could retaliate in anger. With her lips pressed together she stomped to the shack, already reclaimed by the cat, and her interrupted reading, and I stomped to my favourite tree, a cedar with bushy, low-growing branches which overhung the path. I climbed as high as my fear of heights allowed and sat in a green cave, peeling strips of bark off the trunk, crushing needles one at a time until my nostrils were filled with pungency, knowing the world to be a cruel and unfair place and my mother its inimical manifestation.

Slowly, as the branch turned my leg first frizzy-feeling and then numb, I remembered the hole I'd been going to dig, or the candies left in the box the company had brought, or that I'd not been able to climb my favourite rock or read my comics in peace, and maybe the fort would make a better hermit's cave than soldier's bunker.

I opened the door and my mother looked up from her book. I studied her face; guilt prompted my apology. "Yes," she usually said, sounding impassive, but she held out a hand and I advanced and put my head on her shoulder, my face in the softness of her neck. "You have your father's temper, you must learn to control it, he did, he was a gentle person." I vowed I would learn, but then, with greater guilt for now he was dead, thought he could have left his daughter better gifts than red hair and temper, he could have left her height and slimness.

After the inevitable mention of controlling my temper, I could feel her neck muscles tighten into a smile. I stepped back and smiled at her and we shared the remaining candies, one for her and one for me, whether there were two or nine and if the number were uneven, I got a knife and divided the last, half for her and half for me. Still hungry, I offered to make her a sandwich as well but she usually declined, still smiling, and I got out the bread and peanut butter and the other most important ingredient, pickle or apple or lettuce or cucumber, whatever was my fancy of the week. At home my mother made popsicles in flat, coffin-shaped aluminum containers, out of strawberry, lime or cherry Kool-Aid, and once, only once, out of tomato juice. She never made popsicles at the shack; we had no electricity, no ice, no running water. We washed dishes, clothes and ourselves in the ocean with cakes of special salt water soap which never seemed to lather. Occasionally I and whatever children were visiting were made to take the soap with us on our swims. Those were the best baths, washing each other's hair, the soap bar skipping out of our hands, rinsing our hair by diving for the soap, sometimes finding it before the undertow dragged it to the middle of the Inlet where I imagined some mother fish delighted, her babies not. It did not float. We lost a lot of soap.

We brushed our teeth in the sea as well, the company children trying to use their Colgate or Ipana, spitting white blobs among the phosphorescence we stirred up with our toothbrushes until either the taste or my mother convinced them salt water was a better cleanser than their commercial products.

My mother must have had some deep alliance with the ocean — which she called salt chuck with west coast pioneer familiarity — for there was not an ailment it could not cure, not a mineral it did not contain, not a beneficence it could not bestow. Scraped legs, cut hands, gouged knees, all were sent into the chuck where the iodine, she said, was a better antiseptic than bottled mercurochrome. Headaches, mild fevers were cured by brisk swims, although the sufferers were watched to ascertain that in their weakened state they avoided the clutches of both Rip Tide and "blue lips," and if the ailment were too severe — though I cannot imagine what that might have been — pneumonia perhaps? — a good dose of brisk salt air was next best.

My mother's trust in natural cures might have been consolidated by Rena. For the three years before his death my father had been in and out of hospital, which necessitated my mother's return to work and a succession of housekeepers who cooked and cleaned and looked after me. One was Kate from Switzerland whose idea of making toast was to cook only one side of the bread, but it was Rena, a short, fat, East European woman of indeterminate age but determined ideas, who might have influenced my mother's naturopathy.

I fell when I was seven, pretending I could ride a friend's two-wheeler, and exchanged half the gravel of the road for the skin on my arm. Rena's cure was plantain which she picked from the boulevard in front of our house and I attended school in utter mortification with green leaves peeking out of the gauze bandage. Every day when she changed the limp leaves for fresh ones she dragged me to my mother saying, "See Missus? Real good now, God gives us best," and my mother was so impressed by the cleanliness of the wound she ignored my pleas that Johnson & Johnson's cure, if not more efficacious was at least less obvious, and off to school I went to have my pride hurt worse from laughter than my arm had hurt from the fall. Definitely the cure overshadowed the ailment and I finally understood my mother's expression, "adding insult to injury."

The salt chuck could not provide drinking water and it was my job to trek up the trail, up the rutted bumpy road and along the highway to a gas station, where I could also buy real popsicles, the most surprising of which were root beer and blueberry.

Years later at friends' cottages in Northern Ontario when we emerged from cool woods to hot, hot highway, my mind was unwillingly assailed by those early emergences from cool to hot, pails clanking against my legs, and then, on the return trip, from hot, tar sticky macadam to the relief of the forest trail, pails now pulling my shoulder muscles, digging into my hands, slopping water on my sneakers. In Northern Ontario I squelched the unwanted memories, but sometimes wondered at their constant rise from the basement of my mind, for the birch and spruce and pine, lakes and rocks of Ontario were so unlike the cedar, maple, fir, gentle rotting humus and salt tang of Dollarton; only the contrast of hot and cool remained; was that enough, I wondered, to return me with phoenix-fullblown-ness to this earlier time?

Once, coming down the trail in the early morning, the water pails slipping and slopping from a stick across my shoulders, I surprised a deer. I stopped, but must already have made too much noise, pails rubbing bushes, feet clicking rocks, for it dashed away immediately. After that I stalked everywhere slowly and silently, a deerhunter, but although I was allowed within five feet of birds, the deer always eluded me. So did the raccoons and, fortunately, the bears. I caught slow salamanders on the muddy path, and tried for a while to salt a crow's tail, followed our cat on mystery tours, short because I lost him or grew bored while he sat.

Once I found an injured squirrel and carried it to the shack rolled up in my tee shirt. It lay so still I was afraid it was dead but then it twitched and I knew I could save it, held it gently against the warmth of my chest, and showed my mother, whispering as one does near the ill. But she said it was dead, and I said, "no, it moved," and she said that happened — an after twitch. I didn't believe her and wanted to say so, but the last time I had was on top of my memory. "Your father is dead, he died in the night." "I don't believe you, you're lying," and I'd run to my room. It was empty. "Where is he?" I'd asked and she'd told me they'd taken his body in the night. Now I wanted to ask if he'd twitched like the squirrel, if everything twitched when it died, but there are some things not safe to ask, some things one does not want to know.

The squirrel was stiffening and there was blood on my shirt so I found an empty candy box, dug a hole and had a funeral with a doll and a Mortimer Snerd puppet for pallbearers. We sang *Onward Christian Soldiers* as we had at my father's funeral and then *Hark the Herald Angels*. I covered the box with earth and made a popsicle stick cross on which I carved *SQUIRREL R.I.P.* Later I dug up the box and poked the squirrel to make sure it was really dead.

Company at the shack consisted primarily of women and children, friends of my mother who came for a week, leaving their husbands at work in the city, or career women like her who had married late and been widowed early, who had only children about my age. These women, social workers and nurses, were the dominant decision-makers of my youth, the hewers of wood, wielders of machetes and hammers, and men were the background shadows, loved, enjoyed, considered and occasionally deferred to — as were the children. It was the natural order to me that King George would die and the Princess become ruler of Canada with all that televised pomp and ceremony. I doubt I had even heard of St. Laurent.

Both my parents had large families and I had many uncles who came to visit and whose questions my mother's frown made me answer politely before I was dismissed to play. Later I was summoned for leave-taking which consisted of a kiss and a quarter, but my uncles had military moustaches and moist lips and the latter gift barely compensated for the former. Once I ran away from an exiting uncle, trying to appear for my mother's sake, teasing and silly, but clearly aware that if left to me, I would not return to submit to the rape-like humiliation of that kiss. Just as clearly however, I was aware that a man's kiss was something women put up with, like dirty dishes and dust, soon disposed of and worthy of no further attention in the real business of running the world. I returned, I submitted.

Men might have seemed strange creatures with unpleasant demands but boys were my favourite company. Some of the girls who came to the shack were afraid of snakes, bothered by sandflies and crabs, preferred to stay inside reading my comics — although they complained there were too many Superboys and not enough Katy Keenes. The girls sometimes cried when scratched by bushes or barnacles, but the boys saved their tears for importances, fights usually initiated by me — with boys not only did I not have to control my temper, it gave me enough strength to push and kick them to the ground, in one instance to rip the shirt off my friend's back, buttons popping in Clark Kent fashion.

We played complicated games involving knives and sticks, forts and axes, that went on for days, then with sudden consensus switched to the beach where we constructed boats out of scrounged wood, nails, popsicle sticks and string for railings. Sometimes the warships were elaborated into houseboats with the addition of curtains attached so they really opened. The boys, away from their neighbourhoods, would play with my dolls, but here their imaginations flagged, and we usually switched to cars in the dirt at the edge of the forest.

I don't think I thought of myself as a boy, but neither particularly as a girl. I was fully aware of the anatomical differences which we had discussed and illustrated far away from the shack, but other than that minor and obvious difference, which I thought more a nuisance for a boy than a lack for a girl, I regarded us as the same, and whether I felt closer to boys or to girls depended on our activity: pirates or dolls, warships or houseboats. However, I must have wondered what it felt like to be a boy or thought that with practise I could compete in the forest, for once, early in our time at the shack, I walked into BIDEAWEE, pulled down my pants, thrust my hips forward, and tried, as I had observed, to direct the stream forward. I then had to wipe the seat and floor and reach the shack unnoticed, there to change my shorts, pants, socks and shoes. Even the fact that no one knew of my failure did not lessen the humiliation that there was something I would never master, no matter my desire or practise. It was after that I deliberately turned my back when boys had to pee in the woods, and told them they were disgusting.

Later, perhaps the following year, my mother introduced a further complication in my denial of sex differences by insisting I stop running around in public without a shirt. I stared hard at the boys' chests, cool and free in the sun; mine no longer looked the same. From then on I wore an undershirt as well as blouse or tee shirt, began to hunch my shoulders, continued to beat the boys in fights or races, continued to try to believe there were no differences, but when my conviction waned or reality impinged, I was, for a very long time, angry that this was the way it was.

Although my remembered images of the shack are always bright with summer sun, we did spend Thanksgivings and winter weekends there as well, and then the grey waves beat up the beach, inexorably chewing at the rocks' thin snow cover until all lay nude and abject under the vanquisher's retreat. We walked along the beach at low tide, around the Point as far as Dollarton pier then back again, our feet growing numb in cold gumboots, but this discomfort ignored in the delights a winter sea threw up: seaweed of course, brown kelp, green sea lettuce, dark purplish dulse, and mixed with this glass floats from Japan, old fish net, corroded boom chain, rubber boots and summer sneakers, things from houses and wrecked boats — red and yellow chair backs, mugs, plates, shirts, unidentifiable metal pieces, rusting stoves and dishpans.

On these beachcombing expeditions we saw the permanent denizens of Dollarton, a private group of people who shunned the summer residents. One man and woman we met quite regularly, at first only risking a smile above our acquisitions: a glass float, gnarled driftwood, or chairback; and then, later, stopping to talk. The man wore a red and black tartan mackinaw and the woman a faded green knit hat. They lived, we thought, in the shack with window box geraniums — the only window box on the beach. They were friendly; the woman and my mother talked, the man smiled at me, but I always walked away, continuing our search if we had just set out or heading home if we were done, for the man had a moustache like my uncles.

After that I seemed to see them everywhere, singly or together, as with the selective perception of learning a new word which then jumps into the air from every page or conversation.

As well as a favourite tree, I had a favourite rock, one of two left behind on the beach by a retreating glacier. It was about five feet high with handholds and a gentle upwards slope. The tide reached it first and I frequently sat until the rock was an island and water had inched up its barnacle skirt, sat looking across the Inlet until the water behind me had climbed as far up the beach as I could jump.

The other rock, farther to the west and from the water, was nearly seven feet high with steeper and smoother sides. A taller, older company child had claimed it as her rock and truly it was, for I could not scale it without help and that was only grudgingly and occasionally forthcoming.

Every few months when she was not around I attempted to climb the rock; one day, cold and raw in the fall or spring, the man was suddenly there. He said, "shall I give you a leg up" and held out his hands cupped together. I must have been concentrating on my scrabbling failures for I had not heard him approach and I jumped with shock and fear. The rock hid both of us from sight of the shack and there was no one else on the beach. I wanted to run away but I would have had to dash by him and risk his grabbing me; more than that, I would have had to manifest my fear and I knew somehow, as with my uncles' kisses, that to let the enemy know my fear would increase its power over me. Since I could neither let him touch me nor accept his help, silently I shook my head and with a gargantuan struggle made easier from the force of fear, I gained a previously unnoticed toehold and threw myself on top of the rock.

From there I could see the green shack, smoke from the chimney, a corner of BIDEAWEE behind, could look down on my old favourite rock and the man. He still stood there, smiling. He said, "good for you," as if he understood, and I smiled back, embarrassed in case he understood it all.

Head Cook at Weddings and Funerals

VI PLOTNIKOFF

"THE MOST WONDERFUL DAY IN A MOTHER'S LIFE IS WHEN HER DAUGHTER MARRIES into a good family," I often heard Aunt Florence say. "Because she knows her girl will be taken care of for the rest of her life."

My mother would agree with her sister, then look around at her three daughters with a somewhat worried expression.

Aunt Florence, predictably, had married well. Her husband's relatives were all pillars of the Doukhobor community, while my mother had married a man who, although devout and hardworking, had relatives on his mother's side who were not as desirable as those of Aunt Florence's in-laws. However, I enjoyed visiting my father's family in their small house with its faint aura of decadence much more than I did Aunt Florence's home in the Doukhobor village.

Aunt Florence and Uncle Fred had a son, Fred Junior, who'd married well to an agreeable and pretty girl named Tina, from an upstanding Doukhobor family. They proceeded to move into the apartment right across the courtyard from Fred's parents and produce little Fred, much to the delight of Aunt Florence.

Aunt Florence's other child was a girl, my cousin Marusa, four years older than I. Her mother had great expectations of Marusa, who was extraordinarily pretty with her dark curls, sparkling brown eyes and tiny figure — a figure much enhanced by the fitted gabardine skirts she wore, the delicate nylon blouses with little artificial bouquets of flowers at the throat, or the soft, fuzzy pastel sweaters. I felt awkward and plain next to her. I was a giraffe with straight blonde hair and pale blue eyes.

When I visited her house, Marusa could sometimes be pleasant, even fun. Not stuck-up like she was at school. She let me try on her earrings and makeup, but only if she was in the mood.

"She can have her pick of all the nicest Doukhobor boys," Aunt Florence would say. "You should see Saturday morning at our place. The fancy cars and pickup trucks come in a stream, asking Marusa to go to the movies that night. She'll marry well."

Marusa was almost seventeen by now and dating for nearly a year. Aunt Florence hoped to have her settled down before her nineteenth birthday. Marusa would be finished high school next spring and had already filled her soondook, for she'd learned to knit at six, embroider at eight.

She was taking the General Program in high school — typing, shorthand and business math. No use studying university courses when your ambition was to be married soon. A girl could get a job in a local office until she married and began raising a family, usually within a year of the wedding.

Aunt Florence would visit our chaotic little house outside of town, listen to mama's pleas for us girls to help with the work, and say with a touch of smugness, "My Marusa is so cheerful, she likes helping me."

However, I knew Marusa could be stubborn, even mean-tempered.

That winter, which was a cold one, my father decided I was old enough to go to Sunday night sobranye with him, while my mother stayed home with Sara and Lisa.

One particularly frigid night, I was sitting at the back of the meeting hall near the airtight heater, sweaty in my long woollen coat, wiggling cold toes in the tight overshoes. The two pairs of socks hadn't helped.

I wasn't paying attention to the hymns or the speeches, which were especially lengthy tonight. Several men had attended an important sezd, a convention, in Saskatchewan and had much to report.

Instead, I was watching my cousin who was sitting on a wooden bench, third row second from the end on the women's side, making eyes at Peter Zarubin. She was looking remarkably pretty in an embroidered platok, headshawl, her eyes dancing as she smiled at Peter.

Peter was a tall, gawky young man with a too-short haircut and a pleasing personality. He wasn't very good-looking except when he smiled and showed his dimples. He was showing a lot of dimples tonight.

Peter was considered an exceedingly good catch, especially by the mothers of marriageable daughters. His parents had a small tidy farm, vast apple orchards, a large ranch house with many bedrooms to accommodate their four sons. Mable Zarubin, Peter's mother, was a hard-working opinionated woman who kept a clean home and was a renowned cook. In fact her borsch became so famous, she'd graduated to head cook at weddings and funerals.

Most of the women in the Doukhobor community helped out with cooking at these important events. The huge wedding feast required several settings, depending on the number of friends and relatives invited, as did the after-funeral meal serving the singers, gravediggers and family of the deceased.

Always at these occasions, in the place of honour at the dining table, there was the borsch. The special soup, thick with vegetables, laced with rich cream. The dish every young girl learned to cook at her mother's side.

Peter's mother had impressed the older women with her knowledge as to the right amount of butter and whipping cream, the correct pinch of dill, the quick and pretty way she shredded the cabbage, diced potatoes. So it was at an early age that she became head cook, instructing the other cooks, tasting, giving the final nod to the borsch before it was carried out to the tables by the serving women.

After the sobranye that cold night, I followed my father to our pickup, waited while he started the motor, cleared frost off the windshield. I saw Peter follow Marusa outside, tug at the silken fringes of her shawl, watched her jerk away and toss her head. A Doukhobor courting ritual I'd seen many times.

Marusa and Peter began going steady that spring and the following Christmas she received an engagement ring with a tiny diamond.

"Waste of money," papa said. "Better to buy a new stove for their home."

"Marusa let me try it on." I'd waited until my father had gone outside before imparting this important news. "And it cost fifty-four ninety-five. Second most expensive in Eaton's catalogue."

"Page seventy," said Sara. "Ordered from Toronto. Not Regina like our boots and underwear."

"A ring is hardly important to a marriage, but a good cook is," — my mother's voice was caustic, envious of Aunt Florence whose children had chosen well, while she still had three young daughters to marry off. She was chopping borsch cabbage, showing us how to cut the strands long and fine.

"Mable will expect her daughter-in-law to help with the cooking at home. You know there's a house full of men there." But she sounded pleased instead of sympathetic with Marusa.

It was late spring and Aunt Florence and mama were stitching Marusa's wedding quilt in our living room, when Marusa said, "I want to wear a wedding gown." Just like that. As if she were announcing she was hungry and wanted a cheese sandwich.

It was so unexpected that for a minute we kept on doing what we had been doing. Needlework, reading, playing checkers. When the meaning had sunk in, we all stopped, looking not at Marusa but at Aunt Florence.

Aunt Florence took a big breath, her bosom getting large. She turned and looked at Marusa, then at mama, and let her breath out long and slow, making a funny wheezing noise like Uncle Fred's accordion when he closed it. "Well, you can't," she said in a mild way.

This time we all looked at Marusa. Her cheeks were red and she wore her stubborn look.

"Ever since I was very little I've wanted to wear a wedding gown and a veil when I got married, mama." The words came out precisely.

Aunt Florence put down her needle, got up from the floor, faced her daughter with an equally stubborn look.

"You'll wear a Doukhobor skirt and blouse as planned. As for the veil, I'm embroidering a new shawl."

"I picked out a wedding gown in Eaton's. Only sixty-nine dollars and it's got lace flounces."

"I've already ordered lace from the cloth salesman. We won't talk about it anymore."

"Rosie wore a gown."

"Rosie didn't marry a Doukhobor boy. You have to go with tradition. What would people say. And your mother-in-law head cook too. You'll ruin your marriage before it's even started."

Aunt Florence got down on her knees, began stitching, not looking at us.

Marusa, still red-faced, stared at her mother's ample back end, then walked out of the room, through the kitchen, slammed the door so that the ornaments on the wall rattled. Not at all like someone who'd just decided to agree with her mother.

Soon afterwards, Marusa graduated from high school and obtained a summer job at Fogle's Garage doing basic bookkeeping and answering the phone. I'd see her that summer around town, in her crisp cotton dresses, hair pulled back in a ponytail, tiptoeing around the grease in the garage, enjoying the admiring looks of the mechanics. Or sometimes on her lunch hour, she'd be at the co-op, in serious discussion with a clerk about tea towels and pillow cases. After work I'd see her riding with Peter on her way home, sitting so close "she's almost in his lap," " ... but they're engaged," my friends said with envy.

On a hot evening, a few days after Marusa's eighteenth birthday, just as we were finishing supper dishes in the stifling kitchen, Peter's new pink and white Pontiac with the chrome fins drove into our yard. Peter had quit school and got on at the sawmill, making payments to the credit union on the car.

Through the screen door, we watched Marusa lift a big box from the back seat, give it to Peter and hand in hand they walked up the steps.

"Come in, come in both of you," mama bustled about, taking off her stained apron and shoving shoes into a corner. "Have you had your supper? It won't take me a minute to set the table, heat the soup. I made it with fresh peas from the garden."

I stared at mama. Now that Marusa was almost a wife, she'd suddenly acquired a dignified new status. Above waitress or store clerk or even secretary. Only a teacher or nurse were superior to a well-married woman.

"Thank you, tyota, but we've already eaten at Peter's place. His mother taught me to make galooptsi."

"Yours were even better than my mother's," Peter said.

Peter must be blind in love, I thought. Unless she'd improved vastly, Marusa was a careless cook. I'd seen her vareniki come apart in boiling water, fillings bubbling on top, pastry wrappers floating merrily.

"I want to show you something," Marusa said.

She untied string from the box, pushed aside tissue, lifted out lace and satin.

"Page 352, Eaton's catalogue," I breathed.

"Marusa, what have you done?" Mother's shocked voice.

"Isn't it beautiful? And look at the veil."

"But I saw your mother sewing your wedding clothes," mama said.

"She doesn't know. I borrowed the money from Peter."

"You should tell your mother right away. I don't think she'll let you wear it."

"It's my wedding and I should wear whatever I want. But I want you to tell her. She won't listen to me." Marusa had her stubborn look.

"Oh Marusa, you should wear it. It's just beautiful."

"Quiet, Ana, this is none of your business. Marusa," she turned to her niece, "you must tell your mother yourself."

"She's too worried about what Peter's mother will say." She looked at Peter, who was fidgeting with his car keys. "Well? Don't you think I should wear what I want for my own wedding?"

"Your mother and mine won't like it," he said in a mild, hesitant voice.

"Whose wedding is it anyway? I thought it was ours."

She scooped up the gown, stuffed it into the box and marched outdoors, ponytail bobbing. Peter followed, looking worried.

"Do you think they'll break up?" Lisa asked. "And what will happen to the wedding cake?"

"We'll eat it," said Sara practically.

"Maybe Marusa will be an old maid."

Two weeks before the wedding, the zapoy, engagement ceremony, was held at the home of the bride's parents and the betrothed couple was officially blessed by their families.

Marusa was a demure bride-to-be, virtuous and pale and virginal in her pink Doukhobor blouse and skirt, her fringed shawl. Eyes downcast, she and Peter knelt and bowed to their parents.

Nothing was said about the wedding gown since the visit to our place, and we assumed it had been returned to Eaton's unworn and that Marusa had decided to be pliant. We'd admired the wedding blouse and skirt Aunt Florence had created, with its white lace over satin, dozens of pearl buttons, and tiny nipped-in waist. Marusa would be a radiant bride.

It was a clear and dewy summer morning. A beautiful day to be married. We were up early, rushed through chores and breakfast, dressed in new clothes purchased at the co-op. Hurried to the bride's home to help with the cooking and the table setting.

Wonderful smells came from the vast kitchen. Huge loaves of bread and a dozen varieties of cakes and pies were sitting on the counter, waiting to be cut. The pirahi, light pastries filled with vegetables or cottage cheese then baked pale golden, were piled high in a pan, making my mouth water. Rice and raisin plov was being stirred on the stove, salads and trays of fruit were sliced, chopped, arranged, set out on the tables.

The centrepiece of the meal, the borsch, was being cooked that very minute to be served fresh and fragrant at the wedding feast. The woman in charge of the borsch was not as famous as Mable Zarubin, and Aunt Florence eyed the proceedings apprehensively during her frequent trips to the kitchen.

The entire village was a beehive. Cooks were chopping, tasting, "Will it be as good as Mable's borsch? We can't let our family down." Long tables were set in the living room. Pincurled cousins considered important questions — should the bride and groom eat borsch from the same bowl according to tradition, or be modern and use two bowls? And where should the ceremonial table with bread, salt and water be placed?

Finally, everyone ran outdoors as the streamered cars and pickup trucks honked into the yard. The big Zarubin family and their friends walked across the courtyard and up the steps of the verandah. We watched Peter, unfamiliar in his new suit, and his parents, approach the bride's family, Mable holding an enormous loaf of bread in front of her.

Formal greetings. Low bows.

"We've come for the bride."

"She's here," Uncle Fred said, "Come in." Aunt Florence stood beside him, holding her own large loaf of bread.

And from the back of the crowd ... Marusa walked out, head high, looking straight ahead, and stood beside her parents. She wore the wedding gown from Eaton's.

Looking back on that moment, I can remember the silence which followed Marusa's appearance. The almost-fainting look on Aunt Florence's face. Marusa's defiant look. I felt a numbness at the time, but thinking about it today, I can recall the divided thoughts I had as Marusa made her appearance — excitement because it was so totally unexpected, so deliciously sinfully disobedient, and the sinking feeling as I saw Mable Zarubin's shocked expression. Would she take her son, unmarried, and go home? The wedding day over before it had begun? Only Peter seemed oblivious, smiling at his bride, taking her hand.

Uncle Fred, his face red all the way up his bald forehead and into the hair combed carefully across the thinnest part, cleared his throat, said, "Let us start the prayers" in a funny strangled voice, clasped his hands over his plump stomach, closed his eyes and began to recite a psalm.

As the ceremony proceeded, I heard murmurs, "Ona yamoo pakazsha," she'll show him. "Ona krasaveetsa," too pretty. "She'll wear the pants in the family." "Mable will teach her what Florence didn't." "Maybe she'll have bebeechka next year and that'll settle her down."

After the psalms had been recited, the hymns sung, Aunt Florence unrolled the prayer rug which had been brought over all the way from Russia so long ago, and Marusa and Peter began the bowing. They knelt on their knees and bowed to their parents, to their grandparents, to every aunt and uncle and cousin, touching their foreheads to the ground, kissing everyone.

Marusa and Peter stood up and faced us and we all shouted "maladim dobrai chass" to the newlyweds, good luck.

The ceremony at the bride's home was over. It was time for feasting. From my place near the foot of the table I could see the enormous steaming bowl of borsch set down in front of Mable.

She ladled her borsch. Only one ladle? Did it look greasy? Perhaps not the right shade of orange? Too many tomatoes ... the cabbage coarse ... too much dill? Mama and Aunt Florence looked at each other.

Then everyone turned and looked at Mable. Mable buttered a slice of bread, looked down at her bowl with a slight frown. She held the fringes of her shawl to one side as she bent her head over the bowl, lifted the spoon with borsch in it, put it into her mouth, withdrew it, chewed the contents, a thoughtful look on her face.

Mable Zarubin, head cook at weddings and funerals, swallowed, looked unsmilingly across the table at Aunt Florence, solemnly said, "it is good ... very good," and, still holding the fringes aside, began eating her borsch, stopping now and then for a bite of bread. She refilled her bowl, smacked her lips and continued eating. Aunt Florence took a big breath and beamed.

After the meal I helped clear the table, mindful of my new wedgies and striped taffeta dress with the big crinoline.

Mable and her sister Doonya came into the kitchen, loaded with dirty dishes.

"It was good borsch, very good. But two bowls? I tell you, Doonya, it's hard being head cook," Mable sounded satisfied. "But what of my new snaha? So headstrong. And we have to live together, cook in the same kitchen."

Doonya spotted me openly listening, jabbed Mable in the ribs, jerked her head toward me. They left the kitchen, talking low.

Loud voices broke out directly overhead in Marusa's bedroom. Aunt Florence's sounded mad. I dropped the pans in the sink, went through the living room, past guests who lolled on couches and chairs which were pushed back against the walls to make room for the dining tables.

Everyone was sleek and drowsy after the feast and looking forward to more feasting after the ceremony at Zarubins that night. They were discussing Maxim Dutoff's cow which had escaped from a nearby pasture and had just galloped through the village, Maxim in pursuit.

"A bawling cow means a bossy starushka," mother-in-law.

"Nyet, it means a willful snaha," daughter-in-law.

Peter's brothers were carrying the soondook out to the truck, followed by Peter's father with the tooke containing the bridal quilt. It would be placed on the groom's quilt by the mothers and the bed would look high and soft and inviting. Everyone would laugh and tease, and the bride and groom would blush, pretend they weren't interested, that they had loftier thoughts today.

Upstairs I skimmed along the corridor, past bedrooms with their tall narrow windows, spare whitewashed walls, where Marusa's grandparents and parents slept. And I thought it no wonder Marusa often complained everyone knew when she came in on a Saturday night, for each squeaky tiptoe, each cautious footstep could be heard on the creaking floorboards as she crept past all those disapproving doors.

The small commotion brewing around Marusa's door consisted of the bride, her aunt and her mother. Aunt Florence had her turkey look on. Face all red, neck long, saying in a loud voice that she was so ashamed, and to change right away and maybe just maybe not too much harm was done even though it would be all over town by Monday. Marusa was weeping, ruining her rouge, and my mother was standing ineffectually between them, clasping and unclasping her hands.

Then Marusa, who'd looked right through me at school and kept on talking to her friends, who'd ignored me during family visits unless she was bored and then taken me upstairs, told me ghosts were seen floating along the dim hallways, even told me I'd been a foundling abandoned by my real mother near the cemetery, suddenly became Marusa my friend. She reached out and took my hand.

In that instant, as we faced our mothers, I became her ally. Us against them. Cousins forever. I felt her cool fingers, the pressure of the unfamiliar wedding band.

"Yes. Wear what you want, Marusa. It's your marriage."

Was that me sounding profound and grownup? Aunt Florence and my mother looked at me for the first time, not knowing what to make of this unexpected alliance.

"It's your wedding, after all."

"Ana," my mother had recovered. "It's none of your business, or mine either. I'm not going to take sides, Florence," she said, then turned to Marusa, "Although it will be easier on everyone if you give in to your mother, dear." Diplomatic. No one could ever get mad at my mother.

Marusa let go of my fingers, smiled at me as I said one last "do it," shrugged her shoulders.

I went downstairs, thinking I'd do the same some day. When my turn came, I wouldn't give in either. For I'd felt Marusa's strength. Through her I could reach my dreams, unformed as they were. Maybe I'd take the university program at school, go on to college. I wouldn't even marry before I was twenty. I could do as I wanted and Marusa had shown me how. She'd opened the door a crack and I had slipped through after her. And the best, most wonderful part of all was that she had turned to me.

"I am ready," a voice said, and there she was, in her traditional outfit, as demure as she'd looked at the zapoy. She searched the group of people around the steps, seeking approval, smiling when she found it. She didn't look at me.

I followed the crowd to the cars, my unformed dreams dying inside me.

It was fleeting, Marusa's independence. Just those few hours in the wedding gown when she lived her dream. And mine. For after the wedding, after the ceremonies and the feasting, she became a dutiful wife. Within a year she bore a son. Within five years, she had three little boys tugging at her while she shopped at the co-op.

Under Mable's tutelage, Marusa was becoming an expert cook, her pirahi pastry light, her borsch renowned. It was rumoured, according to Aunt Florence, that Marusa would eventually take over her mother-in-law's position as head cook at weddings and funerals.

Mill-Cry

PATRICK LANE

THE YOUNG MAN SITS AT A PINE TABLE PLAYING SOLITAIRE WITH A WORN PACK
of cards. His son, three years old, stands by the chair, his small hand
clenched upon his father's knee. The boy doesn't look at his brother, who
sits in a wooden highchair with a smile on his round face. Fat, with his
first year barely behind him, the baby paddles his hand in a pool of
spilled food and milk.

Standing at the sink with her back to them all, her thin hands deep in
soapy water, the young man's wife washes diapers. The ammonic smell
of bleach and urine lifts with the steam into her nose and eyes. Her belly
is already pushing her back from the counter and she has to lean slightly
forward, a seven-month foetus high up against her heart.

She lifts a strand of hair, leaving a film of soap on the curve of her
cheek. The baby raises his pudgy hand and brings it down in the puddle
of soiled milk and mashed carrot on the board before him, yellow drops
splashing upon his bare chest. The older boy grips the hard blue cotton
seam of his father's pantleg.

The child's eyes barely reach the table. What he sees are the curled
edges of cards, an ashtray with a rolled cigarette in it, and a cup of cold
coffee. His eyes follow the blue smoke that spirals upward from the
cigarette to where it flattens against the air.

In a moment the woman will ask the man to give the diapers a final
wringing. Her hands and arms are tired from dishes and diapers and
lifting her sons from whatever griefs they have fallen into over the long
cold day.

Outside snow falls from darkness. The wet flakes drift down on the
aluminum roof of their narrow trailer. It's snowed for a night and a day

and shows no sign of slowing. There is more than a foot on the gravel reach in front of the trailer. Months ago it was their garden. Now only withered corn stalks lean muffled in the drifts.

If there was a radio the young man and the woman would know the storm will last for another day or two, but there is no radio. They are living between two mountains three miles below Blue River Canyon. There is no radio here. The mountains are too high, the valley too narrow. The weather that surrounds them has its own life and the five of them live inside it.

The snow will stop when it stops. They are used to this, snow or rain, or the slowness of the sun when it at last moves above the mountain at ten in the morning. Half their day is spent in shadow.

The woman squeezes out what water she can from the last diapers and looks into the window above the sink. She can't see the snow through the grey glass, though she knows it's there. What she sees is her face and for a moment it seems as if a ghost stares at her from the night. Steam has covered the window and as it drips down the glass it cuts the ice, creasing her image with crooked vertical lines, the high cheeks and the eyes that stare back at her.

The child inside her moves, striking out with its hard heels, and the woman steps back, placing her wet hand upon her belly, feeling the body within her. She presses down and the heels push back.

Two more months.

It seems to her she's been pregnant all her life. This child, like the two before, is an accident. It's something that has happened to her in the way a leg gets broken or a hand burned.

Each time has been like a blow, as if someone has punched her hard in that place just below the ribs where her heart sits.

She's willed herself to bleed but nothing has happened. She's asked God to stop it, but her tired body is obdurate. It is separate from her. It grows what it grows.

The woman thinks what is between her legs is an enemy, something with a life of its own, a mouth with a terrible "yes" that is not affirmation but affliction.

The man goes through the deck one last time, lifting the cards off in threes and laying them down. He's unaware of the boy and the hand that grips his leg. It's his seventh game and he isn't winning again. He feels a victory in the loss. It rises in him, a perversion, a kind of pleasure. He could cheat if he wanted but he doesn't. Instead, he lays what is left of the pack on the scratched table and pulls the other cards into it.

He's had enough. Soon it will be time to put the children down.

In a moment his wife will ask. When she does he will rise, lift diapers from the puddles on the counter and twist them violently in his hard hands. She will take them from him and hang them on the lines he's strung across their living room. The diapers will hang all night and into the next day until they dry stiff and hard, only to be taken down and replaced by others.

The man is tired. He has worked all day at the mill office adding columns of log scale on a hand-cranked adding machine. He is numb from repeating the same action thousands of times over nine hours.

But at least he's off the mill floor. He isn't just a worker like the rest of them. Not any more. He's on salary now. One hundred and seventy-two dollars a month. He could make more working shifts but he knows that's no answer.

A strike could destroy them.

Welfare or worse.

He's the first-aid man at the mill. Even though he's at home he's on call, and while he sits there gazing at the stack of cards there's a part of him listening to the scream of whistles crying into the night.

The whistles go all the time. If there are six in a row he has to go down through the snow to the mill because six whistles mean an accident, six whistles mean someone's made a mistake and broken something or lost something — a finger, a hand, a bone in a chest or leg — or it could be simply the flesh, a muscle opened up to the air, an ear torn partly off, an eye cut across the cornea by a slash of splinter.

The whistles seem to happen far away.

He's been a first-aid man for barely six months. The course lasted five weeks. Twenty hours of practical and suddenly he had a ticket and ten dollars more a month. The nearest hospital is six hours away in Kamloops. It's only one hundred and eighty miles south but the road is narrow, a thin track of shattered stone. Even driving at night as fast as he can it takes hours, the truck crawling over the mountains and through the canyons.

For a moment, far back in his mind, he glimpses the heavy blue arms of spruce and cedar reaching for him as he pushes a pickup south, a man beside him close to death, in shock or past it and crying out, talking gibberish, or worse, saying nothing, that steady glazed stillness of the badly injured.

He glances out the window and sees through the falling snow a faint red glow. It seems as if the snow is burning somewhere, as if there were a cold fire hanging far off in the night.

It's the mill burner a quarter mile away. The scream of metal on metal is all around them, dulled by the falling snow.

And the whistles?

The whistles cry out every few minutes, sometimes reaching all the way to five, and when they do the young man stops and waits through silence until it stretches past the sound he waits for, the sixth whistle, the one that means shock and blood and helplessness, a man lying in saw-dust and grease staring stupidly at some part of his body disappeared, severed from himself.

None of them can remember a time when the diapers weren't there. It's been two months since winter began but they don't try to remember the fall or the brief summer before that. The past doesn't live inside them. What they have surrounds them, a narrow room eight feet wide and eleven feet long.

Beyond the tight lines of sodden grey diapers is a small couch set against the front of the trailer. The woman has scrubbed the stained fabric arms so many times she's worn through to the brown stuffing below.

There is nothing else in the room, only the table with three chairs and the wooden highchair where the baby sits splashing his hand in the last of his food. A coarse dribble of curdled milk and carrot seeps out of the corner of the baby's mouth and the man, without thinking, reaches and wipes it away with his fingers. The baby gurgles and tries to grab the hand that touches him, but the huge fingers elude his awkward grasp and he flutters his short arm in the suddenly empty air.

Behind a thin plywood door is the rest of the trailer, a tiny room with two narrow bunks against the wall, the lower boarded for a crib, then another door and a bathroom, and beyond that a bedroom at the end where the man and woman sleep. The bed takes up the whole space. It's too short for the man. His feet hang off the end. When he sleeps he wears heavy socks to protect them from the wall and the ice.

The woman who sleeps beside him there curls tightly into a ball each night, though now, with the baby growing larger and larger inside her, she has to stretch out her legs. She's a small woman, barely five foot two, and, pregnant, weighs only a hundred pounds.

What they have is here. The day they've lived through is gone. What is in the room is the present minute, the present hour. It lives in their lives, a small trapped animal without shape or substance that's given up strug-gling against what holds it in its place.

It's been like this for three years, since the first child was born, the one who stands beside his father with his hand gripping fiercely the pantleg beside him. He's not a noisy child just as his brother isn't. The world around the little boy is a silent world with once in a while, each month or so, a violence — abrupt, full of screaming and tears — and then silence again, deeper, more protracted.

The silence weighs heavily upon him, upon them all.

The diapers wrung and hung on the lines, the woman watches her husband go into the night. The door closes and she listens to him shovelling, the soft crunch of ice beneath the wet snow. The boys are in bed now. A moment ago she stood by the upper bunk singing the oldest a song from her childhood.

When she finished, the boy lay there on his back and she covered him and told him to sleep tight. He looked at her gravely and told her he would.

It's only nine o'clock but she is deeply tired.

She stands naked in the bathroom, her clothes on a hook beside her. There is barely room to turn around. The bathtub behind her is four feet long and a foot deep. The new one will sleep there.

Taking a washcloth from a nail, she dips it in cold water. The tank is empty, the hot water used up on the diapers.

She cleans herself slowly, her armpits, the creases below her heavy breasts, the veins and the nipples already swelling, her shoulders, face, and arms. Then she reaches between her legs and washes there. She lifts the cloth and looks at it. She's been doing this for months, hoping the cloth will come away with blood as it had when she was fifteen and miscarried.

She pulls on a heavy flannel gown and steps to the bed.

It's cold at the back of the trailer. The heat doesn't reach here and the walls are covered with thin sheets of ice. It's been weeks since the windows were clear. The bed is piled with blankets and towels and coats. She gets in and lies for a moment under the heavy covers and then rolls to her side. Down the hall through the thin doors she hears her husband come in, the front door banging shut, his boots falling to the floor, and then the long moment of quiet before a match is struck.

Silence.

He will come to bed eventually. She closes her eyes and falls instantly into deep sleep, her mouth sagging, her breath heavy and thick.

The man sits at the table staring at the cigarette he's rolled. Like the boy earlier in the evening, he watches the smoke rise and flatten against the air. The afternoon shift is almost over. After the last whistle he will go to bed. The graveyard shift will start up after cleanup. If there's an accident someone will come to wake him. If there's no trouble he will sleep as he always does, fitfully, turning and moving beside his wife's slack body.

He follows the blue spiral up to where it stops and then he takes a deep drag and blows a ring into the quiet. It moves away from him, a sluggish hole that falls to the table and changes shape, becoming a thin stream that tries to find a place to fall from, an edge, somewhere to go other than the surface it's trapped on.

He waits, and when the shutdown whistle blows he snubs the end off his cigarette with his thumbnail and puts the butt beside the ashtray. There is only a bit of tobacco left in the can and payday isn't till Friday.

Everything has to be saved. There's no waste in his world, only a watchfulness, a husbanding of things around him.

He thinks he could go to his wife and wake her. They could talk, but about what?

Talking is the most dangerous thing they can do. All their words are traps. Talk turns from the moment — the children's day, an owl seen, or a bear — into other things, the maybe, the what if, or worse, the how and why.

It's a place they no longer go.

It leads to tears and argument and, if it goes far enough, to the other silence, the cold one he moves into. To go anywhere else is to release a violence waiting just beyond his life.

He can't go there.

He can't risk that.

The last time they tried to talk was a week ago. After the yelling and screaming he had stood in the centre of the room as she flailed him with her hands. She had slapped him across the face until, weeping with rage and frustration, her arms grew tired and she could no longer lift them. He stood there, eyes closed, waiting for her to finish, a familiar numbness in his body, barely hearing his flesh turn into sound, feeling the blood in his mouth where his teeth had torn his lips and the inside of his cheeks, the way the blood tasted thick on his tongue.

He can't tell her about Yaneck.

Yaneck, the sawyer on the graveyard shift who'd moved into town five months ago with his young wife.

The mill values Yaneck. A good sawyer is hard to find at the best of times and Yaneck is one of the best. The mill pays him well. The mill wants him to be happy. That's what Claude, the boss, told him that afternoon when Yaneck had asked the first-aid man to come to his house.

Months ago Yaneck moved into one of the houses reserved for sawyers, and after that first day no one had seen his wife. There were some in town who said she wasn't real at all. No one, they said, had seen her come down off the train.

He'd seen her.

He'd helped load the sawyer's things into the company pickup when the train arrived, and he'd helped the dark woman climb into the truck. She hadn't spoken. Yaneck told him she didn't speak and he wondered at the time what the man had meant.

Did he mean she was mute or that she didn't speak English, or what? He'd only nodded when Yaneck said it and didn't look at the woman again except when she'd walked to the house. She'd been swaddled in a shapeless coat with a black kerchief pulled tight around her face and knotted at her chin. Yaneck had followed her down the path, closed the door, and that was it.

No one but Yaneck had gone in or out since. The curtains were always pulled, the front door closed.

He'd spoken about her to Claude but the boss told him to leave it alone. The woman's his wife, he'd said. It's his business. Claude had told him Yaneck was his best sawyer and he didn't want anyone interfering with him. Did he understand?

He could wake his wife, he thinks. He could try to talk to her.

He could say he'd done one hundred and forty-three stitches, the woman sitting rigid and trembling only a little while the curved steel needle went in and out of her flesh, the stitches like small black insects climbing across her wounds. He could tell his wife the woman wasn't mute, that she'd made mewling noises in a language he couldn't understand.

But he can't tell his wife.

What would he say?

That he didn't yell at Yaneck and didn't insist she go out to hospital? Should he say he'd begged Claude to do something about it? Should he tell her he left the woman sitting in the bathroom while Yaneck yelled at him?

She's a crazy, this one. A crazy woman. That's what Yaneck had yelled. Damn her, he'd said, damn her.

And then he'd gone, leaving Yaneck and his wife inside their house.

The oldest child cries out in his sleep and the man goes to him, rolling the small body over and stroking until the child's eyes close. The small forehead below the red hair is creased with worry. The little one below has kicked his covers off and he tucks him back in. This one never makes a sound, never cries.

He walks back to the front of the trailer and strips to his underwear, throwing his clothes over a chair in front of the stove. He keeps his socks on. He is going to walk down the hall through the bathroom and to the bed, but he doesn't. Instead he sits at the table again, picks up the deck of cards and begins laying out another hand of solitaire.

As the cards lie down in their ordered rows in front of him the sawyer goes from his mind. The image of Yaneck's wife goes away as well. Just before she does he thinks of how clean her house was, how everything in it shone, the pine floors, the tables and chairs, everything. He remembers how strange he'd thought that was as he went into the bathroom and found her in her blood.

In the distance the mill starts up again. He hopes it will be a quiet night. He lays out the cards and turns the stock over three at a time. Three on the four. Ace of clubs up. Seven on the eight.

The trailer is silent and he thinks of his wife in the bed at the end of the hall. He lays down the cards and then, without thinking, pulls his underwear aside, releasing his cock. He looks down at himself, the cock hard in his rough hand, and, turning sideways on the chair, pumps himself, spreading his white legs and curving his back forward until he ejaculates into the cup of his left hand. He straightens then, stripping the last semen into the pool on his palm. With his free hand he pushes himself back into his underwear, glancing briefly down the hall.

He sits for a moment, shudders, and goes to the sink to wash his hand. Leaning against the counter, he stares at the pale fronds of ice climbing alive across the window.

Part of him knows he should sleep, but he's unaware of it. The mind he thinks with is blank, full of something he has come to know as waiting.

He moves into it.

The mill fills the night, the chains clanking heavily across metal and the shriek of the saws moving sharp and high through the falling, muffling snow.

He doesn't hear them. There are only the whistles and his counting of them, one, and then two, and then three.

Silence.

Only three.

A millwright is needed.

He's heard the mill-cry for years. It's a part of him. It's who he is, his wife in the icy room at the end of the hall, his children, his son who looks out from his small thin body with a grave seriousness at what world there is, and his other son, the little one who won't talk, who never cries.

Somewhere in the room where his wife sleeps is another child. He felt it once while she was sleeping. He placed his hand on her belly and felt the child move. What was in there was alive. For a moment his hand felt protective and then he'd wanted to reach inside her, take the child out and kill it.

When the child comes it will cost one hundred dollars at the hospital in Kamloops. He doesn't have that money. He's still paying for the last one at three dollars a month. That debt and the debt to come stretches out in a long impossible line.

Beyond him, inside the red glow in the falling snow, a thirty-foot spruce slams down on the headrig, the dogs are set, and the log is rammed into the saws. Cants crash onto the gang-saws and edger-feed as men pull and push raw lumber through the mill. Someone swears at nothing, at everything. It is a man on the trimsaws or a man pulling two-by-twelves off the drain.

The young man sits at the table, picks up the deck of cards, then puts it down.

A whistle blows.

He counts until it stops.

A Short Story

GEORGE BOWERING

SETTING

It was that slightly disappointing moment in the year when the cherry blossoms have been blown off the trees, or shrunken to brown lace out of which little hard green pebbles are beginning to appear. The orchardists were running tractors between the rows of trees, disking the late spring weeds into the precious topsoil left there by the glacier that long ago receded from the desert valley.

Starlings were growing impatient with the season, tired of competing for scraps behind the Safeway store in town, eager for those high blue days when the cherries would be plump & pink, when they could laugh at the sunburnt men in high gum boots, who would again try to deceive them with fake cannons & old shirts stretcht between the branches.

High over Dog Lake a jet contrail was widening & drifting south. The orchards on the west bank were in shadow already, & sunlight sparkled off windows of the new housing development on the other shore. The lake was spotted with brown weeds dying underwater, where the newest poison had been dumpt by the government two weeks before.

Evening swallows were already dipping & soaring around the Jacobsen house, nabbing insects in their first minutes of activity after a warm day's sleep. The house was like many of the remodelled orchard homes in the southern part of the valley, its shiplap sides now covered with pastel aluminum, metallic screen doors here & there, a stone chimney marking the outside end of the living room. Fifteen years ago the living room had been used only when relatives from other valley towns came to visit. Now it was panelled with knotty

117

cedar, animal heads looking across at one another from the walls, & the Jacobsens sat there after all the evening chores were done, watching Spokane television in colour, and reading this week's paper, or perhaps having some toast & raspberry jam.

The rug was a pastel shade fairly close to that of the outside surface. The Jacobsens lived with it, though neither of them particularly liked it. One of them had, once, when it was new; the other never thought of offering an opinion, or holding one.

CHARACTERS

The Jacobsens did not discuss things. They spoke short sentences to one another in the course of a card game, or while deciding which re-run was more worth watching on the mammoth television set parkt under a deer head on the west wall of the living room.

"We haven't seen this Carol show, have we?" suggested Mrs. Jacobsen. "I think it must have been on the night we played bridge with Stu & Ronnie."

"No, we saw it," said Mr. Jacobsen from behind his sixteen page newspaper. "This is the one where her & Harvey are on that jet plane that gets highjackt to South America."

"Sky-jackt."

"The same thing. But if you want to watch it again, go ahead."

"I can't remember a sky-jack one."

"Go ahead. I'll probably fall asleep in the middle, anyway," said Mr. Jacobsen.

Art Jacobsen was tired every night. As soon as the after-supper card game was over, & his short legs were up on the aquamarine hassock, his eyes would begin to droop. He was sixty-one years old, & still working eleven hours a day in the orchard. Like most valley orchardists, he wore a shirt only during the early hours of the morning, when the dew was still on every leaf. His body was tanned & muscled, but it was getting more rectangular every year.

Audrey Jacobsen was ten years younger. She had only recently taken to colouring her hair, often a kind of brownish-red she mistakenly remembered from her youth. Her first husband used to tease her about having red hair, though it wasn't true. By the time that Ordie Michaels had died & Art Jacobsen had started courting her on rainy days, her hair was a good plain brown, usually under a kerchief.

She'd taken to wearing the kerchief, as all the women did, while sorting fruit at the Coop packing-house. By the time Donna was five, Audrey had assumed the habit of wearing it all the time, except when she went for drives with Art Jacobsen.

They had been watching Carol on television for five years now, & she didn't know whether she liked the show.

POINT OF VIEW

It is not that I know all about the Jacobsens & Donna Michaels before I start telling you about them. I am what they call omniscient, all right, but there isnt any Jacobsen family until I commit them to this medium. I have some hazy ideas or images, rather, of their story, a sort of past & a present, I suppose, but really, for me the story is waiting somewhere in the future. Or I should say that I'm waiting for a time in the future when I will have the time to come to it, here. As a matter of fact, you dont have to, now, wait as long for it as I do.

So I am in the position ascribed to the narrator with the totally omniscient point of view. A know-it-all. Dont you believe it! "God-like." Dont you believe it!

For instance, I've been thinking about writing this story for two years. Just a month ago I began to imagine a woman visiting her mother & stepfather at their orchard home, & that common emotional violence later on. But I just got the names while I was writing the first parts of the story, & I didn't imagine the Jacobsen house near the lake — I thought it would be forty kilometres farther south.

Do I have to mention that there is something difficult to explain about a third person omniscient narrative having all these "I's" in it? Point of view dictates distance. Well, I would like to keep you closer than your usual "god" will allow (except for people such as yourself, Leda) (no, that's not what I'm trying to do to you, reader: dont be so suspicious).

From up here I can see the Jacobsen house as a little square surrounded by trees that have nearly lost their blossoms & are just producing leaves. I have good eyes; I need them to see all that thru the drifting jet contrail.

By the way, have you noticed that when the narrator speaks in the first person, he makes you the second person? When he speaks of others in the third person, you are perhaps standing beside him, only the parallax preventing your seeing exactly what he is seeing. That makes for a greater distance produced by the first-person narrative. You must have noticed that.

PROTAGONIST

Donna Michaels, an attractive honey-blonde in her early twenties, was about four kilometres from the Jacobsen house, driving along the lakeside road in her dented Morris Minor convertible. She had already gone thru her rite of passage between innocent childhood & knowledgeable maturity, involving strong Freudian implications. Now she was driving thru a warm valley evening, wishing that she had come a week ago, when the cherry blossoms were still at the beginning of their decline.

She had not been home during blossom time for seven years, & perhaps this more than anything else told her that she had really ceast to be a valley kid, that she was a Coast person. Looking to her right she could see, even in the shadows made by the hills over the water, splotches of brown weeds under the surface of the lake. A part of her that still wanted to be a valley person was hurt by that.

She thought about taking a Valium before she got there, only two kilometres to go now. It was not really the time to appear. She should have arrived while Art was still out in the orchard, so she could have a calm talk with her mother. When Art was there, making his blustery remarks or criticisms about her language, her mother could be depended on to remain silent, just as she had always done during family hassles, just as she had done then.

"I love him, Donna. What am I supposed to do?" she had said.

"More than you love me?" That newcomer.

"I *chose* him."

That was the last time her mother had ever said anything so devastatingly open.

She got out of the car & took a Valium. One gets adept at swallowing them without water. She was mildly surprised that she was walking slowly toward the single little Ponderosa pine that used to be her going-to-be-alone place in the far corner of their orchard. It had perhaps grown four inches taller. Looking farther up, she could see Star Bright. She made a trivial wish & walkt slowly back to the dusty car.

What a beautiful sight she was, with her long legs & summer dress, sunglasses percht on top of her short feathery blondish hair.

SYMBOLISM

Donna got back into the dented Morris Minor, & before she let the clutch out, she unaccountably thought about the animal heads protruding from her stepfather's walls. The first time she had seen one, she had gone to the room next door, to see whether the elk's body stuck out from that side. What had ever been done with the bodies, she wondered now. Were they discarded, left on the forest floor for the delectation of ants? Did the family eat them? She couldn't remember eating mountain goat or moose, & she had been a picky eater as a child.

She decided that whatever had been done with the torso & legs, Art was only really interested in the trophy. He talkt about nature a lot, but he was quite comfortable under the stare of the big glass eyes.

Her dog Bridey passed away after a fit when she was twelve. Quickly, before he would have a chance to take her to the taxidermist, Donna put the heavy & limp body along with an adult's shovel into a wheelbarrow & pusht it for half an hour thru the crumbling earth, to the Ponderosa. There she wasted no time looking at Bridey's fur & tight-closed eyes. She dug a deep hole & dropt her in & covered her up, without looking. She left no marker. She knew where Bridey was, & that was all that was necessary.

Now, she reflected, looking at the sagebrush growing around her tree, they probably knew too, he probably saw the wheel tracks the next morning.

She let out the clutch & drove the last kilometre slowly, having pulled on the lights. Just in time, a mother quail & her five little ones raced in a line to the safety of the roadside weeds. She smiled as she imagined the mother there, counting them.

Then she was at the turn just before their driveway, where the truck & the new Toyota were parkt in a sharp vee. People here along Rawleigh Road never pulled their drapes. Thru the window she could see Mr. & Mrs. Jacobsen, an over-coloured Carol, & a deer she used to call Bambi, first childishly, then later to needle her stepfather.

Her car's wheels cruncht over the driveway. Before she got out she did up her two top buttons.

CONFLICT

Donna had driven four hundred kilometres to be there, but she didnt want to go inside the house. Of course in a setting such as this, they would know that somebody had driven up the gravel driveway, & one of them, probably her mother, would be walking to the door at this moment.

Donna wanted to be with her mother, & especially because she never wrote letters home. She did not even imagine writing "Mrs. A. Jacobsen" on an envelope. She felt as if, yes, she still loved her mother, that strange older woman in polyester slacks, though they had not once spoken to each other on the telephone since Jacobsen had mounted her as his casual season's trophy. What ambiguity in the delivery of the thought. When it was accomplisht, & all three knew, what depressing decisions & solitudes.

Donna could not stay in that family where her first love, her first world face, lost all hope & fell in, decided to stay with the bringer of death. What polluted language in the formerly unchallenged eden. Why? How, rather.

"But I chose him. I made my choice."

"Do you love him? Can you?"

"I chose him."

She was not a woman then, but she was not a valley girl, either. She left Dog Lake, she had to, & there was no question but the city on the coast, several ruinous jobs & some solitary education.

Now the door opened & it was Audrey who was illuminated by the porch light. Donna was momentarily ashamed with disappointment that her mother, Mrs. Michaels, was not the picture of a defeated lustreless farm wife, the sensitive buffeted by life, such as one expected to find in the Canadian novels she had been reading.

"Donna! For the Lord's sake! Why didnt you tell us you were coming? Come in, you rascal," the woman said, her arms outstretcht as if offering the red knitting she had been doing while watching television.

Donna held her mother's elbows & kissed her nose as she felt the screen door bat against her rear. Her mother chattered with a little confusion as the pretty blonde deposited her purse & a book & something wrapt in party paper on the telephone table.

"Well, well," said Art Jacobsen, looking up from his paper, his feet still stretcht out on the hassock.

DIALOGUE

"I wish I'd gotten here while the blossoms were in full bloom," said Donna. It was the perfect little bit of business to get thru the awkwardness of their surprise.

"Oh, we had a wonderful year for blossoms," said her mother. "When a breeze came up the whole valley smelled like a garden."

"It *is* a garden," said Donna, getting herself a cup of coffee from the pot on the stove. She came back thru the arch into the living room, where her mother was still standing with the knitting in her hands. "At least that's how we Coast people think of it."

Art shook his paper to a new page.

"It's not the blossoms that count. It's the bees."

"The workers, you mean," said Donna, a little edge on her voice. She sat down with her coffee, not looking at him.

"Yeah, the queen sits at home, getting fatter & fatter, while the workers bring her the honey," said Art, his eyes looking at a news photo of the local skeet-shooting champs.

"Have you had any supper, dear?" Audrey piped in.

"Yes, I stopt at the Princeton bus station café, for old times sake," said Donna.

That was a nice shot. It was there that she had abandoned Art's truck that night, with the keys in the dash. She'd taken the bus to Vancouver with no baggage, not even clean underwear. Just two apples & her purse.

Art didn't say a word now.

"Well, well," said Audrey Jacobsen.

There was a silence. Even the knitting-needles crosst & opened without a sound. It was pitch dark outside. A mirrored deer lookt in from between two young Lombardy poplars.

"How are all your aches & pains, Mom?" Donna askt at last, idly looking at snapshots from a glass bowl on the table beside her chair. Carol was over, & Art raised his remote control & shot the set off.

"Oh, the osteopath in Penticton said I did something to my lower spine when I was a girl, & I can never expect to be a hundred percent."

"Does that mean you're not all there?" askt Art.

FLASHBACK

When he seemed absolutely ready to give it up, give up on it, to settle for some costly talk then, she offered him a cigarette, which he took politely, & lit one herself. It was the only sort of occasion upon which she smoked, anything. They were always grateful, the talkers, when she by her gestures allowed them a certain comfort, a freedom from embarrassment.

"Thank you," he said, & lay on his back beside her, carefully sharing the ashtray she kept on her belly.

"You needn't feel badly." Her voice was soft & sure, caring & casual, it seemed. "You might be surprised how often it happens. You had a lot to drink, I would imagine, it was only enough to make you think you wanted me. Happens quite a lot."

"No, that's not it. Well, it might be a little, but that's not really it. It's … "

She did not offer the interruption he was waiting for. She just smoked her cigarette. She butted it out in the ashtray, & handed the ashtray to him. So he had something to do with his free hand.

"It's just that you are about exactly the age of my daughter," he said.

"No kidding," she said, with a twiggy edge to her voice, & that was his first hint that it was time to go back to his hotel.

FORESHADOWING

After he had left, she got the scissors & clipped her toenails. Having done five, she lay back & imagined the john walking back to his hotel. He did not seem like the taxi-taking kind.

She pictured him lying on her, brought by her to the margin of success. Then she yanked the scissors toward her, fetching a jolt as they sank into the flesh of his back. It was not an old movie on midnight television. The points of her scissors were just below the joining of her ribcage, forcing the skin a little.

I wonder whether I could just throw a few clothes into the car & drive to Montreal, she thought.

Maybe you could work your way across the country, she replied.

She clipped five toenails again. They were the same ones.

PLOT

The spare bedroom of the Jacobsen house was also a kind of store room. It contained a gun-rack in which one could find a pump-action shotgun, a .22 calibre repeater rifle, an old .303 that once belonged to the Canadian Army, a .44 handgun in a tooled holster, a 30-30 with a scope sight, & a collector's .30 calibre machine-gun with a plugged barrel. This is where Donna was, taking off her light cardigan & shoes, finding the toothbrush & dental floss in the bottom of her big-city street bag, looking at herself, untanned, in the vanity mirror. A severed goat head lookt over her shoulder.

Thru two walls she could hear the Jacobsens disputing. Art's voice rose & rose, & at the end of a declarative sentence fragment it uttered the word "slut," followed by an exclamation point.

One would expect the ammunition to be lockt up, & it was, in a cabinet with glass-panel doors. Donna shook the pillow out of one of the pillowcases, wrapt the pillowcase around her fist, & puncht one of the glass panels three times, each time with greater force.

The male voice rose to the word "hell!" & stopt. A door banged against a wall, & heavy footsteps approach. Donna threw the pillowcase onto the bed beside her sweater. When Art propelled the bedroom door open, Donna was pointing a loaded shotgun at his head.

Art backt out of the bedroom & walkt backward all the way to the living room. There he observed a slight movement of the dark holes he had wiped clean just the night before, & sat down in his favourite chair. He was on top of Audrey's knitting, but he felt convinced that he should not bring attention to such a minor problem.

Audrey Jacobsen, usually a chatterbox, found it hard to find the words she should say.

She said, "Donna ... "

It was very frightening that Donna did not say a word. Art looked depressed. He was a heavy man in his chair. Donna blew out her breath.

"For God's sake, girl, that's my husband!"

Donna did not breathe in.

"He's my husband, he's all I have!"

Donna turned a smooth quick arc, & shot her mother's face off.

THEME

Donna walkt from the house & into the orchard, the shotgun still dangling. She had no shoes on. No one followed her, & she did not look behind. She was walking between two rows of cherry trees, so that when a quick hard breeze came around a rock outface it blew a snow of exhausted blossoms over her head.

Donna walkt down the slope, not flinching when a clacking sprinkler spun slowly & soakt her dress from the waist down. It was really dark out now, & she could see the lights of the retirement village on the far side of the lake.

The gun had made a dreadful noise. But now the night life was speaking again, crickets nearby & frogs from down by the lake. They were calling each other to come & do it.

Donna walkt till she came to the dirt road with the row of couchgrass down the middle, & followed it till she arrived at her ponderosa. There she sat down with her back to its narrow trunk, & dropt the shotgun to the dry ground. The sky was filled with bright stars that seemed to have edges, & black behind them. One never saw anything like that from the streets in Vancouver. She thought of the universality speaking thru her condition.

Nearby, her dog lay curled, waiting for her to signal something to her. But she ignored her, as she fought to remember what had happened in the last hour, or was it some years? An airline jet with powerful landing lights appeared from the other side of the hills & descended over the lake, heavily pulling back on its fall toward the airstrip at the end.

Now that her eyes were adjusted to the late spring darkness of the valley, she saw a bat flipping from direction to direction above her. She remembered the fear that it might get caught in your hair. Bats dont get caught in your hair.

I'm not very old, Donna thought, I'm not very old & here I am already. She pickt up the shotgun & fired the other barrel, & threw it over the side of the hill.

Kill Day on the Government Wharf

AUDREY THOMAS

"I ONLY WISH," SHE SAID, REFILLING HIS COFFEE MUG, "THAT IT WAS ALL A little more primitive."

The man, intent on his fried bread and tomato, did not hear or chose to ignore the wistfulness in her voice. Mouth full, he chuckled, and then, swallowing, "All what?"

"All *this,*" she said impatiently, gesturing toward the inside of the little cabin. They were sitting by the window, having breakfast. It was nine o'clock on a Sunday morning and the sky outside bulged and sagged with heavy bundles of dirty-looking clouds. He wanted to get back out on the water before it rained.

"I thought you liked it here," he said, challenging her with a smile. She was playing games again.

"I do. I love it. I really don't ever want to go back. But," she said, looking at him over the rim of her mug, "seeing that the old man died only a few months later, don't you think it was rather unkind of Fate to have suggested plumbing and electricity to him? I mean," she added with a smile, "also seeing as how we were going to be the reluctant beneficaries of all that expense."

"You may be reluctant," he said, wiping his mouth, "I'm not. I think we were damned lucky myself."

She shrugged and stood up to clear the table, rubbing the small of her back unconsciously. She had acquired a slight tan in the ten days she'd been away and he thought how well she looked. There was a sprinkling of pale greeny-coppery freckles across her nose and along her arms. She looked strong and self-reliant and almost pretty as she stood by the window with the stacked plates in her hand. It was not myth, he thought, or a white lie to make them feel better. Women really do look lovely when they're pregnant. Sometimes she would say to him, quite seriously, "Tom, do you think I'm pretty?" or "Tom, what would you say about me if you saw me across the room?"

Her questions made him impatient and embarrassed and he usually ended up by returning some smart remark because he was both a shy and a truthful man. He wished she would ask him now, but he did not volunteer his vision. Instead he got up and said,

"Where's Robert?"

"Right on the porch. I can see him. He has a dish full of oysters and clams and a hermit crab in a whelk shell. He's been fascinated by it for two days now. I didn't know," she added, "that barnacles were little creatures. They've got little hand-like things that come out and scoop the water looking for food."

"Yes, I believe those are actually their feet," he said. "My grandfather told me that years ago. They stand on their heads, once they become fixed, and kick the food into their mouths for the rest of their lives. Now *that's* primitive for you." He drew on his pullover again. "How would you feel if I had another little fish-around before it rains? Then I'll take Robert for a walk and let you have some peace."

"Oh he's all right, except sometimes when he wants to crawl all over me. He's actually better here than at home. Everything excites him. He could live here forever as well."

"You must go back soon," he reminded her gently, "whether you like it or not."

"I don't want to. I hate the city. And I like it better here now," she said, "than later on, when all the summer people come."

"You don't get lonely?"

"No, not at all." She was embarrassed to admit it and irritated he had asked. "I walk and sit and look and read my books at night or listen to the radio. And there's Robert of course. He's become afraid of the dark, though," she said thoughtfully, "I wonder why. He wakes me up at night."

"Weren't you?" he challenged. "I was."

She turned, surprised. She had been of course, but she was a very nervous, sickly child.

"Yes." She stood at the sink, soapy hands held out of the water, poised over a plate, remembering. "I used to lie very still because I was absolutely sure there was someone in the room. If he knew I was awake, or if I should call out, he would strangle me or slit my throat."

"Footsteps on stairs," he said, rolling a cigarette.

"Faces outside windowpanes," she countered.

"And don't forget," he added, "the boy may actually have seen something. A deer, or even the Hooper's dog. I've seen him stand up and pull that curtain back after his nap. Leave the light on." He put the tobacco tin back on the window sill and got up. "Leave the bathroom light on. It won't break us."

"Won't that make him weak?" she cried. "Isn't that giving in to his fears?"

"Not really. He'll outgrow it. I think maybe that kind of strength comes from reassurance." He kissed the back of her hair. "See you later on."

"Bring us back a fish," she said, reminding him of his role as provider, knowing in her heart it was all one to him whether he landed a fish or not. She was jealous of his relationship with the little boat, the oars, the sea. He would come back with a look of almost sensual pleasure on his face.

He went out banging the door, and she could hear him teasing the little boy, explaining something. She left the dishes to dry and poured herself another cup of coffee. The baby kicked and she patted her abdomen as if to reassure it. Boy or girl, dark or light, she wondered idly but not very earnestly. It was out of her hands, like the weather and the tides. But would she really like to have it out here, maybe alone, with Robert crying from the prison of his crib or huddled at the foot of her bed, marked and possibly scarred forever by the groaning and the blood? Robert had been quick, amazingly and blessedly quick for a first child; the doctor had told her this indicated a rapid labour for the second. In her own way she was shy, particularly about physical things. Could she really go along to old Mrs. Hooper's and ask for help, or accept the possibility of being taken off the island by one of the local fishing boats, observed by the taciturn, sun-baked faces of the men to whom she would be, if known at all, simply another of the summer folk.

It was easier in the old days, she felt, when there were no choices. She smiled at herself, for Tom, if he had been listening, would have added "and childbed fever, and babies dying, and women worn out before they'd hardly begun." He called her a romantic and accused her of never thinking things through. *He* was the one who could really have survived here without complaint, in the old days. He was the one who had the strength to drag up driftwood from the little rocky beach, and saw it up by hand, and the knowledge that enabled him to mend things or to start a perfect fire every time. He hauled his rowboat down to the wharf below their place on a triangular carrier he'd made from old wheels off a discarded pram, pulled it down the narrow ramp, which could be very steep when the tide was out, lowered it over the side, stepped in carefully and rowed away. When he was around she was jealous of his strength and his knowledge — he had grown up in the country and by the sea. She was a city girl and forever yearning after the names of things. She dreamed; he did. Her hands were clumsy, except when loving her husband or her son, and she often regretted that she had never learned to knit or weave or even to play an instrument. She liked to read and to walk and to talk and felt herself to be shallow and impractical.

Yet since they had found the cabin she had experienced a certain degree of content and growing self-respect. She had learned to bake good, heavy bread in the little two-burner hotplate/oven which she hoped to replace, eventually, with an old, iron, wood- or oil-burning stove; she had learned about ammonia for wasp stings and how to recognize the edible mushrooms that grew in profusion near the abandoned schoolhouse. She could even light a fire now, almost every time.

She had bought a booklet on edible plants and was secretly learning something about the sustaining nature of the various weeds and plants that grew so profusely around her. She had started an herb garden in an old bureau drawer and already had visions of bunches of herbs drying from the kitchen ceiling, jars of rose-hip and blackberry jam, mushrooms keeping in brine in heavy earthenware crocks. Things could be learned from books and by experiment. She got a pencil and jotted down on a piece of drawing paper a list:

cod	thistles	pick salal
salmon	stinging nettles	?maybe sell some of our apples
oysters	blackberries	?my bread
mussels	apples	
mushrooms		
dandelions		

plant a garden, make beer, ?a goat and chickens for Robert and the baby.

Then she laughed and crumpled up the paper and threw it in the potbelly stove (her pride and joy and a present discovered for her by Tom) which heated the little kitchen. The fire was nearly out. She would set some bread and then take Robert down on the dock until Tom returned.

"Robbie," she called, knocking on the window, "d'you want to help me make bread?" From his expression she could tell he hadn't heard so she went to the other side of the room — Tom had knocked most of the wall out to make one big room out of two — and opened the front door. It was chilly and she shivered. "Hey, d'you want to help me make some bread?"

He nodded, sturdy and solemn like his father, but with her light skin and hair. She undid his jacket and kissed him. His cheeks were very red.

"Your ears are cold," she laughed, holding his head, like a ball between her hands. "And you smell like the sea. Where did you put your cap?"

"I dunno, I want some juice." He wriggled away from her and she thought with a stab of regret, "So soon?" and tried to fix him as he was at just that moment, red-cheeked and fat, with his bird-bright eyes and cool, sea-smelling skin, to remember him like that forever.

"Come on," he said, tugging at her skirt, "juice and cookies."

"Who said anything about cookies?" she asked in mock severity.

"Juice," he repeated, quite sure of himself. "And two cookies. I'm allowed two cookies."

"Says who?"

"Juice and two cookies," he said, climbing onto a chair by the kitchen cable.

Afterward, after they had smelled the yeast and kneaded the dough and made a tiny loaf for Robert in a muffin tin, she covered the bread and left it near the still-warm stove and took the child down to the wharf to watch the fishermen. There were three boats in: the *Trincomali,* the *Sutil* and the *Mary T* and they jostled one another in the slightly choppy water. She looked out toward the other islands for Tom, but couldn't see him. Then carefully she and the little boy went down the ramp to the lower dock, where most of the activity was taking place. A few of the Indians she knew by sight, had seen them along the road or in the little store which served that end of the island; but most of the ten or so people on the dock or sitting on the decks of boats were strangers to her and she felt suddenly rather presumptuous about coming down at all, like some sightseer — which was, of course, exactly what she was.

"Do you mind if we come down?" she called above the noise of the hysterical gulls and a radio which was blaring in one of the cabins. Two young men in identical red-plaid lumberjackets were drinking beer and taking a break on the deck of the *Mary T.* They looked up at her as she spoke, looked without curiosity, she felt, but simply recognizing her as a face, like the gulls or the flapping fish, of their Sunday morning.

"Suit yourself, Missus," said an older man who seemed to be in charge. "But mind you don't slip on them boards."

She looked down. He was right, of course. The main part of the lower dock was, by now, viscous and treacherous with blood and the remains of fish gut. The men in their gumboots stepped carefully. The kill had been going on for at least an hour and the smell of fish and the cry of gulls hung thick in the heavy air. There was an almost palpable curtain of smell and sound and that, with the sight of the gasping fish, made her dizzy for a moment, turned the wharf into an old-fashioned wood-planked roundabout such as she had clung to, in parks, as a child, while she, the litte boy, the Indians, the gulls, the small-eyed, gasping fish, the grey and swollen sky spun round and round in a cacaphony of sound and smell and pure sensation. She willed herself to stop, but felt slightly sick — as she often had on the actual roundabouts of her childhood — and buried her face in the sweetsmelling hair of her child, as if he were a posy. She breathed deeply, sat up, and smiled. No one had seen except perhaps the two young Indians. Everyone else was busy. She smiled and began to enjoy and register what she was seeing.

Everywhere there were fish in various stages of life or death. Live cod swam beneath the decks of the little boats, round and round, bumping into one another as though they were part of some mad children's game, seeking desperately for a way out to the open sea. Then one of the men, with a net, would scoop up a fish, fling it onto the wharf where it would be clubbed by another man and disembowelled swiftly by a third, the guts flung overboard to the raucous gulls. Often the fish were not dead when they were gutted. She could see that, and it should have mattered. The whole thing should have mattered: the clubbing, the disembowelment, the sad stupid faces of the cod with their receding chins and silly Chinamen's beards. Yet instead of bothering, it thrilled her, this strange Sunday morning ritual of death and survival.

The fish were piled haphazardly in garbage cans, crammed in, tails any old way, and carried up the ramp by two of the men to be weighed on the scales at the top. The sole woman, also Indian and quite young, her hair done up in curlers under a pale pink chiffon scarf, carefully wrote down the weights as they were called out. "Ninety-nine." "Seventy-eight." Hundreds of pounds of cod to be packed in ice until the truck came and took them to the city on the evening ferry boat. And at how much a pound, she wondered. Fish was expensive in the city — too expensive, she thought — and wondered how much, in fact, went to these hardworking fishermen. But she dared not ask. Their faces, if not hostile, were closed to her, intent upon the task at hand. There was almost a rhythm to it, and although they did not sing, she felt the instinctual lift and drop and slice of the three who were actually responsible for the kill. If she had been a composer she could have written it down. One question from her and it might all be ruined. For a moment the sun slipped out, and she turned her face upward, feeling very happy and alive just to be there, on this particular morning, watching the hands of these fishermen, hands that glittered with scales, like mica, in the sunlight, listening to the thud of the fish, the creaking and wheeling of the gulls. A year ago, she felt, the whole scene would have sickened her — now, in a strange way, she understood and was part of it. Crab-like, she could feel a new self forming underneath the old, brittle, shell — could feel herself expanding, breaking free. The child kicked, as if in recognition — a crab within a crab. If only Tom — but the living child tugged at her arm.

"I'm hungry."

"Ah, Robert. Wait a while." She was resentful. Sulky. He knew how to beat her.

"I want to pee. I want to pee *and* poop," he added defiantly.

She sighed. "Okay you win. Let's go." She got up stiffly, from sitting in one position for so long. A cod's heart beat by itself just below the ramp. Carefully she avoided it, walking in a heavy dream up the now steeper ramp (the tide was going out already) and up the path to her cabin.

Still in a dream she cared for the child and wiped his bottom and punched the bread, turning the little oven on to heat. After the child had been given a sandwich she put him down for a nap and sat at the kitchen table, dreaming. The first few drops of rain began to fall but these she did not see. She saw Tom and a fishing boat and living out their lives together here away from the noise and terror of the city. Fish — and apples — and bread. Making love in the early morning, rising to love with the sun, the two of them — and Robert — and the baby. She put the bread in the oven, wishing now that Tom would come back so she could talk to him.

"You only like the island," he had said, "because you know you can get off. Any time. You're playing at being a primitive. Like a still life of dead ducks or partridges or peonies with just one ant. Just let it be."

"What's wrong with wanting to be simple and uncluttered?" she had cried.

"Nothing," he had replied, "if that's what you really are."

She began a pie, suddenly restless, when there was a knock on the door. It startled her and the baby kicked again.

"Hello," she said, too conscious of her rolled-up sleeves and floury hands. "Can I help you?"

It was one of the young Indians.

"The fellows say you have a telephone Missus. Could I use it? My brother-in-law wuz supposed to pick us up and he ain't come."

"Of course. It's right there." She retreated to the kitchen and sliced apples, trying not to listen. But of course there was no wall. Short of covering her ears there was little she could do.

"Hey. Thelma. Is that you Thelma? Well where the hell is Joe? Yeah. All morning. Naw. I'm calling from the house up above. Oh yeah? Well tell him to get the hell up here quick. Yeah. Okay. Be seeing you."

She heard the phone replaced and then he came around the big fireplace, which, with the potbelly stove, divided the one large room partially into two. "Say," he said, "I got blood all over your phone. Have you got a rag?"

She looked at his hands, which were all scored with shallow cuts, she could see, and the blood still bright orange-red and seeping.

"You're hurt."

"Naw," he said proudly, standing with his weight on one leg, "it's always like that when we do the cod. The knives is too sharp. *You* know," he added with a smile, as if she really did. Little drops of blood fell as he spoke, spattering on the linoleum floor.

"Don't you want some Band-Aids, at least?"

"Wouldn't last two minutes in that wet," he said, "but give me a rag to clean up the phone."

"I'll do it," she said, bending awkwardly to one of the bottom cupboards to get a floor cloth. She preceded him into the living room. He was right: the receiver was bright with blood, and some spots of blood decorated an air-letter, like notary's seals, which she had left open on the desk. Snow White in her paleness. He became Rose Red. "What am I thinking of?" she blushed.

"I sure am sorry," he said, looking at her with his dark bright eyes. "I didn't mean to mess up your things." She stood before him, the cloth bright with his blood, accepting his youth, his maleness, his arrogance. Her own pale blood drummed loudly in her ears.

"If you're positive you're all right," she managed.

"Yeah. Can't be helped. It'll heal over by next Sunday." He held his hands out to her and she could see, along with the seeping blood, the thin white wire-like lines of a hundred former scars. Slowly she reached out and dipped two fingers in the blood, then raised them and drew them across her forehead and down across each cheek.

"Christ," he said softly, then took the clean end of the rag and spit on it and gently wiped her face. She was very conscious of her bigness and leaned slightly forward so he would not have to brush against her belly. What would *their* children have been like?

Then the spell broke and he laughed self-consciously and looked around.

"Sure is a nice place you've got here," but she was aware he didn't mean it. What would his ideal be? He was very handsome with his coarse dark hair and red plaid lumber jacket.

"Well," she said, with her face too open, too revealing.

"Well," he answered, eager now to go. "Yeah. See you around. Thanks for the use of your phone."

She nodded and he was gone.

When Tom returned the little house was rich with the smells of bread and rhubarb pie and coffee.

"Any luck?"

"Yes," he said, "and no. I didn't catch anything, but you did."

"I did?" she said, puzzled.

"Yeah. One of the fishermen gave me this for you. He said you let him use the phone. It was very nice of him, I must say."

And there, cleaned and filleted, presumably with the knife that had cut him so, was a beautiful bit of cod. She took it in her hands, felt the cool rasping texture of it, and wondered for an alien moment if his tongue would feel like that — cool, rough as a cat's tongue, tasting of fish.

"What did he say?" she asked, her back to the man.

"He said 'give this to the Missus.' Why?"

"Nothing. I thought he was kind of cheeky. He made me feel old."

Later that night on their couch before the fire, she startled him by the violence of her lovemaking. He felt somehow she was trying to possess him, devour him, maybe even exorcise him. And why hadn't she cooked the cod for supper? She had said that all of a sudden she didn't feel like fish. He stared at her, asleep, her full mouth slightly open, and felt the sad and immeasurable gulf between them, then sat up for a moment and pulled the curtain back, looking vainly for the reassurance of the moon behind the beaded curtain of the rain. The man shook his head. There were no answers, only questions. One could only live and accept. He turned away from his wife and dove effortlessly into a deep, cool, dreamless sleep. The rain fell on the little cabin, and on the trees and on the government wharf below, where, with persistence, it washed away all traces of the cod and the kill, except for two beer bottles, which lolled against the pilings as the two young Indians had lolled earlier that day. The rain fell; the baby kicked. The woman moaned a little in her sleep and moved closer to the reassuring back of the puzzle who was her husband. And still the rain fell on, and Sunday night — eventually — turned into Monday morning.

Les Rites

SEAN VIRGO

THE APPLE-WOOD PEG HAMMERED INTO THE BANK ABOVE THEIR MUDSLIDE had reeked of beaver-cast seductively on the wind. The big dog-otter had nosed it, breaking water at the head of his family. He galloped up the bank towards the scent, undulating his sleek length over the moss while five cubs trod water, watching. At the last moment his mate whistled from the opposite bank and he swerved, distracted, to romp down the slide. So the trap, instead of breaking his back, closed on the hind legs and the great rudder, flinging a spray of wet fur a yard away. The otter rolled, thrashing and yickering, down to the water, uprooting the peg; and the cubs dived to join the game.

A coneybeare trap is no great weight, but the otter could only hold its own for so long, straining with his front paws. After twenty minutes the mate and her cubs left off nosing the tethered shape which swung with the current in the sombre gut of the pool. The last red bubble of breath had gone winking off down Kumdis Creek.

With the next freshet, body and trap had washed free of the pool, bumping and tumbling downstream with the sticks and moss-rafts through the coffee-dark water. It travelled a mile in the next three days, passing below the Tlell roadbridge and on into the darker forest. Two pools down, the trap lodged in the roots of a fallen hemlock and the stiff ottershape stretched with the flow in the deeper water. A week later the body rotted free and the head itself snagged on a sunken branch, wrenched off and drifted to the floor of the pool. Leeches seethed in its brain, the fur scummed off and followed the lost limbs downstream, and in the next rains the skull tumbled against a gravel bar and was left there, facing upstream, when the water subsided.

Kumdis Bottom is the most ruinous tangle of forest on the islands. Dark and saturated, it is a senseless grid of fallen trees smothered with mosses; and the ground a succession of trapped black pools, seeping into each other beneath a blotched and treacherous mask of liverworts. Most of the dead trees are young; stretched unnaturally in their search for light and finally starved out; leaning against each other and rotting swiftly in the humid air. There are entire husks of trees, in lichen and bark, thirty feet tall and crumbling into nothing about your face if you should lean on them.

Only the most ancient cedars and hemlocks, whose skins themselves are fire-scarred and marsh-textured, have stability; and as the ground lifts sharply to the south the original unfettered forest permits walking through the giantsleep silence. But down by the creek they stand half drowned or on islands of their roots' own making, blocking out all the light. When they fall they choke the water, which flows in places for many yards, invisible under the overlapping and half-sunken trunks. There is never any wind here, except when a raven, floating down through the cedar crests, breaks the air with its creaking pinions. That sound is like bats in a cave, and when the ravens call, their belling cries hang echoing for minutes in the heavy silence. The texture is almost submarine.

Yet there is life. Underwater it is all one and the dwarf cutthroat trout arrow across the pools at any stir; while autumn brings a few lost dog salmon blundering up the shallows to spawn in the rare clean gravels. The beavers are young to the islands but they work half-heartedly along the creek; and the deer (who are immigrants too) find pathways some-how — their slots are printed everywhere among the liverworts and on the mudbanks, and bright piles of their droppings lie like berries among the sodden litter of hemlock cones.

Moss takes the animals as it does the trees. You will find the shoulder-blades of deer, bleached white with the first green lacing of the forest across their palms. Or the skull, in furry green, of a young buck with lattices on its eyes and bristling plumes on its antler hefts. Bone seems a finality, a certain resolution with the elements, but the mosscloak devours swiftly. Everything leaches back into Kumdis Creek through the filter of moss and rain.

But the otter's skull on the gravel escapes the moss, takes on the colour and feel of its stony bed, and stares back up the covered stream while a deer slips past on the bank with lowered head; and a little later, stumbling over the windfalls, a young man follows with a clamouring heart and a gun.

This pedigree of otter and riverbank must stand, because only an earth-quake, trundling the Queen Charlotte Islands back onto the dark sea bed, will prevent Kumdis Creek, which flows into and out of my story, from pursuing its slow and rack-choked way to the slough when our race, and perhaps the otter's, is quite forgotten.

2

The hotel coffee shop in New Masset faces the volunteer fire hall and the R.C.M.P. station. On the wall, above the vinyl seats and Formica table tops, is a picture of the Creation. It is in felt appliqué, white and black and red, a quaint and clumsy rendering twelve feet long of the Raven, hatching first man and first woman from the clamshell out on North Beach. The picture is by two ladies from Old Masset and their scene is bracketed by the two great clan figures of their people — Raven and Eagle, stiff and uneasy above the heads of the tourists, the loggers, the servicemen, the hippies, the natives.

The hotel bears the name of a great hereditary chief, and in the beer parlour that makes up the other half of the ground floor, there is a list a hundred strong of native people who are banned from the premises.

Behind the hotel is the sprawling reserve of the naval station. The crescents and circles of the married quarters, inturned and inspired as a turkey farm; the three-sided plaza of swimming pool, instruction rooms, and administrative offices; and all dependent on a little blockhouse five miles away on the same North Beach where Raven uttered his fiat. That building is ringed by a towering woodhenge of cedar poles and contributes doubtless to the vigilant security of the great white Lie.

The servicemen do not get involved in fights with loggers or Indians: they are mostly overweight improbable warriors, lounging in the coffee shop or driving through the town. Their wives seem to huddle in their Ottawa-plan homes — eating, dreaming, shopping through the catalogues or at the Capex built tactlessly on the high street. At weekends they may drive with their husbands and children out along North Beach in their dune buggies. It is their only contact with the environment, and in their suburban hearts they whine at the isolation, the rain, the mud, the monotony, the schools, the natives.

Often in the coffee shop you will see a table filled with young men in green clothing, passing the time over coffee and soft drinks, communicating in their closed circle with a foreign tongue. They are so young, so clean-cut and gauche, that their potential as fighting men seems if anything more unlikely than their chubby superiors'. They pass the time, they pass the time, they do not get into fights, they do not explore the wilderness, and they are French.

It is a pedigree of younger sons from families in St. Urbain, or Chicoutimi or the townships of Belchasse. Economic blankness, claustrophobia, perhaps an echo of vingt-douze legends, bring them into the forces. They group, they school, they take courses perhaps in radio technology; they are posted to the Pacific, to the furthest west point of Canada where, if they ever hiked up the beach to Rose Spit, they could see Alaska on a clear day. They pass the time.

One of them is Raoul Forrestier. He has been sitting here for an hour and a half, discussing cars, Guy Lafleur, the prime minister's wife; watching the other customers coming and going over his companions' shoulders. He drifts away from the group, his mind rewaking a dream from the night before as he hears two truckloggers talk:

"I tell you — the rack on him. Seven points, no kidding. Biggest I ever seen!"

"Branch Seven is the place ... "

"No I'm telling you, this feller stays put. Got to be the one I seen there last spring. Even in velvets he was built like an elk. Next fall for sure I'll get him."

"Get him in the morning ... "

"Fuckin' rights: camp out all night on the ridge. I'll get him."

And Raoul Forrestier has been dreaming of the deer too. Of endless dun herds, hooves clicking, passing before him over the muskeg. He has lingered in the Capex at the gun-rack, lovingly taken to himself a 30.30, seen himself tugging down the martini lever to reload, firing into the wave-like herd. It is the old glamour of childhood crazes at work. He is a boy still.

And he withdraws further, pale and certain in his vision, while his eyes take in abstractedly a table full of young natives. Normally he would watch them only in glances, covertly. The full mouth and body of one young girl, with her laughing black eyes, her carelessness of the destiny which leads her — they all know — down her mother's path. And the beautiful young men, with naked gums, ten years away from beer-bellies and broken complexions.

But his mind is with the gun, with the two days, duty-free, ahead of him. The young Indians sit, laughing, in their separate boredom, and he sees that he has money for the gun and the time to use it. He will rent a car — a pickup — he will go out and hunt deer on the muskeg. Most importantly, though he does not realise it, he will do this alone for his dream. He will brag to no one of his plans and he will go alone.

3

The dark blade settled between the rear sight's shoulders and travelled a little to the right. It dipped across the pale brow and steadied on the dark left eye. He eased it away slightly, aiming exactly between the staring eyes. One part of him remembered in time that the rifle was shooting four inches wide; another part noted how everything but the gun and the motionless face across the stream had lost focus, even the running water sound. In that instant the strain broke in — he realized he'd been holding his breath the whole time — and the rifle began to leap slightly with each heartbeat. He lowered it and breathed deeply. The sound of the water rushed in. And a raven called, circling above the high forest roof.

The face before him merged back into its place on the bright gravel. He stepped out gingerly over the dark water on a rafting cedar bough, and along the crumbling bank. The shot would have been wasted anyway. Would have warned the deer.

He squats on the gravel spit, laying the rifle with care, and picks up the skull. Small enough to hold on the flat of his hand, it is still built massively in its own scale. It is the colour of its gravel perch — dry from within though wet to touch from the lapping flicks of the stream. A flat head, snaky, the lower jaw hinged firmly into the skull, clacking in a dead bite when he releases it. The great overbite of the canines is a cold emblem of savagery — like a saurian fossil or a shark's jaw trophy — and he frowns at its mystery, his eyes going slightly out of focus as if he might clothe it again that way with flesh and fur and learn its name. The word comes suddenly — *loutre; l'outre* — as a blaze of dark, fearless eyes. Otter. It was a good omen not to have smashed it with an idle bullet. He eases it into his side pocket and picks up the rifle.

It has not felt right in these woods. His feet have betrayed him at every turn. Not just that he is a stranger under the trees, but that he has failed to condense himself into one simple being. He is out of balance. He had dreamed and foreseen how it would be, but now the clutter of his realities is a trammelling maze where he would walk straight.

And he had felt so straight, so clear this morning as he drove beside the calm inlet, with the truck and the gun, and the sun strobing along the spruce ridge to his left. Till he had stopped by Blue Jackets Creek to give a ride to the young couple squatting by their rucksacks. They settled into the cab and within a minute their cool glances, their patchouli odour, their ease with themselves, upturned his patronage. He lost his grip on the helm, jarring the clutch clumsily as he climbed away from the inlet.

He lost himself, and his thoughts oscillated wildly between contempt, affection, communion, envy, confusion. He despised them as he would have on the base: then he was a generous, tolerant Worldly Wiseman; then they held the answer to everything; secretly he was their brother: they were free spirits; he was a novice.

The 30.30 rested against the hippy's knee. "Going hunting?"

Raoul nodded, defensively. He did not like someone else to touch his gun. Or his dream.

"Bad time for it," the hippy said, easily. "Not much meat on them and you might get a doe."

"Sure, I'll be careful," he said. "Just look around."

"We got all ours canned back in November," the girl said. "It's really good with rowanberries."

The hippy's hand rested on the gun barrel. Raoul winced. The hand was twice as big as his. The young man was huge and calm and knowledgeable. It seemed wrong and unfair.

He was rolling a cigarette now with a careful precision that belied the heavy fingers. "Remember the buck holds his head high" — he ran his tongue delicately along the paper — "though even then you can't be sure."

Raoul said, "Sure, I know." He didn't know; he absorbed the lore. The girl looked out the window, laughing at the great parliament of Ravens out on the gravel pits by the garbage dump.

"New gun?" the hippy gestured.

"Yes, I bought him this morning."

The girl moved to laugh at the "him" but smiled and turned instead: "You're from Quebec?"

Raoul nodded.

"Quebec City?"

"Not too far. Across the river you know. Then Montreal for a while."

"Quebec is beautiful," she nodded gravely. "Really beautiful. Next to here."

Her friend murmured agreement, smiling as he inhaled from his smoke, ducking his chin. The rank Drum tobacco filled the cab. It seemed as exotic and dangerous as dope.

"You sighted the Winchester in yet?"

"No." Raoul was in doubt.

"Should do, man — they get really shagged up in the crates sometimes. You want to stop along here someplace and I'll mark for you?"

He could not be unfriendly. He wanted these people to accept him. But his day was spoiled. He pulled over just past Watun Bridge, feeling as though he were following orders.

The other man picked two beer cans out of the ditch and walked up the road about fifty yards. Across the ditch was a big log pile, a mouldering mass of wasted timber from when the road went through. He set the cans up in front of a log's butt end and stepped back onto the highway. "O.K." he waved.

Raoul was shooting diagonally across the road. He was nervous of the girl beside him at the truck window, and of the hippy down the road not quite safely out of the way. He eased six shells into the gun, trying not to fumble, and yanked at the martini lever. That felt better. He was, after all, good with an FN on the ranges. What would the hippy make of that? Control was coming back.

He aimed the light gun, breathing carefully, sighting low on the can because of the short range. He fired and missed. The sound of the shot came crackling back from some echo point on the muskeg. He aimed higher this time and missed again. He flushed and lowered the rifle to inspect the sights. The girl grinned vaguely, unconcerned. He flicked the lever again but when he aimed, the trigger wouldn't pull. He couldn't close the lever, pulled it down again, and the shell in the breech jerked upright, clamped in by its flange. He could not release it, shame overcoming his tenuous poise. "The son of a bitch jammed hup," he muttered to the girl.

The hippy sloped easily, bored, back down the pavement, buttoning his collar. He took the gun. "Yeh, they do that," he nodded. "You've really gotta slam the lever up." He took a Russell knife from his belt. Raoul fell at once in love with its leaf-shaped blade. This young man was so easy with his world, knowing the mysteries. The knife point twisted and the shell fell out onto the road. The hippy slammed the lever home twice and replaced his knife. "You're shooting wide," he said. "I saw your second bullet hit the wood."

He turned casually and aimed back across the road. His left hand did not even close on the stock. He fired and the lower can leaped, spouting ditch-water. Again, and the other flew out onto the verge. He handed the rifle back. "About four inches to the right," he said, his calm grey eyes resting for the first time straight on Raoul's. "Aim to the left, and you can fix it when you get home. See — the fore sight slides in that groove if you take the guard off." He smiled down at the soldier: "I'll set you up some more cans."

But it was not Raoul's weapon anymore. He ejected the last shell. "No, it's OK," he said. "I'll do it later." And rushed on: "Where you guys heading?"

"Down to Port," said the girl. "Are you going that far?"

"Oh, sure," he shrugged, "I'll take you. I've got nothing to do."

He dropped them outside Port Clements and drove on south towards Tlell. He'd go for ten minutes and when they were out of the way he'd come back. He didn't know what to do with his day.

And down the hill, by Kumdis Bridge, a deer crossed the road. It was big and unhurried; did not look up. It must be a buck.

The hunting spell re-awoke: he pulled the truck in by the bridge, and slithered fast down the bank into the trees. Inside there was frost on the moss still and smothering silence. There was no sign of the deer.

He carried the gun at port across his body like a movie soldier; knelt to touch a bright pile of droppings like a movie Indian. The hard black pellets were cold. He followed what might have been a trail once and floundered, breathing heavily, over logs and oozing pools, along the river bank and so to the resting place of the skull.

Now, he must take control of his day. He looks around. There is a trail, or clear ground anyway, across the stream again where a solitary crab-apple tree lies beaver-felled on the moss. He jumps from the gravel with a bootful of water and looks down at the litter of adze-shavings the beavers have left. The tree's stump points nakedly upwards, chipped round symmetrically as if by axe strokes. He would like to see a wild beaver.

He follows the untidy line of the river bank. There is more sky ahead, more light. For the swamp is not interminable. Someone, sixty years ago, cleared half an acre of the bottom, cut dykes and put stone drains down, and then left his forlorn dream of a homestead and family to die in a different ditch on Passchendaele. And Raoul is approaching a clearing of sorts — a space of matted couchgrass, hedged in by the grey embrangling of the wild apple trees. The ditches are vestigial now — the roots of the coarse grass lie in water — but the clearing is firm. Frost has eaten into the mud and the grass mat will preserve it till nearly midsummer. The crabapples braid into one another — they are cruel, thorny trees and Raoul's toque is snatched by one branch, his left eye gouged and streaming from its neighbour.

He crouches almost to his knees to win the clearing. When he rises the deer is watching him, thirty feet away across the grass patch. A phenomenal, alert stillness awaits him in the grey head and huge black eyes. The animal is poised for panic, but its nature wills stillness upon it. Raoul's mind is a bloody, racing confusion, but his nature, which he reaches for within, teaches him not to extend that to the deer. His heart knocks, but he fixes his eyes steadily on the animal's and keeps them from the gun which now — unprepared — he must load. He eases down the lever, imperceptibly, then with a prayer slams the breech closed. He winces at the sound, the movement, but his eyes hold steady. A muscle jumps on the deer's shoulder. The hind legs almost gather, but not quite.

He brings the gun around; touches the butt to his shoulder while the muzzle still points away across his body. His left arm swings slowly upwards. The deer holds still, staring. Raoul's left eye streams from its twig-lashing. He brings the sights to rest above the deep alert eyes. Then his finger jerks. Echoes rifle the clearing. The deer's ear is fanned by the bullet. Incredibly, the animal does not move.

Raoul has reworked the lever without thinking, straight after firing. The gun is still up and he is allowed another chance. *Four inches wide* he curses himself. The sights settle by the deer's right eye. He fires. The deer's whole neck and head flail backwards as though to a great hammerblow, and the body crumples down. The rifle breech is open, oozing cordite, and he has killed his deer. He steps towards the body.

But then, horribly, the deer is up again, or its hind quarters are up. Panic seeds the little grass plot. The animal forces its broken head, its paralysed front limbs forward with a frenzied rabbit-like working of its back legs. It ploughs itself forwards, colliding with a young spruce tree, through the crab-apples and into another open space beyond. It rams itself into a choked ditch and on again.

Raoul is dancing behind it in an agony of remorse and fear and the deer panic charging his own blood. He would like to run away. He rushes upon the creature, the pathetic upturned tail, and does not know what he should do. But the seconds pass — from a mere foot away he fires the heavy bullet into the back of the deer's skull. The head is nailed to the grass, the body leaps once, electrically, and is still. It is over.

He lays the rifle in the grass and walks around and around the body, beside himself. He is waiting for his heart to still, for the possibility of balance to return. He knows that his crime is not to have done the thing but to have done it wrong. And when the next part comes, the cleaning of the carcass, he must be at peace with himself and calm among the witness trees.

He has not done this before but he knows how to. He kneels with his sheath knife and slices at the side of the deer's throat. The eyes are glazed into an impossible deep blue of their own — there is none in the sky. He watches his own face and hands, foreshortened in the blue mirror as in a teapot's side. Not very much blood rolls from the jugular: so much has been wasted already through the shattered skull and the pumping, running legs.

The stomach next. He tugs the deer onto its side and the legs swing against him, following gravity as if they were scarcely joined to the body. He wills himself into calm, rightness. He cuts from the breastbone, down through the long hammock of the belly. Already he knows that it is a doe (that had glared back at him as he chased the poor cripple down the clearing) but he notes the mild genital now, seeing human anatomy as he has all along.

He plunges his hands around the slick heat of the bowels. The smell comes up at him of rabbit guts, his only reference. Do people smell so? The bundle of intestines comes out heavy, but easily. There is no blood in the body. Only when he pulls the vivid liver free of its roots. He wipes his hands, front and back along the grass. A pink, flecked membrane covers the breast-cave, taut. He pierces it with his knife, and with a long sigh the warm, moss-scented breath comes back at him. The human heart is there, and after the lungs, with two more knife strokes the body is clean. He has done this right. He is redeeming himself.

But a shape has fallen free with the last knife stroke. Shrouded in its caul, the still eye and the smiling, lipless rabbit mouth of the foetus discovers him. He stabs the knife again and again into the frosty grass roots — to clean it, to clean himself. He is almost numb. Under one of the apple trees he slices out turf with his knife and chilled fingers and reburies the fawn in limbo. He would pray for its rest and his atonement if there were words.

Carrying the carcass out is clumsy too, but the woods do not entrap him. He guesses at a drier route, circling around on the higher ground through the big trees; and soon he hears a truck thundering over the road bridge ahead and knows that he has chosen well. His load lightens. And as if in token of that, another deer trots through the shadows at his right, slips round an old cedar and stops to stare back at him. He is seduced, outside himself, considering the feat of the hunter who, with one deer yoked across his shoulders, brings down another.

The deer is facing him directly and something in the forest air decrees that it shall not move. Raoul lets the body slip off his shoulders — it falls fast, top-heavy, and heaps against his leg. He has the hammer on half-cock this time. He pulls it back as he raises the gun, aims wide and fires. The deer falls and then, like a shadow, is gone.

He comes back to himself — that the stricken animal may escape to die in pain is like a knife-stroke. He lurches down the slope, jolting over tree-roots, his breath coming in gasps in a dowse of his victim's state. There is fur scattered everywhere — down the fibrous cedar bark and over the moss — and then, a few feet off, the first great scarlet star of blood upon the ground. And despite himself his brain begins to reason that the creature cannot get far, thus hurt; despite himself the thrill of tracking by a blood-spoor whispers to him out of his childhood reading. His breath comes easily. He is detached and keen.

The track is easy to follow. The blood is brilliant against the moss, the dead wood, the huckleberry stems. But when, across a log, he sees the deer, it is no longer a voyageur's quarry. It is so small and mute, furled gently on the ground, like a faun breathing. He kills it. A doe again, and very small, scarcely a yearling. He cleans it efficiently, his hands working across a cold distance, and drags it back up the hillside. Overhead and back the way he comes, two ravens invoke the forest's echoes. He is observed.

He leaves the smaller carcass and carries the first deer the last two hundred yards to the road. He lays it on the grass verge and tugs down the tailgate. A car is cresting Kumdis hill and his impulse is to leap like a thief to cover, but there isn't time. The driver sounds his horn three times, cheerily, as he swoops past; a passenger waves. Raoul slides the corpse along the truck bed.

Back in the forest he loses his way. It seems an hour of casting around on the slopes, looking for a landmark. As the afternoon wanes the shadows seem to spill out and eddy across the roots and brushwood. His eyes remember nothing. He is almost ready to work down to the river and retrace his whole journey when a marker leaps at him. Draped on a low stump is a long, gritty shred of lung-flesh. And a few feet further on the gun and the deer at last.

Yet both piles of guts were far from this place. Something (the ravens?) had dropped this in his path. There is no sound from them now. The offal gleams obscenely against the moss as he trudges back to the road.

4

He'll drive up past Port Clements with his window rolled down, steering with one hand. He'll stop at the other bridge over Kumdis on the Masset road to wash the stink off his hands. And some Haida kids will be waiting across the bridge for a ride and he'll wave them over. There'll be three in the cab with him and one behind with the deer.

For a while they won't talk much, the two girls embarrassed, murmuring and giggling to each other, the boy remote, staring out with his cheek amidst the window glass. Raoul will be intensely aware of the girl next to him, her thigh pressed to his, her mocking eyes (however shy) when he glances her way. And the two of them off again in uncontrolled giggling.

Then there'll be a hand slamming on the roof of the cab and, jittery, he'll tread hard on the brakes and throw them all forward. Behind him the rear window will be running wet and red, and through that film the boy in the back grinning sardonically with teeth gaping, and brandishing a jug of Kelowna Red.

The boy in the cab will roll down the window and reach out and back for the wine. As they speed up he'll offer it across the girls. Raoul will hesitate and then take it, tilting it awkwardly, squeezed between the girl Mary and the steering wheel. The wine will go back and forth, and the boy behind will hammer for his share, and they'll all begin to talk and laugh, while Raoul's speech slurs and the dusk grows happy.

The furthest girl, Teresa, will say, "Hey come on down to the village, blue eyes." And he'll say, "Sure, I always meant to go there." And all four of them in the cab will be laughing wildly while the girls chant, "Beautiful blue, beautiful blue!"

"Hey, good-looking," Teresa will say, "you gonna come to a party?" The boy will laugh nakedly in the darkening cab and say, "Yeah, we'll stop at the bakery first," and they'll be laughing again because the bakery's next door to the liquor store.

It'll be dark almost at the top of Garbage Dump Hill, and a deer's eyes will glow out on the road. Raoul will swerve madly and the truck's wheels will wrench and skid on the gravel shoulder and almost lose control. But they'll laugh, laugh helplessly with the jug almost empty and the boy in the back beating on the cab roof and yelling, "Goin' down fast, goin' down faast," as they plunge down towards the inlet where New Masset is fairy lights on the dark running tide.

Mary will lay her head on his shoulder and the boy, Adam, will put his arm round her sister and the postilion Henry will scream "Yee-aiii," as they tear along the inlet. "He's my cousin," Mary will say. "He's reeal crazy." Laughter will take them into the town to Collison Avenue: "Collision Corner, Collision Corner," the girls will chant, and Adam will roll the window down and fire the dead bottle onto the church lawn.

At the liquor store the postilion will jump down and Raoul will fumble a ten-dollar bill from his pocket — "Put that in the kitty" — and hold it out. And Adam will smirk, "Yeah, put it in your pussy," and Teresa will slap him hard on his brow and he'll laugh.

Then they'll run the dark and alien mile down to the village and on a ways, up the hill over the church, till the girls shout "Stop." The truck will come to a jolting halt and Raoul will know he's had too much already and his dream of Mary beside him will start to fade even as she grabs his arm by the house door.

They'll troop into the neat warm room where an old woman looks up from the stove. And she'll mutter *Tchi-ay* in disapproval at their state, yet grin in welcome too. She'll nod and nod her head at Raoul and ask his name and when he says it Mary will cry, "No, he's Beautiful Blue Eyes," and Teresa will say, "A reeal French lover," and the old lady will cluck and chuckle and tell him to sit down, they've got no manners, they're *lumga* drunk.

In that small room, with its mirrors and gleaming stove and a photograph on the mantel of an old Haida man with a Hawk frontlet, the old one will take him over and say he must call her *Nonnie*, Grandmother, like the girls; and she will chuckle a lot but disapprove of the bottles going around. And Henry, the postilion, will stand apart by the door, sneering.

To Raoul the words will come harder as the girls chatter on and the wine keeps ending up in his hand. But he'll cling to the immense affection that wells out of him to the old lady. To be able to sense the mother in this stranger from a hostile race, to feel what home and belonging mean after this year of prison life on the bases; after the rivalries, the bravado, the pinups on the walls.

He'll make of her the respectable Gaspé matriarch she resembles, and blush for her protectively when the youngsters make lewd jests and say they've brought down "a French stud for Nonnie." But she will laugh and laugh at that with them and poke his arm and pinch his chin and say he's "too skinny for me — I need something I can get a good hold on." Raoul will love her the more for breaking his illusion of age and restraint.

He'll know he's letting go of something. That tomorrow he'll be starting in an empty square. Or he'll believe this anyway, and a wave of vertigo will wash around the walls upon him, as though he were poised to jump from a cliff and take his chances with the tides.

Another grandson, Jimmy, maybe thirteen years old, will bang into the house and grow shy instantly at the company. He'll ask about the deer in the truck and Raoul will say, "Do you want them? Can you use them? Sure — they're yours. They'd only waste I mean." Nonnie will say she'd really like some fresh meat. "Henry never hunts for me no more." She'll glare at the door: "Lazy dog!"

The two boys will go out with Jimmy and carry the carcasses around to the back porch, kicking the dogs away. Raoul will offer to help and half rise only to sink back to the couch as they laugh at him.

He will feel so fond of these people, yet struggle to keep his eyes from rolling upwards out of weariness and liquor.

Then Henry of the glittering eyes and impatient frame will be back at the door. "Hey, Row, I got to get down to Delkatla and pick up some shakes. Can I take the truck? I won't be half an hour."

He'll see he could never like Henry, but he's included. "Oh sure," he'll wave and fumble anxiously for the keys, but they're still in the dash.

Teresa will say, "No, don't you let him take it — he'll smash it up for sure. He's always pulling mad stunts like that — he's crazy."

"No, it's O.K," he'll say.

And Mary: "Henry, you know you got no license now. You stay here." But Henry will have gone.

Raoul will slip down to the floor, his back against the chesterfield, and try to catch all their eyes. Maybe a minute later, it seems, he'll half-clamber up again, jolting out of sleep and realize he has been talking steadily but won't be able to remember what or for how long. He'll see some echoes in the others' eyes of the lanes and fields of his uncle's farm. And he'll realize that he has not been pretending to anyone and that they accept this and that it has all slipped by. He drifts again.

Then the girls will be by the door suddenly, saying "See you Nonnie" and "Goodnight." Mary of the full mouth and limbs will catch his gaze for a moment and his eyes will reach up feverishly to salvage from the drunken shuttle a moment's touch for the darkness of her eyes.

There'll be no one in the room but himself and Nonnie, and he'll mumble that he must leave her.

"You ain't going to do your Nonnie no harm," she'll say. "You stay now. You're not going *any*where." And she'll squeeze his shoulder, laughing softly, as she limps by.

He'll hear her moving in the other room and he'll struggle out of his jacket from the stove's heat before he lapses into sleep. Maybe tomorrow, on the street, they won't even know him. Maybe they don't trust the things he has been learning. Never mind the truck and the gun — bad thoughts — never mind tomorrow.

His pocket will knock hollowly against the chesterfield's arm and he'll fish out the forgotten skull of the otter. The glow from the stove's grill will play over its deep eyes as he struggles to focus on them and bring back into his grasp the day's contrarities.

And Nonnie will be back at her door saying, "What *is* that you got. *Geee* you're a funny feller, eh?" And he'll relinquish the otter's mask to the trembling hearthrug and slip away from everything while the old woman's voice is still speaking.

The tenses dissolve on that tableau in the hushed living room. Thirty miles down the inlet, over the muskeg, a raven shifts on its roost, dreaming under the cedar canopy high above Kumdis Creek. The water below checks and swirls blindly around the sunken branches. The stars of Orion hang, angled in the sharp January sky. The islands linger on the Pacific.

Summer Wages

CAROLINE WOODWARD

FIRST OFF, LET'S PUT IT INTO PERSPECTIVE, AS JOSIE USED TO SAY. I, GERALDINE, have worked nine waitressing jobs and have taken the vow never to do it again. Sure, I make these tired old jokes about support hose and roller skates supplied by management but I've got other things I can do for less work and more money. No more shiftwork either.

I do the books for five businesses right out of my own home. Claim office expenses for one-third of this doublewide trailer under the self-employed category on income tax and I sign off with a nice flourish, let me tell you. It's better that the money comes back to me, hard-working mother of three, than to the lousy government just lusting to squander it on their corrupt friends or some U.S. kickass submarine thing.

But here's the kicker. My oldest, Carrie-Lynn, wants to get a job. Fine. Grade ten, smart as a whip, takes after Ab for brains and Josie for looks, like she used to look before she got into the booze. But the job she wants is waitressing up the highway this coming summer. "Just like you and Aunt Josie did."

I'm building up to spilling the beans on her, sitting her down in the next hour when she gets home and telling it like it is. Was, anyway. She's too innocent and the world is meaner and trickier than it was in 1969. I'm going to let loose with the scuzzy side of me and Josie's adventures in Service With A Smileville so she'll clue in and get a decent job. Like being a lifeguard. That's classy and the money is two and a half times minimum wage. She's still got time to get the swim ticket she needs. I'd pay for it, no ifs or buts.

She wouldn't get tips unless she served booze and she's still underage so that's that. The kid's only fifteen now, sixteen in June, runs like a deer, swims like a guppy, brings home ribbons every sports day and swim meet. Lifeguard badge be a cinch for an athletic kid like her.

Getting the damn pool job is another story though. I got to be realistic on that score. Carrie-Lynn doesn't have a high-up Daddy, or Mommy, to pull strings at City Hall. Ab is the *janitor* at City Hall for crying out loud. Plus he invents things like the automated scarecrow. But until he makes some indecent amount of money, people will just laugh at him. "How's it goin', Ab?" "Built a better mousetrap yet, Ab?" And Ab will just miss how entirely mean they are and smile and say he's not that interested in mouse-traps, his current project is this or that, keeps me busy, keeps me busy, he says, nodding and smiling at the snickering sons of bees. They don't know who they're talking to. Ab's halfways a genius and he's got the kindest heart in the West, not a mean bone in his body. Me, I'm mean, let me tell you.

Me, I should join the Business and Professional Women's Club, get on the power lunch and business card swapmeet circuit but I'm afraid they'd turn me down. I couldn't take that. It kills me because I'm so proud to finally get to be a bookkeeper but that might not be enough for them. A chartered accountant and on up is what to be for them. Carrie-Lynn, Carrie-Lynn, that's where you come in.

I started by default, waitressing, because they hired me to chambermaid. It was new then, it's closed now, a gas station and about ten cabins plus a café with a good reputation. Exactly halfways between Fort St. John and Fort Nelson with Pink Mountain looming up out of the muskeg some miles away. The Beatton River began a hundred yards from the café, just a little brown stream coiling around the willows and stunted spruce trees.

Josie was actually thrilled to be a waitress even when she found out there was no uniform, just a long green apron to tie on over her blouse and jeans. Still, she fixed up her hair and did her nails and worked a full shift an hour after we got there. Petticoat Junction is what the truckers called our place on account of the five young women between sixteen and eighteen that worked there. But by the first of August, Josie and I were the only employees left. The Mister had picked a fight with Henry, the gas jockey whose girlfriend was the head waitress and whose sister was the second cook. The second cook's best friend was the main cook, a farm kid from Tom's Lake who had cooked for her family since she was eleven and that Esther could cook, let me tell you.

All four of them left in a huff because of Henry being fired. They headed back to Dawson Creek and big summer dances with Bim and The Crystal Ship and maybe even Anthony and The Romans. Lucky bums. We didn't realize how much fun July had been until we watched them leave in Henry's souped-up car and the café was suddenly dull. No more Social Centre. Josie and I were on our own with the Mister and the Wife.

The Mister drank at least once every two weeks and was out of commission for three or four days at a time. The Wife was a bible-thumper and an excellent cook but she holed up in one of the motel units whenever he hit the bottle so he wouldn't hit her. Josie and I had orders to leave him be and to bring her meals three times a day. No problem. We avoided him like the plague, sober or drunk.

We never told our parents. We needed the dollar ten an hour and all this booze and sex and violence, just like the TV, only made us feel more grown-up and on our own. We didn't want to worry the folks. Hear what I'm saying? You got that little smile on.

So. After the big You're Fired! Like Hell I Am, I Quit! We All Quit! episode, Josie and I pretty well ran the place. We'd get up at 5:30 a.m., dash from our unheated shack to the café, get the grill and the coffee on, eat a stack of toast, and go our separate ways. If a tour bus to Fairbanks pulled in, Josie would holler from the back door of the kitchen. I'd set down my toilet scrubber or whatever and run over to ladle out soup and make a bunch more pots of coffee. Josie kept a clean green apron by the door for me so I'd look more or less like a waitress. We'd go flat out getting upward of fifty people fed and watered, answering their dumb questions about where we went to school and how come we didn't have pecan pie and was the soup in the crockpot homemade like the sign hanging over it said?

In July when all five of us had worked, a couple of us could have a break, walk up to the Sikanni Chief airstrip, climb up the old forestry lookout until we lost our nerve around thirty feet up. Henry made it to the top once and so did Josie. It took them forever to get down and I had to run back to cover her shift which pissed me off. It was a whole day off for me and something didn't sit right with me, down on the ground, looking up this ancient creaking tower, and them up there laughing.

Josie and I would hitch the one hundred miles down to Fort St. John every Friday afternoon at four o'clock and on Sunday afternoons we'd hitch back up to work in less than two hours usually. We got rides fast. Two blondes with our thumbs out with no *idea* we were two blondes standing with our thumbs out on the highway! I can't believe it but no kid of mine would stand out there, male or female, not in these times. Only so many angels on duty per innocent kid.

By mid-August we figured out we were putting in close to eighteen-hour days and then it dawned on us we'd just worked seven days a week for two weeks straight. We were missing the really huge parties at the Old

Fort and had romances to tend to. Or we liked to think we did. Pink Mountainview Motel or Pink Elephant Lookout as we called it behind the Mister's back was seriously interfering with our futures, and we each had two hundred dollars clear, a small fortune.

Now listen up. Our Dad phoned us right at a busy lunch spell and told us to quit if we'd had enough, give them a week's notice, come home and have a week off before school started. The Wife came in and gave me a dirty look for being on the phone, my only phone call all bloody summer. So I looked at her, said "Uh, huh," when Dad said goodbye and then I said, "Dead?! Where?" Beat. "Mile 109? Mile 136? Omigod!" Beat. "Hitchhikers? Have they got the murderer yet?" Beat. "Okay. Yes. Okay. Yes, we will. Bye Dad."

The Wife pretended she wasn't eavesdropping and scuttled out the door again. Something fell in the garage (closed again) and the sliding door came up and banged down. No Mister though. We waited a couple minutes, cleaning up the last of the lunch specials for a bunch of campers from Idaho and then it was just the two of us.

We got spinny, plunking quarters in the box and dancing to Little Green Bag three times in a row. Dancing like a pair of banshees until another camper pulled in. I settled down and marched out to where the Wife was holed up in Cabin Three and told her through the door that Josie and I had to quit.

I heard the toilet flush. Quit! Flush! Like an exclamation mark. Spent half her life on the can I swear. She opened the door and glared at me.

"There's two weeks left in the season," she says in her snappy boss voice. Her breath reeked of American cigarettes. Took me hours to air out a cabin after she'd holed up in it.

"Our Dad says you owe us four percent holiday pay," I say in my most polite and careful voice.

"But you girls didn't give us two weeks' notice," she says, folding her big huge arms over her big huge bazooms.

"Our Dad says it's the law and you didn't give us notice to work fifteen days straight either." Her mouth makes an O.

I take the plunge and make a decision for Josie and me. "If you give us our pay with the four percent, we won't charge overtime. Our Dad," I say, watching her squinty little eyes, using my most extremely polite voice now that I'm lying like a sidewalk, "Our Dad will come up tomorrow morning for us and I guess he'll talk to you about it if Mister isn't, ahh, around." I raise my eyebrows at her with this last bit.

That did it. She gave me a long, hard look and slammed the door in my face. I started running up to the kitchen, leaping from plank to wooden plank so I wouldn't sink into the mud lake between the cabins and the café.

There were some customers, the geologist guys from the Pink Mountain site, so I held it in until Josie took out their orders and came back into the kitchen. I retell the whole exchange with the Wife and we both get so excited our whispers shot up to squeaks and we tried to jump up and down without making noise, her in her wooden clogs and me in my gumboots.

Josie had big dark circles under her eyes and she'd lost fifteen pounds in a month and a half. She was more burnt out than me because short-order cooking and waitressing and night clean-up was all inside work, breathing a steady diet of grill grease and Pine-Sol. At least I could cart towels and linen in the fresh air between cabins. For the first few weeks there was a truck, the Alaska Highway Laundry Express, but then it folded and yours truly used an industrial washer and an outside clothes line about fifty yards long because their dryer had broken down. I liked doing laundry better than making beds and scrubbing toilets.

Outside the air smelled like spruce tea with the late summer mists hanging low and the roots dangling into the little river, steeping it a coppery brown colour. I could hear trucks downshifting miles and miles away, that throaty roar with a silent breath between gears. I stood up on the laundry line perch, singing my head off, pulling wet sheets, towels, pillow slips and kitchen cloths out of my basket and onto the line, or vice versa.

Back inside I tried to keep my mood light and summery, battling relief and giddiness and drawing a blank when it came to what to do next. I put the apron on to help Josie with night clean-up, strolling over to the juke-box to punch in some Creedence and Three Dog Night and Greenbaum's "Little Green Bag," our theme song. The geologists chit-chatted about rocks and bone hunters, one of them insisting that this place was smack in the middle of an ice-free corridor during the last glacier age. I poured their refills and kept my ears open because these guys always had the most interesting arguments. Then I heard the Wife giving Josie hell in the kitchen and so did the customers. I set the coffee pot down none too gently and marched back there, do or die.

Josie was looking white and shaky, holding a piece of order pad with some figuring on it.

"You got your hopes up, girlie," says the Wife, standing with her feet splayed apart and her arms hoisted over her bazooms. She launched into a major bullying session with a tired little Grade Ten waitress. Honestly!

"And what's the problem here?" I snap out in a loud voice that shocks even me. Josie looks at me like we've got one last chance to live and hands over the slip of paper.

"I figured out what I've got coming to me and they won't give it," she says, close to crying.

Josie is very smart with math and so I (no genius) quickly check the end result. I pause just a few seconds. Not for nothing was Drama my best subject.

"Looks right to me," I say in my new loud way and stare the skinflint down. By this point I am amazing myself!

"I'm paying her for nine hours a day and that includes breaks and meals," she says, looking past me at the heads of the geologists who are lining up at the till. She starts to move but I jump in front of her, wanting witnesses in case Mister crawls out of his cubbyhole in the garage and things get really weird. The Wife is scary enough but I got to her earlier with the yak about our Dad and the law and I know it.

"This poor kid works more hours than the fourteen a day she's claiming," I say. "She's opened up and closed down this joint for half the summer and she better be paid for it." Then I step aside so she can face the geologists over the cash register. Let the old bag simper and coo about how they like her homemade soup now, the frigging hypocrite!

To make a long story shorter, we got our cheques that night without one word of thanks. By 7 a.m. the next morning we were facing a chilly north wind blowing gravel grit in our faces but in no time flat we were climbing into a big fuel tanker truck. Listening to Buck Owens and Merle Haggart on eight-track stereo. Homeward bound!

It was a deluxe truck with a cabover for sleeping, tons of seat space, tinted windshield, little orange balls across the top that some truckers called Calgary willnots, don't ask me why, and swinging dice cubes in oversized green and white foam stuff. And then there were the naked ladies.

Once I saw them I couldn't stop staring at them out the corners of my eyes because they were cut up into parts and glued onto the dash and the middle of the horn and the ashtray. Mostly breasts, no heads or arms. I was glad the trucker, Al, he said he was, didn't want to talk much because I was sitting next to him. Josie always pulled the shy act when a ride slowed down for us and started whining for the outside seat. The music blared out of four speakers and Al tapped one finger on the wheel but he didn't keep time with the music, just kept the same beat. I had to make myself stop staring at that finger too.

I made myself look out at the scenery rolling by, the miles of stunted muskeg spruce and swamp tamarack giving way to taller spruce and pines and poplars. We passed a jackknifed rig and a squashed station wagon, burnt to a grey crisp. Ugh. And there was a bunch of wild-looking horses in the ditch, at least twenty of them escaped from who knows where, up to their bellies in good grass, sly and happy-looking the way horses are when they're on the lam.

The sun was pouring into the cab even with the tinted windshield. Al put on sunglasses which made him look even more sinister with his pock-marked jowls and hooked nose, an overweight parrot in an Hawaiian shirt and dirty jeans. He asked Josie to reach into the glove compartment for his pills.

"Gotta speed up my eyeballs," he said. "Hyuh, hyuh. Don't know your ass-pirin from your elbow, do ye, girlie?" Josie's giving him a confused, rabbity look because she can't get the lid of the flat black pillbox open. He asks her to fish two pills out for him. She still can't get the bloody little box open. I could scream.

The inside of the glove compartment is completely papered over with cut up women's crotch shots from magazines. You've got to understand that I'd never seen anything like this filth in my entire seventeen years. This was beyond the regular girlie magazines in the drugstore in 1969 is what I'm saying. I know, it's everywhere today, the TV, everywhere. Makes me puke.

Josie broke a precious fingernail and finally opened the pillbox. Al gulped down two and sucked on an orange he kept up on the dash within reach.

He was really booting it, pedal to the metal, wanting to get to Edmonton by midnight. We roared through the village of Wonowon at eighty miles an hour. That's way over a hundred and twenty kliks to you. Too damn fast. Dogs and gas stations and trailer courts and little Indian kids on trikes blurred by us until a siren drowned out the Buckaroos.

Josie dug into my ribs. When Al cursed and started pumping the airbrakes and downshifting, she mouthed "Out, out, out." Her face had gone white and every zit she'd ever had sprouted in purplish scar galaxies across her forehead and chin.

When the rig ground to a halt, we jumped out with the big brown suitcase we shared and yelled our thanks. The young constable waved us on and motioned Al down from the truck for their little talk. Josie yanked at the suitcase and my arm at the same time and broke into a run.

"Do you hafta pee or what's the panic?" I yelled. A red stock truck slowed down before I could even catch up to Josie and in it were two young guys with cowboy hats on. When I got closer I could see it was the Wayling brothers, rancher types from near the Blueberry Reserve. I didn't know them except to look at them and that was fine by me. Dark curly hair, cut short except for sideburns, grey eyes, gorgeous noses. They were, I told Josie later, like Zane Gray heroes minus their buckskin stallions.

We hopped in the truck and tried our damndest to get them to talk in full sentences for the fifty miles into town. Josie loosened them up with jokes about jogging on the highway to keep the pounds off and I, usually the yappier of us two, sat back and laughed and laughed. Josie was never funnier except they didn't get the one about hippies being living proof that cowboys screwed goats, which was just as well considering their occupation. I don't think they liked girls to swear or talk dirty and Josie figured that out in seconds. She hammed it up about disasters in the café kitchen when the only thing left to cook was freezer-burned hamburger and stale white bread. I bragged about her and Esther turning out fifteen pies at a time, cherry, apple, blueberry and lemon meringue. Josie flirted with them way worse than I ever did with the geologists. I had the outside seat too, did I mention that? Anyway, it was amazing what a summer of waitressing did for her confidence!

But once we got to Fort St. John, the brothers asked us to go cabareting and that's when they found out we weren't old enough to get in the bar and that was the end of that but it was fun while it lasted. They dropped us off at the end of our block like we asked because we didn't want our folks to see the truck and get ideas and besides, we had to talk.

She told me there was a convex mirror on her side of the window and she'd looked into it and seen a pair of eyes between the curtains of the cabover, staring at her. That was just as we started to barrel through Wonowon. She stared back at the eyes, paralyzed with fright, and then the police siren saved the day. When I asked if it was men's eyes or women's eyes, she said she couldn't tell because of the warping of the mirror. Holy doodle. And here I was freaked out by the dirty magazine scissor work!

We tried not to dwell on it and we didn't tell our folks because the chances of us going further north to, say, Muncho Lake the next summer and earning really decent money would be shot down for sure. See? Not a brain in our heads — or more guts than brains is a better way of putting it.

Look, Carrie-Lynn, I'll spare you my grown-up jobs, nineteen years and up, the classy night spots like the Oil King Cabaret where I pranced around in red polyester hotpants. Sure, laugh. Where I got bonked on the head by a flying beer glass for stepping between my friend Ella and a very hefty, very drunk woman who'd already yanked off Ella's frosted blonde short'n'curly wig. Poor Ella, standing there in her red hotpants suit with bobby pins holding down her greasy brown hair. Don't laugh. A little giggle is all you're allowed. Now that's enough.

You could be a lifeguard. Or go down to the Tourist Information booth. You're smart, you're pretty, you've got a nice personality. Don't leave this godforsaken town until you're eighteen. Promise me that. You got the rest of your life.

Please?

There Are More Dark Women
in the World Than Light

KEATH FRASER

THAT SPRING HE BEGAN CALLING ON HER OFTEN ENOUGH TO LEAVE HIS LOCK and chain wrapped around the Japanese cherry tree by her building. He saw no point in carrying the chain home every night. He would pedal home and park behind his Toyota Celica in the locked underground garage. Then in June she went away on holidays to visit relatives in Utrecht. She didn't *want* to go — she said leaving the West Coast in June was like eating curry for Christmas. "You know, Sad City." When she returned he pumped over and discovered his lock and chain had disappeared.

"Well, Dimwit, you'll have to park in the lobby from now on." She said the interesting thing about the Netherlands was how *many* people rode bicycles. "With wicker baskets, full of cheese wheels and glads." In Amsterdam she saw Anne Frank's house again, the Red Light District, and far too many twenty-course Indonesian *reistafels*. He could see she had put on weight. She bemoaned her trip because of what had happened to her forehand since going away. And over coffee she made him open his present. "It's not anything great," she told him. A lavender candle, he discovered, shaped like a phallus. "They're for sale all over the Rembrandtsplein," she explained. He lit it, with a smile, and before it burned halfway down they'd made a homecoming of love. The candle cast a guttering, mellow light at dusk. Except its smoke got in their eyes, and she licked her thumb and forefinger to snuff the flame. The lustre slid from her eyes and her hair came down in ringlets. If only she didn't have to go back to work until at least her tennis improved, she murmured. She disliked the Trust Company and was thinking of going over to a real bank. "You know, an old-fashioned one with marble columns and chandeliers?" She wondered how many of those institutions were left.

He took his own holidays in August, though he would have preferred October, and went fishing in Ontario. The acid rain in the lake had killed all the fish. He was surprised and told his brother they should think of selling the family cottage. His brother, who had black spots in his nails from banging up wallboard, said no one wanted to buy into a dead lake. He should have warned him to stay in Toronto. Anyway, it was still an okay lake for water-skiing and reading books, but if he wanted trout fishing to try Algonquin Park.

Instead he flew to San Francisco. Casting around in bars for a little action, he got off a few good lines with a young woman in pearls, who told him she was engaged to a financier in Connecticut. "Wants to retire by the time he's forty," she said. Adding, "I don't really know why I come here, I know all these people." From her office, she meant, but standing there with a Heineken in hand she wasn't talking to anyone he'd noticed. They shared a few laughs, she liked Sissy Spacek and he didn't, and then she left, taking along her dry-cleaning in cellophane from the coat rack. The bar was crowded and loud. A young Vietnamese with nobody to talk to said hi. He was in marine insurance, finishing a college degree at night in business administration, about which he wasn't sanguine. "People tell me to count on future," he said. "Now is first time in history population of San Francisco is not mainly Caucasian." He dropped his articles and drank pernod, looking uneasy among these lawyers and brokers. The bar was on Union Street.

In October he bought another lock and chain to bind his ten-speed Norco to the cherry tree. As before, he left the chain behind in the grass when he rode home at night. He really only used the bike to ride to her place, or occasionally around the park. But driving home from work one afternoon he noticed someone had stolen his bike from the garage. Luckily it was December then and raining every day, so what he didn't much ride he never really missed. In fact he rarely thought of cycling till the warm March sun returned, and he felt his legs could have done with a good pump. The police never phoned him back.

By this time he had known her a year and a half. She was still with the Trust Company and wondering now if they shouldn't take their holidays together. Trouble was she had August, and he October. He told her if she had come up with her bright idea last January they might have co-ordinated their plans. "You sound just as happy I didn't," she said. Anyhow, it didn't matter that much because she was thinking of going to this tennis ranch in Scottsdale with John Newcombe. "Jealous?"

He walked back to his own apartment, sometimes as late as midnight in the middle of the week. One night he remembered to look for his chain in the uncut grass under the flowering cherry. But as he squatted to unfasten the lock he couldn't remember the combination. He had one of those blank moments when he knew if he waited for it, the name, or in this case a set of numbers, would come back. Presto. But his thighs ached and he abandoned it.

Every time he visited her after that he tried to remember his combination in the grass. Trying to remember was a game and he refused to look up the card he had with the numbers written down. It annoyed him he couldn't recall three numbers memorized six months earlier. His business was to remember numbers the way a squash player remembers angles. "Hey, Ben, can we live with these numbers?" Figures in his world were numbers just as chairmen were chairpersons. (The salespeople at meetings who were women insisted on the title.) At lunch he would sometimes grow absent, not hear his gesturing companion, and listen instead like a safe-cracker for the tiny sounds of tumbling digits. Once over Sanka he thought he smelled freshly cut grass, and dog urine. He sniffed his cup. By May the cherry blossoms had all gone.

On a Sunday morning that month he phoned to ask if she wanted to try for a court. "I've got on an apron and pancakes," she said. "Thought you were coming over." He'd forgotten. "If you'd rather play tennis," she told him, "go ahead." He thought it sounded like a test, so he apologized and walked over in his Adidas and whites and had pancakes. He enjoyed them more than he expected to, and spilled syrup on his shorts.

When she was running hot water over the stain he removed the rest of his clothes and waited for her in bed. Listening to her toothbrush he got up and drew the curtains closed on their cedar rings. As soon as she came into the room smelling of Dial and Ultrabrite he gathered her long, thick hair in his hand and bit the back of her neck. "That's how the Japanese do it," he growled. "Bullshit," she said. "They do it like this." He laughed. They both made big bellies and denounced pancakes as disgusting and probably immoral. "Think of the squatters starving in Calcutta," he told her. She sighed. "Mother Teresa isn't getting me," she said. "Besides, she only takes movie stars and pop singers." Standing there on a little rug from Jakarta they rubbed their stomachs together like inflated beach balls. He looked down her back and admired the long dark leg, bent at the knee, poised on its toes. "You exotic cunts are all alike," he said. "You'll go down on your back for a pancake."

Afterwards, lying there, they drifted off. The Dutch clock in the kitchen went cuckoo eleven times. Helpless with laughter she turned to him with love in her eyes. "I ought to tell you," she said.

She said the only time she'd ever gone out with a guy she didn't know was last night on a stupid date her friend Katie at work had set up. She gave this guy her number, and when he phoned he asked did she remember him from August? "I didn't remember him at all. It was a really stupid date." He picked her up in his brother's Rambler, she said, with these spotty seatcovers that felt Mexican to sit on. All he could talk about was when he was going to get a Mazda and how great she looked, but he kept saying it in the stupidest way, like she was a Liberty scarf or a packet of spangled panty hose. Besides he didn't even know her. They went to Humphrey's, which was stupid because he said he couldn't afford the appetizers. She didn't care if she had an appetizer or not, but why go to a restaurant you can't afford in the first place? The view maybe. Or maybe he was razzing her. "I ended up ordering stuffed sole and I *hate* fish. He kept asking me the stupidest questions." Like what was her favourite food? Or were the colour of the sheets on her bed mauve like her blouse? And how come she wore her hair behind her ears, or did it just go that way? "This guy is supposedly a university graduate in forestry. He turned me right off." They ended up at a Whitecaps' game under the dome and sat in seats a mile up in Section 32, which was stupid because you couldn't see the game and he wouldn't move to better seats that were empty.

"God, he was a joke! His conversation consisted of what he was having, like, for lunch at the plywood plant where he's supposedly learning management." She snorted with laughter at the recollection, and the bed shook gently. "Fruitcake! It was insane. The only interesting thing he said all night was he knew Doug's sister, or Doug's cousin, or Doug's *something* of Doug and the Slugs. And she wants to start a band called Movement. On the way home I could hardly listen to him. He asked me did I want to go someplace for coffee and dessert? No. Could he kiss me goodnight? No. Could he maybe see me again because, well, he was really intrigued by somebody different? No. It was stupid, really stupid."

She took his hand and placed it fondly on her stomach. "This morning I decided that's the last time I go out with anybody who isn't a friend of mine already."

Then she said, "A trust company's funny for friends like Katie. I mean I really like Katie, but our tastes are just different. She's younger I guess." She thought awhile. "I'm tired of withdrawals and standing up all day." She lay back and stared at the old schooner reproduced a hundred times in the wallpaper. "The men get careers. The girls just disappear. At a trust company you either quit or get shoved off to another bench. I'd like to get into mortgages."

He listened to what she told him. "I'm glad you're seeing other men," he said. "But this guy sounds like a liability."

She laughed. "Isn't that what you wanted?"

"What."

"I feel guilty, though. That's why I lied about breakfast. I wanted to make it up to you."

He said, "I thought my memory was going." And told her about forgetting his combination around her tree outside.

She found this touching, the lock with no Norco to mind, and they slept until the cuckoo roused them at noon. They woke up smiling. He looked into her dark eyes. "You exotic cunts," he said. He made her breast large by lifting it like a custard. "Is this," she asked, "what losing your memory does for an appetite?" Later, on their way out to a court in the park, she bent down in her white tennis dress and played in the grass with his numbers. She was twenty-three.

He remembered her birthday in June when she turned twenty-four. He bought her roses, dinner and a modest remembrance. "I've never kept a diary," she said. "Keep it in your vault," he warned her. In July when he turned thirty-two she hired a chauffeured limousine and stopped by his office tower to pick him up. Last year she hadn't done anything she said on account of her being in Europe. "Besides, I didn't know you as well."

He told her it was pricey on her salary to be treating him to this. She took him to the Four Seasons for Broiled Sockeye under Bernaise Sauce (she had Veal Oscar) and afterwards told the chauffeur to drive them up the mountain. They parked at an angle on Hollyburn and looked down at the lit-up freighters and city. She handed the driver, who even wore a chauffeur's cap, a bunch of dinner mints. They all gazed down and listened to old Rock 'n' Roll songs on speakers hidden inside the grey-flannel roof. She had requested this particular tape because she thought he'd remember the songs. "Hey," he laughed. "I'm not your father." He sank back into the upholstery smoking her Schimmelpenninck cigars. "This evening must have cost you a month's salary," he said. "About," she shrugged. "Anyway, I'm not going anywhere this year. I told John Newcombe to buzz off." There was a chance she might get out of telling soon, into a desk job. She looked down over the sparkling world, up into the firmament. A group called The Platters were singing *My need is such, I pretend too much, I'm lonely but no one can tell* ... "I really like these old songs," she said. On their way back down to the bridge she asked the chauffeur to park at Ambleside, where they walked barefoot in the black sand. The Beatles crooned through the rolled-down windows of Yesterday, and the driver's cigar glowed like a paper lantern.

In August she took local tennis lessons to get rid of the loop in her serve and to improve her footwork. After dinner they often met in the park to play a set before dusk. She was a gifted athlete and beat him more often than he liked. Later on they walked to Ping Pong's on Altamira and had Italian ice cream in small aluminum dishes. She said that after tennis with him, and the hour and a half lesson before that, she could eat a whole tureen of Malaga. But she kept a paring knife handy to remind her of the destiny of fat girls. Meryl Streep had a peach-and-cabbage diet she admired.

In October he dropped into Canada Trust to buy American Express travellers cheques, waved at her behind a till and went away on his holidays to Hawaii. Not, however, before catching sight of a thin boy up the street with a ten-speed Norco. "This is mine," he said, grabbing the saddle. The thin boy and his friends turned to him with avid curiosity. He had jay-walked through four lanes of rush-hour traffic to nab the thief, who had his knee hooked over the crossbar.

The next day he flew to Honolulu in need of rest and recuperation. The Norco was not his at all. The pedals had toe-straps and the saddle under his hand felt bony it was so narrow. He apologized to the boy who just smirked. His friends, sea cadets, laughed abusively. That evening, packing his suitcase, he phoned her and let the phone whir nine, ten times before hanging up. He wondered if he had the right number, for the exchange he reached sounded custodial and distant.

It was a pleasure to think it was raining at home. He sun-bathed on Waikiki, toured a few clubs, bought himself white loafers and then flew to Maui for the last week of his holidays. In Lahina, where he stayed at the Pioneer Inn, he struck it lucky with the piano player downstairs, a green-eyed doctor on leave from Los Angeles playing her way through the islands. She was living on a thirty-foot Yamaha with her poet husband. Meeting her was lucky because of the girl she introduced him to, her husband's flaxen-haired sister, who served beer in the same pub. Together they all went sailing one day to Molakai, the old leper island across the strait. They were into the sauce. The blonde poet sucked unlit Lucky Strikes and pointed out where the whale pods arrived in January, asking Ben if he knew *Typee*. He hadn't heard of it. Just off a coral reef on Molakai they dropped their sails and the rest of their clothing. He and the poet cooked frankfurters over propane in the galley, rubbed Coppertone into the girls' backs, and gave them the whole day off. The doctor asked herself why she was playing the piano in a bar every night when they still had savings. She laughed. Her sister-in-law, tanned dark from spending every afternoon in the sun, and before this two years in Africa, said, "I hope we can hang around these islands forever." She'd just finished teaching with the Peace Corps in Nigeria, where her eyes had been opened. He gazed a little drunkenly into her blue irises. She sliced pieces of watermelon and he admired her pale gardenia breasts. "Over there," she concluded, "we're definitely in a minority."

The three strangers mentioned books they were reading, and he felt left out. The doctor's breasts perked up like baby owls. The poet put his head in her lap and bit into the flesh of his watermelon rind. He gave Ben a volume of his verse to look through, neatly cut stanzas of long lines and no punctuation, each poem addressed to a different girl whose name always began with I. Iris, Ivy, Ianthe, Isadora, Irene ... "All Greek," said the poet. "All tried and true." He put aside his rind and spoke earnestly to his new friend. "Every woman has a year in her life," he said, "month, week, even — dare I whisper it — a day, when she reaches a summit of perfection, a rare point in time like a peak in the Sierras, when she's neither child nor adult in any strict sense, and from which her body will begin to slide imperceptibly away. This is a sexist observation, Benjamin, certainly not a balanced one, because in toto a woman is a whole moun-tain range." He smiled appreciatively at his dozing wife. And later on, dopey with sun, he turned to his sister and murmured, "What you noticed in Africa, Hel, was there're lots more dark women in the world than light." To go swimming — in water as inviting as Helen's eyes — they hung an aluminum ladder off the stern and snorkelled down to coral.

Returning to Vancouver he learned she was planning to move at the end of November. Because of the recession more vacancies existed now than when she'd taken her present apartment. The new place, she told him, had a small view of the bay and she was surprised to be taking a step *up* in the world since her real reason for moving was the cheaper rent. She was also checking out a sales job at a downtown radio station. They were looking, she'd heard, for better balance in their staff, and she guessed a woman who was ethnic might have a fair chance of success. She rented a U-Haul and he helped her park it. Her heaviest things were a sofa and the bricks she used to make a board planter. He took apart her bed and found the futon lighter to tote than the kitchen clock.

In one of the last boxes to be loaded into the elevator, lying among herb jars and a rolling pin, was the diary he'd given her. Riding down alone he opened it to see if she ever used it. Most pages that year were blank. There were a few entries like *Went swimming today at Aquatic Centre with Katie, promised myself exercise classes. And Met Ben down-town to see* Stardust Memories, *with supper afterwards at Las Tapas. Home for a juicy something, but it wasn't a screw, both bushed. He went home.* The longest entry read *Sometimes I feel like a mistake. Loneliness is a bad city inside you. I don't understand how so much can be going on with so many people doing it and I have nothing to do with anything except gloom. Bought a blouse at the Bay.*

That night to ease the transition she stayed over at his place. She'd forgotten how big his apartment was and what a view of the park he had, even in the rain. She loved his plants, his white rattan furniture, his full refrigerator. She remembered the Markgraf prints and the decanter of sherry. They drank some sherry. "Everything's so magic here," she said. "I envy your touch." He smiled like a pirate, his dark hair shorter than Richard Gere's by a businessman's inch. Later she woke up beside him in bed and asked what he was reading. "Melville," he said. "The Greenpeace Grandaddy who wrote *Moby Dick*." Outside on the balcony the cold rain was puddling, but inside by the bleached glow of his chrome lamp it was warm.

"I love the south seas," she said, snuggling closer to the light.

At a meeting that year before Christmas he tried to remember the phone number of her old apartment. He wrote down different combinations of the last four digits, and none looked right. He remembered the prefix all right since it was the same as his own. That evening he phoned her new number and she seemed surprised to hear from him. He told her he'd been away on trips to Toronto and Montreal trying to make his boss some money. Tomorrow he was going to Calgary to see if he could make some more. And her? "Okay, I guess. Still at the Trust Company." An aunt of hers from Rotterdam was coming for Christmas, and tonight she was picking her up at the airport, in a new old car she'd bought from a friend at work. "Do you know anything about Crickets?" she asked. "Don't tell me if you do." She wondered when they would see each other again. "Over New Year's," he promised. "When I get my act together." She told him she had recently had her legs waxed. "Let me tell you," she said.

He ran into her in March at the tennis courts. He was driving home and saw her playing, striding into the ball with litheness and grace. Her brown limbs shone under her white tennis dress, and her brief blue anklets flew over the green sunny asphalt. She saw him at the fence and waved. Azalea and magnolia blossoms filled the air. When it was her turn to serve she corralled the lime Dunlops at her feet and spoke through the wire. "Katie," she said, "is now better than I am. She took lessons in Colorado." He told her she looked pretty good herself. She smiled shyly. "This year I'm definitely going to Arizona, in October." Hooking her finger in the mesh she asked him how he was. He said he figured the recession had finally bottomed out and things were on their way back up.

"You forget my number or what?" she said.

He didn't pretend he had forgotten it, and rattled it off. She laughed. "That's my old number," she said.

"Is it?" He seemed pleased.

She looked relieved. He took down her new number again and said he would call.

A week later driving by her old building he stopped along the No

Parking curb and switched on his emergency flasher. The Japanese cherry was in full flower. He had thought of it again at a performance of *Madama Butterfly* the other night with a lawyer he'd met in January at a party. He got out of his car and crossed over to the grass. He knelt down in the fallen blossoms and picked up his lock and chain. But the face was encrusted with rust so thick he couldn't dial the numbers in either direction, not even a hair.

Cadillac at Atonement Creek

KATHRYN WOODWARD

WE HAVE COME OUT ONTO THE PORCH TO WAIT FOR THEM. THE LATE AFTERNOON sun, caught behind some aspens, feels its way through new green leaves. It touches our legs as we sit against the cabin's wall, making up games about their arrival. We have each chosen a favourite conveyance in which they would come. Phoebe's is a helicopter. Her eyes shine with the excitement of noise and rushing air. She thinks my own pick, a chariot pulling the sun, is silly, and what is worse, stupid, since everyone knows it is the earth that moves and not the sun. While she frowns at what she takes to be my sport of her, a long, white car moves slowly up the driveway and comes to rest in front of the house.

My mother, and Sparrow the man who has driven her across the continent to visit us. It is her first visit because we are, mother and daughter, estranged. For years we have corresponded by notes and talked only on certain holidays. The granddaughter she has seen just in an occasional picture presses tightly against my side. I can feel the child's anxiety through our thin clothes.

It is Sparrow who gets out of the car first. I am not surprised but I expected that he would walk around to the passenger side and open my mother's door. Instead he stays where he is, leaning against the white fender of his car, lighting a cigarette. The car is not new but it is a Cadillac, and from his pose I assume I am meant to connect the two, man and car. It is difficult because the Cadillac is large and white. It takes up the whole width of my driveway and gleams as if recently washed, while Sparrow is small and chinless, with hair a city-drab brown, that lies across his scalp like wet hay. Perhaps what Sparrow sees when he looks into a mirror is large and white and gleaming, I couldn't say. We have never met, and I

am not really interested in him, not at the moment at least, not until I
have confronted my mother again. She is still inside the car struggling
with her door. My driveway slopes upward, following the mountain's rise
and one has to work hard against its angle. My mother, as I well remember,
does not like hard work. Every snagged zipper, every hopelessly knotted
shoelace I offered her brought bitter complaints, and she hated breaking
in a new girl to clean house. When Dewey was shipped home dead from
Vietnam, it was Mary Rose and I who packed away his short life, the
button-down shirts and limp ties, the football trophies, the aftershave
lotion evaporating into the stale air of his bedroom, while my mother sat
on his bed and directed us. The rifle to Cousin Fred. The shotgun to a
neighbour's boy. The boxes of clothes out back to the gate. Those were
to be picked up by the Salvation Army.

"But Mama, it's too hot," Mary Rose had whined. "Why can't we just
leave them up here for the men."

"Because they let niggers into these organizations," my mother answered her, "and I'm not having those kind of niggers upstairs seeing
where we keep our things."

Now on my driveway, twenty-five hundred miles from that old house
with its many rooms and its gates, she has given up on the car door.

"Help me with this darn thing, Sparrow," I hear her growl.

I get up to go to her aid but Sparrow has heard her. He saunters
around the car, taking his time, mocking her, as he opens the car door,
with a bow low enough to bring his lips within reach of her rising breasts.
I find myself shocked as if I have come down in my pajamas and caught
them doing something indecent on the back porch.

"What's with you two?" My mother is annoyed that we have not as yet
moved to greet her. "You'd think we were from outer space."

She is squinting at us across the car's immense hood and now that she
is no longer a shadowy figure inside the car, I notice how she has gained
weight, soft, pliable weight, rounding the corners of her body and enlarg-
ing her breasts. Those breasts, the same ones he almost brushed with his
lips, shimmer in the heat waves rising from the car's metal.

I take Phoebe's hand and together we walk down the front steps and
around to the other side of the car. My mother has made the long trip out
here but in the end she waits, as she would at home, to receive us. She is
an incongruous figure on the packed earth of my driveway, immaculate
in a roseate pant-suit, her purse and a brown paper bag in her hand. Her
hair, still the same pale blond it was when I was a child, has been dyed
by a master. It retains just the barest hint of grey, a sop perhaps to good
taste because my mother, who is vain, would never want to be thought of
as aging undecorously. I am disturbed at what seems her permanent

beauty. It will not help our re-acquaintance.

She bends down and points to a spot on her well-creamed cheek. "Kiss me here, darling," she says to Phoebe, "so I can show you my surprise."

Poor Phoebe is confused. No one has ever ordained exactly where they would like one of her kisses, but Phoebe is, above all, a kind and obedient child. Stretching, she dabs at her grandmother's smooth skin. That done, my mother straightens. Each time she moves the paper bag rattles as if filled with dried bones. Opening it my mother pulls forth a host of plastic spoons, all labeled: A&W, Arby's, pancake houses, Kentucky Fried, Pizza Hut, McDonald's, and one spoon which is not white like the others, from The Daniel Boone Café.

Phoebe is in ecstasy. She receives this last spoon as if it is a holy sceptre and she is being invested with office. The Daniel Boone Café I can make out from the spoon's reverse side is in Topeka, Kansas.

"Let's not forget this one."

My mother leans into the car to pluck another pale eating tool off the dashboard.

"It's from the Dairy Queen in Nelson. The border being so close we didn't stop but once since crossing, so I guess this is your only Canadian spoon."

That word, *Canadian*. It gives my mother trouble, something I noticed the few times we talked on the telephone. She finds it a difficult word to shape to her Southern accent, so that in her mouth the syllables become that much more alien. Probably she has found substitutes — *those people, that place, up north* — but only for times when she cannot avoid my new nationality. Out of spite I have taken to printing that colonial appellation in my return address, British Columbia, in bold, capital letters.

"That spoon you'll have to wash yourself, Phoebe," she says, pointing to the one from the Dairy Queen. "I scrubbed all the others so you won't get Sparrow's bad germs. Those spoons you have are all his. I've got my own in here."

She opens her purse and shows my daughter an identical collection, this time in a plastic bag. "I wanted to get more but Sparrow wouldn't leave the freeways. But you know, honey, on the way home I'll do the same thing and when I get back to Louisville, I'll wrap them all in a package and send them out to you."

I am truly amazed. In all my infrequent dealings with my mother I have been careful, very careful, not to give my child away. How can she know, then, what a perfect gift a collection of plastic spoons is for my earnest Phoebe? My mother has no other grandchildren — Mary Rose has husbands but no offspring — and it is twenty-five years, longer for Dewey, since either Mary Rose or I were seven.

"Mother?"

"I'm not neglecting you, Joyce. I'm merely saving the best for last."

A cruel remark to make in front of Phoebe. A holdover from my childhood. Then as now it was designed to make me forget her slights. The three of them, she and Mary Rose and Dewey, had similar tastes. They made the same judgements. They were as intertwined as a braid, while I was the stray hair. My mother gave me her attention only by pretending the others were suddenly unworthy of it. No one remained fooled for long, and Mary Rose and Dewey developed into an accomplished team. Whenever my mother decided to favour me, they would go into exaggerated sulks and desert the room, leaving me with a mother who smiled indulgently not at me, her sudden supposed favourite, but at her departed two. She wears the same look now, smiling at absent children safe, one on the Eastern seaboard, one in his grave, while in the second before speaking she notes all my old defects: the narrow face, the short nails, the freckles that are bluntly visible, the man who isn't.

"You're looking good, Joyce," she says, which is true but I know she is disappointed that I display no improvements.

I lean over to give her a kiss. She is only slightly shorter than I am, but immediately I feel awkward again as if she is petite and I am overbearing.

"Sparrow, this is my daughter Joyce."

I straighten quickly and extend my hand. He has not anticipated the gesture so that his right hand jerks up as if remotely controlled. The squeeze he gives me is gentle but prolonged and I am forced to exert pressure to withdraw my own hand. Sparrow grins at his own effrontery. Closer now I see how the tips of his teeth are tinged blue-black.

"Open the trunk, will you Sparrow, so I can give Joyce her present."

Mine too comes in a paper bag: a bottle of Jim Beam.

For supper, I have killed a chicken, one of the older hens which, through inertia, I carried over winter. Opening the bird, I found it rampant with grease as if with old age the hen's fat had lost its nerve and melted into the body cavity. We found eggs too inside the hen, a string of them, translucent as yellowed eyeballs and traced with veins. Phoebe was charmed. She rolled them in her hands and squeezed them, testing the strength of their membranes. Lining them up by size she begged me to scramble the four largest for lunch. The smaller eggs I gave to the dog, plus the yellowish, fatty liver and all the grease. He ate with greedy, gulping bites but later threw up in a corner of the porch.

The chicken is cooking now. I am sanitizing it into fricassee, while my mother sits at the kitchen table drinking my bourbon. We are making conversation about other people, about family and my mother's friends, about people she met on her trip here and my Daddy's brother, Horace, who is retarded and still doesn't know my father left us.

"I see Horace once a month like I always did," my mother says. "He wears a diaper now."

Phoebe is out somewhere with Sparrow. After the spoons the child wanted to take her Grandma to see the baby chicks but my mother refused to go.

"I hate chickens, honey," she had said as if Phoebe didn't matter.

"Then you show 'em to me," Sparrow offered.

It was a bitter blow to Phoebe. All weekend long she had prepared. She drew picture after picture of chickens for her grandmother, proudly writing her name at various places on each paper, and regularly checked the chicken house.

"I know which one Grandma will like best," she announced with deadly accuracy. "The one with the brown on its wing because it's the prettiest."

She had accepted Sparrow with reluctance but with grace. I was proud of her. "Your Grandma's nothing but an old hen herself," I heard him say as they took the path that wound behind the cabin. "You gotta understand, she'd much rather cackle with your Mama, than visit with a bunch of her own kind."

The two of them must have ventured further than the chicken house because they've been gone awhile. Probably they are at the duck pond, a marshy oval of water technically on our neighbour's land but which we feel akin to. It is Phoebe's favourite spot, and Sparrow looks like the kind of man who would enjoy shooting ducks. When they return I see that I am right. Sparrow's shoes are wet and muddy, and Phoebe carries like a valentine one of the big lily pads which float on the pond's surface. I offer Sparrow a drink, then serve them dinner. Sparrow eats enthusiastically, but I have made the mistake of telling my mother about the meat's freshness. Suspicious of the fricassee, she picks it apart with her fork.

"I don't think it's quite as white as the meat I'm used to, Joyce."

I promise her I was vigilant. I remind her the meat has cooked for hours but feel as if I am on trial. My conversation becomes stilted. I choose words too carefully; I overexplain. To my relief my mother interrupts me, this time to discredit the marriage of a distant relative. The night before the unfortunate woman's wedding her new husband's first wife committed suicide, thereby spoiling the ceremony. Sparrow crows with delight, thinking this a great tale. In the momentary lifting of the atmosphere I offer him more fricassee and salad. Across the table from me Phoebe, her mouth overflowing with green lettuce leaves, asks, "What does committing su'cide mean?"

"Don't talk with your mouth full," I reprimand her, trying to mitigate the full explanation she will get.

I am unsuccessful. My mother bristles with disapproval. Had I, age seven, asked the same question, I would have been told it meant a walk in the park.

From things my mother says since arriving I gather that Sparrow agreed to make this trip only if he could spend the bulk of his vacation in Las Vegas. It means they are here for just four or five days. To be with them I have taken time off from work. At breakfast I mention scenic drives to lakes and mountain peaks of particular height, but my mother declines them all, even the spots along the highway favoured by tourists as quick viewpoints of what we offer. She seems content to sit at the kitchen table, to drink coffee or bourbon depending on the time of day, and talk about Louisville. Sparrow is more restless. He hooks up the garden hose and washes the Cadillac. He borrows extension cords from my neighbour to vacuum the car's carpets. Astounded that he cannot pick up baseball games on my radio, he takes Phoebe for milkshakes to a café ten miles down the road where the reception is better. I have little, it seems, to offer to these city people accustomed to finite exhibits, to entrances and exits and limited space. Sparrow would probably go anywhere I suggest but just for the chance to be moving.

I spend much of each day listening to tales of my cousins, their marriages to fellow Southerners, their excellent careers, their children's proper births. By the third afternoon my mother has exhausted the success stories and has come to Warren's daughter Nola, whom I remember chiefly for her limp hair and pallid complexion, and for her faded, milky eyes. In Nola our family genes had finally played themselves out.

"I suppose I could be wrong, Joyce," my mother begins, her drawl suddenly deepening as she puts on charm the way one reaches for sunglasses during a break in the clouds. "I could be wrong, but it just doesn't seem right, Nola in the Army."

She has chosen an odd topic to be charming about.

"It's what's happening," I retort, and am rewarded with a flicker of hurt in her eyes.

When she wrote offering this visit I allowed myself to hope for a quick, clean reconciliation. Wishful thinking I see now, like much of what characterizes my relationship to my mother. I once lived on "If onlys ... " My mother is not thinking of Nola. Her concern is for the Army's reputation. And family pride. My father was a career officer, my brother a casualty. In every generation our men have marched themselves off to serve. I can stand just so much of this, and vow that tomorrow I will not spend the day over the kitchen table.

I am in luck. The next morning proves free of clouds. I keep Phoebe home from school and announce that we are driving to the lake. Sparrow insists we take his car and that I navigate from the front seat. At the ferry dock we park the car and board the boat as foot passengers. This gives us an air of leisure, as if we are embarking on a cruise, in contrast to the other passengers who use the ferry as a highway across the lake. The morning is fresh and clear. The sun's light penetrates deep into the lake, emphasizing the clarity of the water. Winter still holds forth on the giant peaks which surround us, but down on the water it is warm for May. The breeze, however, is sufficient to drive my mother into the ferry's lounge where protected she endures the crossing.

I spend the trip over at the front of the boat holding onto Phoebe so that she can see over the railing, and shouting local lore at Sparrow. I point out an abandoned smelter stack sticking up among the trees and the grader that is visible once the boat is halfway across. On the trip back we are joined at the railing by a man in a silly sunhat who snaps pictures as if he believes it possible, even with expensive equipment, to confine this setting. The first clouds of the day are rapidly piling up behind the western mountains and the wind is strong. It whips the flag above the pilothouse and glues our clothes to our bodies. I shout to Sparrow and my daughter to watch for spray and go into the lounge to be with my mother.

It is quieter here. We sit together on the wooden bench. Her back is to the lake but I sit sideways in an attempt to face both it and her. Through the window I watch Phoebe solemnly cup her hands trying to help Sparrow light his cigarette.

For months I had wavered about admitting my pregnancy to my mother. Finally, mid-term, I wrote her a letter. In reply I received a note, rose-scented and to the point: "There are girls here in Louisville, nice girls like Jessie Bates and your father's niece Harriet, who have gone away on little trips and come back empty."

I never answered that letter. After the birth I mailed home one of the handmade announcements everyone received, but heard from neither of them till Mary Rose's note. "Mother has had her hysterectomy," the note said, as if having one was a matter of course, like learning to say thank you or getting married.

I take courage from this plodding, public boat, from the mountains and blue water pasted like a set outside the large windows. Haltingly I begin with generalities of love and maternal need, my voice just loud enough to be heard above the ferry's engines. I do not get far, however, not even to the most dangerous paragraph which is Phoebe's father, because the child, windblown and cold, comes into the lounge and squeezes onto the bench between her grandmother and me. My mother moves away from her. Outside the windows Sparrow is making faces at us, and gulls swoop and scream. Like ourselves, they have ridden the boat across and are returning.

After lunch I suggest that while we are out we should drive to the old mining town of Reco. "Renovated history," I quote to them from a promotional brochure we have at the travel agency where I work. The hour-long drive once again exiles my mother to the back seat. She does not complain but she takes a pack of lemon-scented towelettes from her purse and periodically asks Phoebe to wipe her hands. We travel along a shelf of asphalt. The road has been cut into steep mountains whose slopes fall like landslides straight into the lake. By the time we near the turnoff to Reco the water below us has deadened under swiftly moving clouds and gone opaque.

At the turnoff I become apprehensive. The brochure promised much: reconstructed hotels, a working café, shops stacked with souvenirs, a Mountie outpost not found in the original town. One would expect then a freshly-painted sign to mark the turnoff, something to draw in the tourists, something evoking the glory days of the town. Instead there is only a crude board nailed to a tree, with a slash of red paint pointing us up a pot-holed road. On it we travel deeper into the mountains, through a forest of spindly second-growth, paralleling what we read from another homemade sign is Atonement Creek. Suddenly the valley widens into a small bowl and we are in Reco.

Nothing has been done to the town. Tons of rubble, from the last time Atonement Creek spilled its banks, still lie everywhere. More than any legends we have of the whooping anarchy of towns like Reco in their heyday the rubble bespeaks wildness and violence. In our path splintered wood from a collapsed building lies across the road. Sparrow stops the car.

"Where to now?" he asks.

"Oh just turn the car around," my mother grumbles from the back seat. "There's nothing here." As if it was my fault I apologize for the bleakness.

"Once there were twenty saloons on this street," I tell them trying, by rebuilding, to dispel the dreary sight. I feel unnerved by the desolation, by the abandoned weathered wrecks. "They were supposed to have fixed it up," I add lamely.

Across the creek an unpainted structure stands forlornly on what was once the town's second street. "What about over there?" I suggest, trying to salvage something from the long drive.

We cross the creek on a log and plank bridge. The building, once a house, does not look promising, though it bears the sign: MUSEUM. My mother resigns herself to being mannerly. Looking up at the now-grey sky, she puts on a sweater and joins me on the porch.

I try the front door. It is locked. Self-consciously I peer through dirty windows at the rooms inside. The building houses a jumble of mining artifacts and useless junk. It looks as if old timers in the area drove up to the building and pitched through the front door whatever clutter they found stored in their attics and out-buildings. Rusted gold pans lie on the floor next to hunks of fool's gold surrounded by broken furniture. Everything is layered in dust.

My mother, however, seems to have found something to interest her. She stands before one of the grimy windows cautiously peering inside. I am about to join her when we hear the shot.

"What the hell!" I blurt out.

Immediately I search for my child. She is down by the creek, stone in hand, looking at something around the side of the building out of my line of sight.

A second shot. It echoes against the wall of mountains enclosing the town.

Phoebe starts scrambling toward us over the rocks. I run to the end of the porch. Thirty feet away Sparrow aims a gun at a pop bottle. This time the glass shatters.

"Stop that," I shout at him.

He looks up at me surprised. "Why Joyce, I'm just passing the time. Just passing the time."

Phoebe comes clattering onto the porch and grabs me around the hips. Even in my anger I am relieved at her fear of the gun. I take some pride in it. It is good to see that she can separate the toy from the real. I lean over and kiss her disheveled curls. "Go sit in the car," I order gently.

My mother has not moved. The first report startled her as it did me, but she shows no alarm that in this deserted place someone is shooting a gun. She must know exactly who it is and that he carries a weapon.

"He never goes anywhere without that thing," she says offhandedly, confirming my suspicion. "What can that man be afraid of? It's always loaded."

I am appalled, enraged.

"Are you insane?" I explode. "Around Phoebe?"

She looks puzzled. "What are you so excited about, Joyce. He's just like your father."

The statement is so preposterous I am instantly deflated. My father has his guns to be sure, but he is over six feet tall and a gentleman, as unlike Sparrow as a coast cedar is to the scrub brush that fills in these interior slopes. I feel only depressed now. A little weak in the knees I stand waiting while Sparrow empties the gun into a clump of poplars encroaching upon the town.

"Tell him not to re-load it Mama."

Under her rouge my mother's face has paled. She shakes her head. "Sparrow's gun is Sparrow's business," she says.

"Well then it is also the R.C.M.P.'s. Carrying a handgun across the border is illegal."

I have her attention now.

"Joyce, you wouldn't. Not the police." She seems clearly frightened.

"I most certainly would," I tell her emphatically.

Sparrow is walking back to the car. He reaches through the open window for the leather holster he left lying on the seat.

"We're going home now, Mama, but later you tell him about re-loading."

Suddenly obedient, my mother allows me to take her elbow and lead her to the car. Her face, as if cleansed of makeup, shows papery skin and a network of veins. I help her down the rickety steps and put her into the front seat of the Cadillac, next to Sparrow. He leans across her chest and drops the gun into the glove compartment as casually as if returning a road map he had taken out to consult.

I climb into the back. Phoebe is huddled in a corner of that vast seat, her hands over her ears. "Never mind, honey," I say gently, taking her onto my lap, "no more shooting."

Sparrow starts the car. He drives it slowly across the bridge and onto the gravel road. I think about the gun, lying like a land mine among extra fuses and spare packs of American cigarettes. I feel violated by its presence. My mind jumps with images. Sparrow driving off to the café for his ball scores, my daughter in the front seat. Phoebe playing in the car, honking the horn, pushing buttons. At any time she might have opened the glove compartment.

I cradle my daughter, rocking her as we drive away from the town. Once we are on the smooth pavement of the highway Phoebe falls asleep.

We travel back down the lake on the roller-coaster highway, the water hidden now under a fine, wet mist. It has begun to rain. Sparrow turns on the windshield wipers, and the headlights. Every few miles he tries the radio but can pick up only static. Once past the ferry dock the road flattens and we are back in inhabited territory. The Cadillac slides by houses perched between the water and the road like birds on a strip of exposed reef.

Phoebe wakes up. "I have to pee, Mommie."

I ask Sparrow to stop the car. "Do it quickly," I urge, "so you won't get wet."

While Phoebe squats beside the car I wait for my mother's protests, for her to turn around and carp at me, "Out here in the open, Joyce? Can't you at least find her a tree to go behind?"

Instead she asks if I know what it was she saw in that museum.

"A commode chair, just like the one Granny Haws had. When Granny Haws lost her power of speech, my brother and I would sneak upstairs to her room and try out her chair. We never used it, you understand, we would have been caught, but we sat on the hole with our pants down, making the most awful sounds."

Sparrow smirks and breaks into a fecal ditty I remember from my childhood. "Here we sit broken-hearted ... "

"We were very cruel," my mother finishes, her voice dramatically trailing away.

I cannot keep from smiling, thinking of her on that commode. Dress hiked. Pants down. Not the child who always posed with the mockseriousness of a Twenties movie star, but the woman she is today.

Is this then her peace offering, this slender bone thrown down on the ground between us? Are we now supposed to break off hostilities and declare a truce of sorts? Tall order for one oblique confession, but how like my mother.

Phoebe, her hair glistening from the rain, climbs back inside the car. Sliding onto the cushioned seat she burrows right up next to me as we ease off the narrow dirt shoulder onto the highway.

White Shoulders

LINDA SVENDSEN

MY OLDEST SISTER'S NAME IS IRENE DE HAAN AND SHE HAS NEVER HURT ANYBODY. She lives with cancer, in remission, and she has stayed married to the same undemonstrative Belgian Canadian, a brake specialist, going on thirty years. In the family's crumbling domestic empire, Irene and Peter's union has been, quietly, and despite tragedy, what our mother calls the lone success.

Back in the late summer of 1984, before Irene was admitted into hospital for removal of her left breast, I flew home from New York to Vancouver to be with her. We hadn't seen each other for four years, and since I didn't start teaching ESL night classes until mid-September, I was free, at loose ends, unlike the rest of her family. Over the past months, Peter had used up vacation and personal days shuttling her to numerous tests, but finally had to get back to work. He still had a mortgage. Their only child, Jill, who'd just turned seventeen, was entering her last year of high school. Until junior high, she'd been one of those unnaturally well-rounded kids — taking classes in the high dive, water ballet, drawing and drama, and boy-hunting in the mall on Saturdays with a posse of dizzy friends. Then, Irene said, overnight she became unathletic, withdrawn and bookish: an academic drone. At any rate, for Jill and Peter's sake, Irene didn't intend to allow her illness to interfere with their life. She wanted everything to proceed as normally as possible. As who wouldn't.

In a way, and this will sound callous, the timing had worked out. Earlier that summer, my ex-husband had been offered a temporary teaching position across the country, and after a long dinner at our old Szechuan dive, I'd agreed to temporarily revise our custody arrangement. With his newfound bounty, Bill would rent a California townhouse for nine months and royally support the kids. "Dine and Disney," he'd said.

I'd blessed this, but then missed them. I found myself dead asleep in the middle of the day in Jane's lower bunk, or tuning in late afternoons to my six-year-old son's, and Bill's, obsession, *People's Court*. My arms ached when I saw other women holding sticky hands, pulling frenzied children along behind them in the August dog days. So I flew west. To be a mother again, I'd jokingly told Irene over the phone. To serve that very need.

Peter was late meeting me at the airport. We gave each other a minimal hug, and then he shouldered my bags and walked ahead out into the rain. The Datsun was double-parked, hazards flashing, with a homemade sign taped on the rear window that said STUD. DRIVER. "Jill," he said, loading the trunk. "Irene's been teaching her so she can pick up the groceries. Help out for a change." I got in, he turned on easy-listening, and we headed north towards the grey mountains.

Irene had been in love with him since I was a child; he'd been orphaned in Belgium during World War II, which moved both Irene and our mother. He'd also reminded us of Emile, the Frenchman in *South Pacific*, because he was greying, autocratic and seemed misunderstood. But the European charm had gradually worn thin; over the years, I'd been startled by Peter's racism and petty tyranny. I'd often wished that the young Irene had been fondled off her two feet by a breadwinner more tender, more local. Nobody else in the family agreed and Mum had even hinted that I'd become bitter since the demise of my own marriage.

"So how is she?" I finally asked Peter.

"She's got a cold," he said, "worrying herself sick. And other than that, it's hard to say." His tone was markedly guarded. He said prospects were poor; the lump was large and she had the fast-growing, speedy sort of cancer. "But she thinks the Paki quack will get it when he cuts," he said.

I sat with that. "And how's Jill?"

"Grouchy," he said. "Bitchy." This gave me pause, and it seemed to have the same effect on him.

We pulled into the garage of the brick house they'd lived in since Jill's birth, and he waved me on while he handled the luggage. The house seemed smaller now, tucked under tall Douglas firs and fringed with baskets of acutely pink geraniums and baby's breath. The back door was open, so I walked in; the master bedroom door was ajar, but I knocked first. She wasn't there. Jill called, "Aunt Adele?" and I headed back down the hall to the guest room, and stuck my head in.

A wan version of my sister rested on a water bed in the dark. When I plunked down I made a tiny wave. Irene almost smiled. She was thin as a fine chain; in my embrace, her flesh barely did the favour of keeping her bones company. Her blondish hair was quite short, and she looked ordinary, like a middle-aged matron who probably worked at a bank and kept a no-fail punch recipe filed away. I had to hold her, barely, close again. Behind us, the closet was full of her conservative garments — flannel, floral — and I understood that this was her room now. She slept here alone. She didn't frolic with Peter anymore, have sex.

"Don't cling," Irene said slowly, but with her old warmth. "Don't get melodramatic. I'm not dying. It's just a cold."

"Aunt Adele," Jill said.

I turned around; I'd forgotten my niece was even there, and she was sitting right on the bed, wedged against a bolster. We kissed hello with loud smooch effects — our ritual — and while she kept a hand on Irene's shoulder, she stuttered answers to my questions about school and her summer. Irene kept an eye on a mute TV — the U.S. Open — although she didn't have much interest in tennis; I sensed, really, that she didn't have any extra energy available for banter. This was conservation, not rudeness.

Jill looked different. In fact, the change in her appearance and de-meanour exceeded the ordinary drama of puberty; she seemed to be another girl — shy, unsure and unable to look me in the eye. She wore silver wire glasses, no makeup, jeans with an oversize kelly-green sweatshirt and many extra pounds. Her soft straw-coloured hair was pulled back with a swan barrette, the swan's eye downcast. When she passed Irene a glass of water and a pill, Irene managed a swallow, then passed it back, and Jill drank, too. To me, it seemed she took great care, twisting the glass in her hand, to sip from the very spot her mother's lips had touched.

Peter came in, sat down on Jill's side of the bed and stretched both arms around to raise the back of his shirt. He bared red, hairless skin, and said, "Scratch."

"But I'm watching tennis," Jill said softly.

"But you're my daughter," he said. "And I have an itch."

Peter looked at Irene and she gave Jill a sharp nudge. "Do your poor dad," she said. "You don't even have to get up."

"But aren't I watching something?" Jill said. She glanced around, search-ing for an ally.

"*Vrouw,*" Peter spoke up. "This girl, she doesn't do anything except mope, eat, mope, eat."

Jill's shoulders sagged slightly, as if all air had suddenly abandoned her body, and then she slowly got up. "I'll see you after, Aunt Adele," she whispered, and I said, "Yes, sure," and then she walked out.

Irene looked dismally at Peter; he made a perverse sort of face —
skewing his lips south. Then she reached over and started to scratch his
bare back. It was an effort. "Be patient with her, Peter," she said. "She's
worried about the surgery."

"She's worried you won't be around to wait on her," Peter said, then
instructed, "Go a little higher." Irene's fingers crept obediently up. "Tell
Adele what Jill said."

Irene shook her head. "I don't remember."

Peter turned to me. "When Irene told her about the cancer, she said,
'Don't die on me, Mum, or I'll kill you.' And she said this so serious. Can
you imagine?" Peter laughed uninhibitedly, and then Irene joined in, too,
although her quiet accompaniment was forced. There wasn't any recol-
lected pleasure in her eyes at all; rather, it seemed as if she didn't want
Peter to laugh alone, to appear as odd as he did. "Don't die or I'll kill
you," Peter said.

Irene had always been private about her marriage. If there were disagree-
ments with Peter, and there had been — I'd once dropped in unannounced
and witnessed a string of Christmas lights whip against the fireplace and
shatter — they were never rebroadcast to the rest of the family; if she was
ever discouraged or lonely, she didn't confide in anyone, unless she kept
a journal or spoke to her own God. She had never said a word against the
man.

The night before Irene's surgery, after many earnest wishes and ugly
flowers had been delivered, she asked me to stay late with her at Lion's
Gate Hospital. The room had emptied. Peter had absconded with Jill —
and she'd gone reluctantly, asking to stay until I left — and our mother,
who'd been so nervous and sad that an intern had fed her Valium from
his pocket. Why is this happening to her?" Mum said to him. "To my only
happy child."

Irene, leashed to an IV, raised herself to the edge of the bed and
looked out at the parking lot and that kind Pacific twilight. "That Jill,"
Irene said. She allowed her head to fall, arms crossed in front of her. "She
should lift a finger for her father."

"Well," I said, watching my step, aware she needed peace, "Peter's not
exactly the most easygoing."

"No," she said weakly.

We sat for a long time, Irene in her white gown, me beside her in
my orange-and-avocado track suit, until I began to think I'd been too
tough on Peter and had distressed her. Then she spoke. "Sometimes I
wish I'd learned more Dutch," she said neutrally. "When I met Peter,

we married not speaking the same language, really. And that made a difference."

She didn't expect a comment — she raised her head and stared out the half-open window — but I was too shocked to respond anyway. I'd never heard her remotely suggest that her and Peter's marriage had been less than a living storybook. "You don't like him, do you?" she said. "You don't care for his Belgian manner."

I didn't answer; it didn't need to be said aloud. I fumed away. "I'm probably not the woman who can best judge these things," I said.

Out in the hall, a female patient talked on the phone. Irene and I both listened. "I left it in the top drawer," she said wearily. "No. The bedroom." There was a pause. "The desk in the hall, try that." Another pause. "Then ask Susan where she put it, because I'm tired of this and I need it." I turned as she hung the phone up and saw her check to see if money had tumbled back. The hospital was quiet again. Irene did not move, but she was shaking; I found it difficult to watch this and reached out and took her hand.

"What is it?" I said. "Irene."

She told me she was scared. Not for herself, but for Peter. That when she had first explained to him about the cancer, he hadn't spoken to her for three weeks. Or touched her. Or kissed her. He'd slept in the guestroom, until she'd offered to move there. And he'd been after Jill to butter his toast, change the sheets, iron his pants. Irene had speculated about this, she said, until she'd realized he was acting this way because of what had happened to him when he was little. In Belgium. Bruges, the war. He had only confided in her once. He'd said all the women he'd ever loved had left him. His mother killed, his sister. "And now me," Irene said. "The big C which leads to the big D. If I move on, I leave two children. And I've told Jill they have to stick together."

I got off the bed. "But, Irene," I said, "she's not on earth to please her father. Who can be unreasonable. In my opinion."

By this time, a medical team was touring the room. The junior member paused by Irene and said, "Give me your vein."

"In a minute," she said to him, "please," and he left. There were dark areas, the colour of new bruises, under her eyes. "I want you to promise me something."

"Yes."

"If I die," she said, "and I'm not going to, but if I do, I don't want Jill to live with you in New York. Because that's what she wants to do. I want her to stay with Peter. Even if she runs to you, send her back."

"I can't promise that," I said. "Because you're not going to go anywhere."

She looked at me. Pale, fragile. She was my oldest sister, who'd always been zealous about the silver lining in that cloud; and now it seemed she might be dying, in her forties — too soon — and she needed to believe I could relieve her of this burden. So I nodded, *Yes.*

When I got back, by cab, to Irene and Peter's that night, the house was dark. I groped up the back steps, ascending through a hovering scent of honeysuckle, stepped inside and turned on the kitchen light. The TV was going — some ultra-loud camera commercial — in the living room. Nobody was watching. "Jill?" I said. "Peter?"

I wandered down the long hall, snapping on switches: Irene's sickroom, the upstairs bathroom, the master bedroom, Peter's domain. I did a double-take; he was there. Naked, lying on top of the bed, his still hand holding his penis — as if to keep it warm and safe — the head shining. The blades of the ceiling fan cut in slow circles above him. His eyes were vague and didn't turn my way; he was staring up. "Oh, sorry," I whispered, "God, sorry," and flicked the light off again.

I headed back to the living room and sat, for a few seconds. When I'd collected myself, I went to find Jill. She wasn't in her downstairs room, which seemed typically adolescent in its decor — Boy George poster, socks multiplying in a corner — until I spotted a quote from Rilke, in careful purple handwriting, taped to her long mirror: "Beauty is only the first touch of terror we can still bear."

I finally spotted the light under the basement bathroom door.

"Jill," I said. "It's me."

"I'm in the bathroom," she said.

"I know," I said. "I want to talk."

She unlocked the door and let me in. She looked tense and peculiar; it looked as if she'd just thrown water on her face. She was still dressed in her clothes from the hospital — and from the day before, the kelly-green sweat job — and she'd obviously been sitting on the edge of the tub, writing. There was a Papermate, a pad of yellow legal paper. The top sheet was covered with verses of tiny backward-slanting words. There was also last night's pot of Kraft Dinner on the sink.

"You're all locked in," I said.

She didn't comment, and when the silence stretched on too long I said, "Homework?" and pointed to the legal pad.

"No," she said. Then she gave me a look and said, "Poem."

"Oh," I said, and I was surprised. "Do you ever show them? Or it?"

"No," she said. "They're not very good." She sat back down on the tub. "But maybe I'd show you, Aunt Adele."

"Good," I said. "Not that I'm a judge." I told her Irene was tucked in and that she was in a better, more positive frame of mind. More like herself. This seemed to relax Jill so much, I marched the lie a step further. "Once your mum is out of the woods," I said, "your father may lighten up."

"That day will never come," she said.

"Never say never," I said. I gave her a hug — she was so much bigger than my daughter, but I embraced her the same way I had Jane since she was born: a hand and a held kiss on the top of the head.

She hugged me back. "Maybe I'll come live with you, Auntie A."

"Maybe," I said, mindful of Irene's wishes. "You and everybody," and saw the disappointment on her streaked face. So I added, "Everything will be all right. Wait and see. She'll be all right."

And Irene was. They claimed they'd got it, and ten days later she came home, earlier than expected. When Peter, Jill and I were gathered around her in the sickroom, Irene started cracking jokes about her future prosthetic fitting. "How about the Dolly Parton, hon?" she said to Peter. "Then I'd be a handful."

I was surprised to see Peter envelop her in his arms; I hadn't ever seen him offer an affectionate gesture. He told her he didn't care what size boob she bought, because breasts were for the hungry babies — not so much for the husband. "I have these," he said. "These are mine. These big white shoulders." And he rested his head against her shoulder and looked placidly at Jill; he was heavy, but Irene used her other arm to bolster herself, hold him up, and she closed her eyes in what seemed to be joy. Jill came and sat by me.

Irene took it easy the next few days; I stuck by, as did Jill, when she ventured in after school. I was shocked that there weren't more calls, or cards, or visitors except for Mum, and I realized my sister's life was actually very narrow, or extremely focused: family came first. Even Jill didn't seem to have any friends at all; the phone never rang for her.

Then Irene suddenly started to push herself — she prepared a complicated deep-fried Belgian dish; in the afternoon, she sat with Jill, in the Datsun, while Jill practised parallel parking in front of the house and lobbied for a mother-daughter trip to lovely downtown Brooklyn for Christmas. And then, after a long nap and little dinner, Irene insisted on attending the open house at Jill's school.

We were sitting listening to the band rehearse, a *Flashdance* medley, when I became aware of Irene's body heat — she was on my right — and asked if she might not want to head home. She was burning up. "Let me get through this," she said. Then Jill, on my other side, suddenly said in a small tight voice, "Mum." She was staring at her mother's blouse, where a bright stitch of scarlet had shown up. Irene had bled through her dressing. Irene looked down. "Oh," she said. "Peter."

On the tear to the hospital, Peter said he'd sue Irene's stupid "Paki bugger" doctor. He also said he should take his stupid wife to court for loss of sex. He should get a divorce for no-nookie. For supporting a one-tit wonder. And on and on.

Irene wasn't in any shape to respond; I doubt she would have anyway.

Beside me in the back seat, Jill turned to stare out the window; she was white, sitting on her hands.

I found my voice. "I don't think we need to hear this right now, Peter," I said.

"Oh, Adele," Irene said warningly. Disappointed.

He pulled over, smoothly, into a bus zone. Some of the people waiting for the bus weren't pleased. Peter turned and faced me, his finger punctuating. "This is my wife, my daughter, my Datsun." He paused. "I can say what the hell I want. And you're welcome to walk." He reached over and opened my door.

The two women at the bus shelter hurried away, correctly sensing an incident.

"I'm going with Aunt — " Jill was barely audible.

"No," said Irene. "You stay here."

I sat there, paralyzed. I wanted to get out, but didn't want to leave Irene and Jill alone with him; Irene was very ill, Jill seemed defenseless. "Look," I said to Peter, "forget I said anything. Let's just get Irene there, okay?"

He pulled the door shut, then turned front, checked me in the rearview one last time — cold, intimidating — and headed off again. Jill was crying silently. The insides of her glasses were smeared; I shifted over beside her and she linked her arm through mine tight, tight. Up front, Irene did not move.

They said it was an infection which had spread to the chest wall, requiring antibiotics and hospital admission. They were also going to perform more tests.

Peter took off with Jill, saying that they both had to get up in the morning.

Before I left Irene, she spoke to me privately, in a curtained cubicle in Emergency, and asked if I could stay at our mother's for the last few days of my visit; Irene didn't want to hurt me, but she thought it would be better, for all concerned, if I cleared out.

And then she went on; her fever was high, but she was lucid and fighting hard to stay that way. Could I keep quiet about this to our mother? And stop gushing about the East to Jill, going on about the Statue of Liberty and the view of the water from the window in the crown? And worry a little more about my own lost children and less about her daughter? And try to be more understanding of her husband, who sometimes wasn't able to exercise control over his emotions? Irene said Peter needed more love, more time; more of her, God willing. After that, she couldn't speak. And, frankly, neither could I.

I gave in to everything she asked. Jill and Peter dropped in together during the evening to see her, I visited Irene, with Mum, during the day when Peter was at work. Our conversations were banal and strained — they didn't seem to do either of us much good. After I left her one afternoon, I didn't know where I was going and ended up at my father's grave. I just sat there, on top of it, on the lap of the stone.

The day before my New York flight, I borrowed my mother's car to pick up a prescription for her at the mall.

I was window-shopping my way back to the parking lot when I saw somebody resembling my niece sitting on a bench outside a sporting goods store. At first, the girl seemed too dishevelled, too dirty-looking, actually, to be Jill, but as I approached, it became clear it was her. She wasn't doing anything. She sat there, draped in her mother's London Fog raincoat, her hands resting on her thickish thighs, clicking a barrette open, closed, open, closed. It was ten in the morning; she should have been at school. In English. For a moment, it crossed my mind that she might be on drugs: this was a relief; it would explain everything. But I didn't think she was. I was going to go over and simply say, *Yo, Jill, let's do tea,* and then I remembered my sister's frightening talk with me at the hospital and thought, *Fuck it. Butt out, Adele,* and walked the long way around. I turned my back.

One sultry Saturday morning, in late September — after I'd been back in Brooklyn for a few weeks — I was up on the roof preparing the first lessons for classes when the super brought a handful of mail up. He'd been delivering it personally to tenants since the box had been ripped out of the entrance wall. It was the usual stuff and a thin white business envelope from Canada. From Jill. I opened it: *Dearlingest* (sic) *Aunt Adele,*

These are my only copies. Love, your only niece, Jill. P.S. I'm going to get a job and come see you at Easter.

There were two. The poems were carefully written, each neat on their single page, with the script leaning left, as if blown by a stiff breeze. "Black Milk" was about three deaths: before her beloved husband leaves for war, a nursing mother shares a bottle of old wine with him, saved from their wedding day, and unknowingly poisons her child and then herself. Dying, she rocks her dying child in her arms, but her last conscious thought is for her husband at the front. Jill had misspelled wedding; she'd put *weeding*.

"Belgium" described a young girl ice skating across a frozen lake — Jill had been to Belgium with her parents two times — fleeing an unnamed pursuer. During each quick, desperate glide, the ice melts beneath her until, at the end, she is underwater: "In the deep cold / Face to face / Look, he comes now / My Father / My Maker." The girl wakes up; it was a bad dream. And then her earthly father appears in her bed and, "He makes night / Come again / All night," by covering her eyes with his large, heavy hand.

I read these, and read them again, and I wept. I looked out, past the steeples and the tar roofs, where I thought I saw the heat rising, toward the green of Prospect Park, and held the poems on my lap, flat under my two hands. I didn't know what to do; I didn't know what to do right away; I thought I should wait until I knew clearly what to say and whom to say it to.

In late October, Mum phoned, crying, and said that Irene's cancer had not been caught by the mastectomy. Stray cells had been detected in other areas of her body. Chemotherapy was advised. Irene had switched doctors; she was seeing a naturopath. She was paying big money for an American miracle gum, among other things.

Mum also said that Jill had disappeared for thirty-two hours. Irene claimed that Jill had been upset because of a grade — a C in Phys. Ed. Mum didn't believe it was really that; she thought Irene's condition was disturbing Jill, but hadn't said that to Irene.

She didn't volunteer any information about the other member of Irene's family and I did not ask.

In November, Bill came east for a visit and brought the children, as scheduled; he also brought a woman named Cheryl Oak. The day before Thanksgiving, the two of them were invited to a dinner party, and I took Graham and Jane, taller and both painfully shy, with me to Central Park. It was a crisp, windy night. We watched the gi-normous balloons being blown up for the Macy's parade and bought roasted chestnuts, not to eat, but to warm the palms of our hands. I walked them back to their hotel and delivered them to the quiet, intelligent person who would probably become their stepmother, and be good to them, as she'd obviously been for Bill. Later, back in Brooklyn, I was still awake — wondering how another woman had succeeded with my husband and, now, my own little ones — when Irene phoned at three a.m. She told me Jill was dead. "There's been an accident," she said.

A few days later, my mother and stepfather picked me up at the Vancouver airport on a warm, cloudy morning. On the way to the funeral, they tried to tell me, between them — between breakdowns — what had happened. She had died of hypothermia; the impact of hitting the water had most likely rendered her unconscious. She probably hadn't been aware of drowning, but she'd done that, too. She'd driven the Datsun to Stanley Park — she'd told Irene she was going to the library — left the key in the ignition, walked not quite to the middle of the bridge and hoisted herself over the railing. There was one eyewitness: a guy who worked in a video store. He'd kept saying, "It was like a movie. I saw this little dumpling girl just throw herself off."

The chapel was half-empty, and the director mumbled that that was unusual when a teenager passed on. Irene had not known, and neither had Mum, where to reach Joyce, our middle sister, who was missing as usual; Ray, our older brother, gave a short eulogy. He stated that he didn't believe in any God, but Irene did, and he was glad for that this day. He also guessed that when any child takes her own life, the whole family must wonder why, and probably do that forever. The face of my sister was not to be borne. Then we all sang "The Water Is Wide," which Jill had once performed in an elementary school talent show. She'd won Honourable Mention.

After the congregation dispersed, Peter remained on his knees, his head in his hands, while Irene approached the casket. Jill wore a pale pink dress and her other glasses, and her hair was pinned back, as usual, with a barrette this time, a dove. Irene bent and kissed her on the mouth, on the forehead, then tugged at Jill's lace collar, adjusting it just so. It was the eternal mother's gesture, that finishing touch, before your daughter sails out the door on her big date.

I drank to excess at the reception; we all did, and needed to. Irene and I did not exchange a word; we just held each other for a long minute. From a distance, and that distance was necessary, I heard Peter talking about Belgium and memories of his childhood. On his fifth birthday, his sister, Kristin, had sent him a pencil from Paris, a new one, unsharpened, and he had used it until the lead was gone and it was so short he could barely hold it between his fingers. On the morning his mother was shot, in cold blood, he'd been dressing in the dark. The last thing she had said, to the Germans, was, "Don't hurt my little boy." This was when Mum and I saw Irene go to him and take his hand. She led him down the hall to his bedroom and closed the door behind them. "Thank God," Mum said. "Thank God, they have each other. Thank God, she has him."

And for that moment, I forgot about the despair that had prompted Jill to do what she did, and my own responsibility and silence, because I was alive and full of needs, sickness and dreams myself. I thought, *No, I will never tell my sister what I suspect, because life is short and very hard,* and I thought, *Yes, a bad marriage is better than none,* and I thought, *Adele, let the sun go down on your anger, because it will not bring her back,* and I turned to my mother. "Yes," I said. "Thank God."

Gold Mountain

(A Tale of Fortune-Seeking in British North America)

CAROLINE ADDERSON

SHOWING IN BRIEF MY PRESENT STRAITS AND THEIR PITIFUL ORIGIN

Now, I am a remittance man of the worst kind, the unwitting kind who leaves home expressly to support his needy, but ends up gnawing on their empty outstretched hands. Example: in England my poor mother, before opening my letters, will shake them, listening vainly for a coin-like jangle. Finding instead more beggarly words, she rebukes me by return post. Financial insecurity distresses her digestion. When my father was alive and providing amply, she never so much as broke wind.

My father owned a shoe shop in Salisbury where he dressed men's feet as a priest might souls. His passion for the vamp, the heel and upper I inherited, though not his knack at turning pennies. For sums I have no nerve. Thus my widowed mother's suggestion that I come to the colonies where I might practise a simpler commerce, man-to-man from the back of a horse, my breast pocket for a bank.

Landing in Montreal, I was brash and optimistic. My mercantile scheme I had bolstered with a loftier ideal: the civilizing influence of fine footwear. I heard a wretched plea from deep in the wilderness and so, as the missionary goes bearing The Word to the isolated and deprived, I went to the barefoot and clodhoppered with Bluchers and Balmorals. A season later, having crossed the maddening plains, I had become a ragged peripatetic, my neck scabbed with horsefly bites, a fungal garden growing on my tongue. How in good conscience could I continue thrusting the corns and calluses of peasants into the shoes of lords? I flung my peddler's case into the river and, though never wont to indulge in spirits, vowed to finish my days in the Dominion of Failure on a saloon stool, marinating myself in brandy, then, like a Christmas pudding, setting myself aflame.

That saloon was here in Everlasting, this frontier town, these hundred meanly-shod inhabitants. Everlasting. Try to find it on your map.

IN WHICH, CAJOLED BY DRINK, I SEAL MY FATE AS A GOLD-SEEKER

I am a slight man, two inches and five feet in stacked heels — a near match for the slumbering dog I met in the saloon doorway. Recalling a certain wise old adage, I hastened to retreat. Just then a voice from inside the saloon hailed me.

"Step on over 'im! He's more an angel than a hound!"

The cur's owner proved to be Mr. Bernard Coop. (The day before, ignoring that he wore no collar, that his flies were spotty and partially unbuttoned, I had tried to sell him a truly resplendent pair of Balmorals, the self-same pair now on its way to sea.) He bade me take a seat, then bought a quantum of brandy that plied my shameless tongue. Before long I had disclosed the trouble with my mother's digestion. "Selling dancing slippers never made a body rich," snorted Coop. "All the smart ones are going to Cariboo for staking claims."

Coop had a scheme which he outlined thus: assemble a party of rude young men and lead them into Cariboo. Give them tents and meals and wages for their placer mining. The gold itself, keep yourself — at a handsome profit. Coop was to be the overseer. He was looking for someone to recruit the men and keep the camp tidy. I being, in Coop's words, "runty and very spruce" was just the man. Did I agree?

"Where is Cariboo?" I enquired.

"I've no hell idea."

He refilled my glass, then held his own out to make a toast. There I sat, penniless, my livelihood bobbing down a river — a beggar, not a chooser. Reluctantly I too raised my glass. We drank and afterward, to doubly seal our fate, shook hands. I recoiled. Where on his right hand his middle fingers should have been, were two unsightly stumps. "At least the good one's left, Mr. Merritt," he said, wagging the finger at me, then, with it, reaming out his ear.

HOW, IN A CLEAN AND STARCHED SHIRT FRONT, I AM TRULY SMITTEN

A decent change of boots (capped toes, four gay buttons) was still in my possession, but for clothes I had only those clinging to my back. Needs were, I hired myself a laundress, a sympathetic lady who let me wait undraped in her parlour while the wash water evaporated from my shirt tails. "Funny. I'm not a bit ashamed," she confessed. "You seem more a lady than a fellow. What's your trade?"

"I ease and beautify mankind's weary tread."

"A cobbler?"

"A peddler, alas. But I hope now to try my luck at gold." Then I told her of Coop's and my plan for Cariboo, could we ever find the place.

"My cousin Evaline is a cartographer."

"A lady cartographer?"

"Of sorts."

"Of sorts a lady or of sorts a cartographer?" I jested.

"Both." She hesitated a moment, then divulged to me the rare nature of her cousin's craft. With her head on her pillow here in Everlasting, Miss Evaline could find me Cariboo. She could find it in her dreams.

When my garments were dried and pressed, my laundress buttoned me. "Go and see her," she said.

I had thought a cartographer who dreamed her maps and mapped her dreams would be as airily constructed as an angel. Miss Evaline was a giantess. (Anvil-footed in derby boots, a torso like a stove.) I found her in her barn, arm to her elbow in the backside of a horse. Her mare was late to foal, she bashfully explained, wiping on her skirt the equine slime. "She'll drop before the stars come out. Upon my word."

Then she invited me to tea and in our brief amble to the house I recognized her considerable manly talents. Already demonstrated were her gifts in husbandry. Now I learned that both her barn and house were built by her person alone. Further, she was sole master of this range, a full one hundred and sixty acres.

In her parlour she poured me a cup of mire, then proffered on a washboard her stony biscuits. I cast a glance around — at hides and burlap sacks, sundry implements, unpapered walls. Espying a rack of scrolls, I asked, "Are those your maps?"

She rose to fetch one and together we unfurled it.

"It's just a pastime."

"On the contrary," I declared. "It's a gift!" Here was a sheet of snow-white parchment. Only close inspection revealed minutiae rendered, not in line, but subtle iridescent shading. Any skills she lacked in pure cartography were made up for in artistry. I saw rills and drifts and locked-in floes. It was indeed snow white; it was snow.

"The North Pole," she said.

"But it's undiscovered!"

"If it were discovered, I would have drawn a flag."

Then she showed me the Hawaiian Islands — volcanoes and pineapple plantations — and in New England the terrible charred place where a witch had been burned.

My astonished accolades I could not restrain. Abashed, Miss Evaline set aside the maps and asked if I cared to promenade. At first I mistook her, thinking she meant a dance. "Walk my range," she tittered, all afluster, her big hand covering her face. I helped tie her bonnet strings, for she was trembling with shyness, though once we got out walking she grew braver. She took my arm. I took two steps to her every one. "I have a goodly herd," she said, so we clambered up a grassy butte and viewed them grazing in the distance. Below us was a sere creek bed, lacy as the bas-relief of a fossil fern. Small clouds cast clear shadows on the flatland. I wondered if in those shapes she read countries.

When we returned to the house, the foal, unborn that morning, was standing in the yard on wavering legs. I was struck then by the marvellous workings of a mere handful of hours. What had not previously existed came into being — ineffably, delightfully! Then, as if it heard and liked my thought, the foal twitched with joy.

Miss Evaline agreed to help me, though she said it was nothing she had ever done before. To absorb my dream of Cariboo, she brought me to her bed, and it was nothing I had ever done before. In one eager puff she extinguished both her shyness and the lamp, gathered me in hirsute arms, made fly the dust and straw while I, I lay passive — a virgin maid. Why are women named the weaker sex? In intellect they have always seemed to me superior. And now I knew by experience how a woman's fleshly potency can vanquish a man's heart. A long time I lay listening to her windy snore, for once I fell asleep she travelled on to Cariboo, left me behind — alone in love in Everlasting.

CONTAINING THE ACCOUNT OF OUR TRAVELLING OUT, ITS PERILS
AND THE DROLL CHARACTERS THAT WE MEET UPON THE WAY

It took a week to ride into British Columbia, where other men with a different dog might have done it in four days. Coop called his creature Bruin, for that was the size and strength of him. At night Bruin molested me in my bedroll. By day he strayed off course to mangle squirrels. As for Coop, he imbibed continuously, dismounting on the hour and making water. All the while I pined for Evaline. At least I had her map which guided us as well as any star.

Note, too, how we were unaccompanied by rude young men. I had petitioned every lad in Everlasting, many of whom gave me an attentive ear, but upon hearing Coop's name, recoiled. Truly, I regretted Coop's and my handshake, but, severed fingers notwithstanding, it bound me to him.

Perilous alpine passes, frigid streams, the omnipresent fear of bears — all this so taxed me that when we finally reached Frazer's River, I was spent. I begged Coop to let me take some days recovering, but as we were then sharing the trail with a contingent of seasoned miners, he feared they would beat us to the best claims. We pressed on, tagging these rivals like, not one, but three smitten dogs. It was they, though, who finally relented, not granting us leave to pass, but inviting us to join them.

Sympathetic to my enfeebled condition, they offered me their freight wagon in which to convalesce. There I lay dreaming of my darling Evaline. I recalled, as a poem learnt in childhood, every detail of her person: her ropy hands and plenteous thighs, the whorl of whiskers around her paps. Delight a potent medicine, before long I had recovered, refreshed and idealistic, my fortune waiting to be panned. With the gold I found I vowed to fashion my love a ring, a seal ring with which to mark her maps. And the beauty of the land revived me further — fireweed blazing along our trail, new growth shivering on the pines, a pale green aura. The river itself, sunlight coloured gold.

Since neither Coop nor I had panned before, I was greedy for good counsel. For the next part of the journey I rode alongside the two hoariest of the fellows, life-long miners flattered to impart their combined wisdom.

On panning itself, one instructed, "Dunk yer pan, but not too deep."

The other resounded this advice. "By God, not too deep!"

"Flush out the silt, but not too much."

"By God, not too much!"

To discourage bears sing bawdy ditties, not for the lyrics but the din. Burn green wood to repel flies. They warned me, too, against the villains we might encounter: the travelling pastor, the savage Native and the Gold Commissioner. As for the moon-eyed Chinese, he is the lowest man in the golden economy.

"A scavenger," they told me. "Where you see a Celestial, there's only dregs."

One night, as we sat around a leaping fire, someone took out a violin and began sawing a despondent tune. The clearing — towering columns of trees, vault of branches — might have been the great choirspace of Salisbury. My soul, an even smaller being hunkering down inside me, was greatly soothed. Then one of the men cried, "How about a dance?" Immediately the dirge became a reel and a bale of calico was thrown down from the freight wagon.

When it hit the ground, the bale burst open to reveal a sampling of ladies' dresses. Some of the men stripped to the waist and began donning this unlikely garb with great anticipation. Indeed, the same hoary fellows whose counsel I had esteemed, were now quarrelling over female frippery. Even Bruin, yelping in indignation, was forced into a petticoat.

"Henry Merritt," someone addressed me. "Will you be a lady or a fellow?"

"I'll be neither."

"You dance or you play the fiddle. Can you fiddle?"

"No, sir."

"Then you dance."

And into my arms lunged an obscene partner, Coop himself, straining his calico seams at the waist and oxters. When he took my hand, my fingers mingled with his hideous stumps. Most of that macabre night we jigged and swigged and reeled. One lady pirouetting near the fire was set aflame, but kept on twirling till her very beard was singed. It was a nightmare. I mourned the laws of nature even as I danced.

RELATING HOW WE ARE DUPED INTO MAKING CAMP AND THE
SHOCKING TRUTH ABOUT OUR NEIGHBOURS. ALSO, THE LOW
PARTICULARS OF A PANNER'S LIFE

The Map showed we had not reached Cariboo, but where our party halted, men were panning in the river below. One eager miner cried, "Boys, it must be loaded here!" and a hot discussion followed. Some wanted to make camp and reap this certain bounty, while others held steadfast to the promise of Cariboo. "Henry Merritt, we are bailing out!" Coop suddenly announced. Astonished, I recalled to him our proper destination only to have torn from my hands the precious map. The other fellows then reached immediate accord — they would remain a band and proceed on to Cariboo. This parting advice they offered: exchange with them our horses for staples of victuals and drink. Then Coop and I, against my timid judgement, descended the wooded slope alone.

Of a sudden the mountains reared around us. Their heads, crowned in red, reminded me of a view at ruddy sunset — the line of stony kings on the face of Salisbury Cathedral. And the river, hailing us with its stately roar, magnified my awe. Kneeling at its edge, I saw the mighty workings of that current, how it had ground down the mountains to liberate the gold. For those clear waters were scintillant with gold, with jade too, green nuggets blinking up at me, wildcats' eyes. I pictured the seal on Evaline's ring carved from that verdant stone, the ring upon her sturdy hand, that hand in mine. Then Coop, having gone to investigate the encampment we had seen from the trail, came racing back, hollering and breaking off my vision.

"Celestials! They are Celestials!"

I gaped at him, for this was the import of his discovery: our journey, having worn down equally my boot soles and my nerves, had now ended in an abandoned claim. With neither transport nor lucre, we were stranded, just as sure as Mr. Crusoe.

"This, Mr. Coop, is what comes of going off the map!"

Though I knew it would but augment my despair, I went to see for myself our Chinese neighbours. Approaching through the trees, I spotted them — five in number, toiling by the river. Down each bent back hung a plait like the long tail of a bell. My mother dressed her hair thus when convalescing, and Evaline, too, abed. They were ladies then! Five Celestial ladies! But an incongruity left me blinking: each was clad in *trousers*. Baffled, I drew within an earshot so as to determine their sex from their voices, yet such clangorous speech told me only that they might have had, too, the tongues of bells. At last one chanced to turn and I saw a bony face of unmistakable masculinity. Shuddering then at the queerness of these people, I hastened back to Coop.

I found him huddled close to Bruin, dog from master indistinguishable in their despondency. I made a fire and prepared our customary meal: salt pork fried in suet, beans and gruel. We ate in silence, then Coop, with a percolating sniff, laid his dish down for Bruin to clean. Hitherto in our journey I had not perceived in him an emotion that might signify the presence of a soul. Now, tears glistened on his stubbly countenance. It occurred to me also that our weeks together had made him my familiar, that this mutual predicament at least united us, as did, of course, our race. Reaching out, I patted his mutilated hand.

"We'll make the best of this," I said.

"They'll cut our throats as we sleep!"

"Bruin will be our guard."

That night a perturbing contradiction set me tossing in my bedroll: abandoned claims the Celestials were said to work, yet I had seen the river sparkle, an aquatic coffer. The next morn this same enigma spurred me headlong to the water. Seeing the Celestials already labouring in the stream, I stopped short, pressed my pan to my breast and in this solemn pose vowed to do the work of five. Then I squatted and commenced to earn my fortune as per the instructions of my erstwhile mentors — filling the pan and swirling it, using the current to flush out the silt. Accordingly, the pan should then have brimmed with nuggets; it brimmed instead with gravel, the gold having washed away. The whole course I then repeated to the same worthless result. Only after many dogged efforts did I learn the trouble: the gold was not formed in nuggets, but flakes like the scales of an auriferous fish. Soon Coop came down to pan as well. "It's arse gold," he said, disgusted. "We're the arses, Henry Merritt."

If panning was no good to us, we would try another method. First we endeavoured to cull the flecks directly, but our fingers stiffened hopelessly in that frigid water. More successful was extraction by toothpick; after two days, we were a full teaspoon richer.

In the end, I returned to the old method. Toiling thus, I was one day arrested by a dazzling sight: a gold leviathan gliding through our river shedding as it went the glinting scales of its splendour. Rapt, I dropped my pan and hastened after it. Ahead on the bank I met a Celestial, not panning, but crouching in perfect immobility. Loath to pass him, I stopped and waited for him to move. When he did, it was a most peculiar motion; he cast into the air his own plait. To my further astonishment the plait continued soaring as an angling line uncoiling from a reel. On it stretched, and on, in a wondrous elongation, finally landing with a splash in the river. At the same moment, a monstrous gold tail burst from the water and the Celestial lurched forward violently. Scrambling for purchase among the rocks, he began his tug o' war — a Chinese Jonah against a gilded whale. When I finally awoke, the Celestial reigned triumphant, hauling upon the rocks that priceless catch.

Thus our neighbours' tenacity and good fortune mocked our failure, even in our dreams. We coveted their laughter as they came up from the river, balancing on a pole their teeming baskets. "Children of the Mother Lode," they had no need for teaspoons; she fed them directly from her paps. Coop called them "heathen alchemists." To ascertain their golden secret, he concealed himself near to where they worked, but their method was simple panning, he confoundedly reported, differing from ours in only speed and mirth.

To numb disconsolation and the bombarding effect of Coop's snores, I began to indulge, too, in a nightly tipple. (The sweetness of the whisky I tasted not upon my tongue, but in my thirsting heart. From the first draught I had discovered a thrifty mode of transport; though my love lay a vast distance from me, if I had sufficiently imbibed, when I closed my eyes, I felt her near.) One night as we shuttled the bottle to and fro, an idea, sure as a river stone, struck me on the head. Salvation would come not by angel or Messiah, but in another party of our race. With this end in mind, we agreed that while I panned Coop would keep watch upon the trail. The prospect of delivery cheering us greatly, I allowed myself a double measure of drink.

That night Evaline's tangibility so aroused me, I found myself rolling upon her bosom. Her formidable scent I truly breathed. If these were the delightful workings of an extra dram, I wished I had indulged more frequently! Of a sudden, though, the fancy vanished and I sensed a most unimaginary squeeze. With ardour unmistakable, Coop was gripping me, wheezing hotly on my neck. The last time we had thus entwined had been by the miner's fire a-jigging. The queer semblance (how it had unnerved me then!) now admitted no denial: Coop's embrace and Evaline's were twins. Thus I came to know by experience how loneliness is a dread affliction, worse even than self-disgust.

GOLD MOUNTAIN, IN WHICH I AM ENLIGHTENED TO THE GOOD
HUMANITY OF OUR NEIGHBOURS

"I am ill," I told Coop. "I am dying."

"You don't know their parleyvoo!"

This did not deter me. I set off to the Chinese camp with a need more pressing than even that of gold.

The Celestials had a flock of scabious hens and a garden made from terracing the bank. Approaching, I found a fellow stooping between the rows of greens. "My bowels have not moved in weeks,' I abashedly confessed. "Could I beg from you a — ?" I gestured to the unfamiliar cousin of our cabbage at his feet.

When he straightened, I saw before me my equal in physical insignificance. He squinted, perplexed, so I pantomimed my complaint. Then he bade me wait as he repaired to their tent. (When he drew aside the flap I saw it stacked inside with blankets.) A moment later he returned with a different cure: a handful of foul-smelling sticks and leaves.

"Tea," he said in a toothy exhibition.

Within two days this potion had done the trick. In truth, I might have set a watch by my visits to the earth closet. "Those Celestials are good fellows," I told Coop.

He spat his whisky on the ground. "They're little dandies in their pigtails, just like you! That's why you love them!" Then he crawled into the tent and, till morn, blat not a further word.

I was roused as usual by the insistent buzz of flies and the clack of Bruin's jaws as he caught them. Then Coop issued forth his cheery reveille.

"Shite! Shite! Shite!"

He had taken to wearing a lady's bonnet stolen from the dancers. "It comes to this!" he griped. "Sluicing dregs with Celestials!"

We were not even sluicing. That required an apparatus we did not possess. I hastened to remind him of this and how we had come unfortunately to land there. Pronouncing me a cretin, he stalked off toward the trail, stopping first to make poor Bruin yelp for mercy.

Since first we fell stranded in the wilderness I had maintained that pleasant manners would keep us civilized and therefore sane. That evening I entered the Celestial camp again. I found them by the fire, watching the progress of a kettle, their voices tolling merrily. Perceiving me, though, they at once ceased conversing. I had come to thank the good apothecary, but unable to tell one from the other, was struck as mum. In the eerie silence, the firelight warped and made sinister their features. Somewhere an owl shrieked. Then one leapt up, jabbed his finger at me and made the cruel pronouncement all men loathe to hear.

"Die ... Die."

I swooned. Luckily one nimble fellow arrested my fall. A second applied himself to my revival by a vigorous fanning of his hat. Then, as a flock of birds will wake in one clamorous burst, they resumed their chatter and in a throng helped me to a seat. Finally I recognized the apothecary as the one whose dire utterance had instilled in me such terror. Now he explained himself, mostly by dumb-show. It was my pallor that had startled them; as I had taken them for my murderers, they had supposed I was a ghost.

Ready in the kettle was a manner of dumpling which they served in bowls with cabbage. Though they kindly pressed this meal upon me, I repeatedly declined, for instead of spoons, they ate with sticks. (These implements, I perceived, required no small dexterity. Had poultry been on the menu, however, or even a fresh egg, I might have happily employed my fingers!) When I accepted tea, served likewise in a bowl, they were satisfied and settled down to eat. I soon surmised that the apothecary alone knew a little English. Lee Hon was his name. The others, though, were eager students. Throughout the meal they used their sticks as pointers, asking how I called things.

"Fire," I told them. "Mountain. River. Gold."

I was not the only tutor. Lee Hon opened wide his arms to embrace the lonely place we inhabited, then taught me its Chinese name. Later I informed Coop, "We are at Gold Mountain."

"Ask them then," he retorted, "how they are making their mountain of gold!"

I wondered if something in the Chinese camp recalled to me my darling Evaline, or if disillusionment with my own lot endeared them to me. Once I had felt a kinship with Coop, but could no longer abide his crude manners and philosophies. Though we spoke the same language, and glared at one another through same-shaped eyes, I surely did not love him.

IN WHICH A GOOD FELLOW JOINS OUR JOLLY COMPANY

"Where have all the men gone?" I asked Coop.

I meant the scores of eager miners rushing off to Cariboo. Coop's post on the trail served the hope that we might accost a passing party, yet not a soul had he encountered, not even Natives who I had understood were numerous in these parts. This had begun to irk me as much as the flies and the stones that made their unaccountable entry into my boots. One unprofitable afternoon I therefore put away my pan and clambered up the slope to spy on Coop. I found him nowhere on the trail, but in the wood slumbering behind a tree. Shaking him to consciousness by his slobbery bonnet strings, I roared an ultimatum. Until he came with news of fellow panners, he was banished from the camp; I would henceforth bring his supper to the trail. When he failed to appear that night, I was truly astonished, marvelling that he had actually paid me heed. Then I settled happily into a solitude infinitely less lonely than keeping vexatious company.

Two nights hence I woke to Bruin baying in mortal terror and a frightful crashing in the trees. Both I and the Celestial party dashed from our tents with lanterns lit hastily. Upright and staggering toward us was a maddened and vociferous bear. I held the musket but, ignorant of its workings, stood with clacking knees. With great relief I espied a familiar gleam: the bear was wearing shoes.

He was drunk beyond language (which accounted for his animal roars) and miserably tattered. Coop by then had caught up and together we cajoled him to our tent.

"There he is," said Coop when we had tucked him in. "Yer good fellow."

The following day, when our visitor had regained his wits, Coop recounted to him his words. "Samuel Goodfellow," the stranger rejoined, his grin so blackened he might lately have supped on charcoal. "That's sure enough my name."

I did not believe him. To pry from him a little of his history, I enquired after his excellent and grossly incongruous shoes.

"I kilt a man for 'em in Californee, but it was hardly worth it. They pinch me in the heels."

DESCRIBING THE RISING HOSTILITIES IN AND AMONG THE CAMPS.
REVEALING ALSO A SCHEME OF MINE AND HOW IT IS THROWN OVER
FOR ONE BETTER. FURTHER, THE ACCOUNT OF THE DEATH OF A CERTAIN
CHARACTER FOR WHICH THE READER WILL REQUIRE A HANDKERCHIEF

The presence of the Celestial fowl grieved us all, having known for too long only salt pork for meat. Bruin especially coveted them. (Once daring to enter the Celestial camp, he had been soundly thrashed by Coop.) When Goodfellow joined our company, Bruin's ration became his and Bruin was forced to seek sustenance for himself. Mainly he gnawed our boots, his bulk daily diminishing until love of life surpassed his love of Coop and he went and got himself a hen. Goodfellow, witness to the deed, pursued Bruin and wrested away his banquet. After the manner of the best French chefs, he and Coop impaled it on a stick and roasted it in its feathery jacket. For Bruin's trouble, they tossed him the well-sucked bones.

That night one of the Chinese burst into our camp accompanied by all his fury. Brandishing a knife and with choppy gesticulation, he informed us he was full prepared to quarter Bruin. Goodfellow, by way of rebuttal, issued forth a sonorous belch.

Soon afterward, I found a sign fixed to a tree outside our camp.

NOTTISS! TO SELETEELS!
YOU ARE HEARBI NOTEEFED THAT IFF
YO GOW INTU THIS CAMP
YOU WILL KETCH HELL!

That my own name was not recorded there surprised me. Despite a certain handshake, Coop and Goodfellow were now rightful partners — in sloth instead of gold — and I, I was their object of derision. They retorted upon me noisome slander: if I polished my boots or performed ablutions in the river, I was a "dandy" or a "maid." For my acquaintance with Lee Hon, they called me "Hen Ree."

I loved that sobriquet. My few visits to the Chinese camp had been my only peace. Once, wretched with a longing for Evaline, I had crossed over and like the peddler that I had been, put on display the woeful contents of my heart. I had not expected comprehension, just a sympathetic ear, yet Lee Hon rose and went into the tent. He fetched a tin box and from it took a daguerreotype of his wife. Her hair was pulled tight in the Celestial plait and she wore a striking costume: flowered slippers fitting to tread the ground of the Flowery Kingdom (Lee Hon's name for China), a short jacket that fastened at the side, and, I am decidedly not mistaken — trousers.

Since Goodfellow's arrival and the incident with the hen, my relations with the Celestials had ailed. Lee Hon no longer saluted me if we happened to meet at the river and I dared not pay a visit to their camp. Something cheered me though. With Evaline's map as my true guide I intended to try again for Cariboo. My breast pocket a bank, I had a modest account, enough to quit Gold Mountain. The gold was rightly mine — flake by flake I had extracted it — though Coop and Goodfellow were sure to call it common wealth. My departure would therefore be stealthy; I had already begun to squirrel provisions in the woods.

From my bed by the fire (having been thus displaced), I watched a shadow-show on the tent wall: Coop and Goodfellow, card-sharpers, cheating one another. With no gold to wager, they played for punitive stakes — the winner bashing the loser on the pate. One evening, in the course of this jollification, Coop and Goodfellow began a suspiciously subdued colloquy.

"We'll kill the lot of 'em," was what reached my ears. I sat up alarmed. From the Celestial camp, I could see a fire still burning.

It being so far into night, I had expected to find them reposing, but they were busily at work. Onto several blankets spread out on the ground, they were pouring silt from sacks.

"They plan to take your hens!" I cried, translating with gesticulation.

They stopped short and gaped at me. Then Lee Hon came forward with an exaggerated grin and took me by the arm. "Thank you, Hen Ree," he told me and began to steer me off. Glancing over my shoulder, I saw the others hastening to conceal their occupation. I realized then that Coop had been correct; steady toil alone did not enrich them. I had chanced upon their secret art.

I clutched Lee Hon's hand. "Show me. I beg you, show me."

Why he conceded, I do not know. Perhaps it was to return the favour I had done them in my warning, or that I had already seen the greater part of it. It occurred to me also that there might be a fondness between us, despite his being a Celestial and I a Ghost.

The more they stoked the fire, the hungrier it grew, many tongued, lapping at the night. A glittering silt, a fortnight's panning, they spread across the blankets. When folded, these blankets and their contents became their noble offering and by way of rite were fed into the flames. I was awe-struck. In this simple method I fancied a golden enchantment, heard in their unfathomable parlance incantation. Now I know no manner of utterance can speed or slow this truth: Anything fire loves will burn. For fire has a mouth and a thousand teeth and its bite is all-transforming. In the slow-burning the tiny flakes amalgamated to nuggets. At dawn we sifted through the cool ash, retrieving in handfuls the metamorphosed gold.

My second plan for Cariboo I then abandoned and applied myself to panning with reborn hope. Compared to my previous exacting labour — gleaning pure flake — collecting the silt required little wit. In truth, as I panned a pleasant drowsiness ofttimes suffused me, almost as if I dreamt awake. Then, gazing at the swirling contents of my pan, I would behold an image. Formed not of gold or gravel, they were visions, as in the tales of prophets and saints. I saw, for example, my mother back in England mixing soda tonic for her wind. Also revealed: the ideal shoe. Evaline I saw dreaming, and then I saw her dream. In my half-dream she was smiling at her own dream — at ladies dressed in breeches and fellows wearing plaits.

One morning a raucous commotion from the Celestial camp broke off my reverie. Leaving my pan, I raced to learn the trouble, stood watching from a safe vantage behind a tree. The Celestials were shouting and waving cudgel-like their fists. Lee Hon, in the centre of the camp, was clutching fast to Bruin's tail while Bruin, fuelled by famine and oblivious to his passenger, was pursuing in crazed circles a shrieking hen. This carousel of starvation continued its merry rotations until the fowl finally collapsed. Immediately, Bruin seized hold of his feast. But a second Celestial pounced likewise upon Bruin and with no ado whatsoever plunged into his wasted scruff a knife.

Coop and Goodfellow, also witnesses to this carnage, were strangely gleeful. Coop refused to bury Bruin. He left the corpse to rot under his warning sign, saying the Gold Commissioner would soon pass by and bring justice to the river. Hitherto I would not have believed the flies could plague us worse. Blue-bottles swirled over the swelling carcass, an opaque confusion. In the autumn heat, Bruin's bursting open was the crack of doom.

AN ACCOUNT OF THE SCANDALOUS TRIAL AND ITS FATAL REPERCUSSIONS.
ALSO, MY EXPERIENCE WITH THE CELESTIAL METHOD OF GOLD
RETRIEVAL AND WHAT WAS CAUGHT IN JUSTICE'S PAN

"This was damshur more an angel than a dog!" Coop told the Gold Commissioner who had appeared while on his route downstream. "In cold blood they kilt 'im!" By then Bruin's bones were protruding whitely from his putrid flesh. Bending over to examine them, the Commissioner gagged behind his handkerchief.

"And Yer Highness, look what they done to Coop!" Goodfellow cried.

Coop drew from his pocket a bandaged hand; Goodfellow proceeded to unswaddle it. Then Coop, bawling, a debauched baby in his bonnet, thrust in the Commissioner's face his freshly scored and bleeding stumps.

The Gold Commissioner is the lawful adjudicator of all disputes under fifty English pounds. He seemed a just enough fellow, albeit haggard and with one eye listing sightless in its socket. Declaring Bruin worth two pounds and Coop's severed fingers ten pounds apiece, he drew his pistol and rounded up the terrified Celestials. Having assembled on the river bank both disputing parties, he produced a Bible and set to swearing in the Christians. Coop repeated his libellous testimony with Goodfellow's perfidious corroboration, but since the Celestials could neither utter a language intelligible to the Commissioner, nor be sworn to oath, their defence was disqualified.

I then proceeded to describe in exacting detail how Bruin came to lose his life, for just reason and with due warning. The Commissioner turned his blind eye to me.

"Surely, sir," I protested, "you won't take the word of these vulgarians over that of honest gentlemen!"

"Having no words from them, how can I presume honesty? Furthermore, your title "gentlemen" is the grossest of misnomers. Do you know who these pathetic fellows are?"

I looked to the Celestials, tattered and made even more diminutive by incomprehension and fear. It occurred to me then that I more truly belonged in their party than my own. In truth, welling up inside me was a new allegiance which I now felt called upon to defend. I turned to the Commissioner.

"They are my friends, sir."

"They are slaves," he retorted, "indentured to a coolie broker to repay their passage to this hell! Imagine the hell they come from, if they would go to such expense! And now I shall fine them, Mr. Merritt, for their injury to this man, thus happily prolonging their misery!" He broke off coughing.

"They are innocent of your charge, sir, and my testimony will prove it!" I paused to let him finish retching. His handkerchief, I noted, was stained with bloody sputum. "I had several occasions to remark Mr. Coop's stumps before we ever came in contact with Celestials."

"When, Mr. Merritt?"

"We shook to seal our bargain before we set out for Cariboo. Once, too, I comforted him as he wept."

"Lies!" screamed Coop.

"We danced together! He was a lady and I a fellow!"

Now Goodfellow, too, set to railing, but the Commissioner objected.

"Mr. Coop and Mr. Goodfellow! I shall question this witness without interruption or molestation! Do you mark my words?"

Coop shrunk down in obeisance; Goodfellow expectorated on the ground.

"At any other time," the Commissioner continued, "did you note Mr. Coop's disfigurement?"

This question caused me to blush deeply, but having laid my hand upon the Bible, I was fettered to the truth. The matter of Coop's and my nocturnal tussling, of which we ourselves had never spoken, I now shame-facedly confessed.

"You say he squeezed you?" queried the flabbergasted Commissioner.

"Aye, sir, he did."

"How often?"

"While we shared a tent, sir, almost every night."

(Here Coop and Goodfellow, with violent expletives, renewed their denials, but were silenced once again by threat of contempt of court.)

"And, Mr. Merritt, did you enjoy this treatment?" asked the Commissioner.

"It gave a bit of comfort, sir. I miss so much my lady."

"A moment ago you called Mr. Coop a lady." Then the Commissioner, disgust marring his countenance, dismissed my evidence on the grounds that I was unsound of mind. His judgement: The Celestials were without a doubt guilty of the aforementioned crimes. The confiscation of their gold and its disbursement among the Commissioner and the aggrieved plaintiffs was the swiftest retribution.

Coop and Goodfellow were equally swift in leading the Commissioner to the Celestials' tent and their unsecret cache. Then erupted a most hellish skirmish as the Chinese tried to defend their store. Clearly Lee Hon did not understand my part in these outrageous proceedings; when I approached him, he drew a knife.

I fast retreated to the safety of the nearby trees, but my nostrils were immediately assailed by a potent stench — Bruin's corrupting carcass billowing gas. Although all the men found sufficient air with which to fuel their fight, it nearly stifled me. I fled the tainted atmosphere, stumbling up the wooded slope.

Waiting on the trail was the Commissioner's horse. I grabbed its halter and was about to take up the unlikely trade of pony stealing, when I heard shots fired at the river. I could not go without learning my friends' fate, though nearly an hour passed before the Commissioner reached the trail.

"Who is shot?" I asked.

"Celestials. The whole party."

"Take me with you!" I implored him, feeling my breast pocket for a bribe. To my immense shock I found it empty, all my earnings scattered on the slope. "Sir, I beg you! Take me!"

"Where I am going, Mr. Merritt," the Commissioner replied, "I will no other man to go."

I watched him ride away. I could not run myself, for night was settling like a million flies. Nor did the prospect of the morning's light offer any hope; I was penniless and without a morsel. Coop and Goodfellow, in possession at last of real stakes, would shuffle and deal through the night. Already I could hear their roisterous carousing far below. I felt certain they would not welcome a third player.

In the end I huddled upon the trail, insensible with shock and grief. Above me the constellations were like minuscule flecks of gold set in everlasting patterns in the firmament. As I crouched, I fell to wondering why the Chinese were called Celestials, whether it was their shaved fore-locks that earned them the appellation — their naked brows round and smooth like planets — or that, when smiling, their eyes folded into pleas-ing crescents that brought to mind the waning moon. They had, too, tails like black comets and voices that mimicked the tonal music of the spheres. Then the stars themselves, indeed the whole bespangled sky, seemed to unswirl in an astronomical tribute to my friends. Lying back to watch this wonder, I drifted off to sleep.

In my dream, Smoke Personified was leaning over me in an oppres-sive cloak of black, forcing up my nose its ghastly fingers. I woke gasp-ing. Below in the darkness, gold sparks were shooting. I saw them glinting, as in my pan, but would not touch them, lest I burn: *something in our camp had caught on fire.* The tent. Blazing up of a sudden, it made a mighty pyre, Coop and Goodfellow trapped within.

If the compound of feelings churning in me could have been distilled, it would have made an insanity potion. At once I battered my skull against a tree and hummed a ditty I had learned upon the trail. ("We are dancing girls in Cariboo, and we're liked by all the men … ") Then, thinking of Coop's corpse braising in the embers, I set to wailing, only to find myself a moment later jigging. Thus I passed the remainder of that hellish night.

At daybreak, exhausted and in awful trepidation, I ventured back down the slope. About their camp the Chinese lay in various wracked postures, all bearing monstrous wounds. Lee Hon's very arm was severed from his person as he stared heavenward from a pool of gore. I turned away in horror. They were the sole men with whom I had felt affinity, perhaps in all my sorry life. Now they had travelled on to a place not even Evaline could map.

As for Coop and Goodfellow — drunk, they must have knocked the lamp down in the tent while gambling their booty. I knelt beside the fire's remains. The Celestials' gold, twice consumed by flame, had fused to weighty nuggets. I might have been a rich man. I might have made my love a ring. But gold washed in blood loses all its lustre, makes an ugly trinket and a foul currency. To fund my escape, I was obliged to take a handful. A more grisly chore I cannot imagine, combing through those ashes, sorting gold from charred stubs of bone.

WHEREIN I ARRIVE BACK IN EVERLASTING,
GREATLY DOWN AT THE HEEL

By the time I found my Evaline snow lay upon the ground and I was a tatterdemalion, as much a pauper as when I left her. In my absence she seemed to have accumulated flesh, that or trial and hunger had shrivelled me. And though she greeted me with the same bashful manner I adored, I saw at once I had not been missed. Knowing well she would refuse me, nonetheless I begged her hand, then with my tears I washed her boots.

"It would be too comic, Mr. Merritt," she told me. "As if I were the man and you the lady."

At least she consented to make for me a map. She shooed me to her bed and while I tumbled headlong in its frowzy comfort, she made a coy show of removing her hair pins and letting her plait fall down her back.

"What if I can no longer dream?" I asked her.

"How do you know you are not dreaming now?" Turning, she smiled at me in the lamp-light and for a moment I thought she was Coop.

How true her words! What had happened to me awake was infinitely more terrible and strange than anything I had encountered in a nightmare. As a lad I was wont to contemplate the simple workings of a boot-lace, how eye-to-eye it made its criss-cross pattern — certain, pre-determined and everlasting. So too, I had thought, would be my life. Now even elemental truths — justice, for example, or what defines a race of people, or even, for that matter, a man or woman — all this seemed to me reversed. I was lost and knew not where to go.

We slept like babes and, in dreaming, awoke together to find ourselves upon a forest trail. This sylvan path we trod but a short distance before it opened in a field. In truth, we had reached a vista glittering and vast — a plain of golden stars. Evaline turned to me in amazement. "This is the Celestial Route!" And so I learned my proper destination. I took her hand, she took mine, and as one we ventured forth. In the morn she sat up in the bed, her visage radiant with our shared dream. "Such a lovely place!" she exclaimed. "Are you certain it exists?"

Now I am waiting out the winter in a room above the saloon, replying to my mother's bombastic correspondence, taking her pennies to pay my keep. Sometimes I wax despondent, lamenting what has happened to me and my boots. Mostly, though, I pass the hours studying Evaline's map of China, its mighty wall, the two great rivers wending to the sea. Somehow it stirs me. It seems as much a work of art as of cartography. When first I saw it, I proposed she travel with me to be sure that this time I would not stray off course. She only laughed and told me she could sojourn far more economically.

My boots! Of the original laces, only one remains; the left I now fasten with a bit of string. Part of the stacking on that heel is also gone, giving me a most ungainly limp. As for the right, being so punctured by Bruin's gnawing it would make a perfect sieve. Yet these mean scraps of leather have brought me so great a distance I am loath now to part with them. If they endure this one last journey, then I shall retire them — for a pair of flowered slippers.

The Gridlock Mechanism

REBECCA RAGLON

THIS IS A POST-MODERN STORY SET IN TORONTO AND VANCOUVER, BUT PRIMARILY on a plane shuttling back and forth somewhere in between the two cities. The characters are Louis, who lives in Vancouver, and Geena who also lives in Vancouver, except when she's working in Toronto. Louis is an architect who specializes in house designs for narrow, steep lots, while Geena teaches courses in the aesthetics of post-modernism at the large alternative university in Toronto. According to the official biographical notices that appear on her publications, Geena is one of those lucky and important people who is able to "divide her time between Toronto and Vancouver." Riding the plane back and forth was, of course, really quite tedious, although she could see in the eyes of her colleagues that many of them didn't actually believe it. They could see only her escape from the grimness of the Toronto winter routine, going to a place where cappuccino bars replaced doughnut shops, and buoyant vegetation softened the concrete edges of the city, a place that was pretty. Geena wasn't used to the aggressive ugliness of Toronto: Even the women were ugly, made themselves ugly by putting henna in their long stringy hair, dressing in black and painting their scowling mouths an aggressive shade of maroon. In her heart she had to admit that she was always very glad when the plane penetrated through the cloud cover, and she had her first sight of the green lushness of Vancouver.

To survive the frequent plane rides, Geena normally snapped open her briefcase and read scholarly articles on subjects such as "The Cultural Logic of Late Capitalism" or "The Insecurity of Post Materialism," the headphones clamped firmly over her ears. The headphones, the briefcase, the sharpened pencil that made quick, sharp notations in the margins of the

scholarly articles were all a part of the arsenal she used against the hor-
rific possibility of conversation with the endless stream of parts salesmen,
assistant managers and regional reps, who always seemed to be seated
next to her. They sat with their shirt sleeves rolled up and their ties
loosened, ordered doubles from the liquor trolley and were eager to
share their grievances against taxes and government interference with
any unattached woman: even more eager to explain why they were not
riding business class.

Geena and Louis had been through a great deal together. They had
both worked very hard for years and years to get through school. Louis
had delivered pizza, manned a chip wagon, and stood behind a storefront
for the Insul-King ("Insulate Now, We'll Show You How"). Geena worked
graveyard shifts for the police department, answering the 911 line and
dispatching help to innumerable squalid scenes throughout the city: men
beating their wives, gangs terrifying store owners, old women passed out
on street corners. They had lived in damp little basement rooms, handy-
men specials, with windows buried away in window wells and the smell
of cooking drifting down from the floors above. They lived and studied
together in these rooms for years and even in their hardest times (the
time the car broke down and the Insul-King folded, owing Louis two
weeks' pay, and Geena was in the midst of exams), even then they had
not quarrelled in the way they had when Geena decided to take the job
back east. They had never quarrelled about anything all those years in
school and they had always agreed on the important things: above all to
be absolutely free and equal partners. That meant they had agreed not to
get married. (Geena could never understand why so many of her feminist
friends were married.) They had agreed to share domestic chores; they
had agreed always to support each other in their separate pursuits of
fulfilling, lifetime work.

After they graduated, Louis got a job with a firm of architects and
Geena, less fortunate, was still hanging around the fringes of the university, hanging around, waiting for "something" to come up. This inequality
was not something they had planned for during those long intense dis-
cussions about their "relationship" and their future together. And it was
awkward now when they totalled up their expenses at the end of the
month, or when Louis talked about building their dream house. Louis,
riding the wave of a Vancouver housing boom, was doing very well in his
own work, and she was pleased for him. But she also felt that he did not
really understand her own overwhelming sense of anguish and sadness,
her fear of becoming a dilettante like the "faculty wives" she occasionally
saw at departmental functions, forever working on their theses or writing
poetry in their spare time, and so grateful when they were tossed a course

to teach. Louis was unremittingly cheerful: "Just get on with your own work. Something will turn up." She was both touched and annoyed by his faith — which seemed based upon very little. He would not indulge her sadness or sense of defeat, and met her despair with an unflagging optimism that "something" would turn up.

She was given a course here and there to teach, but noticed that she was greeted less enthusiastically now by the professors she had worked with, less and less enthusiastically until she felt just going into the central office to pick up her mail was an ordeal of huge proportions, one that took a great deal of courage and preparation: She had to wash her hair, and select the right clothing, she had to sit in the cafeteria and slowly sip two cups of coffee and afterwards walk around the campus, very slowly, her umbrella shielding her from the rain. Even so, her heart would start to race as the elevators took her up to the Main Office. Sometimes she didn't see anyone but the departmental receptionist, but even Shirley seemed to treat her a bit differently now, a bit cooler. "No, there were no calls for you." It wasn't the words, so much as the rather satisfied look Shirley wore when delivering such messages. Shirley had a degree in Moderns from Edinburgh, and she felt this qualified her for quite a bit more than answering calls in an English Department at a Canadian University. Geena was not yet inured to Shirley's ever-so-slightly-contemptuous looks, or to the curt nods from her former professors, or to the brusque way the chair of the department had of turning on his heels and becoming deeply immersed in paper work when she wandered by his office on the way to the Xerox machine.

She could see quite clearly that she was an embarrassment to everyone as she plummeted from the high, heady cliffs of a "promising" doctoral candidate, to the desolate and dreary slough inhabited by those who could not find work. She now joined the very ones she had felt such contempt for: Charles, who always wore the same sweater with the unravelling elbows and the same tight, shiny pants, and who was an expert on Anthony Powell; or Peter, with his faded plaid work shirts and jeans and hiking boots, his unkempt curly hair and beard, always carrying his well-thumbed Derrida around and quoting from him like scripture. In spite of their shared scorn for the Philistines, they were a pathetic crew, exchanging bits of information, furtively haunting the bulletin board with its two or three job postings (one in Bellingham, one at a Christian School in Alberta). Charles' strategy was to hang in, teaching composition until some new position opened up. ("If one ever does," he always added hollowly). Peter had applied for a position as a language instructor in Singapore. ("Face it, because of the feminist agenda, no man's going to get a job around here.") It was a revelation to learn that the rest of the world was so thoroughly indifferent to the importance of their work. Every Monday, Wednesday and Friday, Geena stood in front of her class of young engineering students and struggled through "Elegy in a Country Churchyard" or "Richard the Third" as they smirked, snickered and yawned. Her pen skimmed across their papers, marking spelling errors, grammatical errors, errors in punctuation. Their essays were appalling, and at times she felt like weeping as she sat mulling over a sentence that made no sense.

Much to her surprise, something finally did turn up. She was called by the chairwoman of an eastern school and was interviewed by people who had read her articles. She had a chance to talk to a group of graduate students who were interested in what she had to say. It was odd, but she had never realized in all those solitary years as a student just how much she needed a community, not to mention a recognized position or, after years of austerity, the salary such a position would bring. Flying back to Vancouver on the plane that first time, looking sleek and successful, she felt she could finally leave behind the half-apologetic sense of doing something arcane and inessential she had always had when talking to certain people: paint salesmen, hairdressers, manufacturers of bathroom fixtures. Suddenly it seemed as if she too might have a place in that busy jostling world where things got done. She would be a university professor. Now, that was solid. That had substance.

She couldn't remember now when the argument first surfaced but she did remember a certain evening when they were sitting out on the deck of a restaurant overlooking the ocean, a late summer sunset streaking the sky. The air was brisk and salty and they were both wearing sweaters. It was just after the waitress had set the coffee down that Geena was finally able to precisely formulate the dread that had been hanging over them for weeks.

"So, do you mean you wouldn't even consider going east?"

"How can you ask that? My life — our life is here. I thought — I always thought you felt the same way."

"I suppose there aren't challenges back east. Too flat?" She meant it to be light, but it sounded different — almost a sneer.

"It's taken me a lifetime to feel confident enough to design something that really belongs here. You don't just pack up and go off, and do that somewhere else."

"You don't just go off and find someone else to live with, either. What really matters to you?"

"Well, I guess I could ask you the same thing, couldn't I? What really matters to you, Geena?"

It was a question that they were still asking themselves now, a year later. Sometimes she could convince herself that things were really quite wonderful, that she was doing important, exciting work. Somehow the very pace of her life gave it a sense of urgency that made such questions irrelevant. There were the late night arrivals in Toronto, the conferences, stays in strange hotels, the chaotic crush of people in airports and restaurants. There were lectures to prepare, committee meetings, students waiting outside her door. And there was the eeriness of going from a mild spring day, full of blossoming cherry trees, daffodils, crocuses and pansies, back into the dark heart of winter, back into the sullenness of the spreading city, full of angry dreams and hard edges. She could glimpse Louis' profound resistance to Toronto on those nights she returned, skirting the northern edges of the city in the Grey Coach, the chemical toilet reeking, the driver muttering angrily under his breath. There was something unsettling and profoundly depressing in those miles of refineries, warehouses, mini-malls, eyeglass outlets and storage units. Then there was the peculiar smell of the subway, filled with the babble of a dozen different languages, and the long lonely walk up Bathurst Street, before she could finally open the door of her apartment, finding herself inexplicably alone while her body still tingled with the memory of Louis' kisses.

What kind of life was it, going back and forth across a country, muffled in clouds, eating California strawberries and Chilean grapes inside a heated aluminum tube? At times Geena and Louis felt like very smart people, people in control, people who were able to make important choices. They were a part of a legion of important people crisscrossing the country: the senator, the bank manager, the union organizer, the opera singer. They were part of a vast movement of important people doing important things, going to important meetings, making important decisions. Yes, they were making the most of their lives, living intensely and fully.

But there were dangerous moments, too, contradictions that seemed to lie like a crack in the foundation of their life together. Louis designed ecologically responsible houses for rich clients who made their money harvesting vast swaths of trees, while she used her university position to teach a generation of young people that the very concept of "knowledge" was a socially constructed reality maintained by a power elite. They told each other they loved each other when they met, yet most of their time they spent apart. With a few glasses of wine and a moonlit evening Geena could convince herself that their lives were wonderful, more than wonderful, the best of all possible lives. They had everything, the world of city and country, brick and cedar, oak and pine. The same moon shining over Burrard Inlet shone on Lake Ontario, gathering together and embracing them all in its benevolent, unifying light. Some people shook their heads and said, "I don't see how you can do it … " But they were people who didn't know about e-mail, portable phones, modems, faxes and frequent flyer points. From time to time in Toronto, Geena lunched with an old friend whose husband was teaching in Florida. When they talked about their "situations" together over lunch, their lives did indeed seem less strange, almost normal. They all knew friends, and friends of friends, people doing the same thing. (They didn't like to talk about the ones who got divorced, or about the children.) They lived in a world where people talked about going to London for the weekend: They lived in a world full of choice.

There were also the bad times, the times when everything seemed to go flat, and arguments that might have been resolved overnight went on and on, sometimes for weeks. Such times always seemed to crop up unexpectedly. They had lost the ability to read each other's moods, and were always saying or doing the wrong thing at just the wrong time. One November weekend they had their worst quarrel ever, just at a time when Geena felt particularly close to Louis. They were taking the ferry over to Bowen Island to walk a building site together. Louis was considering buying it and designing a place for them, the ultimate dream home. On the ferry were a small brigade of mothers: women her own age with soft, friendly faces, and soft, friendly voices, women who had made their choices and now spent their time taking care of children while their husbands were off in the downtown offices all day. Geena found herself staring at them, a strange irritation welling up inside her. The whole group, women and children, were dressed in bright coloured sweatsuits and running shoes, and they were all chattering in the same high, sweet voices.

"Wouldn't you like Eric to come over and play? Wouldn't that be fun? We can have cookies and milk when we get back … "

"No, no, no, Fiona, you have to share with Anna."

"Oh, Heather, did you remember to order the Playset for the Christmas raffle?"

Geena went and stood out on the deck with Louis and let the brisk wind pull her hair back from her face. She could see it all, the cookies and milk and Christmas raffles, the long bored mornings together over coffee while the kids wrestled around in front of the television set, the sweet smug certainty that they were doing the best thing for their children, and the bickering that would begin when the husbands came home. ("I pay the bills, I expect a hot meal." "Well I've been with the kids all day, you could put them to bed once in awhile." Did people really choose such a life?) The water was choppy and the blue mountains down Howe Sound were wrapped in clouds. "I feel like I'm covered in goo," she said, but Louis didn't laugh.

"Why do you think it would be such a bad life, living here, raising kids?"

"Oh, come on, Louis, they look bored out of their skulls. And did you see the poster inside? They spend their weekends watching films about the Great Goddess and 'getting in touch with their feelings.' Give me a break."

They stared silently down the Sound together, then Louis suddenly said, "We weren't supposed to do this forever, remember?"

That week the plane circled far out over the Pacific ocean before finally banking and making its turn east. It climbed and climbed until even the snow covered mountains looked small. Then they went through the clouds, and Louis was finally gone, and her other life, the life alone began. She supposed many people — most people — lived badly fragmented lives; hers was just more extreme. The problem was how to make sense of the fragmentation. At one time she would have written sprightly sentences celebrating "diversity" but all during that grim November she felt too tired to celebrate anything. She dragged herself through her days at work, Louis' e-mail messages were terse, flights were delayed because of snowstorms. The sense of community she had so eagerly sought seemed to dissolve as she sat through an endless round of committee meetings that seemed to centre on an endless number of petty topics. With a shock she learned that she was really liked by very few of her colleagues; and on her part she found herself confronted by an inexplicably touchy group of human beings. She struck up an acquaintance of sorts with an older woman in the department, a feminist who carried vague resentments around with her. Earlier in her career she had published a book on *Feminism and Phallocentric Imagery* and she felt that the "newcomers" — young women like Geena — did not fully appreciate the sacrifices of her generation or the true depravity of the men surrounding them. Furthermore, they were uninformed about the importance of Phallocentric Imagery. As they sat sampling the sushi at a mini-mall restaurant near the University, Geena listened to the arid recitation of grievances, past and present, and wondered how anyone could live here, in a place so stripped of gaiety. Outside the window was an oil refinery — huge white tanks and pipes looming over them and dented, rusted cars blowing through slush. A woman trying to cross the street stood with bulging plastic bags full of groceries, waiting patiently for the lights to change. Perhaps she was going back to the highrise that stood at the side of the road, a highrise with a meagre metal playground at its base for the children living inside.

Sometimes after a long, fruitless day she would stagger home from work, her head pounding, longing for Louis, for someone *normal* to talk to. Those were the moments when she was particularly vulnerable: She would call him and he would say stiffly, "Well, that's not something we can talk about over the phone." "Well, when can we talk?" "Well, I don't know." Things would end so badly that when she hung up the phone she felt more isolated than before.

Sometimes on her way back downtown to her apartment she would stop at a mall for a salad or to purchase one or two small things. There was something about the mall that seemed to correspond to how she felt; more, it corresponded to what she was, and she tried to find the words for what that was as she spent hours walking up and down, up and down. It was both oppressive and comforting. All that stuff (clothes, shoes, watches, books, food, perfume, records) made her head swim, made her almost dizzy, and she would have to hurry over to a bench to sit down, and stare at the floor, at some bland neutral place. Everywhere around her were people, lots and lots of people, walking around, enjoying themselves. Her mind went spinning from thought to thought as her eyes cruised the displays of cosmetics and sparkling cheap jewellery. Sometimes she'd wait until the mall closed before she'd start back to her lonely little apartment, bone tired, hoping it was late enough to crawl into bed, hoping that *tonight* she wouldn't wake up with a start at three in the morning, wondering where she was, reaching through the dark for Louis.

Christmas that year was not a particularly happy time. She left Toronto in the midst of a really rancorous battle over who would be the next chair. Louis was sullen and it rained in Vancouver for two weeks straight. On the day after Christmas they were invited over to Bowen Island to visit Jonathan Cares and Mary Wilding. Jonathan worked in the same firm with Louis and had been the one to convince Louis about the desirability of living on the Island. Their home overlooked a pretty bay, with cedar trees brushing up against the windows. It was a lovely "rustic" home, with exposed beams and a big stone fireplace. To Geena, though, it all looked slightly overdone, as if every penny that they earned and every spare moment was lavished on this creation. She imagined them on the weekends, hand polishing their oak floors, or hunting through small shops for the perfect piece of pottery to place on the table in the entryway. Mary was a new mother, dressed now in purple harem pants and a cotton tunic, who sat nursing the baby while the rest of them talked. She was a slim, pretty woman who had recently given up her job as a book editor to stay home with the baby but she still had a certain brittle pride that proclaimed her independence. She might be a new mother but she was still going to smoke a cigarette after dinner, and talk bravely about doing some freelance work. Eventually the baby fell asleep and Mary put him in his crib, then curled her legs up under her and joined the conversation about the development occurring on Bowen Island, and how lucky they felt having gotten in on the housing market before the big upsurge in prices.

"Frankly, we couldn't afford a spot like this at today's prices," Jonathan said. "And we have an option to subdivide, if we want."

"You can't get waterfront at any price anymore," Louis agreed. "You were smart to pick this up when you did."

"And we like it here, it's a good place for kids," Jonathan said.

"Though some of the women here are quite awful," Mary said. "Don't try and deny it, Jonathan. I know. They spend all their energy on the kids and are just so out of touch. When I introduced myself to this one woman and she noticed that my last name was different from Jonathan's she just gave me this *look* and said, 'Oh, you're one of those *independent* women.' I mean, what a thing to say."

"I wonder what they'd think of me?" Geena asked.

"Well, I mentioned you once at a Ladies Breakfast," Mary laughed. "They couldn't believe it. They really couldn't. Most of them thought you were — careerist. And they said it wouldn't work if you had kids."

"Careerist?" Geena asked heatedly. "When it gets right down to it, right down to the nitty gritty, that's the one thing men won't compromise on, ever. But who calls them careerists?"

Later, when they were again talking about housing prices (such a safe topic, so endlessly fascinating), Geena took her mug of tea and wandered over to the floor-to-ceiling window. It was a typical dark winter day, with low-hanging clouds and a grey sea, mournful cedars bowing in the wind. Out on the lawn stood a deer. It was a small island deer, inbred and fragile-looking. It stood for a moment in the rain, head raised, listening intently. It was so close that Geena could see its thin sides moving in and out as it breathed, could see its ears twitching. Perhaps it heard the distant roar of bulldozers and gravel trucks, the sound of future development happening. As she watched it, something inside of her knotted, something that almost made her feel like crying. There was something there waiting to surface, something about the way her life was going, if she could just give it a name …

"Oh, the deer," Mary said behind her. "Jonathan says we're going to have to fence our property — they eat everything in sight. 'Hoofed locusts' Islanders call them. You should see what they've done to my roses."

On the way back to Toronto she sat and corrected a stack of students' essays and tried not to think about the generally dismal time she had just had. Halfway across Manitoba they hit turbulence and cups and glasses rattled and the pilot asked the flight attendants to take their seats. Through the window Geena could see the wing vibrating. For forty-five minutes the plane shimmied through rough air and everyone fell strangely quiet as they meditated upon their lives. They were in a small aluminum tube, thirty-seven thousand feet above the earth, shooting exhaust directly into the ozone, being buffeted in return by fierce jet streams. This was certainly not a place they should be — how did they ever allow themselves to get into this ... situation? What madness, what conceit dogged them all? (Important business in Bonn ... have to make the connection to Ottawa ... if I miss the meeting ... might lose the contract. Geena there too, thinking about her morning class but also thinking how much more important it would be to be lying next to Louis right now, their arms around each other, listening to the rain.) Somewhere over Ontario things smoothed out, the meal service was finished and they landed safely — again.

She thought of Louis back in Vancouver at his drawingboard, carefully, precisely taking measurements, designing new buildings for impossible sites, sites where only deer used to walk. Louis loved her, understood her, had never done anything to harm her. She thought of that word love, and the warmth it evoked, starting there in her mouth, tongue pressed against her teeth. Love. When they had met, in their second year of university, they had hitchhiked down the coast together to Mexico. She still remembered those strange intense days together and the first time he had said "I love you" to her. They had found a room in the mountain town of San Cristobal. It was a huge room, with two balconies overlooking the street. Yet it was furnished with only a double bed, which stood in the middle of the room like an altar. They collected bottles and filled them with wildflowers and placed them all around the bed. One morning, when they woke up, the floor of their room was covered with green husks, shed by the dozens of locusts now clinging to the white walls. It was on the morning when the floors were covered with the green husks that he had told her he loved her and she sat stroking his smooth young face, thinking if her life was to be linked with his, her one hope would be that she would never cause him bitterness.

She no longer felt any of that kind of tenderness for him as she thought of him there, in Vancouver, bent over his drawingboard. He was simply there, her partner. An essential leg propping up a table. What they had now was nothing at all like what they had begun with when she felt she couldn't *exist* without him. How extravagant that seemed now. Of course she would *exist*.

The earth turned on its axis and the sunlight began its return to the north. As she sped back and forth across the continent, Vancouver was buoyant with El Nino warmth, and flowers seemed to be bursting out everywhere, weeks ahead of time. In the east she had left in the midst of a snow squall, while in the west daffodils, crocuses, cherry trees and tulips were all in full bloom. Her heart ached as the lushness of Vancouver flashed by: the laurels and rhododendrons, the ferns, salmonberries and bleeding hearts, the tender green aspen. Not until weeks later, in the east, did crocuses push through the mud in the backyard of her apartment building. As she sat preparing a lecture, she felt cold, too, looking at them. Perhaps Louis was right: there was something so *alien* in all of this, something she would never get used to. He was right, and she was wrong, and wrong headed, willing to sacrifice a relationship with another human being for the sake of an inflated sense of her own importance.

Was that the truth?

She thought of all the complaints she had heard over and over again, from women, about men.

Definition of a man: someone who doesn't clean toilets.

And others, much, much *worse*. She pictured those men as slightly overweight and with too much hair — the kind of men who would have hair growing out of their backs.

Geena had never reciprocated these confidences from her women friends, because Geena and Louis were different. Somehow they had escaped the terrible sense of grievance wounding so many others. That's because they were smart, bright people, people who were in control of their lives, people who could make choices and tough decisions.

Maybe that was the truth.

Some nights when she was very lonely, watching the television alone, waiting for sleep to come, she thought of just quitting and returning to Vancouver, waiting again for something to "turn up," or saving her pride like Mary Wilding and doing "contract" work. And of course they'd have children and live in an unpretentious yet environmentally sound house and maybe they'd even be happy. But she could only think of that for a few minutes before Louis started growing larger and larger. She imagined him, the big man, coming home and recounting the events of the day, making pronouncements for her benefit, devouring her, devouring the world. When they were fifty they would grow weary of each other, and he would leave and marry a much younger woman, an architectural student he would meet while she was working in his office one summer.

Was that true?

Maybe she would have the affair. They would continue on and then she would meet someone younger, someone sweet and compliant, without a complicated history, someone who would ease the lonely nights. Afterwards she would write her own bittersweet feminist version of the "Campus Novel." Maybe that is what would happen.

She thought of the deer standing out in the rain on Bowen Island, and she thought of the flights crossing the country and all the people in the airplane, businessmen and managers and government officials with their little laptops, busy working, working, working, administrating life on earth for everyone down below. Somehow Louis had resisted this, the pull of this. He had planted his feet deep into the ground and said, "No." Louis was different, stood for something different. He had been born in Vancouver and loved every nook and cranny of the city. He loved the laurel hedges and the cedars, the Douglas Fir, the November rains. He loved the sea walk around Stanley Park, and the neon signs blooming through the fog. It wasn't egoism that held him, but commitment. She turned that possibility around and around; maybe that was the truth.

Finally she put aside the lecture and went outside. It was a cold spring day and even the daffodils in their gigantic concrete containers looked chilly. People out on the street looked tight, their coats buttoned up tight, with a certain tightness around their mouths. Geena walked and walked and walked, trying to out-walk her tumultuous thoughts: Louis and the deer and the flights back and forth. Everywhere she looked there were dark clothes, tight faces, maroon lips, grit. Grit everywhere. Hotdog stands with the smell of sizzling grease and the tang of onions. She passed one or two streets of specialized shops, their windows offering handwoven wool, shawls or imported cherrywood pipes, highlighted as if each was an *objet d'art*. Sunlight on warm brick, black grillwork, an art gallery. More to the point were the streets that followed with other stores, the kind of stores that let their products slide out onto the sidewalk and pile up. FOR SALE, a bag of one thousand Q-tips. Who would need one thousand Q-tips? Stacks of plastic laundry baskets. Bins full of dusty acrylic sweaters that had been for sale for twenty years. Socks, brooms, plastic measuring cups, china saucers, a tray of cheap tin spoons. All of it out there on the street — who would steal it? She walked and walked, thinking that now she was getting close to it, to some sort of epiphany, some sort of revelation, coming closer and closer to *insight*. Wasn't that always what happened at the end of the story? Why couldn't it happen now, to her? She was walking and walking, past thousands of strange faces, strange faces and strange dreams, getting close to the gritty essence of the city and of her life. She passed Donut Shops with their vinyl-covered stools and hard Formica table tops. Slumped there were people in dark overcoats staring through the greasy steamy windows as they stirred their coffee with plastic stir-sticks. She thought of herself, walking these streets, alone, forever, past the little brick houses with their little pocket yards of dead brown grass. As she walked she felt something shrivelling inside her, as she imagined herself year after year, walking this landscape alone, caught in it, yet always longing to be somewhere else. There was something oppressive about it, something that settled down over her shoulders and over her mind, down over everything. Those houses, and streets, those Donut Shops, those people dressed in black, the stares, the pocket yards, imagine, being here, living here forever ...

She called him on the phone, and sobbed, she was so lonely. And he was so far away, so distant. His voice remained distant. "Well, you made your choice." She saw him back in their apartment, with all the familiar books and plants saying this. "Well, you made your choice." He thought it was a choice, a choice that didn't take him into consideration at all, while for her it wasn't choice but necessity, survival. Good jobs were hard to come by, and bad jobs could ruin your life. But with no work, you didn't even exist, you were just nothing at all ...

On the way to the airport in the airport limousine they got caught in a gridlock on the 401. They simply sat in the midst of the greyness, the grey concrete and grey skies, the stunted leafless bushes hanging on so pathetically to life at the side of the road. (One of them was wrapped in burlap. Someone had crossed eight lanes of traffic to wrap a little bush in burlap.) They sat on the highway, bumper to bumper, some people talking on their car phones ("I'll be late for supper") and Geena was getting more and more anxious about missing her flight. All of them locked into this life by some sort of perverted sense of *necessity*. It seemed insane, it was insane, but there was no way out of it. She thought of her academic posturing, and the meagre wisdom of the age that the "best minds" had created as the world died around them ("when narrative authority is challenged then we can all participate in creating our own stories ... " the words flew up at her from the manuscript spread open on her lap.). All those individual stories, all those new texts, all merging together to create gridlock. Behind them a horn began to blow. Geena turned and saw a beefy, angry red face staring back at her, and for a long time afterwards she carried with her the sound of a horn bleating its message of frustration and rage into the evening sky.

Marriage

EVELYN LAU

HIS GOLD WEDDING BAND CATCHES THE LIGHT BETWEEN THE TWO WALLS OF FLESH that are our bodies in bed. It is a wide band with a perforated design, and it fits loosely on his finger. When he draws his hand up between us to touch me, the band seems to take on a separate entity — as though it is a stranger's hand encountered in a crowded bus on an empty alley, the ring as hard as a weapon. I feel the coldness of it branding my skin. Yet I am drawn to it compulsively, this symbol of his commitment to another, as though it is a private part of him that will derive pleasure from my touch: rubbing it, twisting it, pulling it up to his knuckle and back down again.

In the morning we go for a walk in Queen Elizabeth Park, where a wedding is taking place. There are photographers bent on one knee in the grass, children with flowers looped through their hair, a bride in her layers of misty white. We watch from a bridge over a creek nearby, and then from the top of a waterfall. From that height the members of the wedding appear toy-like, diminished by the vast green slopes, the over-flowing flower beds. When I glance sideways, I see him serenely observing the activity below, his hands draped over the low rail. I want then to step behind him, put my hands between his shoulders, and push him over, if only to recognize something in his face, some anxiety or pain to correspond with what I am feeling.

The people we pass in the park see a middle-aged man in a suit with his arm around a nineteen-year-old girl. They invariably pause, look twice with curiosity. At first I look back boldly, meeting their eyes in the harsh sunlight, but as the walk wears on my gaze falters. I keep my eyes trained on the ground, my pointy white high heels keeping step with his freshly

222

polished black leather shoes. I don't know what people are thinking; I know they don't think I am his daughter. Their stares make me feel unclean, as if there is something illicit about me. Suddenly I wonder if my skirt is too short, my lipstick too red, my hair too teased. I concentrate hard on pretending that there is something natural about my odd pairing with this man.

He is oblivious to their looks; if anything, he is pleased by them, as though people are looking because the girl his arm holds captive is particularly striking. He does not see that the looks are more often edged with pity than any degree of approval or jealousy.

He tells me afterwards that he is proud to be seen with me.

Sometimes when he visits me he is carrying his beeper. He has just completed the crawl to the foot of my bed, drawn up the comforter tent-like over his head and shoulders, and is preparing in the fuzzy dark to attack my body with his tongue. And then from deep in the grey huddle of his pants on the floor rises the berating call of the beeper, causing the anonymous bulk under the covers to jump and hit his head against the soft ceiling of the comforter. I resist the urge to reach out and rub that dome under my comforter, like it is a teddy bear or my own bunched-up knees.

Naked, he digs into the mass of material on the floor, extracts the beeper and seats himself on the edge of the bed. I tuck my hair behind my ear and examine his back as he dials a series of numbers to access his answering service, the hospital, other doctors.

"Good afternoon," he says. "Is this Dr. Martin? Yes ... yes ... how is she? All right, one milligram lorazepam to be administered at bedtime ... " while he remains half-erect between his long white thighs, one hand groping behind him 'til it finds and begins to squeeze my breast and then its nipple. Even though he has tucked the phone between his ear and shoulder so that the hand that flaps the air is not the one that wears the ring, I still feel it belongs to someone other than him as it rounds the blank canvas of his back and pats air and pillow before touching skin. I am reminded of the card in my desk drawer: On Valentine's Day four months ago he gave me a card that read, in a floral script, "I Love You." He said, almost immediately, "I hope you don't get vindictive and send that card to my wife. It's got my handwriting on it."

It never would have occurred to me to do so if he hadn't told me. What he said inspired me to keep the card in a special drawer, where I will not lose it. I put it away feeling reassured that at last I had some power over him. I had something I could hurt him with. I now know I saved the card because it was my only proof of his love for me, it is the only part of him that belongs to me.

The night before his wife's return from the conference she's attending in Los Angeles, we drive to our usual restaurant where the Japanese waiter smiles at us in a way he interprets as friendly, while I recognize amusement dancing at the corners of his mouth. I lift my purse into my lap and politely ask permission to smoke.

"I'd rather you didn't. My wife has a good nose for tobacco."

How much I want his wife to come home to the smell of smoke in the family car. After she has walked off the plane and through the terminal to where her luggage revolves on the carousel, after she has picked out his face among the faces of other husbands waiting to greet their wives and take them home, I can see her leaning back in the passenger seat, rubbing her neck, tired after her night and eager for sleep — then the trace of smoke acrid in her nostrils, mingled perhaps with my perfume. In my fantasy she turns to him, wild-eyed and tearful, she demands that he stop the car, she wrenches the perforated wedding band from her finger and throws it at him before she opens the door and leaves. Give it to that slut, she will say.

"Maybe I'm subconsciously trying to ruin your marriage," I smile as I light a cigarette and watch the smoke momentarily fill up the front of the car.

"Please don't," he says calmly. I think a man whose marriage is in my hands should sound a little more desperate, but in the dark I can only see his profile against the stores and buildings blurring outside the window, and it is unreadable. I wish afterwards that I had looked at his hands, to see if they tightened on the wheel.

He tells me that we will have lots of time together over the years but I have no concept of time. I ask him to leave the city with me.

"Would you really do that?" he asks. "Run off with me?"

"Yes."

"I'm very flattered."

"Don't be. It wasn't meant to be flattering." I pause. I want to say, It meant more than that. "Why can't we just take off?"

"I can't do it right now," he says. "I have people depending on me — my patients. I'd love to. I can't."

"I have just as much to lose as you do, you know," I say, but he doesn't believe me. He has been feeding me whisky all evening, and I am swaying in a chair in front of him. He places my hands together between his own and pulls me out of the chair, collapsing me to my knees. Kneeling, I sway back and forth and squint up at him, my hands stranded in his lap.

"You should go," I say.

"Yes, I have to work tomorrow morning."

"And you have to pick your wife up from the airport," I say, struggling to my feet to press the colour of my lips against his white cheek.

I do not realize I am clutching the sleeve of his suit jacket until we have reached the door, where he chuckles and pries my fingers loose. He adjusts his beeper inside his pocket and walks out into the rain-misted night.

Back inside the apartment I am intent on finishing the bottle of Chivas he left behind on the kitchen counter, but when I go to it I find an envelope next to the bottle, weighted by an ashtray. I tear it open, my heart beating painfully — it could be a letter, he could be saying that he can no longer live without me, that tonight he will finally tell his wife about us. Instead I pull out a greeting card with a picture on the front of a girl standing by a seashore. She is bare-legged, with dimpled knees, wearing a loose frock the colour of daffodils. She looks about twelve years old.

Inside are no words, just two new hundred-dollar bills.

He tries to alleviate his guilt by giving me money: cheques left folded on the kitchen table, crisp bills tucked inside cards. He takes me shopping for groceries and clothes, he never visits my apartment without bringing me some small gift, as though all this entitles him to leave afterwards and return home to his wife. But I have no similar method of striking such bargains with my conscience. The dregs of our affair stick to my body like semen. Because I do think of his wife — of the way she must sink into bed beside him in the dark, putting her face against his chest and breathing him in, his scent carried with her into her dreams. I do think of the pain she would feel if she knew, and I am frightened sometimes by the force of my desire to inflict that pain upon her — this wife who is to be pitied in her faithless marriage, this wife whom I envy.

And tonight I want more than anything to take those smooth brown bills between my fingers and tear them up. Does he think I'm like one of those teen hookers in thigh-high boots and bustiers he says he used to pick up downtown before he met me? My hands are shaking, I want so badly to get rid of his money. Instead I go over to the chest of drawers beside my bed and add this latest contribution to the growing stack of cards and cash I have hidden there.

He often says to me, "If you were my daughter ... " My lips twist and

he has to add each time, "You know what I mean." If things were different, he means. If we weren't sleeping together. We cultivate fantasies for
each other of what a loving, doting father he would have made me; of
what a pretty, accomplished daughter I would have made him. "I adore
you," he says to me. "I wish I could marry you." And then, "I wish you
were my daughter," as he kisses my neck, my shoulders, my breasts, his
fingers slipping between my thighs. As things are, I see we don't have
anything that comes close to the illusion.

His cologne has found places to lodge in my blankets, clothing, cushions.
No matter how many loads of laundry I carry down the back stairs, the
smell of him has taken up residence in the corners of my apartment, as
though to stay.

He tells me little about his activities, but the spare portraits he paints
grow vivid in my mind. This weekend he will visit Vancouver Island with
his family. I picture them on the ferry, with the possibility of grey skies
and rain, the mountains concealed by veils of fog, the treed islands rising
like the backs of beasts out of the ocean. I wonder if his family will
venture onto the deck and look down at the water; I imagine them falling
overboard and being ground to pieces by the propellers, staining those
foamy waves crimson.

He's told me about his three sons and I know they are all teenagers. I
know that the oldest is stronger than his father, handsome with a thick
head of red hair, and that this son's feisty girlfriend reminds him of me. I
know they tease him with the eyeball-rolling exasperation and embarrassment that I've felt towards my own parents.

"Oh, Dad," they'd groan in restaurants where he'd be teasing the waitress. "Don't do that. She's in our class at school!"

I imagine him clambering up the grey steel ladder leading to the top deck
of the ferry. He reaches down towards his wife. When she grips his hand
his ring bites into her palm, a sensation she has grown used to, as though
the ring is now a part of his body.

They walk together behind their children, past rows of orange plastic
chairs in the non-smoking section, past the cafeteria selling sticky danishes
and Styrofoam cups of hot coffee, past the gift shop with the little Canadian flags and sweatshirts in the window. They wrestle open the heavy
door leading onto the deck and the blast of air sucking them out sepa-
rates his hair into pieces plastering forward, backward, tight against his
cheek.

His family races in their sneakers and jeans towards the edges of the ferry, clinging to the railings, and he fights his way through the wind towards them, laughing and shouting. I know for certain that, for once, he is not thinking of me.

Heart Red Monaco

CHRISTIAN PETERSEN

HE YANKS THE NIGHT BACK AS IF IT WERE A RAGTOP. THE SPLINTERED WINDSHIELD is tinged with chlorine light, dawn of the third Sunday in July. We speed over the steel beam bridge, above the green current, through the river mist and mill steam. As the car growls up the hill south of town, stars are just fading in the rearview mirror, way back in the purple black west of the Nazko country.

Thomas whispers, "I'll sleep when I'm dead." He grins, half a cigarette gently clenched between ivory teeth. Then he squints his dark eyes at me and casually with his left hand rips the old car screeching off the highway, down through the scarred log arch entrance to the rodeo grounds. The Monaco crowhops in the dirt ruts, raising a flurry of dust. Muscled quarter horses stand tethered to aluminum trailers, curtains are drawn in the cowboys' campers and the pickup trucks wear wry chrome smiles. He cuts the headlights. We approach the warped backside of the wooden arena, and the corrals where the circuit bucking stock is held, the longhorn bulls and the broncs. There is an over-rich focus to this, angering chemical static in my blood, sporadic shooting flares of hyper green joy, then icy fear, joy, fear. In my jean jacket I slouch against the passenger door, shiver slightly, rub my knuckles in my eyes as the silent tires press over the turf. In draughts through the car vents come scents of trampled bluegrass, fresh-cut sawdust and horseshit. Thomas exhales spicy smoke of his Winstons. A sort of rinsed mind is what I feel, an awakening, and along with it the steady arousal that comes from any night spent on fast miss psilocybin.

Six feet from the corral fence the wide red car halts and the V8 idles quietly for just a few seconds. I watch his hand brush the steering column

228

and turn off the key. Silence rushes the windows. Thomas searches the floor and finds the J&B, the very last of it. No, I can't drink, can't keep up to you, crazy fool. He downs it himself, then drops the empty green bottle over his shoulder, thuds behind the seat. His anger suddenly fills the car interior and I have to get out, open the door, swing my boots in the grass. I stand and lean against the unfailing body of the car, slide myself forward, haul up and sit on the hood with my back against the windshield. The cooling engine ticks twice. The drugs are wearing off smoothly and the sky is now precious silver. Don't change, don't ever go away. After a time Thomas joins me there, our legs stretch out down the hood of the Monaco and the big light at the end of the rodeo arena makes our boots shine. His are made of lizard skin.

The animals are quiet inside the corral, a faint steam rises from their broad warm backs, the bulls have settled in deep sawdust nests and the broncs doze neck to neck. The horses are roughened and musky. Just one is wide awake, curious and stepping forward. He's a dark buckskin, with a black mane and tail, black legs and his thick neck arched attentively. Thomas lights another Winston, the quick flame startles the horse. He swings his head and mane, his muscles roll and the line of his strong flank deepens as he wheels away.

My father was a bush pilot. On the afternoon of October 12, 1979, he got caught in a freak snowstorm and crashed his floatplane while trying to set down on the Blackwater River. The accident made headlines, mostly because his two passengers happened to be the manager of one of our town's largest mills and the representative of a Japanese company looking to invest big money. All three were killed, and some people suggested that my father was at fault, for flying in bad weather.

At school that following winter I stuck to myself, spent lunch hours in the library and pretty much lost touch with the friends I'd had. My studies became an escape, I suppose, from the stupid sort of attention I got after the accident, and from different questions I didn't want to face. But never did I doubt my father's skill or judgement, I'd like to make that clear.

Quesnel was a small place. Rumours ran like stray dogs there, rarely worth much, but sometimes troublesome or mean. And for the rest of the time I spent in that town, the spring of my final year at school and the summer after graduation, it seemed that I lived with different rumours concerning myself. Perhaps we always do, and I was just becoming aware of this. Anyway, rumours first involved my father, as I've said, then my mother's seeing Harold Nelson, and finally they got to my own friendship with Thomas Ross.

The memories of Thomas are what I'm dealing with now — they are disordered and somewhat crazy, as we were then. But certain moments we shared, and words he said, have stayed with me. The time between then and right here seems only as long as one hard screaming all-night drive, though it has been more than fifteen years and I can't say anything about where Thomas Ross might be now.

There was another weird rumour going around that spring, which was that a volcano had erupted out west. Somewhere way off in the endless jackpine, not simply another fire, but an honest-to-god volcano. About forty miles out the Nazko road, someone said, past Puntchesacut. Apparently from there you could see the smoke. I imagined the cone rock lip, rising white ash, orange lava.

"Listen man," I said to Thomas, while chalking my pool cue, "you and me could be the first to actually see this thing. This is like a big chance." I placed my fingers on the green felt, slid the stick excitedly against the rail, and missed a straightforward shot at my last highball. Thomas then snapped the black eight in the side pocket and dropped his cue down on the table. He smirked, "Yeah right. Nothin' else to do, I guess."

We climbed into the Monaco, Thomas swung by the Billy Barker Hotel and I galloped into the bar to buy a case of beer. We were only eighteen, and getting away with that still seemed a terrific heist.

Thomas was not as keen as I was about looking for that volcano. Whatever that country offered he took for granted, even mention of white bears, wild mustangs or spirits that inhabited the canyons and springs of the Itcha mountains. None of that surprised him, and he seemed to know of stranger secrets. His mother was Carrier, and as a kid he had lived for a time out on a reserve. He knew that road. Top down, we blasted out of town and our music mixed with the wind. After a fast hour he pulled over onto the gravel shoulder, shut off the engine, stuck out his hand for another beer. He took off his mirror glasses and glanced up the steepness of the mountain. Then he gave me a look which said: This is going to be a real hike, and it better be worth it.

It was slow going because we were half-drunk and the smooth leather soles of our western boots slipped backwards on the fine speared grass that grew beneath the pines. Already the ground seemed unbelievably dry, yet the slope was shining with that wild grass, blue juniper and waxy, thorny Oregon grape. Thomas was a ways behind, crisscrossing up the slope with a beer in one hand and sidestepping the rocks so he didn't scuff his beloved lizard boots.

Up ahead, wisps of white smoke rose from a blackened crust of rock into the sharp blue sky.

"I see it!" I yelled back excitedly. His expression didn't change.

There were no splashes of lava, but there was a queer smell. My steps had slowed as I got closer; Thomas caught up and stood beside me as I peered over the lip.

He laughed, "You're right, this was some big chance, to see a cave full of smoking bat shit." He laughed harder then than I had seen him laugh before. And I laughed with him. He hurled his beer bottle into the cave. A second passed, then the echoed shatter came out like the cave's own guffaw.

My foolish attention had been so focused on the volcano that when I turned around the view nearly knocked me backward. Thomas turned and grew silent. Vast pine green country swept out before us, countless jagged valleys, and in the distance blue peaks that stretched away like a lifelong promise.

Thomas had a hard leaning to violence. He was as physical, as contained as a cougar, and usually he was that quiet. But you could never be certain what would set him off, and if something did, then he was dangerous. From the time he was sixteen no one in town had nerve to fight him. Whenever any guy got close to it, Thomas would stare at him and softly say, "D'you wanna bad time?" A teacher tried to guide him forcibly out of a grade ten gym class. Thomas dropped him on the floor. The man's collarbone broke and Thomas was expelled.

By then I knew him by reputation, but how we first met was like this. He lived in a house-trailer, in a dumpy sort of trailer court not far from the senior high school, and he sold dope. The trailer was owned by his uncle or someone who was never there. One lunch hour Jimmy Gillam took me along to this place to buy a quarter ounce of grass, and then, he suggested, we'd leave in a hurry. Thomas was unfriendly and stared at me when we went in the trailer. But we smoked a joint, and he and I got talking. Turned out we were both Bruins fans.

After a bit he looked right at me and said, "Your old man, he was in that plane crash?"

"That's right," I replied. A chill crept up my neck and I straightened in the chair. Jimmy was watching me closely and I knew he'd got a bit scared suddenly. What I felt was a mix of tested pride and readiness, because of my father. "He was the pilot," I said.

Quietly Thomas said, "Nobody coulda known that storm was comin'."

I watched my own hands on the table, traced the grain in the arborite with my little finger. Jimmy Gillam was nervous with the silence, and he kept checking his watch, then looking over at me. I paid him no attention.

Thomas started to roll another joint, and as he licked the paper his dark eyes held mine for just a moment. He said, "Jimmy, you're gonna be late for school." Jimmy Gillam picked up his baggie of dope, looked at me curiously when I made no movement, then he left the trailer.

Thomas lit the second smoke and passed it to me. Then he put a record on his stereo and took a bottle of Southern Comfort out of the cupboard. As he poured the liquor into coffee cups he said, "Least you know who your old man was; that's more than I do."

That first day was probably in March. I remember sunshine and wind, with silver ice still thick on the windows of the trailer. The only furniture I recall was the pool table, bought by his uncle from the hotel. The felt was ratty, wood finish gone, and we had to stick quarters in to get the pool balls back, but it was most of our entertainment. There was a small TV too, and I know the Bruins got to the quarter-finals that year, but I do not remember who won the cup.

It was around this same time that Harold Nelson began visiting my mother. He sold real estate and sat as alderman on the town council. Although I can see that situation somewhat differently now, at the time I did hold certain mean feelings for my mother, and I had no use for Harold Nelson. He bought a new car every two years, and he thought that was some big deal. And he seemed to think I needed guidance, which maybe my mother encouraged, I don't know. However they saw it, my view was different. It became simplest to avoid much time at my mother's house.

The last few months of high school I somehow lost the interest I'd had in my studies and began spending more time with Thomas. Often I left school at lunch hour and spent the afternoon at his trailer. The guys that came to buy dope were puzzled to see me. Supposedly I had been a real school boy, but there I was standing in the kitchen with a can of beer, while Thomas divvied up the skunk weed on the table and took their money. They were afraid of him. They saw the two of us as pretty different, which we were I guess, though it didn't always seem like it.

But magic mushrooms or LSD, for instance, were things I had not tried until I met Thomas. Two paper hits: extremely soon the trailer begins humming like a microwave — what day what time is it? Tuesday, 1:43, 44 p.m. — white clay sun — turquoise aluminum windowsills — rusted sink — creased cracked brown fake brick linoleum — 3:14, 15, 16 p.m. — please, let's sit on the April rain soft cedar steps — breathe the textured air — cartoon salamander eyelids — my palms sweat glass — wash my shaking fingers in the honeycomb snow in the shade of the decomposing trailer — see new subdivisions' gravel crossroads encroach on the muddy

Fraser — water flat and fierce — 5:35 p.m. see fear, flood, suffocation —
urgently Thomas says, "Hey it's okay man, this is the peak right now, you
can ride it out from here, just ride it out." — but I feel naked and strapped
to an alien velocity — crawl into the silent Monaco — curl up on the seat
like a child — stare fixated at the red vinyl dash and dials of the Dodge
Music Master — moocow coming down along the road — spring pink
sundown in the mirrors — ride it out ...

One afternoon, when I was not there, two patrol cars pulled up at the
trailer. According to Thomas the police were not polite. When he resisted
their search one of them winded him in the guts with the butt of a shotgun. But they did not find the marijuana, which was stashed in the Chee-
rios box sitting right on the counter.

Thomas and I really did not talk a whole lot, but when we did the topic
always seemed important — like different girls we knew or whether the
Monaco could make it to Cape Horn, the availability of Dodge parts in
South America, or the way to properly pass and catch a football. Thomas
could be stubborn. He would insist on teaching me things he figured I
should have known, how to catch a football, for instance, no matter what
I thought. And he could be funny too, though he did not often intend to
be. In a very straightforward way he sometimes asked questions which at
first made me laugh because they were impossible to answer, yet he
clearly expected a reply from me. As if I knew anything. As if I knew one
way or the other if there was a God, or what time really meant.

The old Texaco garage up from the BCR tracks had been converted into
the town's first nightclub, and we often ended up there on a Saturday
after midnight, because we had nowhere else to go. Music hammered
against the glossy painted walls and coloured lights flickered at the edge
of the dance floor. We tended to kick off with tequila, to try and get in the
mood, and then drank a mean succession of beers. Always we grabbed a
corner table, out of the way, but Thomas still drew a strange amount of
attention. People were wary of him, his cutting eyes like wet chips of
shale, his sullenness and occasional violence. Yet they seemed impelled
toward him too. Led by nervousness, they would show up at the table.
The guys wanted to talk about hockey, or bush work or buying dope,
anything just to talk with him it seemed. Girls would come and ask him to
dance, which was not a customary sort of thing in that town. It was
certain that none of this impressed Thomas.

Sitting there, across from him, I could sometimes feel invisible. And I enjoyed this because it allowed me to look at people more freely, to study them a bit, especially how they responded to the charged quality in Thomas. For their part, they only seemed to wonder why I now was his friend.

As the snow melted and mild breezes carried into the nights, on any weekend there was commonly a party on the outskirts of town. It was often at the stockcar track. Or it happened in a field or a gravel pit where the cops were not likely to appear. Someone would have stereo speakers set out on the roof of their pickup and the volume cranked full. One or two roaring bonfires formed the centre of the gathering and there might be hundreds of people. Drunken faces ringed the fire. Bottles were hurled into the flames where they whined, hissed and exploded. There were always fights going on. It was at these parties, well before I knew him, that Thomas made his name. Rumbling vehicles came and went, with just their parklights peering through the dust. Now and then somebody passed out in the grass and got run over. Once a young girl was crippled this way, but I don't recall that anyone was ever killed.

One green evening in June we sat on the steps outside the trailer, looking across the new town development to the bank of the Fraser and its muddy highwater. The sun just hung around. We'd been stoned and drinking half the day and now faced another aggravated night in town. It was bronze light in the whorls of the river current that made Thomas think of the hotsprings, and he decided we should drive out there. So we yanked the top down and cruised by The Billy for a case of beer.

Jumping into that car always gave me the great sense of doing something. This was partly, I believe, because at that point in my life I really did not know where I was going. But once in the heart red Monaco any direction we headed seemed all right. Plus, with a tailwind that old beast could do a hundred and ten miles an hour.

The hotsprings were a fair distance southwest of town, and the rough road slowed us down, so by the time we arrived, though the air remained warm, the sky was dark. We were not too happy to see the light of a campfire. A new four-wheel-drive was parked in the trees and two couples sat by the fire. They did not leap up to greet us either.

We were bent out of shape, of course, but still eager to be soaking in that sulphury hot water. Weaving around, we managed to tug off our boots and strip and tiptoe grinning into the steamy pool. I had not been out there before, or to any springs, and it was wild to lie back drunk in warm bubbling water and watch the first stars revealed above the jackpines.

The water filtered up between the bed stones, and rippled against the pads of my feet. As the current reached the surface it became visible, faintly traced with silver light. On my tongue the taste was like warm coins and I took a sip of beer.

Wanting a cigarette, Thomas turned his shoulders, looking for his shirt which lay just out of reach. He leaned out of the water and stretched his arm toward his Winstons. The sight of his wet body startled me. I had not seen him naked before, not close like that, and I had not really imagined it — though physically, as I've said, he always made himself felt. Now in one breath I was more conscious of myself, my own body. First came a panic that nearly made me shake. Suddenly those rumours were whispering again, bitterly in my mind — maybe others had seen something all along that I had just not figured out, or had the guts to face? But right away an even stranger rush of faith pushed this aside, as if my fear were unimportant. Thomas' body was chiselled and corded with muscle, extended only for a moment while these things passed through my head. Then he settled back in the water holding the lit cigarette in one raised hand. I was staring up at the stars, aware of him watching me now, as if he might have read my senses. Our hair was curly damp and our faces had begun to sweat.

Before long we were too hot and both pulled ourselves out onto the smooth stony bank to cool, leaving just our lower legs submerged. I still felt his gaze. Finally he said, "D'you know, I got a question for you ... "

Then, right before he asked whatever it was, a woman appeared silently between us at the edge of the spring. It occurred to me that I might be hallucinating, but I shifted forward about to duck into the water when Thomas stopped me with a taunting jab of his dark eyes.

The woman was somewhat older than we were. She waited half a moment, almost as if to get a power over us, which she did. She said something, I don't remember what she said. Then she dropped her hiker's shorts, pulled her tee shirt over her head, and, murmuring softly, she lowered her body into the pool. Her breasts swayed and shadows caressed the curve of her belly and thighs. I was breathing through my mouth, and could feel the pulse at the back of my knees against the smooth wet rock. She had long coppery hair which she held up with one hand at first. Then she snugged her neck against the stone rim of the pool and there could keep it dry. In the heat her lips expressed a deep-lung sigh. Her white arms circled gently through the water. They folded under, lifting her breasts while the water lapped between and into the hollow of her throat. She moved beneath the water, her leg pressed to my own, and within me came a sudden fierce stir.

A breeze parted the steam rising from the spring, and with it drifted

the spicy pitch smoke of the fire at the edge of my vision. Light scamp-
ered like spirits bent on mischief in the pines. Thomas was leaning toward the woman with his weight on one rigid arm, and a perfectly calm
smile on his face. He looked strong, but not at all threatening at that
moment. The woman arched her back, so that for a moment my eyes
touched her breasts, then fastened on the stem of her throat. She was
smiling too. Gradually I caught my breath and then I tried to smile — it
appeared to be the thing to do. All my nerves were keen and focused,
and briefly it seemed that I had a grasp of some mystery, but then of
course she slipped away.

"Barbara? Barbara?!" A man's loud voice, angry and very drunk, in-
truded on the night. Thomas turned his head, I saw the violent glint in his
eye and I thought — oh Jesus.

The woman in the water had a look on her face that seemed uncertain. Moments passed. And they passed too slowly for me now, because
the thought of her husband confronting Thomas had me frightened. We
were out in the middle of nowhere. Finally she stood. We were watching
her closely. Her skin had flushed with heat. The water on her body ran
with starlight. And no trouble did occur, thanks to Barbara, who had the
sense to put her clothes back on and return to her husband. She left us
her smile.

Dawn of the third Sunday in July — Thomas lights another Winston, the
quick flame startles the horse. He swings his head and mane, his muscles
roll and the line of his strong flank deepens as he wheels away.

I shift my back, still reclined against the windshield. Thomas turns his
head, toward me but not far enough to meet my eyes. The edge has gone
from his mood, or the anger has been replaced by another feeling that at
first I can't recognize, not coming from Thomas. His profile is highlit by
the big light at the end of the rodeo arena.

He asks, "D'you ever wonder what's gonna happen later, like, from
now on?" Then he looks right at me, and I nod yes. It is fear. He too is
frightened. He says, slowly, "D'you know, what's gonna happen?"

He keeps looking at me, and all at once seems so much like a young
brother, also without a father, almost innocent — not a tough guy, and
sure not a guy with much idea of a future. I want to touch his hair, put my
hand on his shoulder, but I won't. More than that I want to tell him that
whatever happens it might be okay, the future, but I can't do that either.
I look down at my fingers splayed against the warm red metal hood of
the Monaco.

"No," I say. "I don't."

Thomas stares out at the horses. That buckskin bronc is frisking around with the first rays of light, twisting its meaty neck, glaring at us, but most of the bunch are still dozing. Thomas says, "Fuck it anyway."

Then after a moment his face flashes with a grin, a devilish sort of look. He says, "Hey man, I got an idea." He hops off the hood of the car, swings over the rails of the fence, and walks in his shiny lizard boots in the soft sand and sawdust inside the corral. Just like a fool he goes over and opens the gate. And then starts walking right at that crazy buckskin and waves his arms. Horse bolts and kicks. He walks around behind the bunch clapping his hands. "Gdyap!" And he chuckles.

He moves with a sort of strut, but grace as well. And for all his cowboy boots and jeans and Bruins hockey sweater he looks like some damn Comanche in an old western movie, running off the cavalry's mounts. I laugh aloud. Then I whoop, jump the fence and join in the chase. We run those knot-headed horses helter skelter through the gate. They throw their heels, they whinny and snort, and their hooves pound as they gallop over packed dirt of the parking area.

"Heeyeeeeeah! Heee! HEEYEEOOOAHEE!!" Thomas shrieks and howls, while I laugh with each stride, I stumble and reel from laughing, and it seems my laughter bucks along with the freed horses.

Cowboys and women step out in their underwear from the doorways of the campers. Their legs are much whiter than their arms, and their hair is all askew. They express an irritable wonder at what the hell is going on.

Now Thomas and I are hightailing it for the car.

Say the Word

JEAN RYSSTAD

THE BOY IS TWELVE AND TALLER THAN FRAN BY SEVERAL INCHES NOW. SHE HAS NOT seen much of him this summer since he is trolling with his uncle, away ten days at a time, in town for a day or two, then out, away again. Even when he is home, Fran hardly sees him because he sleeps until the phone rings or until one of the neighbourhood boys hollers up at his open bedroom window. Then he is in the bathroom, at the fridge, and before she can speak with him, out the door, skateboard under his arm.

He used to walk but now, just this summer, he has begun to glide. He is finding a stride that is a little like his father's way of navigating the world but not so sure or sturdy. The way the boy moves down the hall or down the road toward his friends is lighter than the way Joe walks. He seems to float as if he is several inches above the ground, and Fran wonders if time on the water has given him this ability.

The boy has just called from the fishing grounds and though they have said goodbye and hung up, Fran feels as if they are still connected — it's just a time of dead air, each waiting for the other to say something that might make a difference.

How are you, Fran asked him.

Good, he said, but his voice wasn't hearty.

Where are you. Yes, at Zayus, where the blackflies are not so bad as they are at Dundas, but where on the boat, where are you now? Below? In your bunk?

I'm in the wheelhouse. Where the phone is.

She'd heard a hint of sarcasm, a hint of what would come with his changing voice.

And where is Uncle Ronnie?

He's icing fish in the hold.

And was fishing good today?

I'm not going to make as much money as last trip. We're getting lots of humpies.

What else to ask him? What piece of news would give him pleasure, something to mull over?

You got a skateboard catalogue in the mail today.

What's on the cover?

Oh, Jer, she'd said, I don't know if I can find it in this mess. We're still sanding the floors, you know. We're upside down.

Will you try, he'd asked.

Okay. Hold on, she'd said, rummaging through a pile of papers on the table. Jackpot, Jer. You're lucky. It's a dark blue, a nighttime sky and there's tall white buildings, like towers or highrises, and a big steep ramp.

You mean a half-pipe?

I don't know what it is. It's this big curved thing that's joined up to the buildings and there's a boy hanging in the air on his skateboard. He's just come off the ramp and the photographer took a picture of him hanging there in the sky.

What's on the second page?

She'd laughed, flipped the page, and told him a little about the advertising for "completes," tops, trucks, wheels and bearings and then said maybe they'd talked enough for one night. It was good Uncle Ronnie bought that new phone that reached from the grounds to home, wasn't it? Was there anything else he wanted to say?

Will you put the catalogue on my bed?

That's it? That's all? She'd encouraged him to say a little more. After all, they had privacy. Not like on a radiophone where every word you said crackled in the galleys of all the boats on the grounds.

Well, there's *something* else.

And what is that?

I'm afraid I'm going to drown. I'm afraid I'm not going to come home from this trip.

And Fran had said, Of course you will. Do you think we'd let you go fishing if we were even a little bit worried about you? But at the same time she saw the wall at the waterfront park, built with bricks, hundreds of bricks bearing the names of those who were lost at sea, life spans both long and short. Fran wishes Joe had been home. His words might make a difference. What he'd say might help the boy get through it.

Fran stood inside the doorway of the boy's room, looking at the things that represented his spirit at twelve. He collected far less junk than any of them, discarded his past passions and dreams easily and often. Ninja Turtles and that pair of nunchucks he'd ordered from the back of a comic for $19.95, U.S. dollars: Two heavy-duty plastic sticks attached with a chain arrived in a cardboard tube. A weapon. Where would he swing those sticks? At whom? Did they work like a boomerang? Did you swing them and let go? The boy had looked surprised. Enemies? Robbers, maybe. Killers.

Pirate ship and space station Lego sets were long gone. Now his walls were plastered with posters of Pavel and Linden but these were tattered and droopy because the pins and staples had fallen out. They were ready for the garbage. She knew what posters came next: Smashing Pumpkins, Kurt Cobain, Hendrix, Rage Against the Machine.

She got clean sheets, made his bed and flapped the quilt his gran had made for him from old wool coats that had belonged to the men in the family. She watched the quilt float down and settle, smoothed out the wrinkles and sat down facing his CD player. Last summer's fishing had bought it. This icon. The machine and the neatly piled discs held his deepest self, his hopes, fears, dreams. The machine, the music, the shelf: an altar.

Above the CD shelf, he'd hung an 8x10 picture of himself in a deep blue hand-knit sweater and leggings set. The photograph had been taken in Woolworth's on his first birthday. Fran had carried him part-way through the store and then set him down, held his hand while he took head-first topple-over steps. What a beautiful boy, the grandmothers in the store had said that December day. What a beautiful boy.

Beside the portrait was a newspaper clipping of his gran and grampa taken fifty years ago on their wedding day, their heads touching, tilted in toward each other, their eyes startling in their shiny innocence. These three faces had held their places throughout the boy's changes, but this year, Fran thought, he'll take them down from the wall and put them in a shoebox. Of course he has to do this.

Fran reached behind her and turned out the light. The glow-in-the-dark stars on the boy's ceiling were dim from where she sat and she wondered if they shone brighter when Jer lay down, thinking of the faraway future, or if they shone bright just for the next day and were faint and misty, ghostly even, when he thought of the years ahead. Did he imagine what it would be like if she died, if his father died, where he would go, what he would do? She lay down on the single bed with the skateboard magazine across her breasts.

By now he would be in his narrow upper bunk, inside his blue sleeping bag. He would have warmed his hands on the engine pipes after some last chore on deck. He'd have brushed his teeth in the tiny sink, gotten rid of the taste of diesel fuel for a moment, then turned out the light, crawled up, opened the tiny porthole and cranked his neck around so he could see the black water and the dark grey rainy skies. No stars, no dipper, no moon.

And what would he think? Would he take his mind directly to the skateboard catalogue, remember that she'd promised to put it on his bed, or would he have to take the long way to that thought, first listening to the waves elapsing like slow seconds on the sides of the wooden boat, then thinking of falling over the side, how it might happen to him the way it had happened to others. He would try not to think about the men floating in the water with their zippers open, but these dead men would knock and bump and nudge the sides of the boat. He would spend some time hating his dad for telling him about it, for making him show him how he could plant his feet solid, two feet apart, one a little ahead, think about how he hated being given a push, a playful but hard and sudden push which toppled him and proved that he wasn't planted, didn't have his feet or his mind solid or determined, didn't have sea legs yet.

And boots. New yellow and black Helly Hansons, size eleven, the same size as his dad's and his uncle's. Last year just regular gumboots from the back of Zellers, $15.99, and now these new ones, $60 off his crew share. Buying them with his uncle in Fisherman's Supply. He's getting in deeper and deeper. And he never asked for it, except he did ask if he could fish again this summer. For the money. Now he has his own rain gear and six pairs of black gloves and a scar from when one of the hooks flew through the flesh below his thumb. Six pinpoint needle marks from the barbs on a cod. How weird and numb his whole arm went. He would think about crab bait, fish heads, his head, and then about his hand with the two big warts that won't go away even though the doctor dropped stuff on them twice this summer.

His father and uncle had made him practise kicking his boots off. Faster, they yelled at him. See how fast you can get them off. You gotta kick hard. And even a survival suit now. For him. Uncle Ron said it was for the boat, but then why did he have to try it on in his living room. Lay it out like it's your shadow and get in as fast as you can, his dad said.

The fisherman who drowned just before they'd left on this trip. He fell off the dock, slipped or something coming down the ramp, boards greasy with rain and oil, and fell into the harbour right beside his own boat and no one was there to help him.

What would it be to lose him? Fran panicked, feeling as though she had fallen in herself. She kicked away from those thoughts. Did she think she could travel with the boy all his life, be his life ring? No. But she imagined she could go a long distance with him, maybe all her life, all of his, if she just floated. His dreamy way invited this kind of quiet companionship, knowing, didn't it?

This boy. He didn't use words. It wasn't his way. When he was nine, they'd been doing dishes together. He was washing. The radio was tuned into the local pop station, low, part of the air. And the air between them was easy as it mysteriously always has been — a live and let live. Lots of space and air, a sink full of water and suds. The boy liked the dishes to be clean. He didn't hurry. And she didn't say c'mon c'mon, speed it up, get the job done. He had pushed his hand and the dish cloth into a glass and let it fill up with water. After a bit of turning and swishing he'd held the glass up for her. His fist was crammed against the side and his thumb and finger made a kind of sad dreamy smile.

This is how I'd look if I drowned, he said.

He'd been swimming in the town pool earlier that week, he told her. The words came slowly. She'd pumped and pressed them out of him, a few at a time, as they carried on washing and drying. Shane, that bully, had held him under in the deep end. Jer dried his hands, pulled the neck of his tee shirt down onto his shoulder, and she saw the bruises on his back, his collarbone, faint blue fingerprints. She loathed that boy Shane, but kept drying and setting the dishes in the cupboard. He had struggled but Shane had held him down harder so he stopped fighting and waited.

After that watery revelation, she and Joe began to preach. You've got to get mad. Say no. Say to yourself: I will not sink. I will not go under. This will not happen to me. Find that place in your head, Fran had said. No, said Joe, find that place in your body.

Had any of these words sunk into his skin? Or did they drift through him, in one ear and out the other?

Words. He doesn't use them but Fran has noticed how the boy is drawn and held by the way she and his sister talk sometimes, as if he is warming his hands at a fire. He comes in close but he rarely adds wood. Perhaps he knows that the beach has been combed and that there is enough on the fire to keep it burning without his help. This thought makes Fran sad. How can you survive without words to keep you warm when you are shivering with cold after falling in? Still, lately, when the four of them gathered by chance at the kitchen table, a girl and a boy, a man and a woman, they'd built some rip-roaring fires and the laughter had leapt like cinders between them.

Before the boy left on this trip, there'd been a flare-up between Joe and Julie, some normal thing like Julie used all the hot water when Joe needed to have a shower too. Normal and then escalated, Julie storming upstairs to her room and Joe retreating to his basement quarters. That left Fran and Jer on the middle deck. Jer headed for the television in the front room and Fran turned on the radio in the kitchen and began to wash dishes. Vicki Gabereau was live on the Fraser River, rushing down through white water. Her squeals of fear and exhilaration rose and fell in Fran. She dried her hands on the tea towel and went to check on Jer. He was lying on the couch watching *Dumb and Dumber*, hands cupped behind his head. He paused the movie with the remote.

Do you feel sad or anything, he'd asked.

No, she'd said. And they had gazed at each other, amused, amazed. They had floated through the storm untouched, dry as a bone.

Yes, what she knows of him so far is his calm floating soul. If you don't tell me things, she'd said to him recently, I just think, Oh, Jer — his life is perfect. He'd looked at her as if she were insane. Not long ago, when the four of them were together at breakfast, Jer said he'd had a dream about falling down a deep hole and the more he tried to climb out the deeper the hole grew. And then somebody mentioned a jogger, how his wife had said he ran in his sleep and the sheets and blankets got all whipped up. Joe had talked of flying. How joyous to look at the stick-on stars and think of him soaring over Grassy Lake, flying high and tilting down into the cove where Duffy has set up his bachelor camp, watchman at the dam. Fran soared too, circled. She saw two teenage boys, a case of beer, a canoe, a moon. The boys were laughing and then the canoe, the canoe tipped and the boys struggled in the icy water, laughing at first and grasping for the boat. Laughing and then gasping, unable to believe what was happening.

This country has become treacherous now, Fran thought. Before kids, she'd decided that to think too much about what might happen would be to invite disaster. If your number was up, it was up. Still, on the seaplanes crossing the Hecate Straits in storms, she'd made deals with God. I'll do this if you will do this. The engine stalled on a plane Joe was on. He didn't mention any deals. He said he put his duffel bag in front of his face and chest, thinking it might cushion the blow when it came.

And the Skeena River. Every year, sometimes twice a year, someone, sometimes families, slid in. Old cars, brand new cars, four-wheel-drive all-terrainers, logging trucks. And lives, swallowed whole by this huge grey whale. If it wasn't the river side of the highway, it was the mountains that slid down once a year, twice a year, caving in on travellers whether they were making business deals or going to a hockey tournament with all intentions of bringing home a trophy for the town.

Now any story of survival, of how people kept their wits about them, seems important to repeat, to discuss.

Last year at the end of the summer, two boys had left their village in a canoe. They packed for an overnight adventure, intending to paddle to the far side of an island and set up camp. Their canoe tipped in the breakers as they approached what they thought was the spot they wanted and though they made it to shore, they weren't found for three days. Their grandfather, who was aboard the rescue boat, told the crew where the boys would be and there they were, wet, cold and hungry. "You went the wrong way," the grandfather said. "Well, why didn't you tell us?" the boys said. "You watched us leave. You heard us planning. Why didn't you tell us?"

"You didn't ask," said the grampa.

Fran keeps remembering this story and telling it to her kids. Now after what happened to them, the boys will ask, she says. *Wanting* to know is so much better than being *told* what you should know, she says to them. But she wonders: How did the grandfather keep his mouth shut? Where did he find his trust? How could he risk so much?

Fran wonders if Jeremy remembers the fire lesson, the day they went out for blueberries, filling an ice cream bucket along the tracks, and then climbing higher onto the rock bluffs above the harbour, scrambling on those cliffs. They found a sheltered place to rest, and the kids had said, Let's make a fire. Okay, said Joe. But you only have one match. Pretend you are lost and you only have one match. How would you make the best of your one chance? The kids had the right instinct —they'd gathered small twigs and propped them up like a teepee — but the match didn't catch. Look under the trees, go into the bush a little, look for the driest finest smallest burnable things. Dry brown needles, anything like that. The wind off the water was really cold when the sun disappeared. Did Jer remember that time on the bluff? Would he remember it if he needed it?

What would it be to lose him? Could she hold on to the story, the making lost into found, that the singer for the Haida dancers had explained before the dancers danced the story in their red and black, this life and that other one? How all the village mourned as they searched for a little lost girl, how in spring they saw the first salmon jump in the creek, joyful, and they knew it was their little girl, come back to them. She had heard parents say that after a while, after the passing of several seasons, they saw their lost children appear in spring, not in a fish, perhaps, but in a flower, the first purple crocus raising its head through the snow.

Every mother and father goes to the place in them where the child is lost. If they do not imagine it, fall into it through events around them, through a neighbour, a friend, a relative, then it happens through the news, the falling into that empty unimaginable pit. And if they refuse to fall in waking life, then the descent comes in dream. The child about to fall from a cliff, drown in the lake, be murdered by ... and the hopeless grasping, stretching out to reach the hand of the child, kicking, swimming toward him, never getting there, the sheets and blankets churning. Nobody speaks of these dream deaths. Fran has never told hers to anyone but Joe, and even then, she left out details and went straight for the interpretation — "worry," a need making itself known through dream to make sure the boy, the girl, had survival skills.

The boy will come home. What is happening to him now is natural and good and at twelve he must walk through it on his own. He has to learn to manage fear—waking and sleeping — to fear in dreams and wake from them, to fear before sleep, and in all the long days on the water. He needs to remember and invent survival, to imagine himself as eagle, otter, boy in a canoe paddling to an island for a weekend adventure.

She can't do anything but wave goodbye, go with him in spirit. He will walk through it, glide through the door as he has done at the end of every trip this summer. She knows he can and will. He must. She rises, smooths the bed and lays the magazine on his pillow.

That new boat phone. The cellular. Did it help or hinder the walking through?

Did you tell Uncle Ron you were afraid of drowning? she'd asked.

Yes, he said. I have a whistle around my neck.

Out on Main Street

SHANI MOOTOO

JANET AND ME? WE DOES GO MAIN STREET TO SEE PRETTY PRETTY SARI AND BANGLE, and to eat we belly full a burfi and gulub jamoon, but we doh go too often because, yuh see, is dem sweets self what does give people like we a presupposition for untameable hip and thigh.

Another reason we shy to frequent dere is dat we is watered-down Indians — we ain't good grade A Indians. We skin brown, is true, but we doh even think 'bout India unless something happen over dere and it come on de news. Mih family remain Hindu ever since mih ancestors leave India behind, but nowadays dey doh believe in praying unless things real bad, because, as mih father always singing, like if is a mantra: "Do good and good will be bestowed unto you." So he is a veritable saint cause he always doing good by his women friends and dey chilren. I sure some a dem must be mih half sister and brother, oui!

Mostly, back home, we is kitchen Indians: some kind a Indian food every day, at least once a day, but we doh get cardamom and other fancy spice down dere so de food not spicy like Indian food I eat in restaurants up here. But it have one thing we doh make joke 'bout down dere: we like we meethai and sweetrice too much, and it remain overly authentic, like de day Naana and Naani step off de boat in Port of Spain harbour over a hundred and sixty years ago. Check out dese hips here nah, dey is pure sugar and condensed milk, pure sweetness!

But Janet family different. In de ole days when Canadian missionaries land in Trinidad dey used to make a bee-line straight for Indians from down South. And Janet great grandparents is one a de first South families dat exchange over from Indian to Presbyterian. Dat was a long time ago.

When Janet born, she father, one Mr. John Mahase, insist on asking de

Reverend MacDougal from Trace Settlement Church, a leftover from de Canadian Mission, to name de baby girl. De good Reverend choose de name Constance cause dat was his mother name. But de mother a de child, Mrs. Savitri Mahase, wanted to name de child sheself. Ever since Savitri was a lil girl she like de yellow hair, fair skin and pretty pretty clothes Janet and John used to wear in de primary school reader — since she lil she want to change she name from Savitiri to Janet but she own father get vex and say how Savitri was his mother name and how she will insult his mother if she gone and change it. So Savitri get she own way once by marrying this fella name John, and she do a encore, by calling she daughter Janet, even doh husband John upset for days at she for insulting de good Reverend by throwing out de name a de Reverend mother.

So dat is how my girlfriend, a darkskin Indian girl with thick black hair (pretty fuh so!) get a name like Janet.

She come from a long line a Presbyterian school teacher, headmaster and headmistress. Savitri still teaching from de same Janet and John reader in a primary school in San Fernando, and John, getting more and more obtuse in his ole age, is headmaster more dan twenty years now in Princes Town Boys' Presbyterian High School. Everybody back home know dat family good good. Dat is why Janet leave in two twos. Soon as A Level finish she pack up and take off like a jet plane so she could live without people only shoo-shooing behind she back ... "But A A! Yuh ain't hear de goods 'bout John Mahase daughter, gyul! How yuh mean yuh ain't hear? Is a big thing! Everybody talking 'bout she. Hear dis, nah! Yuh ever see she wear a dress? Yes! Doh look at mih so. Yuh reading mih right!"

Is only recentish I realize Mahase is a Hindu last name. In de ole days every Mahase in de country turn Presbyterian and now de name doh have no association with Hindu or Indian whatsoever. I used to think of it as a Presbyterian Church name until some days ago when we meet a Hindu fella fresh from India name Yogdesh Mahase who never even hear of Presbyterian.

De other day I ask Janet what she know 'bout Divali. She say, "It's the Hindu festival of lights, isn't it?" like a line straight out a dictionary. Yuh think she know anything 'bout how lord Rama get himself exile in a forest for fourteen years, and how when it come time for him to go back home his followers light up a pathway to help him make his way out, and dat is what Divali lights is all about? All Janet know is 'bout going for drive in de country to see light, and she could remember looking forward, around Divali time, to the lil brown paper-bag packages full a burfi and parasad that she father Hindu students used to bring for him.

One time in a Indian restaurant she ask for parasad for dessert. Well!

Since den I never go back in dat restaurant, I embarrass fuh so!

I used to think I was a Hindu *par excellence* until I come up here and see real flesh and blood Indian from India. Up here, I learning 'bout all kind a custom and food and music and clothes dat we never see or hear 'bout in good ole Trinidad. Is de next best thing to going to India, in truth, oui! But Indian store clerk on Main Street doh have no patience with us, specially when we talking English to dem. Yuh ask dem a question in English and dey insist on giving de answer in Hindi or Punjabi or Urdu or Gujarati. How I suppose to know de difference even! And den dey look at yuh disdainful disdainful — like yuh disloyal, like yuh is a traitor.

But yuh know, it have one other reason I real reluctant to go Main Street. Yuh see, Janet pretty fuh so! And I doh like de way men does look at she, as if because she wearing jeans and tee shirt and high-heel shoe and makeup and have long hair loose and flying about like she is a walking-talking shampoo ad, dat she easy. And de women always looking at she beady eye, like she loose and going to thief dey man. Dat kind a thing always make me want to put mih arm round she waist like, she is my woman, take yuh eyes off she! and shock de false teeth right out dey mouth. And den is a whole other story when dey see me with mih crew cut and mih blue jeans tuck inside mih jim-boots. Walking next to Janet, who so femme dat she redundant, tend to make me look like a gender dey forget to classify. Before going Main Street I does parade in front de mirror practising a jiggly-wiggly kind a walk. But if I ain't walking like a strong-man monkey I doh exactly feel right and I always revert back to mih true colours. De men dem does look at me like if dey is exactly what I need a taste of to cure me good and proper. I could see dey eyes watching Janet and me, dey face growing dark as dey imagining all kind a situation and position. And de women dem embarrass fuh so to watch me in mih eye, like dey fraid I will jump up and try to kiss dem, or make pass at dem. Yuh know, sometimes I wonder if I ain't mad enough to do it just for a little bacchanal, nah!

Going for a outing with mih Janet on Main street ain't easy! If only it wasn't for burfi and gulub jamoon! If only I had a learned how to cook dem kind a thing before I leave home and come up here to live!

2

In large deep-orange Sanskrit-style letters, de sign on de saffron-colour awning above de door read "Kush Valley Sweets." Underneath in smaller red letters it had "Desserts Fit For The Gods." It was a corner building.

The front and side was one big glass wall. Inside was big. Big like a gymnasium. Yuh could see in through de brown tint windows: dark brown plastic chair, and brown table, each one de length of a door, line up stiff and straight in row after row like if is a school room.

Before entering de restaurant I ask Janet to wait one minute outside with me while I rumfle up mih memory, pulling out all de sweet names I know from home, besides burfi and gulub jamoon: meethai, jilebi, sweetrice (but dey call dat kheer up here), and ladhoo. By now, of course, mih mouth watering fuh so! When I feel confident enough dat I wouldn't make a fool a mih Brown self by asking what dis one name? and what dat one name? we went in de restaurant. In two twos all de spice in de place take a flying leap in our direction and give us one big welcome hug up, tight fuh so! Since den dey take up permanent residence in de jacket I wear dat day!

Mostly it had women customers sitting at de tables, chatting and laughing, eating sweets and sipping masala tea. De only men in de place was de waiters, and all six waiters was men. I figure dat dey was brothers, not too hard to conclude, because all a dem had de same full round chin, round as if de chin stretch tight over a ping-pong ball, and dey had de same big roving eyes. I know better dan to think dey was mere waiters in de employ of a owner who chook up in a office in de back. I sure dat dat was dey own family business, dey stomach proudly preceeding dem and dey shoulders throw back in de confidence of dey ownership.

It ain't dat I paranoid, yuh understand, but from de moment we enter de fellas dem get over-animated, even armorously agitated. Janet again! All six pair a eyes land up on she, following she every move and body part. Dat in itself is something dat does madden me, oui! but also a kind a irrational envy have a tendency to manifest in me. It was like I didn't exist. Sometimes it could be a real problem going out with a good-looker, yes! While I ain't remotely interested in having a squeak of a flirtation with a man, it doh hurt a ego to have a man notice yuh once in a very long while. But with Janet at mih side, I doh have de chance of a penny shave-ice in de hot sun. I tuck mih elbows in as close to mih sides as I could so I wouldn't look like a strong man next to she, and over to de l-o-n-g glass case jam up with sweets I jiggle and wiggle in mih best imitation a some a dem gay fellas dat I see downtown Vancouver, de ones who more femme dan even Janet. I tell she not to pay de brothers no attention, because if any a dem flirt with she I could start a fight right dere and den. And I didn't feel to mess up mih crew cut in a fight.

De case had sweets in every nuance of colour in a rainbow. Sweets I never before see and doh know de names of. But dat was alright because I wasn't going to order dose ones anyway.

Since before we leave home Janet have she mind set on a nice thick syrupy curl a jilebi and a piece a plain burfi so I order dose for she and den I ask de waiter-fella, resplendent with thick thick bright-yellow gold chain and ID bracelet, for a stick a meethai for mihself. I stand up waiting by de glass case for it but de waiter/owner lean up on de back wall behind de counter watching me like he ain't hear me. So I say loud enough for him, and every body else in de room to hear, "I would like to have one piece a meethai please," and den he smile and lift up his hands, palms open-out motioning across de vast expanse a glass case, and he say, "Your choice! Whichever you want, Miss." But he still lean up against de back wall grinning. So I stick mih head out and up like a turtle and say louder, and slowly, "One piece a meethai — dis one!" and I point sharp to de stick a flour mix with ghee, deep fry and den roll up in sugar. He say, "That is koorma, Miss. One piece only?"

Mih voice drop low all by itself. "Oh ho! Yes, one piece. Where I come from we does call dat meethai." And den I add, but only loud enough for Janet to hear, "And mih name ain't 'Miss.'"

He open his palms out and indicate de entire panorama a sweets and he say, "These are all meethai, Miss. Meethai is Sweets. Where are you from?"

I ignore his question and to show him I undaunted, I point to a round pink ball and say, "I'll have one a dese sugarcakes too please." He start grinning broad broad like if he half-pitying, half-laughing at dis Indian-in-skin-colour-only, and den he tell me, "That is called chum-chum, Miss." I snap back at him, "Yeh, well back home we does call dat sugarcake, Mr. Chum-chum."

At de table Janet say, "You know, Pud (Pud, short for Pudding; is dat she does call me when she feeling close to me, or sorry for me), it's true that we call that 'meethai' back home. Just like how we call 'siu mai' 'tim sam.' As if 'dim sum' is just one little piece a food. What did he call that sweet again?"

"Cultural bastards, Janet, cultural bastards. Dat is what we is. Yuh know, one time a fella from India who living up here call me a bastard-ized Indian because I didn't know Hindi. And now look at dis, nah! De thing is: all a we in Trinidad is cultural bastards, Janet, all a we. *Toutes bagailles!* Chinese people. Black people. White people. Syrian. Lebanese. I looking forward to de day I find out dat place inside me where I am nothing else but Trinidadian, whatever dat could turn out to be."

I take a bite a de chum-chum, de texture was like grind-up coconut but it had no coconut, not even a hint a coconut taste in it. De thing was juicy with sweet rose water oozing out a it. De rose water perfume enter mih nose and get trap in mih cranium. Ah drink two cup a masala tea and a lassi and still de rose water perfume was on mih tongue like if I had a overdosed on Butchart Gardens.

Suddenly de door a de restaurant spring open wide with a strong force and two big burly fellas stumble in, almost rolling over on to de ground. Dey get up, eyes red and slow and dey skin burning pink with booze. Dey straighten up so much to overcompensate for falling forward, dat dey find deyself leaning backward. Everybody stop talking and was watching dem. De guy in front put his hand up to his forehead and take a deep Walter Raleigh bow, bringing de hand down to his waist in a rolling circular movement. Out loud he greet everybody with "Alarm o salay koom." A part a me wanted to bust out laughing. Another part make mih jaw drop open in disbelief. De calm in de place get rumfle up. De two fellas dem, feeling chupid now because nobody reply to dey greeting, gone up to de counter to Chum-chum trying to make a little conversation with him. De same booze-pink alarm-o-salay-koom-fella say to Chum-chum, "Hey, howaryah?"

Chum-Chum give a lil nod and de fella carry right on, "Are you Sikh?"

Chum-chum brothers converge near de counter, busying dey-selves in de vicinity. Chum-chum look at his brothers kind a quizzical, and he touch his cheek and feel his forehead with de back a his palm. He say, "No, I think I am fine, thank you. But I am sorry if I look sick, Sir."

De burly fella confuse now, so he try again.

"Where are you from?"

Chum-chum say, "Fiji, Sir."

"Oh! Fiji, eh! Lotsa palm trees and beautiful women, eh! Is it true that you guys can have more than one wife?"

De exchange make mih blood rise up in a boiling froth. De restaurant suddenly get a gruff quietness 'bout it except for a woman I hear whispering angrily to another woman at de table behind us, "I hate this! I just hate it! I can't stand to see our men humiliated by them, right in front of us. He should refuse to serve them, he should throw them out. Who on earth do they think they are? The awful fools!" And de friend whisper back, "If he throws them out all of us will suffer in the long run."

I could discern de hair on de back a de neck a Chum-chum brothers standing up, annoyed, and at de same time de brothers look like dey was shrinking in stature. Chum-chum get serious, and he politely say, "What can I get for you?"

Pinko get de message and he point to a few items in de case and say, "One of each, to go please."

Holding de white take-out box in one hand he extend de other to Chum-chum and say, "How do you say 'Excuse me, I'm sorry' in Fiji?"

Chum-chum shake his head and say, "It's okay. Have a good day."

Pinko insist, "No, tell me please. I think I just behaved badly, and I want to apologize. How do you say 'I'm sorry' in Fiji?"

Chum-chum say, "Your apology is accepted. Everything is okay." And he discreetly turn away to serve a person who had just entered de restaurant. De fellas take de hint dat was broad like daylight, and back out de restaurant like two little mouse.

Everybody was feeling sorry for Chum-chum and Brothers. One a dem come up to de table across from us to take a order from a woman with a giraffe-long neck who say, "Brother, we mustn't accept how these people think they can treat us. You men really put up with too many insults and abuse over here. I really felt for you."

Another woman gone up to de counter to converse with Chum-chum in she language. She reach out and touch his hand, sympathy-like. Chum-chum hold the one hand in his two and make a verbose speech to her as she nod she head in agreement generously. To italicize her support, she buy a take-out box a two burfi, or rather, dat's what I think dey was.

De door a de restaurant open again, and a bevy of Indian-looking women saunter in, dress up to weaken a person's decorum. De Miss Universe pageant traipse across de room to a table. Chum-chum and Brothers start smoothing dey hair back, and pushing de front a dey shirts neatly into dey pants. One brother take out a pack a Dentyne from his shirt pocket and pop one in his mouth. One take out a comb from his back pocket and smooth down his hair. All a dem den converge on dat single table to take orders. Dey begin to behave like young pups in mating season. Only, de women dem wasn't impress by all this tra-la-la at all and ignore dem except to make dey order, straight to de point. Well, it look like Brothers' egos were having a rough day and dey start roving 'bout de room, dey egos and de crotch a dey pants leading far in front dem. One brother gone over to Giraffebai to see if she want anything more. He call she "dear" and put his hand on she back. Giraffebai straighten she back in surprise and reply in a not-too-friendly way. When he gone to write up de bill she see me looking at she and she say to me, "Whoever does he think he is! Calling me dear and touching me like that! Why do these men always think that they have permission to touch whatever and wherever they want! And you can't make a fuss about it in public, because it is exactly what those people out there want to hear about so that they can say how sexist and uncivilized our culture is."

I shake mih head in understanding and say, "Yeah. I know. Yuh right!"

De atmosphere in de room take a hairpin turn, and it was man aggressing on woman, woman warding off a herd a man who just had dey pride publicly cut up a couple a times in just a few minutes.

One brother walk over to Janet and me and he stand up facing me with his hands clasp in front a his crotch, like if he protecting it. Stiff stiff, looking at me, he say, "Will that be all?"

Mih crew cut start to tingle, so I put on mih femmest smile and say, "Yes, that's it, thank you. Just the bill please." De smartass turn to face Janet and he remove his hands from in front a his crotch and slip his thumbs inside his pants like a cowboy 'bout to do a square dance. He smile, looking down at her attentive fuh so, and he say, "Can I do anything for you?"

I didn't give Janet time fuh his intent to even register before I bulldoze in mih most un-femmest manner, "She have everything she need, man, thank you. The bill please." Yuh think he hear me? It was like I was talking to thin air. He remain smiling at Janet, but she, looking at me, not at him, say, "You heard her. The bill please."

Before he could even leave de table proper, I start mih tirade. "But A A! Yuh see dat? Yuh could believe dat! De effing so-and-so! One minute yuh feel sorry fuh dem and next minute dey harassing de heck out a you. Janet, he crazy to mess with my woman, yes!" Janet get vex with me and say I overreacting, and is not fuh me to be vex, but fuh she to be vex. Is she he insult, and she could take good enough care a sheself.

I tell she I don't know why she don't cut off all dat long hair, and stop wearing lipstick and eyeliner. Well, who tell me to say dat! She get real vex and say dat nobody will tell she how to dress and how not to dress, not me and not any man. Well I could see de potential dat dis fight had coming, and when Janet get fighting vex, watch out! It hard to get a word in edgewise, yes! And she does bring up incidents from years back dat have no bearing on de current situation. So I draw back quick quick but she don't waste time; she was already off to a good start. It was best to leave right dere and den.

Just when I stand up to leave, de doors dem open up and in walk Sandy and Lise, coming for dey weekly hit a Indian sweets. Well, with Sandy and Lise is a dead giveaway dat dey not dressing fuh any man, it have no place in dey life fuh man-vibes, and dat in fact dey have a blatant penchant fuh women. Soon as dey enter de room yuh could see de brothers and de couple men customers dat had come in minutes before stare dem down from head to Birkenstocks, dey eyes bulging with disgust. And de women in de room start shoo-shooing, and putting dey hand in front dey mouth to stop dey surprise, and false teeth, too, from falling out. Sandy and Lise spot us instantly and dey call out to us, shameless, loud and affectionate. Dey leap over to us, eager to hug up and kiss like if dey hadn't seen us for years, but it was really only since two nights aback when we went out to dey favourite Indian restaurant for dinner. I figure dat de display was a genuine happiness to be seen wit us in dat place. While we stand up dere chatting, Sandy insist on rubbing she hand up and down Janet back — wit friendly intent, mind you, and same time Lise have she arm round Sandy waist. Well, all cover get blown. If it was even remotely possible dat I wasn't noticeable before, now Janet and I were over-exposed. We could a easily suffer from hypothermia, specially since it suddenly get cold cold in dere. We say goodbye, not soon enough, and as we were leaving I turn to acknowlege Giraffebai, but instead a any recognition of our buddiness against de fresh brothers, I get a face dat look like it was in de presence of a very foul smell.

De good thing, doh, is dat Janet had become so incensed 'bout how we get scorned, dat she forgot I tell she to cut she hair and to ease up on de makeup, and so I get save from hearing 'bout how I too jealous, and how much I inhibit she, and how she would prefer if I would grow my hair, and wear lipstick and put on a dress sometimes. I so glad, oui! dat I didn't have to go through hearing how I too demanding a she, like de time, she say, I prevent she from seeing a ole boyfriend when he was in town for a couple hours *en route* to live in Australia with his new bride (because, she say, I was jealous dat ten years ago dey sleep together). Well, look at mih crosses, nah! Like if I really so possessive and jealous!

So tell me, what yuh think 'bout dis nah, girl?

Queen of the North

EDEN ROBINSON

FROG SONG

Whenever I see abandoned buildings, I think of our old house in the village, a rickety shack by the swamp where the frogs used to live. It's gone now. The council covered the whole area with rocks and gravel.

In my memory, the sun is setting and the frogs begin to sing. As the light shifts from yellow to orange to red, I walk down the path to the beach. The wind blows in from the channel, making the grass hiss and shiver around my legs. The tide is low and there's a strong rotting smell from the beach. Tree stumps that have been washed down the channel from the logged areas loom ahead — black, twisted silhouettes against the darkening sky.

The seiner coming down the channel is the *Queen of the North*, pale yellow with blue trim, Uncle Josh's boat. I wait on the beach. The water laps my ankles. The sound of the old diesel engine grows louder as the boat gets closer.

Usually I can will myself to move, but sometimes I'm frozen where I stand, waiting for the crew to come ashore.

The only thing my cousin Ronny didn't own was a Barbie Doll speedboat. She had the swimming pool, she had the Barbie-Goes-to-Paris carrying case, but she didn't have the boat. There was one left in Northern Drugs, nestling between the puzzles and the stuffed Garfields, but it cost sixty bucks and we were broke. I knew Ronny was going to get it. She'd already saved twenty bucks out of her allowance. Anyway, she always got everything she wanted because she was an only child and both her parents worked at the aluminum smelter. Mom knew how much I wanted it, but she said it was a toss-up between school supplies and paying bills, or wasting our money on something I'd get sick of in a few weeks.

We had a small Christmas tree. I got socks and underwear and forced a cry of surprise when I opened the package. Uncle Josh came in just as Mom was carving the turkey. He pushed a big box in my direction.

"Go on," Mom said, smiling. "It's for you."

Uncle Josh looked like a young Elvis. He had the soulful brown eyes and the thick black hair. He dressed his long, thin body in clothes with expensive labels — no Sears or K-Mart for him. He smiled at me with his perfect pouty lips and bleached white teeth.

"Here you go, sweetheart," Uncle Josh said.

I didn't want it. Whatever it was, I didn't want it. He put it down in front of me. Mom must have wrapped it. She was never any good at wrapping presents. You'd think with two kids and a million Christmases behind her she'd know how to wrap a present.

"Come on, open it," Mom said.

I unwrapped it slowly, my skin crawling. Yes, it was the Barbie Doll speedboat.

My mouth smiled. We all had dinner and I pulled the wishbone with my little sister, Alice. I got the bigger piece and made a wish. Uncle Josh kissed me. Alice sulked. Uncle Josh never got her anything, and later that afternoon she screamed about it. I put the boat in my closet and didn't touch it for days.

Until Ronny came over to play. She was showing off her new set of Barbie-in-the-Ice-Capades clothes. Then I pulled out the speedboat and the look on her face was almost worth it.

My sister hated me for weeks. When I was off at soccer practise, Alice took the boat and threw it in the river. To this day, Alice doesn't know how grateful I was.

There's a dream I have sometimes. Ronny comes to visit. We go down the hallway to my room. She goes in first. I point to the closet and she eagerly opens the door. She thinks I've been lying, that I don't really have a boat. She wants proof.

When she turns to me, she looks horrified, pale and shocked. I laugh, triumphant. I reach in and stop, seeing Uncle Josh's head, arms and legs squashed inside, severed from the rest of his body. My clothes are soaked dark red with his blood.

"Well, what do you know," I say. "Wishes do come true."

Me and five chug buddies are in the Tamitik arena, in the girls' locker room under the bleachers. The hockey game is in the third period and the score is tied. The yells and shouting of the fans drown out the girl's swearing. There are four of us against her. It doesn't take long before she's on the floor trying to crawl away. I want to say I'm not part of it, but that's my foot hooking her ankle and tripping her while Ronny takes her down with a blow to the temple. She grunts. Her head makes a hollow sound when it bounces off the sink. The lights make us all look green. A cheer explodes from inside the arena. Our team has scored. The girl's now curled up under the sink and I punch her and kick her and smash her face into the floor.

My cuz Ronny had great connections. She could get hold of almost any drug you wanted. This was during her biker chick phase, when she wore tight leather skirts, teeny weeny tops and many silver bracelets, rings and studs. Her parents started coming down really hard on her then. I went over to her house to get high. It was okay to do it there, as long as we sprayed the living room with Lysol and opened the windows before her parents came home.

We toked up and decided to go back to my house to get some munchies. Ronny tagged along when I went up to my bedroom to get the bottle of Visine. There was an envelope on my dresser. Even before I opened it I knew it would be money. I knew who it was from.

I pulled the bills out. Ronny squealed.

"Holy sheep shit, how much is there?"

I spread the fifties out on the dresser. Two hundred and fifty dollars. I could get some flashy clothes or nice earrings with that money, if I could bring myself to touch it. Anything I bought would remind me of him.

"You want to have a party?" I said to Ronny.

"Are you serious?" she said, going bug-eyed.

I gave her the money and said make it happen. She asked who it came from, but she didn't really care. She was already making phone calls.

That weekend we had a house party in town. The house belonged to one of Ronny's biker buddies and was filled with people I knew by sight from school. As the night wore on, they came up and told me what a generous person I was. Yeah, that's me, I thought, Saint Karaoke of Good Times.

I took Ronny aside when she was drunk enough. "Ronny, I got to tell you something."

"What?" she said, blinking too fast, like she had something in her eye.

"You know where I got the money?"

She shook her head, lost her balance, blearily put her hand on my shoulder, and barfed out the window.

As I listened to her heave out her guts, I decided I didn't want to tell her after all. What was the point? She had a big mouth, and anything I told her I might as well stand on a street corner and shout to the world. What I really wanted was to have a good time and forget about the money, and after beating everyone hands down at tequila shots that's exactly what I did.

"Moooo." I copy the two aliens on *Sesame Street* mooing to a telephone. Me and Uncle Josh are watching television together. He smells faintly of the halibut he cooked for dinner. Uncle Josh undoes his pants. "Moo." I keep my eyes on the TV and say nothing as he moves toward me. I'm not a baby like Alice, who runs to Mommy about everything. When it's over he'll have treats for me. It's like when the dentist gives me extra suckers for not crying, not even when it really hurts.

I could have got my scorpion tattoo at The Body Hole, where my friends went. A perfectly groomed beautician would sit me in a black leather dentist's chair and the tattoo artist would show me the tiny diagram on tracing paper. We'd choose the exact spot on my neck where the scorpion would go, just below the hairline where my hair comes to a point. Techno, maybe some funky remix of Abba, would blare through the speakers as he whirred the tattoo needle's motor.

But Ronny had done her own tattoo, casually standing in front of the bathroom mirror with a short needle and permanent blue ink from a pen. She simply poked the needle in and out, added the ink and that was that. No fuss, no muss.

So I asked her to do it for me. After all, I thought, if she could brand six marks of Satan on her own breast, she could certainly do my scorpion.

Ronny led me into the kitchen and cleared off a chair. I twisted my hair up into a bun and held it in place. She showed me the needle, then dropped it into a pot of boiling water. She was wearing a crop top and I could see her navel ring, glowing bright gold in the slanting light of the setting sun. She was prone to lifting her shirt in front of complete strangers and telling them she'd pierced herself.

Ronny emptied the water into the sink and lifted the needle in gloved hands. I bent my head and looked down at the floor as she traced the drawing on my skin.

The needle was hot. It hurt more than I expected, a deep ache, a throbbing. I breathed through my mouth. I fought not to cry. I concentrated fiercely on not crying in front of her, and when she finished I lay very still.

"See?" Ronny said. "Nothing to it, you big baby."

When I opened my eyes and raised my head, she held one small mirror to my face and another behind me so I could see her work. I frowned at my reflection. The scorpion looked like a smear.

"It'll look better when the swelling goes down," she said, handing me the two mirrors.

As Ronny went to start the kettle for tea, she looked out the window over the sink. "Star light, star bright, first star — "

I glanced out the window. "That's Venus."

"Like you'd know the difference."

I didn't want to argue. The skin on the back of my neck ached like it was sunburned.

I am singing Janis Joplin songs, my arms wrapped around the karaoke machine. I fend people off with a stolen switchblade. No one can get near until some kid from school has the bright idea of giving me drinks until I pass out.

Someone else videotapes me so my one night as a rock star is recorded forever. She tries to send it to *America's Funniest Home Videos,* but they reject it as unsuitable for family viewing. I remember nothing else about that night after I got my first hit of acid. My real name is Adelaine, but the next day a girl from school sees me coming and yells, "Hey, look, it's Karaoke!"

The morning after my sixteenth birthday I woke up looking down into Jimmy Hill's face. We were squashed together in the backseat of a car and I thought, God, I didn't.

I crawled around and found my shirt and then spent the next half hour vomiting beside the car. I vaguely remembered the night before, leaving the party with Jimmy. I remembered being afraid of bears.

Jimmy stayed passed out in the backseat, naked except for his socks. We were somewhere up in the mountains, just off a logging road. The sky was misty and grey. As I stood up and stretched, the car headlights went out.

Dead battery. That's just fucking perfect, I thought.

I checked the trunk and found an emergency kit. I got out one of those blankets that look like a large sheet of aluminum and wrapped it around myself. I searched the car until I found my jeans. I threw Jimmy's shirt over him. His jeans were hanging off the car's antenna. When I took them down, the antenna wouldn't straighten up.

I sat in the front seat. I had just slept with Jimmy Hill. Christ, he was practically a Boy Scout. I saw his picture in the local newspaper all the time, with these medals for swimming. Other than that, I never really noticed him. We went to different parties.

About mid-morning, the sun broke through the mist and streamed to the ground in fingers of light, just like in the movies when God is talking to someone. The sun hit my face and I closed my eyes.

I heard the seat shift and turned. Jimmy smiled at me and I knew why I'd slept with him. He leaned forward and we kissed. His lips were soft and the kiss was gentle. He put his hand on the back of my neck. "You're beautiful."

I thought it was just a line, the polite thing to say after a one-night stand, so I didn't answer.

"Did you get any?" Jimmy said.

"What?" I said.

"Blueberries." He grinned. "Don't you remember?"

I stared at him.

His grin faded. "Do you remember anything?"

I shrugged.

"Well. We left the party, I dunno, around two, I guess. You said you wanted blueberries. We came out here — " He cleared his throat.

"Then we fucked, passed out and now we're stranded." I finished the sentence. The sun was getting uncomfortable. I took off the emergency blanket. I had no idea what to say next. "Battery's dead."

He swore and leaned over me to try the ignition.

I got out of his way by stepping out of the car. Hastily he put his shirt on, not looking up at me. He had a nice chest, buff and tan. He blushed and I wondered if he had done this before.

"You cool with this?" I said.

He immediately became macho. "Yeah."

I felt really shitty then. God, I thought, he's going to be a bragger.

I went and sat on the hood. It was hot. I was thirsty and had a killer headache. Jimmy got out and sat beside me.

"You know where we are?" Jimmy said.

"Not a fucking clue."

He looked at me and we both started laughing.

"You were navigating last night," he said, nudging me.

"You always listen to pissed women?"

"Yeah," he said, looking sheepish. "Well. You hungry?"

I shook my head. "Thirsty."

Jimmy hopped off the car and came back with a warm Coke from under the driver's seat. We drank it in silence.

"You in any rush to get back?" he asked.

We started laughing again and then went hunting for blueberries. Jimmy found a patch not far from the car and we picked the bushes clean. I'd forgotten how tart wild blueberries are. They're smaller than store-bought berries, but their flavour is much more intense.

"My sister's the wilderness freak," Jimmy said. "She'd be able to get us out of this. Or at least she'd know where we are."

We were perched on a log. "You gotta promise me something."

"What?"

"If I pop off before you, you aren't going to eat me."

"What?"

"I'm serious," I said. "And I'm not eating any bugs."

"If you don't try them, you'll never know what you're missing." Jimmy looked at the road. "You want to pick a direction?"

The thought of trekking down the dusty logging road in the wrong direction held no appeal to me. I must have made a face because Jimmy said, "Me neither."

After the sun set, Jimmy made a fire in front of the car. We put the aluminum blanket under us and lay down. Jimmy pointed at the sky. "That's the Big Dipper."

"Ursa Major," I said. "Mother of all bears. There's Ursa Minor, Cassiopeia … " I stopped.

"I didn't know you liked astronomy."

"It's pretty nerdy."

He kissed me. "Only if you think it is." He put his arm around me and I put my head on his chest and listened to his heart. It was a nice way to fall asleep.

Jimmy shook me awake. "Car's coming." He pulled me to my feet. "It's my sister."

"Mmm." Blurrily I focused on the road. I could hear birds and, in the distance, the rumble of an engine.

"My sister could find me in hell," he said.

When they dropped me off at home, my mom went ballistic. "Where the hell were you?"

"Out." I stopped at the door. I hadn't expected her to be there when I came in.

Her chest was heaving. I thought she'd start yelling, but she said very calmly, "You've been gone for two days."

You noticed? I didn't say it. I felt ill and I didn't want a fight. "Sorry. Should've called."

I pushed past her, kicked off my shoes and went upstairs.

Still wearing my smelly jeans and shirt I lay down on the bed. Mom followed me to my room and shook my shoulder.

"Tell me where you've been."

"At Ronny's."

"Don't lie to me. What is wrong with you?"

God. Just get lost. I wondered what she'd do if I came out and said what we both knew. Probably have a heart attack. Or call me a liar.

"You figure it out," I said. "I'm going to sleep." I expected her to give me a lecture or something, but she just left.

Sometimes, when friends were over, she'd point to Alice and say, "This is my good kid." Then she'd point to me and say, "This is my rotten kid, nothing but trouble. She steals, she lies, she sleeps around. She's just no damn good."

Alice knocked on my door later.

"Fuck off," I said.

"You've got a phone call."

"Take a message. I'm sleeping."

Alice opened the door and poked her head in. "You want me to tell Jimmy anything else?"

I scrambled down the hallway and grabbed the receiver. I took a couple of deep breaths so it wouldn't sound like I'd rushed to the phone. "Hi."

"Hi," Jimmy said. "We just replaced the battery on the car. You want to go for a ride?"

"Aren't you grounded?"

He laughed. "So?"

I thought he just wanted to get lucky again, and then I thought, What the hell, at least this time I'll remember it.

"Pick me up in five minutes."

I'm getting my ass kicked by two sisters. They're really good. They hit solidly and back off quickly. I don't even see them coming anymore. I get mad enough to kick out. By sheer luck, the kick connects. One of the sisters shrieks and goes down. She's on the ground, her leg at an odd angle. The other one loses it and swings. The bouncer steps in and the crowd around us boos.

"My cousins'll be at a biker party. You want to go?"

Jimmy looked at me like he wasn't sure if I was serious.

"I'll be good," I said, crossing my heart then holding up my fingers in a scout salute.

"What fun would that be?" he said, revving the car's engine.

I gave him directions. The car roared away from our house, skidding a bit. Jimmy didn't say anything. I found it unnerving. He looked over at me, smiled, then turned back to face the road. I was used to yappy guys, but this was nice. I leaned my head back into the seat. The leather creaked.

Ronny's newest party house didn't look too bad, which could have meant it was going to be dead in there. It's hard to get down and dirty when you're worried you'll stain the carpet. You couldn't hear anything until someone opened the door and the music throbbed out. They did a good job with the soundproofing. We went up the steps just as my cousin Frank came out with some bar buddies.

Jimmy stopped when he saw Frank and I guess I could see why. Frank is on the large side, six-foot-four and scarred up from his days as a hard-core Bruce Lee fan, when he felt compelled to fight Evil in street bars. He looked down at Jimmy.

"Hey, Jimbo," Frank said. "Heard you quit the swim team."

"You betcha," Jimmy said.

"Fucking right!" Frank body-slammed him. He tended to be more enthusiastic than most people could handle, but Jimmy looked okay with it. "More time to party," he said. Now they were going to gossip forever so I went inside.

The place was half-empty. I recognized some people and nodded. They nodded back. The music was too loud for conversation.

"You want a drink?" Frank yelled, touching my arm.

I jumped. He quickly took his hand back. "Where's Jimmy?"

"Ronny gave him a hoot and now he's hacking up his lungs out back." Frank took off his jacket, closed his eyes and shuffled back and forth. All he knew was the reservation two-step and I wasn't in the mood. I moved toward the porch but Frank grabbed my hand. "You two doing the wild thing?"

"He's all yours," I said.

"Fuck you," Frank called after me.

Jimmy was leaning against the railing, his back toward me, his hands jammed into his pockets. I watched him. His hair was dark and shiny, brushing his shoulders. I liked the way he moved, easily, like he was in no hurry to get anywhere. His eyes were light brown with gold flecks. I knew that in a moment he would turn and smile at me and it would be like stepping into sunlight.

In my dream Jimmy's casting a fishing rod. I'm afraid of getting hooked, so I sit at the bow of the skiff. The ocean is mildly choppy, the sky is hard blue, the air is cool. Jimmy reaches over to kiss me, but now he is soaking wet. His hands and lips are cold, his eyes are sunken and dull. Something moves in his mouth. It isn't his tongue. When I pull away, a crab drops from his lips and Jimmy laughs. "Miss me?"

I feel a scream in my throat but nothing comes out.

"What's the matter?" Jimmy tilts his head. Water runs off his hair and drips into the boat. "Crab got your tongue?"

This one's outside Hanky Panky's. The woman is so totally bigger than me it isn't funny. Still, she doesn't like getting hurt. She's afraid of the pain but can't back down because she started it. She's grabbing my hair, yanking it hard. I pull hers. We get stuck there, bent over, trying to kick each other, neither one of us willing to let go. My friends are laughing their heads off. I'm pissed at that but I'm too sloshed to let go. In the morning my scalp will throb and be so tender I won't be able to comb my hair. At that moment, a bouncer comes over and splits us apart. The woman tries to kick me but kicks him instead and he knocks her down. My friends grab my arm and steer me to the bus stop.

Jimmy and I lay down together on a sleeping bag in a field of fireweed. The forest fire the year before had razed the place and the weeds had only sprouted back up about a month earlier. With the spring sun and just the right sprinkling of rain, they were as tall as sunflowers, as dark pink as prize roses, swaying around us in the night breeze.

Jimmy popped open a bottle of Baby Duck. "May I?" he said, reaching down to untie my sneaker.

"You may," I said.

He carefully lifted the sneaker and poured in some Baby Duck. Then he raised it to my lips and I drank. We lay down, flattening fireweed and knocking over the bottle. Jimmy nibbled my ear. I drew circles in the bend of his arm. Headlights came up fast, then disappeared down the highway. We watched the fireweed shimmer and wave in the wind.

"You're quiet tonight," Jimmy said. "What're you thinking?"

I almost told him then. I wanted to tell him. I wanted someone else to know and not have it locked inside me. I kept starting and then chickening out. What was the point? He'd probably pull away from me in horror, disgusted, revolted.

"I want to ask you something," Jimmy whispered. I closed my eyes, feeling my chest tighten. "You hungry? I've got a monster craving for chicken wings."

BLOODY VANCOUVER

When I got to Aunt Erma's the light in the hallway was going spastic, flickering like a strobe, little bright flashes then darkness so deep I had to feel my way along the wall. I stopped in front of the door, sweating, smelling myself through the thick layer of deodorant. I felt my stomach go queasy and wondered if I was going to throw up after all. I hadn't eaten and was still bleeding heavily.

Aunt Erma lived in East Van in a low-income government housing unit. Light showed under the door. I knocked. I could hear the familiar opening of *StarTrek,* the old version, with the trumpets blaring. I knocked again.

The door swung open and a girl with a purple Mohawk and Cleopatra eyeliner thrust money at me.

"Shit," she said. She looked me up and down, pulling the money back. "Where's the pizza?"

"I'm sorry," I said. "I think I have the wrong house."

"Pizza, pizza, pizza!" teenaged voices inside screamed. Someone was banging the floor in time to the chant.

"You with Cola?" she asked me.

I shook my head. "No. I'm here to see Erma Williamson. Is she in?"

"In? I guess. Mom?" she screamed. "Mom? It's for you!"

A whoop rose up. "Erma and Marley sittin' in a tree, k-i-s-s-i-n-g. First comes lust — "

"Shut up, you social rejects!"

" — then comes humping, then comes a baby after all that bumping!"

"How many times did they boink last night!" a single voice yelled over the laughter.

"Ten!" the voices chorused enthusiastically. "Twenty! Thirty! Forty!"

"Hey! Who's buying the pizza, eh? No respect! I get no respect!"

Aunt Erma came to the door. She didn't look much different from her pictures, except she wasn't wearing her cat-eye glasses.

She stared at me, puzzled. Then she spread open her arms.

"Adelaine, baby! I wasn't expecting you! Hey, come on in and say hi to your cousins. Pepsi! Cola! Look who came by for your birthday!"

She gave me a tight bear hug and I wanted to cry.

Two girls stood at the entrance to the living room, identical right down to their lip rings. They had different coloured Mohawks though — one pink, one purple.

"Erica?" I said, peering. I vaguely remembered them as having pigtails and making fun of Mr. Rogers. "Heather?"

"It's Pepsi," the purple Mohawk said. "Not, n-o-t, Erica."

"Oh," I said.

"Cola," the pink-Mohawked girl said, turning around and ignoring me to watch TV.

"What'd you bring us?" Pepsi said matter-of-factly.

"Excuse the fruit of my loins," Aunt Erma said, leading me into the living room and sitting me between two guys who were glued to the TV. "They've temporarily lost their manners. I'm putting it down to hormones and hoping the birth control pills turn them back into normal human beings."

Aunt Erma introduced me to everyone in the room, but their names went in one ear and out the other. I was so relieved just to be there and out of the clinic I couldn't concentrate on much else.

"How is he, Bones?" the guy on my right said, exactly in synch with Captain Kirk on TV. Captain Kirk was standing over McCoy and a prone security guard with large purple circles all over his face.

"He's dead, Jim," the guy on my left said.

"I wanna watch something else," Pepsi said. "This sucks."

She was booed.

"Hey, it's my birthday. I can watch what I want."

"Siddown," Cola said. "You're out-voted."

"You guys have no taste at all. This is crap. I just can't believe you guys are watching this — this cultural pablum. I ... "

A pair of panties hit her in the face. The doorbell rang and the pink-haired girl held the pizza boxes over her head and yelled, "Dinner's ready!"

"Eat in the kitchen," Aunt Erma said. "All of youse. I ain't scraping your cheese out of my carpet."

Everyone left except me and Pepsi. She grabbed the remote control and flipped through a bunch of channels until we arrived at one where an announcer for the World Wrestling Federation screamed that the ref was blind.

"Now this," Pepsi said, "is entertainment."

By the time the party ended, I was snoring on the couch. Pepsi shook my shoulder. She and Cola were watching Bugs Bunny and Tweety.

"If we're bothering you," Cola said. "You can go crash in my room."

"Thanks," I said. I rolled off the couch, grabbed my backpack, and found the bathroom on the second floor. I made it just in time to throw up in the sink. The cramps didn't come back as badly as on the bus, but I took three Extra-Strength Tylenols anyway. My pad had soaked right through and leaked all over my underwear. I put on clean clothes and crashed in one of the beds. I wanted a black hole to open up and suck me out of the universe.

When I woke, I discovered I should have put on a diaper. It looked like something had been hideously murdered on the mattress.

"God," I said just as Pepsi walked in. I snatched up the blanket and tried to cover the mess.

"Man," Pepsi said. "Who are you? Carrie?"

"Freaky," Cola said, coming in behind her. "You okay?"

I nodded. I wished I'd never been born.

Pepsi hit my hand when I touched the sheets. "You're not the only one with killer periods." She pushed me out of the bedroom. In the bathroom she started water going in the tub for me, poured some Mr. Bubble in, and left without saying anything. I stripped off my blood-soaked underwear and hid them in the bottom of the garbage. There would be no saving them. I lay back. The bubbles popped and gradually the water became cool. I was smelly and gross. I scrubbed hard but the smell wouldn't go away.

"You still alive in there?" Pepsi said, opening the door.

I jumped up and whisked the shower curtain shut.

"Jesus, don't you knock?"

"Well, excuuuse me. I brought you a bathrobe. Good thing you finally crawled out of bed. Mom told us to make you eat something before we left. We got Ichiban, Kraft, or hot dogs. You want anything else, you gotta make it yourself. What do you want?"

"Privacy."

"We got Ichiban, Kraft, or hot dogs. What do you want?"

"The noodles," I said, more to get her out than because I was hungry.

She left and I tried to lock the door. It wouldn't lock so I scrubbed myself off quickly. I stopped when I saw the bathwater. It was dark pink with blood.

I crashed on the couch and woke when I heard sirens. I hobbled to the front window in time to see an ambulance pull into the parking lot. The attendants wheeled a man bound to a stretcher across the lot. He was screaming about the eyes in the walls that were watching him, waiting for him to fall asleep so they could come peel his skin from his body.

Aunt Erma, the twins and I drove to the powwow at the Trout Lake community centre in East Vancouver. I was still bleeding a little and felt pretty lousy, but Aunt Erma was doing fundraising for the Helping Hands

Society and had asked me to work her bannock booth. I wanted to help her out.

Pepsi had come along just to meet guys, dressed up in her flashiest bracelets and most conservatively ripped jeans. Aunt Erma enlisted her too, when she found out that none of her other volunteers had showed up. Pepsi was disgusted.

Cola got out of working at the booth because she was one of the jingle dancers. Aunt Erma had made her outfit, a form-fitting red dress with silver jingles that flashed and twinkled as she walked. Cola wore a bobbed wig to cover her pink Mohawk. Pepsi bugged her about it, but Cola airily waved goodbye and said, "Have fun."

I hadn't made fry bread in a long time. The first three batches were already mixed. I just added water and kneaded them into shapes roughly the size of a large doughnut, then threw them in the electric frying pan. The oil spattered and crackled and steamed because I'd turned the heat up too high. Pepsi wasn't much better. She burned her first batch and then had to leave so she could watch Cola dance.

"Be right back," she said. She gave me a thumbs-up sign and disappeared into the crowd.

The heat from the frying pan and the sun was fierce. I wished I'd thought to bring an umbrella. One of the organizers gave me her baseball cap. Someone else brought me a glass of water. I wondered how much longer Pepsi was going to be. My arms were starting to hurt.

I flattened six more pieces of bread into shape and threw them in the pan, beyond caring anymore that none of them were symmetrical. I could feel the sun sizzling my forearms, my hands, my neck, my legs. A headache throbbed at the base of my skull.

The people came in swarms, buzzing groups of tourists, conventioneers on a break, families and assorted browsers. Six women wearing HI! MY NAME IS tags stopped and bought all the fry bread I had. Another hoard came and a line started at my end of the table.

"Last batch!" I shouted to the cashiers. They waved at me.

"What are you making?" someone asked.

I looked up. A middle-aged red-headed man in a business suit stared at me. At the beginning, when we were still feeling spunky, Pepsi and I had had fun with that question. We said, Oh, this is fish-head bread. Or fried beer foam. But bullshitting took energy.

"Fry bread," I said. "This is my last batch."

"Is it good?"

"I don't think you'll find out," I said. "It's all gone."

The man looked at my tray. "There seems to be more than enough. Do I buy it from you?"

"No, the cashier, but you're out of luck, it's all sold." I pointed to the line of people.

"Do you do this for a living?" the man said.

"Volunteer work. Raising money for the Helping Hands," I said.

"Are you Indian then?"

A hundred stupid answers came to my head but like I said, bullshit is work. "Haisla. And you?"

He blinked. "Is that a tribe?"

"Excuse me," I said, taking the fry bread out of the pan and passing it down to the cashier.

The man slapped a twenty-dollar bill on the table. "Make another batch."

"I'm tired," I said.

He put down another twenty.

"You don't understand. I've been doing this since this morning. You could put a million bucks on the table and I wouldn't change my mind."

He put five twenty-dollar bills on the table.

It was all for the Helping Hands, I figured, and he wasn't going to budge. I emptied the flour bag into the bowl. I measured out a handful of baking powder, a few fingers of salt, a thumb of lard. Sweat dribbled over my face, down the tip of my nose, and into the mix as I kneaded the dough until it was very soft but hard to shape. For a hundred bucks I made sure the pieces of fry bread were roughly the same shape.

"You have strong hands," the man said.

"I'm selling fry bread."

"Of course."

I could feel him watching me, was suddenly aware of how far my shirt dipped and how short my cutoffs were. In the heat, they were necessary. I was sweating too much to wear anything more.

"My name is Arnold," he said.

"Pleased to meet you, Arnold," I said. "Scuse me if I don't shake hands. You with the convention?"

"No. I'm here on vacation."

He had teeth so perfect I wondered if they were dentures. No, probably caps. I bet he took exquisite care of his teeth.

We said nothing more until I'd fried the last piece of bread. I handed him the plate and bowed. I expected him to leave then, but he bowed back and said, "Thank you."

"No," I said. "Thank you. The money's going to a good cause. It'll — "

"How should I eat these?" he interrupted me.

With your mouth, asshole. "Put some syrup on them, or jam, or honey. Anything you want."

"Anything?" he said, staring deep into my eyes.

Oh, barf. "Whatever."

I wiped sweat off my forehead with the back of my hand, reached down and unplugged the frying pan. I began to clean up, knowing that he was still standing there, watching.

"What's your name?" he said.

"Suzy," I lied.

"Why're you so pale?"

I didn't answer. He blushed suddenly and cleared his throat. "Would you do me a favour?"

"Depends."

"Would you — " he blushed harder, "shake your hair out of that base-ball cap?"

I shrugged, pulled the cap off, and let my hair loose. It hung limply down to my waist. My scalp felt like it was oozing enough oil to cause environmental damage.

"You should keep it down at all times," he said.

"Goodbye, Arnold," I said, picking up the money and starting toward the cashiers. He said something else but I kept on walking until I reached Pepsi.

I heard the buzz of an electric razor. Aunt Erma hated it when Pepsi shaved her head in the bedroom. She came out of her room, crossed the landing, and banged on the door. "In the bathroom!" she shouted. "You want to get hair all over the rug?"

The razor stopped. Pepsi ripped the door open and stomped down the hall. She kicked the bathroom door shut and the buzz started again.

I went into the kitchen and popped myself another Jolt. Sweat trick-led down my pits, down my back, ran along my jaw and dripped off my chin.

"Karaoke?" Pepsi said. Then louder. "Hey! Are you deaf?"

"What?" I said.

"Get me my cell phone."

"Why don't you get it?"

"I'm on the can."

"So?" Personally, I hate it when you're talking on the phone with some-one and then you hear the toilet flush.

Pepsi banged about in the bathroom and came out with her freshly coiffed Mohawk and her backpack slung over her shoulder. "What's up your butt?" she said.

"Do you want me to leave? Is that it?"

"Do what you want. This place is like an oven," Pepsi said. "Who can deal with this bullshit?" She slammed the front door behind her.

The apartment was quiet now, except for the chirpy weatherman on the TV promising another week of record highs. I moved out to the balcony. The headlights from the traffic cut into my eyes, bright and painful. Cola and Aunt Erma bumped around upstairs, then their bedroom doors squeaked shut and I was alone. I had a severe caffeine buzz. Shaky hands, fluttery heart, mild headache. It was still warm outside, heat rising from the concrete, stored up during the last four weeks of weather straight from hell. I could feel my eyes itching. This was the third night I was having trouble getting to sleep.

Tired and wired. I used to be able to party for days and days. You start to hallucinate badly after the fifth day without sleep. I don't know why, but I used to see leprechauns. These waist-high men would come and sit beside me, smiling with their brown wrinkled faces, brown eyes, brown teeth. When I tried to shoo them away, they'd leap straight up into the air, ten or twelve feet, their green clothes and long red hair flapping around them.

A low, grey haze hung over Vancouver, fuzzing the street lights. Air-quality bulletins on the TV were warning the elderly and those with breathing problems to stay indoors. There were mostly semis on the roads this late. Their engines rumbled down the street, creating minor earthquakes. Pictures trembled on the wall. I took a sip of warm, flat Jolt, let it slide over my tongue, sweet and harsh. It had a metallic twang, which meant I'd drunk too much, my stomach wanted to heave.

I went back inside and started to pack.

HOME AGAIN, HOME AGAIN, JIGGITY-JIG

Jimmy and I lay in the graveyard, on one of my cousin's graves. We should have been creeped out, but we were both tipsy.

"I'm never going to leave the village," Jimmy said. His voice buzzed in my ears.

"Mmm."

"Did you hear me?" Jimmy said.

"Mmm."

"Don't you care?" Jimmy said, sounding like I should.

"This is what we've got, and it's not that bad."

He closed his eyes. "No, it's not bad."

I poured myself some cereal. Mom turned the radio up. She glared at me as if it were my fault the Rice Crispies were loud. I opened my mouth and kept chewing.

The radio announcer had a thick Nisga'a accent. Most of the news was about the latest soccer tournament. I thought, that's northern native broadcasting: sports or bingo.

"Who's this?" I said to Mom. I'd been rummaging through the drawer, hunting for spare change.

"What?"

It was the first thing she'd said to me since I'd come back. I'd heard that she'd cried to practically everyone in the village, saying I'd gone to Vancouver to become a hooker.

I held up a picture of a priest with his hand on a little boy's shoulder. The boy looked happy.

"Oh, that," Mom said. "I forgot I had it. He was Uncle Josh's teacher."

I turned it over. *Dear Joshua,* it read. *How are you? I miss you terribly. Please write. Your friend in Christ, Archibald.*

"Looks like he taught him more than just prayers."

"What are you talking about? Your Uncle Josh was a bright student. They were fond of each other."

"I bet," I said, vaguely remembering that famous priest who got eleven years in jail. He'd molested twenty-three boys while they were in residential school.

Uncle Josh was home from fishing for only two more days. As he was opening my bedroom door, I said, "Father Archibald?"

He stopped. I couldn't see his face because of the way the light was shining through the door. He stayed there a long time.

"I've said my prayers," I said.

He backed away and closed the door.

In the kitchen the next morning he wouldn't look at me.

I felt light and giddy, not believing it could end so easily. Before I ate breakfast I closed my eyes and said grace out loud. I had hardly begun when I heard Uncle Josh's chair scrape the floor as he pushed it back.

I opened my eyes. Mom was staring at me. From her expression I knew that she knew. I thought she'd say something then, but we ate breakfast in silence.

"Don't forget your lunch," she said.

She handed me my lunch bag and went up to her bedroom.

I use a recent picture of Uncle Josh that I raided from Mom's album. I paste his face onto the body of Father Archibald and my face onto the boy. The montage looks real enough. Uncle Josh is smiling down at a younger version of me.

My period is vicious this month. I've got clots the size and texture of liver. I put one of them in a Ziploc bag. I put the picture and the bag in a hatbox. I tie it up with a bright red ribbon. I place it on the kitchen table and go upstairs to get a jacket. I think nothing of leaving it there because there's no one else at home. The note inside the box reads, "It was yours so I killed it."

"Yowtz!" Jimmy called out as he opened the front door. He came to my house while I was upstairs getting my jacket. He was going to surprise me and take me to the hot springs. I stopped at the top of the landing. Jimmy was sitting at the kitchen table with the present that I'd meant for Uncle Josh, looking at the note. Without seeing me, he closed the box, neatly folded the note, and walked out the door.

He wouldn't take my calls. After two days, I went over to Jimmy's house, my heart hammering so hard I could feel it in my temples. Michelle answered the door.

"Karaoke!" she said, smiling. Then she frowned. "He's not here. Didn't he tell you?"

"Tell me what?"

"He got the job," Michelle said.

My relief was so strong I almost passed out. "A job."

"I know. I couldn't believe it either. It's hard to believe he's going fishing, he's so spoiled. I think he'll last a week. Thanks for putting in a good word, anyways." She kept talking, kept saying things about the boat.

My tongue stuck in my mouth. My feet felt like two slabs of stone. "So he's on *Queen of the North?*"

"Of course, silly," Michelle said. "We know you pulled strings. How else could Jimmy get on with your uncle?"

The lunchtime buzzer rings as I smash this girl's face. Her front teeth crack. She screams, holding her mouth as blood spurts from her split lips. The other two twist my arms back and hold me still while the fourth one starts smacking my face, girl hits, movie hits. I aim a kick at her crotch. The kids around us cheer enthusiastically. She rams into me and I go down as someone else boots me in the kidneys.

I hide in the bushes near the docks and wait all night. Near sunrise, the crew starts to make their way to the boat. Uncle Josh arrives first, throwing his gear onto the deck, then dragging it inside the cabin. I see Jimmy carrying two heavy bags. As he walks down the gangplank, his footsteps make hollow thumping noises that echo off the mountains. The docks creak, seagulls circle overhead in the soft morning light, and the smell of the beach at low tide is carried on the breeze that ruffles the water. When the seiner's engines start, Jimmy passes his bags to Uncle Josh, then unties the rope and casts off. Uncle Josh holds out his hand, Jimmy takes it and is pulled on board. The boat chugs out of the bay and rounds the point. I come out of the bushes and stand on the dock, watching the *Queen of the North* disappear.

CAROLINE ADDERSON grew up in Alberta but now lives in Vancouver where she teaches at Vancouver Community College. In addition to her fiction, she has written *Humans and the Environment*, about ecological issues, and a feature-length screenplay. In 1988, she won the CBC Literary Competition and her story "Oil and Dread" appeared in *The Journey Prize Anthology 5*. Her first book, *Bad Imaginings*, was published in 1993. It was nominated for the Governor General's Award and won the Ethel Wilson Fiction Prize. "Gold Mountain" is taken from *Bad Imaginings*. W.H. New has said that the narrative form emulates John Bunyan's 17th-century allegory, *Pilgrim's Progress*, but that Adderson re-creates the world of imperial history only to subvert its claims on truth.

GEORGE BOWERING was born in 1935 in Penticton, a small city in the Okanagan Valley. He was educated at the University of British Columbia and quickly established his reputation as a prolific, experimental writer. Two poetry collections, *Rocky Mountain Foot* and *The Gangs of Kosmos*, together won a Governor General's Award for 1969. Bowering has also achieved a reputation as a prose writer. His collections include *Protective Footwear* (1978), *A Place to Die* (1983), from which "A Short Story" is taken, and *The Rain Barrell* (1994). Bowering's post-modern techniques and his origins in B.C.'s Okanagan Valley are evident in "A Short Story." Longer prose works include the novel *Burning Water*, which won the Governor General's Award for 1980, and several books of criticism. Bowering has taught in Calgary, Montreal and at Burnaby's Simon Fraser University. He lives in Vancouver and continues to work on a wide range of literary projects.

EMILY CARR (1871-1945) was born into a prominent merchant family in Victoria, B.C., then a small colonial settlement. She matured into one of Canada's most gifted artists, a painter who created a new vocabulary to represent the peoples and landscapes of the Pacific Northwest. Although Carr began writing in the 1920s, it was only after a severe heart attack in 1937 that she turned most of her attention to her prose. *Klee Wyck* won the Governor General's Award in 1941 and became a Canadian classic; the stories trace Carr's physical and imaginative journeys up and down the West Coast in search of the aboriginal peoples she so admired. "Sophie" is a portrait of Carr's long friendship with Sophie Frank, and at the same time a symbolic meditation on the death of a culture; in "D'Sonoqua" Carr sets out on an autobiographical journey toward the many faces of the "wild woman of the woods." "Silence and Pioneers," from *The Book of*

Small (1942), recreates the first stirrings of a Canadian sensibility impatient with colonial perspectives. Carr's writings include *The House of All Sorts* (1944) and other autobiographical works, all published posthumously.

WAYSON CHOY was born in Vancouver's Chinatown and was raised there in the 1930s and 1940s. He attended the University of British Columbia and subsequently moved to Toronto where he has taught English at Humber College for more than twenty-five years. "The Jade Peony" was a story written for a UBC creative writing class conducted by Carol Shields in 1977. It was reprinted in Carole Gerson's *Vancouver Short Stories* in 1985 and has been anthologized more than twenty times since. It eventually formed the nucleus of a successful novel with the same title which was published to high praise and won the Trillium Award in 1995. Choy is currently working on a sequel.

SANDY FRANCES DUNCAN was born in Vancouver in 1942. After earning degrees at the University of British Columbia, Duncan worked for ten years as a clinical psychologist. She began writing in 1973, publishing novels for young readers as well as adult fiction such as *Dragonhunt* (1981) and *Finding Home* (1982). "Was That Malcolm Lowry?" recalls her summer residence as a child in the Dollarton area of North Vancouver. Duncan describes the genesis of the story "as a conversation with some local writers. The topic, Malcolm Lowry's influence on the West Coast literary scene, soon degenerated into 'who had known Lowry,' and except for one writer who took pride in never having met the man, it seemed everyone else had some personal contact with him — in short, had a Lowry story... This story is the result of that conversation." (*Room of One's Own* 6, no. 3 [1981]). Frances Duncan lives with her daughter on Gabriola Island.

KEATH FRASER was born in Vancouver in 1944. After earning a doctorate in English from the University of London, he returned to Canada to teach at the University of Calgary. He retired from teaching in 1978 and moved back to Vancouver to devote himself to writing. His first collection of stories, *Taking Cover*, was published in 1982. It was followed by *Foreign Affairs*, which was nominated for a Governor General's Award and won the Ethel Wilson Fiction Prize for 1985. Fraser has travelled extensively and has edited two anthologies of travel essays: *Bad Trips* (1991) and *Worst Journeys: The Picador Book of Travel* (1992). Travel is also at the heart of *Popular Anatomy*, which was the 1996 winner of the Chapters/ *Books in Canada* First Novel Award. His most recent books are *Telling My Love Lies* (1996) and a memoir about his friendship with writer Sinclair

Ross, *As For Me and My Body* (1997). Fraser lives in Vancouver and is a director of Canada India Village Aid.

JACK HODGINS was born in 1938 in the Comox Valley on Vancouver Island, the son of a logger and the grandson of pioneer farmers. After earning a degree from the University of British Columbia, he taught high school in Nanaimo and began publishing short stories. His first collection, *Spit Delaney's Island*, appeared in 1976 and was followed by *The Invention of the World* (1977) and *The Resurrection of Joseph Bourne*, which won the Governor General's Award for fiction in 1979. A second collection of stories, *The Barclay Family Theatre*, was published in 1981, followed by several more novels. Hodgins has found much of his material in his knowledge of Vancouver Island. "Earthquake" recalls the quake of 1946 which had its epicentre in the Strait of Georgia near Comox. It was first published in *The Canadian Forum* in 1986. Jack Hodgins lives in Victoria where he teaches at the university and works on a variety of literary projects.

PAULINE JOHNSON, or *Tekahionwake* (1861-1913), was born at Chiefswood, her family home on a bluff overlooking the Grand River near Brantford, Ontario. Johnson's family heritage and personal life are inextricably linked to the rise of a Canadian national identity. The daughter of a Mohawk chief and an English cousin to the American novelist W.D. Howells, Johnson achieved fame for her poetry performances throughout Canada, the United States and England between 1892-1908. Dressed in buckskin and received as an "Indian Princess" by London society, Johnson presented a romanticized image of First Nations people after colonization. She was best known for her poetry collections *White Wampum* (1895), *Canadian Born* (1903) and *Flint and Feather* (1912), and for her *Legends of Vancouver* (1911), from which "The Two Sisters" and "The Lost Island" are taken. This book grew out of Johnson's friendship with Chief Joe Capilano whose oral telling of West Coast tribal mythology she transformed into her own poetic voice. These stories of memory, elegy and loss reveal Johnson's narrative powers at their best. From 1910 until her death from cancer in 1913, Johnson lived in Vancouver where she was a much loved figure. After her death, Pauline Johnson's ashes were placed in the earth at Ferguson Point overlooking Siwash Rock in Stanley Park. A large stone bearing her image marks the final resting place of a Canadian legend.

PATRICK LANE was born in Nelson, B.C. in 1939, and spent his childhood in small towns in the B.C. interior. Influenced by his brother Red Lane, who died young, and by the poets bill bissett and Seymour Mayne, Lane helped found Very Stone House Press in Vancouver in the mid-1960s. His first collection of poetry, *Letters From the Savage Mind* (1966), was published by this press. In the books of poetry that followed, Lane established himself as one of the best poets in this or any other country. He received the Governor General's Award in 1978 for *Poems New and Selected* and was nominated again in 1990 and 1991, most recently for *Mortal Remains*. Lane's first book of fiction, *How Do You Spell Beautiful? and Other Stories*, was published in 1992. The twenty stories in this volume chart human violence, pain and love in the working class towns of B.C., the very places where Lane worked as labourer, truck driver, miner and mill first-aid attendant. Lane lives in Victoria and teaches at the University of Victoria.

EVELYN LAU was born in 1971 into a traditional Chinese family in Vancouver. She was fourteen years old and an honours student when she ran away to live on the city's streets. Two years later, at seventeen, Lau chronicled her experience of drugs and prostitution, and her discovery of a literary voice, in the bestselling *Runaway: Diary of a Street Kid* (1989), which has been translated into French, German and Spanish, and made into a CBC movie. Lau's precocious talents have brought her personal notoriety, literary success and numerous awards. Her first book of poetry, *You Are Not What You Claim*, published when she was twenty, was selected for the Milton Acorn Memorial 1990 People's Poetry Award. In 1992, at the age of twenty-one, she was short-listed for the Governor General's Award for Poetry, the youngest writer ever nominated for that honour. Lau's *Fresh Girls and Other Stories* (1993) is a brutal exploration of sex, obsession and love. "Marriage" examines the relationship between a "fresh girl" and a married doctor. Lau's descent into the worlds of passion, compulsion and elusive dreams of acceptance continues in her most recent poetry, *In the House of Slaves* (1994), and in her first novel, *Other Women* (1995). Lau lives in Vancouver.

MALCOLM LOWRY (1909-1957) was born on Merseyside in northern England and educated at a private school in Cambridge. After working his way to the Far East on a freighter, he entered Cambridge, graduating in 1932. *Ultramarine*, a novel about his experiences at sea and written during the Cambridge years, was published in 1933. Escaping from an unhappy family life, Lowry lived in France, the United States and Mexico while writing three novels which failed to find publishers. A 1934 marriage ended in divorce. In 1939 he came to Canada with his second wife, the novelist Marjorie Bonner, and lived in a squatter's shack on the beach at Dollarton in North Vancouver. There, while battling alcoholism, he completed his famous novel, *Under the Volcano*, published in 1947. Between 1950 and 1954, he wrote most of the short stories which were collected and published posthumously as *Hear Us O Lord From Heaven Thy Dwelling Place*. "The Bravest Boat" is taken from that collection. Lowry died in England in 1957; *Hear Us O Lord* won the Governor General's Award for fiction in 1961.

SHANI MOOTOO was born in 1957 in Ireland and grew up in Trinidad where she was part of the Indo-Trinidadian community. She now lives in Vancouver, where she is engaged in several art forms. Her visual art has been exhibited in solo and group shows and she has written and directed several videos, including *English Lesson* (1991), *Wild Woman in the Woods* (1993) and *Her Sweetness Lingers* (1995). Her poetry has been anthologized in *The Very Inside*, and other writings have appeared in *The Skin on Our Tongues* and *Forbidden Subjects*. Her first book of stories, *Out on Main Street,* was published in 1993. Jane Rule has written that "Shani Mootoo explores racial and religious diversity, and ambiguities of gender, to pose fundamental questions about who each of us is." Mootoo's first novel, *Cereus Blooms at Night*, was published in 1996 and nominated for the Giller Prize. Mootoo divides her time between Vancouver, B.C. and Brooklyn, New York.

HOWARD O'HAGAN was born in Lethbridge, Alberta in 1902 and grew up in a series of towns from California to northern Alberta. His family finally settled in Jasper in 1919 and thereafter O'Hagan spent vacations there, for a time working as a mountain guide and packer. He graduated with a law degree from McGill, but decided on a career as a writer. He and his wife moved to Victoria in 1951, where he wrote stories and general interest articles but was never able to make his living by writing. His literary output consists of two novels and two collections of stories. His masterwork, the novel *Tay John* (1939), is a haunting tale of a man born mysteriously from his Shuswap mother's grave. "The Woman Who Got on at Jasper Station" is the title story of his first collection, published in 1963. Most of the stories reflect the author's abiding love for the mountain country of his youth. Recognition came late: *Tay John* was not published in Canada until 1974. O'Hagan was awarded an honorary doctorate by McGill University a few months before his death in 1982.

CHRISTIAN PETERSEN grew up in Quesnel and has lived there and in neighbouring Williams Lake. He studied at the University of Victoria and at the University of New Brunswick, and currently works in adult education. He is one of a number of talented young writers who have chosen to live far from major literary centres. Petersen's stories, often set on the dry interior plateau of the province, resonate with a deeply felt sense of place. "Heart Red Monaco" first appeared in *Prism International (30:4)* and is a story of youthful male friendship tested by social convention and sustained by the freedoms of the road. But "Monaco," like much of Petersen's work, suggests worlds beyond those on the page. There is often an elegiac tone, an undercurrent of sexual attraction and ambivalence, and a sense of missed human connections. Petersen's fiction has appeared in various journals and e-zines, and has been selected for anthologies such as *Key To The Highway* and *97: Best Canadian Stories.*

VI PLOTNIKOFF was born near Verigin, Saskatchewan but as a young girl moved to Grand Forks in the Boundary region of British Columbia. She has lived for many years in Castlegar, B.C., a small Kootenay community where she and her husband have raised a family, worked in radio and become well known for their artistic and musical accomplishments. Plotnikoff was born into the Canadian Doukhobor community, a pacifist Christian sect which emigrated from Russia at the end of the nineteenth century. In her book *Head Cook at Weddings and Funerals and Other Stories* (1994), she explores the social issues, histories and beliefs which have shaped her people, offering a fully imagined portrait of a traditional people living on the edge of mainstream Canadian life. Plotnikoff is working on a new book about the Doukhobor community in the 1930s and 40s.

REBECCA RAGLON was born in Indiana but came to live in Vancouver when she was still in her teens. For a time, she worked as a newspaper reporter in Hay River, NWT. Living in that pristine wilderness, "by a lake so pure you could dip your cup and drink," had an enormous impact on the future writer and her choice of themes. She has written that "the chance to see the original brooding face of the planet is a chance to be transformed — it certainly is a chance to question what humans have made of it." Since completing degrees at UBC and Queen's University, Raglon has taught courses on ecofeminist issues at York University, Simon Fraser University and UBC. Since 1991 Raglon has lived on Bowen Island with her husband and two children, and she hopes never to move again.

BILL REID (1920-1998), acclaimed Haida artist, and ROBERT BRINGHURST (1946), poet, editor and cultural linguist, collaborated on the book of Haida stories, *The Raven Steals the Light*, from which "The Raven and the First Men" is taken. Although he suffered with Parkinson's disease for many years, Reid gained a worldwide reputation as an artist who revitalized traditional Haida art forms. He made remarkable carvings in gold, silver, argillite and wood, and produced monumental sculptures such as *Haida Village* and *Raven and the First Human Beings*, both at the University of British Columbia. His epic sculpture *The Spirit of Haida Gwaii*, installed at the Canadian Embassy in Washington, D.C. (with a copy at the Vancouver Airport), has focussed international attention on the cultural history of the Northwest Coast. Robert Bringhurst possesses a deep fund of knowledge concerning the mythologies and oral narratives of indigenous peoples. His growing reputation as a poet is based on books such as *The Shipwright's Log (1972), Cadastre (1973), The Beauty of Weapons: Selected Poems, 1972-82 (1982),* and *Pieces of Map, Pieces of Music (1986).* With photographer Ulli Steltzer, he collaborated on *The Black Canoe: Bill Reid and the Spirit of Haida Gwaii* which received the Bill Duthie Bookseller's Choice Award in 1992. Bringhurst lives in Vancouver.

EDEN ROBINSON was born in 1968 on the Haisla Nation Kitamaat reserve in northwest British Columbia. No other young First Nations writer in Canada has entered onto the literary scene with more critical acclaim, or with more expectations concerning her future work. Robinson refined her talents in advanced writing classes at the University of Victoria and at UBC, and her early work was awarded the *Prism International* Short Fiction Prize. Her first book, *Traplines* (1996), was selected as a *New York Times* Notable Book of the Year. In the words of her publisher, Robinson takes us into "homes ruled by bullies, psychopaths, and delinquents; families whose conflict resolution techniques range from grand theft to homicide ... a world where the fast food, banged-up cars, and grunge of modern adolescence barely camouflage the dark extremes of sex, fear, and desire." "Queen of the North" contains the blood of more than one victim, but is also an account of spiritual strength and personal survival. Robinson has supported herself as a mail clerk and receptionist but now works full-time as a writer.

JEAN RYSSTAD was born in Kintail, Ontario in 1949 and spent her childhood near Port Huron, Ontario. After graduating from the University of Windsor in 1971, she worked for several weekly newspapers, then moved to Prince Rupert in 1975. She has lived in this coastal fishing community since that time, working at a variety of jobs, marrying a local fisherman and starting a family. She began writing fiction in her mid-thirties. The sea, and life on or near it, plays a prominent role in her imagination, as do work and creativity, family life and passion. These themes are explored in her first book of stories, *Travelling In* (1990), and are deepened in her most recent collection, *Home Fires* (1997). "Say the Word" appears in the latter book and is an elegant meditation on the changes within a family when a young son goes away to work on the boats. Rysstad's stories have appeared in the *Journey Prize Anthology* and *Coming Attractions*, and have won the CBC Radio Literary Competition. She has adapted Ethel Wilson's *The Innocent Traveller* for radio and had her own dramatic work produced on CBC's *Morningside*. In 1997, two of Rysstad's stories were performed on the Bravo!-TV Spoken Arts Program.

LINDA SVENDSEN was born in Vancouver in 1954. She graduated from the University of British Columbia and moved to New York City, where she received a Masters of Fine Arts degree from Columbia University. Her stories have been published widely in some of North America's most prestigious magazines, and she won first prize in 1980 in the American Short Story Contest. Her work has been anthologized in *The O. Henry Prize Stories* (1983) and *Best Canadian Stories* (1981, 1987). *Marine Life*, published in 1992, is a collection of connected stories about a lower-middle class family in Vancouver. The book received high praise from critics and fellow writers. Alice Munro wrote: "Linda Svendsen's stories are stunning — so easily embodying such terrific power. The last story ["White Shoulders"] left me shaking." Svendsen returned to Vancouver in 1989 and now teaches creative writing at the University of British Columbia. She has also worked as a screenwriter, adapting Margaret Laurence's *The Diviners* for a CBC movie.

AUDREY THOMAS was born in Binghamton, New York in 1935 and was educated at Smith College and St. Andrews University, Scotland. She worked for a time in England before immigrating to British Columbia in 1959. She completed an M.A. in English at U.B.C., spent two years in Ghana, Africa, then returned to B.C. and began Ph.D. studies. She eventually settled with her three daughters on Galiano Island, where she still lives. Thomas is a prolific writer who has published nine novels including *Mrs. Blood* (1970), *Songs My Mother Taught Me* (1973), *Blown Figures* (1975) and *Intertidal Life* (1984). Her story collections include *Ten Green Bottles* (1967), *Ladies and Escorts* (1977), *Real Mothers* (1981), and *Goodbye Harold, Good Luck* (1986). "Kill Day at the Government Wharf" appeared in *Ladies and Escorts*. In its subtle examination of the tensions between men and women, it is typical of much of Thomas' fiction. She has won the Ethel Wilson Fiction Prize three times — in 1985 for *Intertidal Life*, again in 1991 for her story collection *Wild Blue Yonder*, and in 1995 for her novel *Coming Down from Wa*.

SEAN VIRGO was born to Irish parents in Mtarfa, Malta in 1940. His life and art has been shaped by an expatriate experience. He lived and received his education in South Africa and in England before emigrating to Canada in 1966 to take up a teaching position at the University of Victoria, where he remained until 1970. While living on B.C.'s West Coast, Virgo became interested in aboriginal narratives, and in the conflict between traditional and occupying cultures. After spending a year in Connemara, Ireland, Virgo returned with his family to the Queen Charlotte Islands and lived there until 1975. His experience of traditional Haida culture had a rich effect on Virgo's artistic pre-occupations during this time. He produced *Deathwatch on Skidegate Narrows and Other Poems*, and, with Susan Musgrave, a limited edition book entitled *Kiskatinaw Songs*. Several stories in Virgo's first story collection, *White Lies and Other Fictions* (1980), date from this time. "Les Rites," a CBC prize-winning story for 1979, is a subtle examination of time, landscape and the cultural fantasies which separate one people from another, and individuals from themselves. In 1983 Virgo published a second book of stories, *Through the Eyes of A Cat*. His ambitious experimental novel, *Selakhi,* was published in 1987.

ETHEL WILSON (1888-1980) was born to missionary parents in Port Elizabeth, South Africa. Her mother died when she was two and she was taken back to England by her father, who died seven years later. In 1898 she was sent to Vancouver to live with her maternal grandmother's family. She attended the Vancouver Normal School and taught in local elementary schools until her marriage in 1921 to prominent Vancouver doctor Wallace Wilson. In the 1930s she published a few short stories in English magazines and began a series of reminiscences, including "Down at English Bay," which were published in 1949 as *The Innocent Traveller*. Her first book, *Hetty Dorval*, did not appear until 1947 when Wilson was nearly sixty years old. Her career ended fourteen years later with the publication of *Mrs. Golightly and Other Stories*. Her stories are remarkable for their playful blend of irony and compassion and for their delight in language. In setting they range throughout the province. Wilson's husband died in 1966 and she spent the last fourteen years of her life in seclusion and ill-health. Her work is aptly celebrated in the Ethel Wilson Fiction Prize, presented annually by the B.C. Book Awards Association.

CAROLINE WOODWARD was born on a homestead near Cecil Lake in the Peace River Country in 1952 and began writing articles for the *Alaska Highway News* in the late 1960s. She has travelled widely in Canada,

Europe and Asia, and her writing has been published in magazines, news-papers and several fiction anthologies. Her books are *Disturbing the Peace* (1990) and *Alaska Highway Two-Step* (1993), which was nominated for the Arthur Ellis Award for Best First Mystery Novel. Woodward has gained a loyal readership because of her focus on rural lifestyles and her ability to merge comic invention with serious human insights. "Summer Wages" charts the sentimental education of two teenage girls as they move down the Alaska Highway in search of work and experience. The story has been televised by Bravo!-TV. Woodward has played an important role in the B.C. arts community as writer, editor and teacher. She lives in the Kootenay region of B.C. where she and her husband own and manage the Motherlode Bookstore in New Denver. She is also working on a sec-ond mystery novel and a collection of short stories.

KATHRYN WOODWARD was born in New York City in 1942 and completed a degree in chemistry in Boston. From 1963-1967, she volunteered as a Peace Corps teacher in Liberia and Micronesia and also worked in Nairobi on the first indigenous African publishing house. Woodward married a Peace Corps volunteer and together they moved to Canada in the late 1960s. Through the 1970s, Woodward lived in Winlaw, B.C., and began to write about her experiences of country life. "Cadillac at Atonement Creek," her first published short story, was included in *Common Ground: Stories by Women* (1980). Set in Nelson and the Slocan Valley, "Cadillac" is about the psychic borders which separate Canadians and Americans, parents and children. Over the past twenty years Woodward has compiled a body of deeply felt, intellectual fiction. Her work has appeared in *Carolina Quarterly, Malahat Review, Descant* and *Event*. "Of Marranos and Gilded Angels" was included in the *Journey Prize Anthology* for 1994. Woodward divides her time between writing and a career as an x-ray technician at St. Paul's Hospital in Vancouver.

Acknowledgments

"The Raven and the First Men" reprinted from *Raven Steals the Light* by Bill Reid and Robert Bringhurst (©1984, 1996), published by Douglas & McIntyre. Reprinted with permission of the publisher.

"Down at English Bay" reprinted from *Innocent Traveller* (© 1949) by Ethel Wilson. "Hurry, Hurry" reprinted from *Mrs. Golightly* (© 1961) by Ethel Wilson. Reprinted by permission of Macmillan Canada.

"The Woman Who Got On at Jasper Station" reprinted from *Trees are Lonely Company* (© 1993) by Howard O'Hagan, published by Talonbooks, Burnaby, BC.

"The Bravest Boat" reprinted by permission of Sterling Lord Literistic, Inc., © 1987 by Malcolm Lowry.

"Earthquake" by Jack Hodgins was first published in *Canadian Forum*. An altered version appeared in *The Macken Charm* (McClelland & Stewart, 1995). Reprinted by permission of the author.

"The Jade Peony" © 1977 by Wayson Choy. Reprinted by permission of the author.

"Was that Malcolm Lowry" by Sandy Frances Duncan was first published in *Room of One's Own*, v. 6, no. 3, 1981. Reprinted in *Vancouver Short Stories* (UBC Press, 1985).

"Head Cook at Weddings and Funerals" by Vi Plotnikoff reprinted from *Head Cook at Weddings and Funerals* (©1995), published by Polestar Book Publishers.

"Mill-Cry" reprinted from *How Do You Spell Beautiful* by Patrick Lane, published by Fifth House Publishers. Reprinted with permission of the author.

"A Short Story" by George Bowering reprinted from *A Place to Die*, by permission of Oberon Press.

"Kill Day on the Government Wharf" reprinted from *Ladies and Escorts* (© 1977) by Audrey Thomas, published by Oberon Press. Reprinted by permission of the author.

BRIGHT LIGHTS FROM POLESTAR

Polestar Book Publishers takes pride in creating books that enrich our under-standing of the world and ntroduce discriminating readers to exciting writers. These independant voices illuminate our history, stretch the imagination and engage our sympathies.

FICTION

Broken Windows by Patricia Nolan
"When I think of successful literary portrayals of devastated lives, I think of Raymond Carver, Dorothy Allison ... After reading *Broken Windows*, I will also think of Patricia Nolan" — *Quill & Quire*
1-896095-20-8 • $16.95 CAN/$14.95 USA

Comfort Zones by Pamela Donoghue
"Donoghue establishes herself as a masterful observer of humanity ... she is bursting with knowledge about the shades of dark and light in human hearts."
— *Vancouver Sun*
1-896095-24-0 • $16.95 CAN/$13.95 USA

Crazy Sorrow by Susan Bowes
" ... an astonishingly vivid portrait of small-town childhood. Everyday scenes are so detailed that anyone with an ounce of Maritime history will wax nos-talgic." — *Vancouver Sun*
1-896095-19-4 • $16.95 CAN/$14.95 USA

Disturbing The Peace by Caroline Woodward
Evocative stories from the spirit of the Peace River valley. "... a series of memory, imagination and wit that leaves you thumping the table for more."
— *Vancouver Sun*
0-919591-53-1 • $14.95 CAN/$12.95 USA

Head Cook at Weddings and Funerals by Vi Plotnikoff
These simple and authentic stories reveal the heart of a young woman, and the Doukhobor community.
0-919591-75-2 • $14.95 CAN/$12.95 USA

Our Game: An All-Star Collection of Hockey Fiction by Doug Beardsley, ed.
Thirty stories — from writers such as Roch Carrier, Morley Callaghan, Roy MacGregor, Audrey Thomas and others — that capture the essence of hockey.
896095-32-1 • $18.95 CAN/$16.95 USA

Rapid Transits and Other Stories by Holley Rubinsky
"[These stories] will return to haunt the reader in the middle of the night. Forceful and beautifully evocative ... these finely crafted stories grab the reader about the throat." — Sandra Birdsell
0-919591-56-6 • $12.95 CAN/$10.95 USA

...rling by M.A.C. Farrant
"...nt is a writer readers can trust: she's got the skills of a
...er] stories engage, and her satire stings." — *The Georgia Straight*
...28-3 • $16.95 CAN/$14.95 USA

...TRY

Hand to Hand by Nadine McInnis
"McInnis takes on the body's engagements — sex, birthing, death — with
considerable vigour." — *Quill & Quire*
1-896095-31-3 • $16.95 CAN/$14.95 USA

Love Medicine and One Song by Gregory Scofield
"[Scofield's] lyricism is stunning; gets within the skin. Be careful. These songs
are so beautiful they are dangerous." — Joy Harjo
1-896095-27-5 • $16.95 CAN/$13.95 USA

Thru the Smoky End Boards by Kevin Brooks and Sean Brooks, eds.
This collection of sports poetry features the work of Margaret Atwood, George
Bowering, Al Purdy, Bronwen Wallace, Michael Ondaatje and others.
1-896095-15-1 • $16.95 CAN/$14.95 USA

Time Capsule by Pat Lowther
Time Capsule consists of excerpts from a manuscript Lowther had prepared
for publication at the time of her death, as well as poems selected from her
earlier books. An important collection by a strong and passionate poet.
1-896095-25-9 • $24.95 CAN/$19.95 USA

To This Cedar Fountain by Kate Braid
A revealing and insightful series of poems that celebrate the life and work of
artist Emily Carr.
1-896095-25-9 • $24.95 CAN/$19.95 USA

Whylah Falls by George Elliott Clarke
Clarke writes from the heart of Nova Scotia's Black community. Winner of
the Archibald Lampman Award for poetry.
0-919591-57-4 • $14.95 CAN/$12.95 USA

Polestar titles are available from your local bookseller.
For a copy of our catalogue, contact:

POLESTAR BOOK PUBLISHERS, publicity office
103-1014 Homer Street
Vancouver, BC
Canada   V6B 2W9
http://mypage.direct.ca/p/polestar